To Bodo

Thanks for all your
encouragement & pestering
I hope you enjoy the fruits
of my toil.

Best regards
Iain        18/02/2014

# Clouds In The Wind

*Ian Mackenzie*

authorHOUSE®

AuthorHouse™ UK Ltd.
1663 Liberty Drive
Bloomington, IN 47403 USA
www.authorhouse.co.uk
Phone: 0800.197.4150

Published by AuthorHouse 01/30/2014

ISBN: 978-1-4918-9212-1 (sc)
ISBN: 978-1-4918-9217-6 (hc)
ISBN: 978-1-4918-9213-8 (e)

Text editor:- Peter Merrington

*I would like to dedicate the book to "My dear wife Rose"*

# FOREWORD

## *This book is a work of Fiction*

*The attitudes, statements, phrases and ideas expressed by the characters in this work do not represent the views of the author. Rather, they are based on research done into the thoughts and attitudes as they appear to have existed and were being articulated at the various periods during which the story is set.*

*None of the characters in the book are real people. Any resemblance that may be perceived or applied to any person living or dead should be seen as unpremeditated and entirely co-incidental.*

*Where the names of actual people or places are mentioned, it should be taken in the context of poetic licence and the use of those names is purely for the purpose of allowing the reader to gather an understanding of how those persons were viewed against the background of the conflict central to the book.*

**Ian Mackenzie**

# PROLOGUE

## Cape Town South Africa
### February 1960

T he distinguished guest rose gracefully from his seat on the green leather benches and strode to the podium. He carried about him an air of dignified self assurance, characteristic of his lifetime in offices of influence and power.

His surroundings in the ornate oak-panelled hall, the crystal chandeliers, heavy satin drapes and soft thick carpeting, symbolized the prosperity and solidity of a long-standing colonial heritage.

This was the eighth country that this man had visited in ten days, and his keen blue eyes betrayed his fatigue. His features were handsome though ageing and a gaunt pallor was barely concealed behind the flush of colour from recent unaccustomed exposure to the harsh African sun. During his mission he had been met with reverence, and he had encountered hostility. He was on a hugely challenging assignment and his encounters had left him both enlightened and disturbed.

Experience told him that his message today would not rest easily with the present audience. Thirty-three years of tough political engagement had, three years previously, brought him at last to the ultimate reward, the office of Prime Minister of Great Britain. In this role, he was now charged with the thankless task of attempting to unbundle the empire that had been created through centuries of colonization.

He turned at the lectern and drew a sheath of notes from the inner pocket of his Saville Row suit. Glancing up, he took stock of his auditors and saw before him an assembly of battle-hardened politicians. These bulky men in their dark double-breasted suits were the sons of Afrikaners who had, six decades earlier, fought the British with Musket and cannon on the battle fields of the Boer war. This was their new field of battle and they were alert, on the defensive.

The speaker was a tall man with immaculately trimmed, wavy grey hair and a fine pencil-line moustache. His mere presence spoke volumes. It spoke of gravity and earnest. It left little doubt in the minds of the waiting audience that he was accustomed to being listened to and taken seriously.

'Honourable members of this House, members of the press and all African members of the Commonwealth,' he began, 'I thank you for this opportunity to present my government's greetings.'

The words were spoken in a clear and resounding timbre. Then he raised his voice to a well-rehearsed pitch and continued in a tone of unmistakable authority:

'Since the end of the war, the world has seen the awakening of a national consciousness in people and nations, who for centuries have lived within the borders of their own land as servants and dependants of some or other foreign colonial power.

'Fifteen years ago, this stirring of awareness spread through Asia and since then, many countries on other continents . . . countries of different races, beliefs and civilisations have pressed their claim to an independent national life and self-governance with demands for an end to colonial rule.'

The speaker paused for effect, glancing with stern appraisal at his audience of South African politicians. Among them, he saw expressions of naked contempt. As far as the majority of those parliamentarians were concerned, they had already claimed their independence from the British Crown. They had already seized their right to sovereignty and self rule. The ardent belief was that God himself had delivered this to them in the South African general election of 1948 when the pro-British, Commonwealth Unionists had been toppled by the Afrikaaner at the polls.

'Today,' continued the speaker, 'the same thing is happening in Africa, and the most striking of all the impressions that I have formed since leaving London, is the strength and resilience of the African National Consciousness. In different places it takes different forms, but it is happening everywhere and it is obvious to me and my government that this awakening of pride and spirit cannot be ignored.'

His powerful voice came across firm and clear through the public address system. It was a full sitting in Cape Town of both Houses of Parliament in the Union of South Africa. For the moment he held sway, but a quiet undercurrent of murmuring from the ruling party benches indicated irredeemably that this august gathering reserved its own views. They would not be ignored either.

The speaker paused again, and then raised his voice for dramatic impact:

'*The wind of change* is blowing through this continent of Africa, ladies and gentlemen, and whether we like it or not the growth of black national consciousness and their right to self determination is a political fact . . . an irreversible fact that our national policies, now and in the future, must take account of.'

He paused once more and stared in deliberate challenge at the upturned faces of his audience.

"As fellow members of the Commonwealth" he proceeded, "it is our earnest desire to give South Africa and the Southern African region our fullest support and encouragement, but frankly there are some aspects of your legislation, the policies of Apartheid and racial segregation which make it impossible for us to do so.'

Harold Macmillan resumed his seat alongside his host, Prime Minister Dr Hendrik Verwoerd. The murmur, which had become a hostile drone, erupted into a hubbub of defiance. Macmillan's and Verwoerd's eyes did not meet but in a hushed tone, Verwoerd spoke to his distinguished guest:

"Sir, we will never surrender our sovereignty." he said. "We fought far too hard and sacrificed far too much to achieve it, and we will fight and sacrifice to keep it. Take that message back to London with you."

It was clear that the words of the leader of Great Britain had re-opened old wounds. More, his words had struck against a people's sense of destiny and conviction. He had fired a warning shot against a bastion of stone and touched a political nerve so profoundly painful as to be intolerable. His warning would be ignored.

\*     \*     \*

## DAR 'E SALAM. TANGANYIKA
## MAY 1960

IN A DINGY COMMUNITY HALL ON THE OUTSKIRTS OF THE CITY an assembly of delegates had drawn together, representing nationalist liberation movements from seven African countries.

The man they had gathered to hear had recently returned from Moscow, where he had undergone extensive military and political training.

The crowded hall was furnished with folding metal chairs set out on a chipped wooden floor. The paint on the walls was stained and faded and the windows were bare and grimy. The space was weakly illuminated by a few naked light bulbs that hung from a sagging ceiling on frayed electric wires.

The speaker was a bespectacled man of medium build. He was immaculately dressed in an expensive navy-blue business suit and a starched white shirt, ornamented with a red tie and a white silk handkerchief that flowed like a bouquet from his breast pocket.

The audience listened to his booming voice as if mesmerised, captivated by his charismatic power and eloquence.

'For four centuries,' he declaimed, 'our African continent has been targeted as a pillaging ground for colonizing forces from Europe. The Portuguese, the French, Dutch, Belgians, Germans, Italians and the British have all laid claim to our land. They enslaved our people. They carved up Africa into borders of their own expedience. They built citadels of white privilege and wealth at the expense of our freedom, which was stolen from us by their greed and exploitation. They have cast us aside in our own land as objects of irritation when we have tried to reason with them on the subject of justice for our people.

'Now the time has come to fight back! . . . We will reclaim our continent! Progressively, we—the Black Consciousness activists, the Peoples' National Revolutionary movements—have intensified our struggle. We now challenge the legitimacy of the colonizers. We are pressing our justifiable demand for self-determination and the rehabilitation of our freedom!

The speaker paused and stared at his audience as if defying them to challenge him. The hall was hushed, but the energy was palpable.

'Comrades,' he continued, 'we are not alone! There is an international groundswell of support. A new international philosophy is calling for Freedom for Africa and the People of Africa! This is even now gathering momentum in the minds of fair-thinking sympathisers. It has support among the foreign sponsors of liberation, and in corridors of power on the global political stage. The grip of white supremacy in Africa is slipping! It is loosening under the pressure of our heroic Revolutionary forces and our struggle can no longer be ignored.'

He spoke for over an hour, and his words goaded his audience, inciting them in a fever, kindled with anger, bloodlust and patriotic devotion.

'The struggle for the liberation of our continent must not falter,' he exhorted them. 'We must not slumber nor grow complacent! The struggle will continue and our victory is certain!'

Timing the climax with the assurance of a showman, his ebony forehead glistening with perspiration, the speaker raised a clenched fist high above his head. Switching to fluent Swahili, he bellowed:

*'Mzungu Aende Ulaya! Mwafrika Apate Uhuru!* Let the European go back to Europe! Let the African regain his Independence!'

Then he concluded his speech in English: 'Our strength is our survival. Our will is akin to an ever intensifying storm that will soon overwhelm the trespassers and blow them away like clouds in the wind!'

A roar of applause went up in a crescendo of frenzied approval. The school teacher turned political militant raised both arms in acknowledgement of his audience. He turned from the lectern to resume his place among the VIPs on the stage behind him. Applauding, they rose from their seats in unison and each in turn embraced the orator, honouring their brother in arms.

# CHAPTER 1

## 1980
## Johannesburg, South Africa

The nightclub was crowded with youthful revellers. At 31 years of age Andrew Mason should have felt out of place here, but he was beyond caring. The liquor that he had consumed in steady measure since early that morning, after a humiliating interview, had mellowed his inhibitions. He tramped determinedly to the bar and ordered another drink.

He raised himself onto a stool with his back to the bar, his elbows resting on the counter top for support. Sipping at his drink, he surveyed the gyrating teenagers who moved like phantoms under the coloured stroboscopic lighting. The music blared so loudly that he was sure nobody would notice if the place were targeted by a mortar attack. It would be a catastrophe if fire broke out. But he would be the only one to have thought of that. These merrymakers were untouchable. Disaster of any kind was the last thing in the minds of this mass of young humanity.

Mason was a man of few words, but his rugged features, vigilant eyes and solid frame spoke volumes. Drunk or sober, this was not a man you'd want to be at odds with. But therein lay a contradiction. There was vulnerability about him, a tangible sadness that diminished the ruthlessness of the image and reflected a portrait of sorrow and loneliness.

His periodic binges were born of a desire to rid himself of the demons that haunted him. Half a decade fighting for survival in a war he'd made his own, coupled with personal tragedy, had moulded him in a way that few would comprehend, and the emotional scars he carried as a result were deep and painful. Few men would understand or even believe the experiences Andy Mason had endured and his silent manner discouraged enquiry.

Absorbed in his private world, he sensed rather than saw the woman. She had sidled up to a seat a few metres away, and when he lifted his head he saw that he was being targeted by a seductive smile.

Andy guessed that she was in her late twenties or early thirties—also out of her age group among the crowd of youngsters who gyrated on the dance floor or clung to each other on the dark periphery. Her clothing suggested elegance and good taste and she wore it with the ease of practised self-assurance. She wore a black cotton tunic with a high collar, cut suggestively to expose a magnetising cleavage between a pair of firm breasts. Her skirt was short, and had ridden high on her crossed legs— long and shapely legs, he noted. She was well groomed. Her make-up was simple but sophisticated and there was a waft of a soft and enticing perfume—a musky fragrance that tingled in Andy's nostrils and was of a quality that did not come cheap.

Mason was not so drunk as to miss the invitation and it occurred to him that it had been too long since he had enjoyed the company of a woman.

He grinned at her, gesturing first toward the blaring music and then to his ears. Raising his eyebrows, his head tilted slightly, he shrugged apologetically. He sat there frowning, not looking at the woman for a few moments, and then he raised his head as if surprised by a sudden flash of inspiration. He clicked his fingers dramatically, leaving his index finger momentarily poised upward. Eyeing her shrewdly, he took a pen and paper from his pocket and scribbled a note which he passed to the woman.

'You're gorgeous,' said the note.

She read it and chuckled delightedly, and then she scribbled on the paper and passed the note back.

'You're drunk,' it said. Andy grinned, scribbled again and passed the paper back along the counter.

'We've barely met and already you know me so well. I'm impressed.'

The woman laughed heartily and got up from her stool to sit on the one beside Andy. He put his head close to hers and yelled, 'If it's a conversation you're wanting you'd be wasting your time in this place!'

'What?' she yelled back.

'See what I mean?' he returned with his mouth close to her ear. She was still smiling: a genuine glowing smile that lit up her eyes and radiated sex appeal.

'Didn't get that!' she yelled. 'Would you like to go somewhere else?'

Andy shrugged and pursed his lips, rolling his head backwards as if undecided and needing to think about it, and then he leant across and took her hand.

When he woke, he was in his apartment with a throbbing booze-induced headache. His mouth was as dry and rough as an emery board. His eyes felt swollen, as if they bulged from their sockets. The sensation was one that he detested but it wasn't unfamiliar; he'd woken up feeling that way too often recently.

He turned over sleepily and cast an arm across the bed, expecting to feel the touch of soft eager flesh. Instead, his reach flopped against an empty sheet. After a moment of contemplation he raised his aching head and stared through bloodshot eyes at the vacant spot where he had expected the woman to be. She was gone.

He instinctively turned and looked at the dresser where he'd left his wallet and watch. They were also gone.

'Bitch,' he muttered, and his head flopped back on the pillow. He tried to remember how much had been in the wallet when he'd entered the nightclub the previous evening, but he was more annoyed by his own stupidity than having been robbed of the money. The watch was a not a valuable piece but the loss of it irritated him as much as the foolishness of falling victim to such an obvious con.

'Maybe I should go looking for the slut,' he muttered. 'Get the stuff back from her? Mmm?' He reflected for a moment. Then— 'Nah! Not a good idea; there's probably a pimp behind this, with a bunch of brawny thugs at his side.' That didn't bother him as much as where it would end up. 'Probably in a police cell.' He pulled a face. 'It's not worth going down that road. The hell with it! Forget the bitch. I'll get over it.'

He rose naked from the bed and staggered from the bedroom to the lounge where he'd left the half drunk bottle of spirits. It was still there on the coffee table and he strode over and eagerly poured a double measure into a tumbler.

Warm relief soaked through his veins as he gulped at the drink. Picking up the bottle, he returned to the bedroom and sat down heavily on the side of the bed trying to piece together the events of the night. All he could remember was being enthralled by the woman and the prospect of getting laid—and then? . . . . That it had never happened.

He didn't know if she'd drugged him or if it was just the booze, but—either way—she'd caught him off guard and clearly had her plans worked out in advance.

'And it cost me around five hundred bucks and my watch,' he muttered.

He sighed deeply and his shoulders sagged under the weight of humiliation. The relief brought on by the shot of liquor quickly subsided, giving way to despair and remorse.

It was a trick he would never have fallen for six months earlier. Then, he would have seen the warning signs. He would have been suspicious of the seductive smile and the unsolicited come-on. He would have scoured the room to see where her minders had positioned themselves and would have played her at her own game—let her think that she had him and then leave her to deal with her own resentment and vexation. In his present state of mind he'd fallen blindly into her trap and paid the price

He stood up unsteadily and caught his reflection in the mirror. The image did nothing to improve his self-esteem. His hair was unkempt and his unshaven face looked unwashed. His eyes were glazed and seemed to haemorrhage from behind both retinas.

'Look at you,' he muttered with disgust. After a moment, he added: 'Loser.'

He lurched across to the tall French window and embraced the splendour of the panoramic view that the apartment afforded him.

The sun had not yet broken above the horizon, but it was heralded by a soft golden glow in the east. The light reflected scarlet off small puffy clouds that floated idly in the vast blue sky. It promised to be a beautiful day.

Staring out at the pre-dawn light, marvelling at the spectacle, he was assailed by memories of a thousand sunrises in a different place, under different circumstances . . . . In another life.

He slumped back on the bed as he mulled over the many images of an existence that he'd left behind, a place in his mind where conflicting ghosts lived on—ghosts of happiness and torment.

He drifted away into a reverie, capturing all too clearly the fateful events that had mapped out his life, moulding his destiny

# CHAPTER 2

## January 1963

IMPOSING WROUGHT IRON GATES TO THE SCHOOL STOOD WIDE OPEN and the stream of family cars, transporting pupils to start their new term, flowed through unimpeded.

The carefully tended sports fields were green and fresh beneath a misty haze cast by irrigation sprinklers and the spray refracted the sharp morning light into dancing rainbows.

A long driveway, lined by giant oaks, led between the fields and up a slope to a stately stone edifice. This, the main building, was like a handsome fortress, a great paternal protector that kept vigil across the grounds. The driveway ended beneath this citadel around a circle that embraced a fishpond set into a rockery shrouded in creeping Ivy. In it's centre, a bronze fountain made in the image of an angel in flight with water streaming from its wings formed the focal point of the circle and from here, a sweeping flight of stone steps led up to the formal entrance, a broad stone archway. Rising above the entrance over the centre of the great facade, was a domed clock tower with a huge timepiece displaying black Roman numerals against a mottled white face.

In every sense the setting was like an English public school, one of those ancient establishments for the sons of English gentry—but these surroundings were ten thousand kilometres remote from England; situated in sunlit South Africa, close to the small town of Pietersburg on the road-and-rail route to Rhodesia.

For half a century the school had served as a seedbed of privilege and excellence, the shaping of thousands of white

Southern African boys. Here was the breeding ground for future politicians, business leaders and industrialists, national cricket and rugby heroes, the ruling caste of white South Africa.

The hallways and cloisters echoed with banter of returning pupils. Boys, shouting greetings to their friends, while in the car park, subdued farewells to parents and siblings marked the end of the long Christmas holidays.

Amidst the bustle of activity, Andrew Mason got down from the back seat of his father's Austin Princess and retrieved his bags from the trunk. He put them down on the verge beside the car and turned to his parents.

'You've done us proud, son,' said his father. He squeezed Andy's hand in a firm grip and clapped him on the shoulder. 'Keep up the good work son. The education you're getting here is important—it'll stand you in good stead for the years to come. Who knows what the future will bring?'

Andy pulled a face at the well-worn clichés. He'd heard more than enough about the 'uncertain future' and 'the advance of communism in Africa and the black puppet politicians who promoted it'. This was a hobby horse of his father's generation. Conversations with family friends and acquaintances invariably drifted towards the 'approaching onslaught of black power and anarchy'. And every single parent who spoke at Founders' Day or Prize giving said 'Keep up the good work. It'll stand you in good stead.'

'I'm only fifteen, dad! Give me a chance! I'll cover the basics before we're overrun. But who knows? I might end up as a civil rights lawyer and champion the cause of black liberty.'

His father shoved him away in mock disgust. 'Talk like that and you'll get arrested, young man,' he scolded, but he grinned fondly at his son.

Andy reached out to his mother who was weeping discreetly into her handkerchief. This too was a regular feature at the start of a new term.

'Cheer up mom,' he said. 'It's only three months until Easter and time flies. Remember, I'm here to be educated, not executed.'

She hugged him tightly and kissed him. 'Look after yourself, my love I miss you terribly.' Then she turned and got back into the car. Andy raised his hand in farewell, retrieved his bags and headed toward the third form hostel.

Andy Mason walked with an air of confidence. At fifteen he was just edging over the latter stages of puberty. He was a tall and well-built adolescent with thick sandy brown hair, trimmed short-back-and-sides in keeping with school regulations. He had clear hazel eyes and prominent dimples in both cheeks when he smiled. He was a popular and active student with good reason to be confident. His parents were caring and supportive; he produced excellent results in the classroom as well as on the sports field. He captained his age-group in rugby and cricket, and he held the schools under-sixteen 1,500 and 3,000 metre track records. He had made many good friends at school and it was generally expected that he would be in the running for Head Boy in his senior year.

As he strode along the roadway in the bright morning sunlight, he was unaware of the Chev Impala with Northern Rhodesian license plates close behind him. The loud, unexpected blast of the car's horn caused him to instinctively leap away onto the sidewalk. He spun around with his heart racing from the sudden fright to identify the source of the intrusion and in the passenger seat of the car, consumed with laughter, sat Alec Bradford

'Nerves, Mason! Nerves!' he called out laughing through the open window as the car drifted slowly passed him. 'You should try moving that fast off the starting blocks, champ! You'd be unbeatable.'

'You should try to be more careful about who you scare the bejesus out of, Bradford,' retorted Andy. 'You're short of friends as it is.'

The Chev pulled to the verge ahead of Andy and three occupants emerged.

One was a tall and ruggedly handsome man who could only have been Alec's father. He had the same wavy blonde hair, though shot through with whitening streaks, and his alert blue eyes gave an impression of perpetual amusement. He wore an open-necked khaki shirt and short pants, with socks pulled neatly up to his knees, and a pair of veldskoen shoes. His resemblance to Alec was remarkable and it wasn't difficult to picture him at the same age like an identical twin.

Next was Alec's mother. She got out from the back seat of the car, a plump cheerful-looking woman, deeply tanned and freckled. Her auburn hair was tied in a bun at the top of her head and she wore a light knee-length sleeveless cotton dress with a floral design and cowhide sandals. She walked briskly up to Andy and embraced him in a demonstrative hug. She kissed him warmly on the cheek.

The third was Alec himself, grinning impudently at his friend.

Alec and Andy had met on their first day at the school. They'd stood together in the registration line in the imposing corridor outside the bursar's office, both feeling anxious and way out of their depth. The walls were lined with row upon row of daunting framed black-and-white photographs—decades of sports teams and school achievers who seemed to look down on the new boys and challenge them. Making a new friend was a relief.

'I'm Alec Bradford' said the other boy, extending his hand.

'Hi. I'm Andrew Mason.'

'Where are you from?'

'Jo'burg. And you?'

'I'm from Ndola in Northern Rhodesia.'

'Wow,' said Andy. 'You're a long way from home! That's on the Copper Belt, isn't it?'

'Just south of the Belgian Congo.' Affirmed Alec.

'Where the mercenaries are fighting?' Andy had heard many news broadcasts about the troubles in the Congo although they meant little to him. But here was someone close to the action.

Alec frowned. 'All we know is when the refugees come across the border. My dad says they're rich colonials who've lost all their money because of the independence war and they leave most of their stuff behind. They come through on tractors and old trucks. But they don't stay long. Ndola's on the doorstep, but it's okay.'

'Gosh. What does your dad do?'

'He manages a mine. We live there. We're in the sticks, about fifteen miles from town. But it's okay, its fun. There's a club with a golf course and tennis courts and a swimming pool. We go hunting in the bush and fishing when my dad's free.'

'Why don't you go to school there?'

'There aren't any,' replied Alec 'No decent schools. All the mine kids get sent to school in Southern Rhodesia or here. Except the black kids from the compounds. They don't go to school at all—or some get taught by missionaries. They sit under trees for their classes.'

That had been two years ago, and since then Andy and Alec had become close friends. But Andy hadn't yet met Alec's parents.

'So this is Andy, is it?' Alec's mother released Andy from her embrace and stood back to inspect him. 'We've heard all about you for so long. It's nice to meet you at last. I'm Jean.'

'I'm Jed' said the man, extending his hand. Andy smiled. The Bradfords were reassuring in their easy familiarity.

'Hi,' he said laughing. 'And I'm very nearly Alec's ex-friend. He's a total delinquent. How were the hols?'

'Brilliant,' said Alec. 'We had four amazing weeks in Lorenco Marques. I swear that place should have pearly gates on the approach roads. It's paradise.'

They took Alec's bags from the trunk of the car and Jed drew a wad of notes from his pocket and shoved them into the breast pocket of Alec's blazer.

'Don't spend it all at once,' he said. 'There might not be more where that came from.' Then he turned to Andy:

'You must come up and visit us. It's long overdue.'

The epic three-day train journey from Pietersburg to Ndola had meant that Alec was often a guest at Andy's home in Johannesburg during the short school breaks in April and September. Andy was invited to visit the Bradfords in return, but nothing had yet come of it.

'We'll organize it with your parents,' said Jean. 'We'd love to have you as our guest.'

'Thank you. I'd like that. It'll be an adventure.'

'Well,' said Jed, 'we've got a hell of a long drive ahead of us. We'd better get moving. I want to reach Salisbury before dark. I don't want to drive at night with all the wild game on the road.'

They said goodbye and the two boys strode off to their hostel.

# CHAPTER 3

## Rhodesia 1963

Parental arrangements were made and Andy was, at last, going to spend the July holidays in Northern Rhodesia. As the mid-year school holidays drew nearer, his excitement grew. He had never been outside the borders of South Africa and Alec had painted a fantasy picture for him with his vivid descriptions of life on the Copper Belt.

The last day of the second term finally arrived—a chilly subtropical winter morning. The Rhodesian contingent, all boarders at the school, embarked at the Pietersburg station on the northbound train and made it throb with their released energies. Three weeks of freedom lay ahead.

The train descended the steep southern escarpment, down the mountains of the Waterberg and into the Limpopo valley. It chugged across the flat basin of the lowveld, towards the small border town of Beit Bridge. Cliff Richard's latest hit single, 'Summer Holiday', played on a portable radio as the train sped northwards, and the boys all sang along.

They reached the Rhodesian border, crossing the railway bridge over the Limpopo River, as the sun was going down.

Andy was amazed by the rugged beauty of his surroundings. He had never seen a sunset with such extraordinary splendour. The sky to the west was a deep orange, stained by sparse lazy grey clouds that hung idly in the warm evening air. Against the sky were the darkening silhouettes of palm trees and the native

Mopane vegetation. It seemed as if the entire world below the horizon was engulfed in an inferno and that the moment had been captured on the canvass of a master artist.

The train chuffed its way farther inland and Andy's excitement welled up. Ignoring the flying smuts from the steam locomotive, he slid open a window; and his spirits rose in elation as the unfamiliar bushveld rolled past.

The train laboured on through the night. It reached the city of Bulawayo a little before eight the following morning, and a scheduled three-hour layover gave the boys a chance to go into the town. They took a taxi from the station into the city centre and Andy found himself marvelling at a town that bustled with unexpected vibrancy. It had a rural atmosphere and yet it bore the stamp of an energetic metropolitan hive. The city streets were spotlessly clean and broad and grand. He'd read somewhere that the streets in Bulawayo had remained as they were in pioneering days, when wagons drawn by teams of sixteen oxen could be turned around without the need to unhitch them.

The architecture showed the distinct stages of historical progress: the infancy of pioneering days and ornate Edwardian-era offices that mingled easily with more modern structures. He was enthralled by the people on the streets who gave the impression of being filled with energy and alive with excitement. Even the sun seemed to shine with a special brightness. He was impressed by the absence of anything vulgarly ostentatious about the town, and yet it seemed to exude a palpable passion and vitality.

They strolled through the wide streets of the small city, lined with flamboyant and acacia trees in winter bloom. Bougainvillea abounded in a bright and glorious blend of colours while the famous avenues of huge jacaranda trees stood quiet and bare in their winter rest. This was a different world from Johannesburg, an older and simpler world where false airs and graces did not seem to exist. The atmosphere was contagious and Andy felt as though he was floating on a cloud of contentment.

They left Bulawayo in the middle of the morning and continued their journey north towards the Northern Rhodesia border at Victoria Falls. Andy was captivated by the natural splendour of the virgin bush through which the railway line had been carved. Sparsely scattered amongst the dense tropical shrubbery, gigantic baobab trees more than a thousand years old stood out against the skyline, magnificent in their ugliness and laden with cream-of-tartar pods.

As they travelled further north, sightings of wild game became frequent. They saw browsing herds of elephant and buffalo who stopped grazing to look up at them curiously as the train sped by. Herds of antelope and zebra, startled by the rattling carriages, bolted off through the bush and drew delighted laughter from the group of boys. Andy didn't think he had ever been so happy. He couldn't remember a time when he'd experienced such a rush of liberty and well-being. If God had a country of his own, then this was surely it.

As evening approached, the train drew into the remote border town of Victoria Falls on the Zambezi River. There was a tangible carnival atmosphere in the air and tourists, laden with cameras and African curios, roamed the streets.

Andy was awestruck by the spectacle of the powerful river and the wall of white water, a full two kilometres wide that plunged into the chasm. It seemed that a billion gallons of water crashed over the precipice every minute, with a thunderous roar, plummeting in a suicidal dive onto the jagged rocks in the gorge 120 metres below. As the water fell, it dispensed a cloud of spray that rose up high above the rim of the gorge. The constant roar of the tumbling torrent echoed off the walls of the gorge and reverberated through the air like the din of an airliner's engines. In the forest along the river banks and around the falls, a relentless drizzle fell in a fine soggy haze as the mist descended gently back to earth.

The train came to a wheezing halt at the small station which overlooked the spectacle, as the sun sank toward the western horizon. As the boys watched, it changed in colour and shape into a huge bright orange ball that seemed to be swallowed by the wide wild waters of the Zambezi, leaving behind it a sky that mourned its passing in a rush of scarlet . . .

'The local tribes of long ago,' said Alec, 'called the falls *Mosi oa Tunya* which means The Smoke that Thunders. Then Livingstone came along and renamed them in honour of his queen. Patriotic kind of guy. In his memoirs he said "scenes so lovely must have been gazed upon by angels in their flight."'

Andy agreed. He had never seen anything of such magnificence. It defied description—the majesty of that watery African sunset blending with the surrounding forest. The rising cloud of mist with an arched rainbow that framed the falls against the backdrop of the golden sky created an unbelievably beautiful vista. The cries of wild birds roosting and the stirring of nocturnal creatures added voice to the glorious setting and Andy was mesmerised.

'God's African lullaby,' came the spontaneous and passing thought.

As they boarded the train for their onward journey to the north, Andy vowed that one day he would come back here with all those whom he loved, to relive and to share the richness and the splendour.

He had no idea, then, that his return would be under very different circumstances.

# CHAPTER 4

## July 1963
## Ndola, Northern Rhodesia

IT WAS SHORTLY AFTER FIVE THE FOLLOWING EVENING WHEN THEY DREW TO A HALT alongside the railway platform at Ndola Station. The small platform was abuzz with parents welcoming their offspring who were arriving home for the first time since Christmas.

Jed and Jean were waiting amongst the throng and as Andy stepped down from the train, Jean welcomed him with her trade mark greeting; A bear hug and a warm kiss on the cheek.

'Lovely to see you, Andy!' she said. 'You're going to have a wonderful time with us. We have some really exciting activity lined up.'

Jed welcomed him with a firm handshake and a broad smile. He turned to Alec with an affectionate grin. He grabbed his son around the neck in a playful headlock and punched him lightly on the shoulder. 'How you doing, soldier?' he asked. 'Good to have you home!'

It was getting dark as they left the station. From what Andy could see, Ndola was a small rural town with buildings not unlike what he'd seen in Bulawayo, impressively clean and neat. They drove through the quiet streets and then away from the town, toward a collection smoke stacks perched high on the top of a hill in the distance.

Twenty minutes later they arrived at the Bradford family home.

It was a brightly illuminated rambling bungalow under a green corrugated iron roof which overhung a wide veranda, supported by ornate wrought iron pillars painted white. They pulled up on a gravel verge next to the veranda across from the front door. This opened as they stopped, and revealed two black men dressed in neat white fatigues. They stood side by side on the veranda step, grinning broadly, and as Alec got out of the car they clapped their hands softly together in respectful greeting, and inclined their heads. 'Welcome Bwana,' they said, clearly delighted to see him, and then they went off in an African language that Andy didn't understand. To his surprise, Alec answered them fluently in the same tongue, and went across to shake their hands. They responded sheepishly, as if being done a great honour. Then Alec turned and pointed to Andy, and said in English:

'This is my friend Andy from South Africa. Andy, this is Joseph and Potboy. Joseph is the houseboy. Pot boy is our cook and what he does in the kitchen makes that stuff we eat at the hostel seem like swill.'

Andy went over and shook hands with the two of them, and they responded politely bending slightly at the knees and clapping their hands softly together. Then they moved towards the car to get the bags.

'I'll introduce you to the rest of the staff tomorrow,' said Alec as the two men manhandled the luggage from the trunk. 'They all knock off at five so they've already gone back to the compound.'

Discreetly positioned spotlights lit up a colourful garden with a huge wild fig at its centre and a number of acacia trees beyond a wide stretch of neatly trimmed lawn. The interior of the house was tastefully furnished with a long, wide passage leading from the front door. On the floor lay a thick pile carpet with soft creams and pinks interwoven in an complex floral pattern. Plain but skilfully placed light fittings adorned the walls, between paintings of African landscapes. The house was old but emanated warmth and discreet elegance. A beautifully kept home.

The holiday sped by and Andy's delight grew daily. The people he met were relaxed, friendly and hospitable to a fault. They were invited out to barbecues and lunches and parties where they danced to the Beatles, Gerry and the Pacemakers, Cliff Richard, Elvis Presley and Pat Boone. They played tennis and water polo at the club, they went fishing in flawlessly clear streams where they stripped down to their underwear and swam in the warm still waters of rocky pools. They went underground at the mine and were taken into the stopes to help clear out blasting residue. They got a first-hand demonstration that the use of a jack hammer was not as simple as a faceman makes it look. They were shown the extraction process and the smelting process. They were taken on a three-day safari to hunt antelope, where they slept under cloudless star filled skies and fished for bream in an unspoilt river, cooking their catch over an open fire.

Whooping with delight and the recklessness of youth, they raced motorcycles from the mine security office up and down the dirt road along the Congo border, and they returned breathless, dusty and windblown to be greeted with cold Cola drinks and cheese sandwiches. The hospitality of the people seemed to be boundless. The freedom of an idyllic lifestyle gave the impression that they didn't have a care in the world. Andy dwelt in a state of continuing euphoria, blissfully ignorant of the political turmoil that simmered just beneath the surface.

As the holiday drew to an end, Andy's thoughts turned to the long journey that would take them back to school. He privately nursed a spiritual vacuum at the thought of leaving this incredible place.

He, Alec, Jed and Jean were sitting on the wide veranda in front of the house, chatting idly over afternoon tea. Andy stretched luxuriously, savouring the last day of what he perceived as paradise.

'I have so enjoyed being here,' he said to Jed and Jean. 'This is such a beautiful part of the world. And the people are unbelievable.'

'Yep,' responded Jed thoughtfully: He was quiet for a moment and then went on, 'I'm glad you've enjoyed it, Andy. Remember it, keep the enchantment safe in your thoughts because you may never see it like this again.'

Andy was taken aback. 'Why?'

'It's Africa, son,' said Jed 'And Africa is changing. We've built a good life here, and we've enjoyed it . . . . and earned it, but I give it another year, maybe two at most, and all this will be in the hands of others.' Jed paused again, then added: 'Government-sponsored management. They'll destroy everything that's taken us years to build. The nationalist movements are staking their claim to the right to govern this country. They want to get rid of colonialism, and they'll do it. It's just sad that it's happening too soon. They're not ready.'

Andy had developed a high regard for Jed. He was a shining example of leadership in the community and appeared to be a man who knew exactly where he stood. He had obviously worked out the difference between what he wanted and what he could realistically have, and having accepted the reality of those limitations he lived right on the very edge of them. Andy was ready to hear him out.

'That's a surprise,' he said. 'Who would want to change anything? I get the impression that life here is perfect for everyone.'

'It would be, Andy,' replied Jed, 'if it weren't for the greed and expedience of politics. But what you see on the surface doesn't necessarily reflect the truth. All the development that you see here, the mines, the farms, the factories and the lifestyle have come together in a relatively short space of time. But everyone in charge of planning, progress and maintenance has been educated and trained and they are all qualified experts in their respective fields. Overall we've done a bloody good job, even if I say so myself—but there's one glaring exception and we should have seen it coming.' Jed paused and thought for a while. 'Have some more tea, and I'll tell you a story.'

Jean rolled her eyes. 'Come on Jed, I'm sure Andy doesn't really need that on his last day here.'

'No, please,' said Andy, 'I'd love to hear. I'm fascinated. And I want to know why I might never see your paradise like this again.'

'You see, Andy,' Jed picked up his narrative, 'the indigenous people of this land have worked as labourers and have drawn a wage as part of the progress that has been made here, but they have never had reason to conserve, preserve or respect any of what has been built.' Jed cast a hand in a broad sweep encompassing the distant mine and its surroundings. 'And frankly they wouldn't know where to start, because we never showed them. They've just done as they've been told which has suited us fine. It's like when a parrot talks: we think the vocabulary we impart which is then repeated is marvellous, but the parrot doesn't have a clue what it's saying or why he's saying it. The African labourer, in almost every situation, does his job in pretty much the same way; because that's the way we've taught him.

'In the not too distant future, like the rest of the countries to the north of us, the black politicians will get their independence from the dreaded colonial masters and then they'll squabble over the spoils of colonial planning, investment and prosperity. They'll ease out or hound out the whites who have been the driving force of progress, and they'll put their own unqualified people in charge, and the whole lot will turn to a bag of shit within a couple of years.'

Andy was puzzled. 'But why should that happen?' he asked. 'It all seems so perfect; surely something can be worked out. Why not just talk to each other?'

Jed chuckled and took a thoughtful draw on his pipe.

'That's dreaming, Andy.' He blew smoke into the air. 'The honeymoon is drawing to an end I'm afraid. The dream of paradise in Africa is built on white man's arrogance. The belief that a debt of gratitude is owed to them for raising the African from an abyss of ignorance; that their right to dominance and ownership is the reward. But that's a white man's perception. Black political activists will tell you that what you see has all been stolen from them by the marauding exploitation of white capitalists. I guess the situation can be compared to a marriage between two incompatible people. Both parties self-righteous and demanding, while one is paternally condescending but selfish with money and power, the other proud and ambitious but downtrodden and impatient. It simply has no chance of success unless the two can change within themselves and agree to co-exist in an atmosphere of trust and common goals. That's not happening and I don't think it ever will. The cultural gap is far too wide. There have been sporadic racial disturbances here and in Nyasaland and Southern Rhodesia, where black political activists are stirring up trouble and seducing the masses by fair means or foul. Even inciting violent resistance against white domination in the territories.

'You know what's happening just across that border?' Jed pointed with the end of his pipe towards the Congo only a few kilometres away. 'And further north? In Ghana, Kenya, Uganda, all these countries have suffered the fate of violent change and progress has hit a wall. It's something of a tragedy, Andy. The white man in Africa has been a reality for three hundred years, and there are people of European descent who can trace their family history on this continent back by up to ten generations. That's probably eight generations more than any indigenous family can, but we are still branded as settlers and intruders. It's only in the last hundred and thirty years or so that the white man has ventured in any meaningful numbers away from the coastal regions of the Cape. In this neck of the woods, the history of white influence only goes back eighty odd years, but in that time the wilderness of southern and central Africa has been unimaginably transformed. What is not acknowledged is what it took to make that transformation.

'When the first explorers came to Central Africa the people they encountered—the tribes of Africa—were people who had existed almost as primitively as the earliest ancestors of man. They had advanced at about the same rate of progression as the herds of game that you see roaming the veld. The march of human progress and civilization had simply passed them by, leaving a primitive culture of marauding nomads that had not even invented the wheel. There was nothing here.

'When the white pioneers and prospectors started their advance into these regions, they brought with them an entirely new vision and culture based on centuries of creative development. They were possessed of technical skills and used those fundamentals to build the infrastructure that supports the lifestyle we have come to enjoy. But in so doing they shaped the foundation of a divide between the races.

'The African, who had been awakened from thousands of years of dormant existence under his own rules of nature, found himself a labourer or servant in a world where a glass wall separated him and the sweat that pours off his aching back, from the privileges and sophisticated indulgences that the white colonizers created for themselves.

'The perception that the early white interlopers formed in their minds, and passed on through the succeeding generations of what became white Africans, was that these people were Neanderthal beings incapable of advancement or intelligent thought. We drove a racial wedge between black and white but expected them to fall into line with our so-called civilised norms and outlawed a tribal system that in its primitive way had worked to maintain a balance in Africa for centuries. What we did not do as part of the development was to offer anything of substance in its place, such as to allow the black labour force to participate in, or benefit substantially from, the spoils of our entrepreneurial endeavours or the sweat off their own backs. In fact laws were passed prohibiting him from having a social, political or financial voice, even on issues that are specific to his own dignity or destiny. The result is that we have a groundswell an awakening consciousness with some very angry black people and among them are some exceptionally clever manipulators. They have risen above the mob and promised the masses deliverance from white domination.'

Jed stared out across the beautifully maintained garden surrounding the house, to the wide open expanse of magnificent wild African bushveld beyond, and sighed.

'The point that seems to be missed Andy,' he went on, 'is the realism and reason for the whites wanting to protect their investment and stay in control. When the black labourer sees production come out of the mines or off the farms that are worked by his calloused hands, he works out roughly what it's worth in hard cash, he whistles silently through his missing teeth and thinks "Eish! My work is making some white bastard very rich!"

'He's dead right, but he doesn't think of the huge investment of time, planning, money and bloody hard work that went into the development of these enterprises. Nor does he see the risks or costs and administrative skills that are involved in sustaining the production and market distribution. The indigenous African, even those with an education, has yet to grasp the basic concept of reinvestment and redistribution. They take what's available and spend it. Tomorrow doesn't count.

'In business, European society has a history of settling differences between themselves around boardroom tables. They draw up contracts against the background of negotiations and debates using highly qualified lawyers and accountants to tie down the details. Politically we deal with leadership conflicts through a process of election, and we accept the outcome. When differences arise amongst the Africans, they settle things by simply killing their opponent and taking what was his. They don't see anything wrong with that—it's an effective way of making the problem go away and it's the way that it was always done before.

'The countries that have achieved the dream of black rule in Africa are governed with the same basic principle of might is right and all the ignorance that goes with it. Party leaders assume dictatorial possession of their countries as if those are their own personal fiefdom and they amass obscene wealth while leaving their countrymen in a state of abject poverty. The select few cling to their power base with a barbaric ruthlessness that defies imagination in Western civilisations. Accountability gets to be replaced by tyranny. Bribery, corruption and nepotism replace integrity, and the law of the jungle returns to rule. The peasant who has put his life on the line for the cause, based on the empty promises of the big house, abundant land and a Mercedes Benz, will have toured the full circle of true exploitation, from peasant to activist to guerrilla fighter to peasant but his protection as a peasant under a well managed, accountable administration will have ceased to exist, his sacrifices forgotten. And that, Andy, is what they call liberation.'

Jed held his cup toward Jean. 'Top that up for me please, love.' While Jean poured the tea, he stroked the side of his face with the end of his pipe.

'Try explaining all this to some fat gin-swilling Colonial Office civil servant and his politician cronies in London who've never set foot on the continent, but who continue to believe that they know what is best for these territories, and you'll find only deaf ears. As far as they are concerned the white man in Africa has become expediently expendable so long as Western values and influence can be sustained, and they will blindly continue to promote black rule in Africa. It's an even greater exercise in futility trying to explain to the young black guy that his life is being used as a pawn in the devious game of power to the people, which in reality will turn out to be power to the few where he won't be included.'

Jed stopped for a few minutes, while he puffed on his pipe and gathered his thoughts. Then he continued:

'To suggest that the autocratic despots who get the house and Mercedes and all the other trappings of power are capable of managing and logistically sustaining the sophisticated economies and enterprises that have been created in Africa, is akin to suggesting that you can give the keys of a fast and expensive car to a child.'

He paused again, pondering his verbal portrayal of the history and emerging conditions, and then after a while said:

'The sad truth, Andy, is that there is enough wealth on this continent for everyone to be more than comfortable—but greed, arrogance and politics have created divisions between the races that will never be healed. As much as we may pretend and ignore the inevitable, the fact is that you cannot suppress and disregard a proud but impoverished and ambitious majority group forever. That's where the seed of revolution germinates. We should have been smart enough to realise from the beginning that Western values and African customs are about as compatible as water and stone: the one can only displace the other. It is rapidly becoming apparent that the pre-conceived idea that Africa was there for the taking needed a whole lot more foresight, and it takes a fool not to see the danger we have created for the entire population of Africa from our failure to share our advanced knowledge in an environment of equality rather than to isolate ourselves from reality. Now we're painted into a corner. No matter what is done at this stage, it will be too little too late and neither side is going to give up without a fight. The unfortunate certainty, Andy, is that there will be a lot of blood spilt before Africa's problems are solved and you boys will be in the thick of it when the fighting starts. And the fighting will start, you mark my words.'

Jed sighed audibly and gazed out upon their beautiful surroundings. Andy was silenced by his narrative. None of what had been described had ever occurred to him before and it rattled him.

As he looked back at Jed he noticed that there were tears in his eyes.

# CHAPTER 5

## Rhodesia 1979

THE LABOURED RASP OF STUART'S BREATHING sounded like the dregs of a milkshake being repeatedly sucked from the bottom of a glass through a straw. The sound was unmistakable—Stuart had taken a lung shot and was breathing through his own blood. Twenty metres farther ahead, Rob had gone down and the manner of his falling indicated that he was dead—probably without ever knowing what had happened.

Sergeant Andrew Mason had taken cover thirty metres away and, in the time he'd been lying there—somewhere close to an hour—he had become immobilized in the grip of rising horror, in the face of an unfolding catastrophe.

Mason could hear movement close by, just ahead of where he lay. The unseen peril was drawing closer, but the darkness was absolute and for what he could see he may as well have been blind.

All he could be sure of was that the slow, soft disturbance of dead leaves and twigs only metres away was not Vern. The fear had slowly crept through him, and it was now a consuming wave of terror. It welled up from his groin, through his tightened guts and chest, and into his throat where it threatened to explode in an anguished scream.

It was five years since Mason had left South Africa to join the Rhodesian army, and in this African theatre of war he'd faced down death in scores of engagements. It was death, in fact, that had driven him from South Africa to Rhodesia—the tragic demise of two people whom he'd loved. He had faced the grim reaper with something very near to flippancy, a confidence born of anger and a desire for retribution. He'd been commended and decorated for his conduct under fire, and he had the emotional ability to endure danger and fear. But this was different. Never before had he been so vulnerable. He was trapped, hunted, and alone in a hostile and foreign country, facing unknown odds in the dark, with no immediate possibility of support or escape.

The emotional control was utterly gone. He had broken out in a sweat that soaked his shirt and denim fatigues, and he trembled as if he'd been lifted from an icy sea and dumped naked onto a cold windy beach. He had involuntarily pissed and shat himself, and the stench assailed his senses and the remnants of his dignity.

There was absolute certainty in Mason's mind that this night he would die; and he was so unprepared for it. A thousand thoughts and images, events and people, raced through his mind. So much left incomplete, so many thoughts unspoken, so many dreams and desires cut short, like pages left permanently and unalterably blank between the covers of a half written book. The present reality held him helpless and his fear blended with a deep sense of profound sadness as he pondered sudden and final oblivion.

And then, through the rush of images and the gripping panic, there came on him a sudden and overwhelming will to survive. It was like the cracking of a whip, and it brought him back to the situation.

'It mustn't happen!' he thought. 'Not now, not here, not like this! Focus, Mason! Focus!'

Drawing on every last resource of character, on his training and experience, and on the thought of all that he held precious, he fought to recover control of his mind and body. He pushed the fear back down, and out of his consciousness.

'Get on top of it! Control it! Think, and stay alive.'

Mason didn't know how far away Vern had been when, a little over an hour ago, they'd walked into the ambush. Nor did he know if Vern had survived the attack.

It was an overcast and moonless night and they had been making their way to a vantage point. Suddenly out of the silent darkness, the gates of hell had been thrown open with muzzle flashes that split the blackness in a hail of green tracer, like a storm of lethal fireflies that lit up the bush with the radiance of a pyrotechnics display.

In the blaze of tracer illumination Mason had seen his two comrades go down. He had instinctively loosed off a burst in the direction of the muzzle flashes and then gone to ground, rolling away on the hard rough surface of the hillside. He'd fired from the hip and he was pretty certain as he rolled for cover that he'd achieved nothing other than to expose his position. He'd drawn fire but it had gone high and wide, smashing through the foliage above him.

To move would be suicide. He could sense the enemy's presence. How many? He had no idea. But he did know that they had a rough idea of his location, and they'd be aware that they'd inflicted casualties. Now they were hunting, looking for survivors and closing in. He, Mason, seemed to be their focus. They seemed to be ignoring Stuart despite the fact that even in the pitch darkness his position could be pinpointed by the gurgle from his bleeding lungs. The hideous noise and Stuart's soft groaning were unmistakeable. He was near his end. Mason tried to focus instead on the tiny sounds that told of an invisible stalker—who was no more than eight or nine metres away, up ahead and to his right.

All of a sudden there was a flash and a single gunshot from where Stuart lay mortally wounded and the harsh bubbling noise abruptly ceased. Mason just made out the muted sound of a figure—the killer, surely—retreating through the bush, in the general direction of the place where the ambush party had first opened fire. But it wasn't over yet. Another person was still moving, ever so softly—the stalker whom Mason had sensed to the right of his position. The abrupt end of Stuart's life tested the limits of Mason's sanity, but he had to keep cool. He had to stay focused.

Doc Morrison's face, and his words, came into Mason's mind. Doc Morrison, combat psychologist attached to the SAS, had given them motivational lectures during their training in enemy tactics and combat discipline.

'There will be times,' he had said casually, in a conversational tone, while he paced the lecture room. 'When conditions or circumstances will strike fear in your hearts. That's nothing to be ashamed of. Anyone who denies being afraid under fire or in a tight situation is a liar.

'Chaps,' he had said, 'fear is an emotion—a condition of the mind like love, jealousy, anger or hate. Like any other emotion it can be controlled. And it must be controlled. If you don't learn to control it, it will control you, and that will lead to panic.'

He then raised his voice an octave to emphasise his next words and bring an element of drama into the subject: '*Panic, gentlemen, breeds panic.* It spreads like an odour. Once it's upon you it will spiral out of control and you will begin to behave irrationally, and that will affect all those around you. If you do that in a combat situation, you will not only endanger yourself, but everybody else as well. Then, you or your friends and maybe all of you, will die.

'Now it may be noble and patriotic to die for your cause and country but, believe me, you will be of far greater use to the war effort by staying alive and helping the guys on the other side make the sacrifice.

'Always remember that they are more afraid of you than you are of them. To coin a phrase, the thing that you should fear the most is fear itself.'

This op was supposed to have been a simple intelligence-gathering reconnaissance patrol. Mason's four-man callsign had been tasked with setting up an observation post in these hills in western Zambia. The hills overlooked an area where a recent concentration of Zipra guerrillas indicated that the enemy was establishing a transit base. Such a base was typically used to re-equip, feed, and brief parties of infiltrators en route from their training facilities further north to the Rhodesian border. The suspected layout and general activities of the base had warranted an in-depth intelligence report, and this required first-hand research from a patrol on the ground.

\*     \*     \*

A NDY HAD BEEN HAVING BREAKFAST IN THE MESS TENT AT THEIR FORWARD BASE CAMP, with the usual morning banter and horseplay among the NCOs, when an orderly had come across to him:

'Sergeant Mason,' he said, 'Sunray wants you in the Ops Room.'

On operations or in forward base 'Sunray' was used in reference to the officer in command. In this case it was Major Dawson. Greg Dawson.

Andy finished his coffee, picked up his rifle and slung his chest webbing with spare magazines loosely over his shoulder.

'It's back to the war I guess,' he said with a casual grin as he rose from the table. 'Let's just hope we don't all get culled.'

He strode down the lines of tents towards the Ops Room, swopping greetings with the troops. He wore an old khaki tee-shirt, faded green shorts and veldskoen shoes without socks, and his webbing hung loose against his broad back. His tee-shirt was already wet with perspiration. Thermals rose off the Zambezi and the humidity was oppressive, even at this early hour, but he strode with a spring in his step.

Andy was just back from two weeks of leave which he'd spent in the intoxicating company of Alyson Carstens. Part of the time was at Lake Kariba and part of it on her parents' farm of citrus and tobacco. Golden Acres was the name of the farm, and for him she was the golden girl. She wasn't a conventional beauty but she was curiously striking. In fact, she oozed sex appeal—and for eighteen months Andy had dated, mated and laughed with her during periods of reprieve from the war.

They had met in the Winged Stagger, the legendary NCOs' Mess at SAS Squadron Command in Salisbury. He wasn't sure if it was love, but he knew without a doubt that he was passionately in lust; and two weeks of Allison's company had left him light headed. The effect she had on him—a new vitality and warmth—was delicious.

They'd parted just the day before, and through the warmth he felt a twinge of pain. She had cried when he left her apartment to report for duty at SAS headquarters. He'd flown in a Dakota supply aircraft from Salisbury to the Air Force base at Wankie, and on by helicopter to this improvised forward base on the banks of the Zambezi River, and all the while she'd been in his thoughts. *I guess it must be love*—this thought struck him through the easy glow of pleasure.

Andy walked into the Ops Room. Dawson was sitting on an upturned ammunition box in front of a large fold-down chart table, plotting positions on a map. On the wall was another much bigger map, in 1:500, 000 scale, of southern and central Zambia.

'Good morning, sir,' said Andy, placing his rifle into the rack at the door and slinging the magazine pouches from it. 'You're looking for me?'

'Yeah. Hi Andy. Welcome back.' Dawson smiled. 'I hope your wallowing in luxury hasn't blunted your soldiering skills.'

Andy laughed. 'It may have blunted my enthusiasm to be nasty to anyone, sir. It was like the Garden of Eden.'

'Well, you may need to eat an apple or something.' replied Dawson with a grin. 'Look—we've got a job for you. It's a walk-in op, about seven to ten days. Will you get a team together? Be back here by 11h00 for briefing.'

'Right, sir. Any special skills needed?'

'Nothing that you can't all handle. It's just a "look-see" job.'

The Rhodesian SAS conducted cross-border intelligence-gathering operations and subsequent lightning-strike raids on external revolutionary command bases. These were combined with the sabotage of supply lines and infiltration routes, prisoner snatches, and extensive external disruption of the enemy's activities. This, in sum, constituted the work of Sergeant Andy Mason of the SAS. They were rarely deployed for ops within the borders of Rhodesia. This small force of highly-trained specialists concentrated their well-honed skills on the surrounding territories of Mozambique and Zambia, where the guerrilla armies of ZANLA and ZIPRA were given sanctuary.

Andy selected a team with whom he'd worked on dozens of missions similar to the one now at hand:

31

Rob Southey, a sandy-haired, freckle-faced twenty-two-year-old who'd played rugby for Rhodesian schools and had his sights set on playing the game at international level. He was of medium height, with powerful shoulders and a heart of gold. He had an infectious laugh and a sharp wit. Apart from being an intelligent soldier he was known for the outrageous tales he told about his escapades as a ladies' man and a war hero. The stories always had an element of truth about them but were hugely exaggerated, and he was known to change the details to suit the occasion. He could be as entertaining as a professional stand-up comedian.

Stuart O'Donnell, who had been on the same selection course as Andy, was an obvious choice. He and Andy had become friends five years previously, in training troop, and they had encouraged each other through the gruelling months of training and selection. Those who stayed the distance physically and mentally were seen as men who had crossed over from the run of the mill into a privileged elite—but in reality the successful candidates were average guys with above-average character, who had to prove their worth in often fatally dangerous conditions.

The fourth member of the team was Vern Dempsey, a New Zealander who had served with the Australian forces in Vietnam. Andy got to know Vern a year back when they had been together on the squadron sniper course. He was a big man in his early thirties and his skill as a marksman was fearsome. Weapons of any sort seemed to be natural extensions of himself, and his effortless use of a rifle and light machine gun was unmatched for speed and accuracy. He stood at six foot three with a pair of shoulders almost as broad as he was tall and formed a pillar of solid muscle. He had grown up in the back streets of Auckland using his wits and fists to get his share of whatever was going around, but he'd mellowed and was the sort of guy that kept pretty much to himself. He'd turned down promotion although he was more than competent and qualified, but he was a ready helper when there was work to be done. He was an excellent soldier and a good man to have on board.

The three were eager to take on the job, and Mason repeated to them what he'd been told by Dawson. The team reported to the Ops Room for their briefing.

The large scale map of Zambia on the Ops Room wall was the focus of the briefing. It had coloured markers pinned over dozens of different locations, and Dawson began by pointing out their location at Deka Drum on the banks of the Zambezi. Deka Drum was a derelict fishing camp about eighty kilometres east of Victoria Falls. Once it had been popular as a resort for anglers going out for tiger fish, but like all the formerly luxurious camps on the Zambezi, Deka had succumbed to the ravages of war. The ruins of the resort now served as base camp for the SAS.

'Chaps,' said Dawson, 'There's unusual activity going on in this region. Enough to worry us.' He placed his pointer on an area about 180 km north of Livingstone, the small Zambian town on the Zambezi River opposite the Victoria Falls. The location was decorated with red pins in the shape of a question mark.

'We've never had troops on the ground there,' Dawson continued, turning to Andy and his team, 'but intelligence reports suggest that a transit base may be on the build—for ZIPRA terrs coming down from training in Zaire. If that's the case, we'd rather not let them settle in too comfortably. The Air Force ran a high altitude photo session over the vicinity a week ago but it's inconclusive. We need detailed information about what's actually going on.

'So,' said Dawson, 'this is the job. We want you to get into the area and set up an observation post in these hills.' He moved the pointer to a pattern of contours that spoke of high ground to the south-west of the objective.

'We want to know about vehicle movement if any, coming and going of personnel, armaments, whether or not there are women and children, and most importantly exfiltration activity.

'Are there groups arriving and swelling the numbers, or are they night-stopping and then moving on? If groups are moving in and out, how big are the groups? What is their mode of transport? Are the numbers consistent—as in platoon strength or smaller? Is there a pattern to movement, like early morning or after last light? If they're moving out, are they all moving in the same direction or does that vary?

'You'll be on the ground so you must use your discretion as to whether or not a close-in recce is wise. If you can get close enough to identify the commander and any senior personnel it would be useful, but not essential—so don't take unnecessary chances. An overview of the situation is all we need for now.'

Dawson looked at each man in turn.

'Right!' he said. 'Execution. You'll be taken in by chopper to this area here.'

He pointed to a flat area a long way south of the target, then looked up and smiled in mock apology:

'Sorry chaps, but you've got a long walk. It shouldn't take longer than two and a half to three days, but we can't take you any closer for fear of compromise. Anyway, that's as far as the choppers can go without having to refuel on the way back, and there's no provision for that so it has to be a long walk-in.'

He scanned the faces of the men.

'If you find what we think you'll find, we don't want to scare them off before we pay them a flying visit. The bush for miles around is pretty thick and it will be impossible to move through it silently—so keep your eyes and ears open.'

'As far as Admin & Logistics are concerned, we expect you to be in position for seven to ten days. So equip yourselves accordingly—you know the drill. We won't be able to re-supply you, so you'll have to conserve your rations. If all goes well, and there's no reason why not, you'll need a week to get the intelligence that we want.

'You'll be deeply clandestine and you're unlikely to run into a contact so don't overload yourselves with ammo—but be prepared. You might consider side arms with silencers in case of people snooping around you. If the shit hits the fan, get out. You're not there to fight a four-man war; you're just there to look. Make sure you have a pre-arranged RV in case you are separated, but—whatever you do—try to avoid that.

'If you look at the map,' added Dawson, 'you can see that there is water en route: these rivers—here, here and here.' He touched the thin crooked blue lines that crossed the general direction of their march. 'None of them are raging torrents, but you'll be able to keep up your supply.

'On logistics,' he continued, 'let's look at an emergency withdrawal scenario. You'll be out of range of the Allouettes, but don't worry. If we need to get to you for an urgent evacuation, at least one chopper will be empty of troops on the way in and can carry spare fuel and dump the drums en route to refuel on the way back. From here it's a long run for the choppers, but if any serious trouble pops up we'll scramble fixed wings from Wankie to give you overhead cover. That shouldn't be necessary, though. When you exfiltrate you'll walk out again and we'll pick you up where we drop you.

'Comms! You'll need to be carrying one big means, so get the signallers to sort you out with a TR48. This call sign is zero, and you'll be two zero. Report in at 06h00 and 18h00 daily unless there's an emergency. Otherwise keep the radio off in between your sitreps. It's up to you guys, but I'd also suggest small means in the form of two A60s in case you need to split up for whatever reason. Any questions?'

'Can I make a suggestion, sir?' asked Andy, putting down the notebook in which he'd been scribbling details.

'Of course.'

'Why don't we do a HAHO drop closer to the target? The moon's down at the moment, which means we'll have to walk from the chopper LZ during the day. If we do a 02h00 high altitude, high opening para drop, here,' he pointed to an area about ten km north-west, 'we'd be unlikely to attract attention. We could use the height to drift, and we'd probably get two to three K closer to the target from our jump position under canopy. Then we can recce the area at first light, lay up for the day and walk into position that night. Don't you think we'd be too exposed to the locals on a three-day daylight walk-in from the LZ?'

We'd thought of that, and it's a good idea. We're just a bit worried about you guys landing all over Zambia and not being able to find one another.'

'Oh come on, sir,' laughed Rob. 'We all know how to read a map. We can set an RV before we leave, and close on it once we've hidden our chutes.'

'Daylight walking, Rob,' said Dawson. 'As Andy's pointed out, there is no moon, which means you'd have to find each other in daylight. Being so close to the target you could run into a patrol and compromise the op. If you're together that's not such bad news but if you're still solo you've got big shit in your life and we don't want to have to come looking for you on a search and recovery op. Let's stick to the original plan, but thanks for the input. Anything else chaps? No? Right, on your bikes, then. H hour from here is 18h30.'

In typical military layout, the camp comprised rows of bell tents under untidy camouflage netting: the Signals tent with a variety of co-ax antennae extending from it at different angles and heights, Medics with a tattered Red Cross ensign fluttering in the wind outside, Admin and Armoury boasting a 'Base Walla' sign hanging from the entrance. The kitchen and dining area were set away from the rest, with a permanent aroma of cooking. The 'desert lilies' were in evidence at varying intervals, with long-drop latrines positioned over a slit trench behind a fence of hessian cloth at the extreme edge of the camp.

A long-abandoned club house, a relic from the fishing resort, had been turned into the Ops Room. Maps on the walls covered the area of operations and two clerks spent their time summarising situation reports that had come in from operational groups out on deployment. Vehicles moved about on a variety of transport tasks, and troops in shorts and tee-shirts occupied themselves playing cards, reading or cleaning their weapons.

The sleeping quarters were low-pitched one-man tents scattered around the perimeter of the camp, where essential kit lay packed for emergency deployment at a moment's notice. Three Allouette helicopters were perched on a makeshift helipad in a clearing behind the Ops Room, under anti-glare netting.

The team made their way through the supply lines, drawing the equipment they needed for the op. They then gathered in the mess tent to sort it and discuss their plan of action. Stuart was tasked with carrying the radio, a heavy and cumbersome piece of equipment. Andy had the medic kit, while Vern was volunteered the extra weight of the RPD and five spare belts. The weapon was a light machine gun of Russian manufacture and thousands of these guns had been captured from the guerrilla forces over the years. It operated on a belt feed from a compact drum beneath the breach and was a favourable alternative to the British-made MAG, which was bigger, heavier and more cumbersome but offered nothing extra in stopping power or rate of fire.

Rob was to carry the spare batteries and an eight kilogramme 'chocolate cake,' the nickname given to an anti-vehicle landmine, whose appearance struck a remarkable resemblance to something upon which one would expect to see birthday candles. Most patrols took some form of explosives with them to cater for the unexpected, and a landmine was stable and compact.

Personal kit was personal choice. Each member of the unit had his own idea of comfort when it came to what went along within the limits of what was sensible in weight and size.

By 12h15 they were ready to move. After lunch they played volleyball, and then they got their heads down for an hour. At 18h00, they'd done their final kit checks and ticked them off. Medical supplies, radios working, radio batteries charged, radio codes, ammunition, rations and maps, compasses etc. They had checked for unwanted rattling from each other's Bergens and light webbing and were moving out to the helipad when Dawson came out of the ops room and called them back in.

'Change of plan,' he said. 'Sorry, lads, but we've had another look at the para drop option and we've decided to go that route, except you'll go HALO. Jump at 20 000 and open at two and a half into that north-west sector you pointed out, Andy.' He touched the map with the pointer.

'Lead jump to use his shoulder strobe set on a two second flash cycle and you can all close on him. It's going to be bloody dark so keep your legs together. Casualties on the DZ are not an option. The choppers will take you to Wankie now. There's a Dak on its way up from Salisbury. H-hour 01h00. Everything else stays the same. Questions? No? Okay! Away you go then! Happy landings.'

They strode off to the waiting Allouettes, their engines already racing, churning up a cloud of dust and leaves and bending the boughs of the trees under the downward force of the spinning rotors. The four of them piled into the lead chopper, bending double as they ran under the rotor tips and heaved their packs on board. They lifted off in a storm of flying debris and dust, the pilot dipped the nose of the aircraft, and they were away—headed out southwest into a glorious sunset of orange and gold.

They got dinner at Wankie in the airmen's mess and then went across to the bar for a Coke before quietly slipping away to the hanger where they'd left their kit. They all put their heads down and settled into a few hours of uneasy sleep. Pre-op nerves never failed to put a squadron of butterflies in Andy's stomach, something that affected them all. He never got used to it. He would joke that at least his butterflies flew in formation, which meant that instead of feeling petrified before an op, he was more than just a little apprehensive.

Part of their training had been how to put those butterflies into order. There was a perception among some other units that SAS operatives were fearless, and for the sake of the image they never let on—but it remained no more than a perception. SAS troops had the same sense of impending danger and doom as anyone else. It was only once they were on the ground that the tension would ease.

They were shaken awake at midnight by the dispatchers who had brought their chutes up from Salisbury in the Dakota:

'Wakey, wakey guys! It's time to go!'

The four-man team rechecked their equipment and harnessed it to their individual para drop containers. Before donning their chutes, they covered themselves with cammo cream, a substance that looked like a mixture of boot polish and face cream. Nobody knew what it was made of, and most didn't want to ask. All they knew was that it could save their white arses if they were seen from a distance—or even from quite close. It made them look like black men. Black men were the enemy in this war, and the enemy of black men was white.

# CHAPTER 6

The Dakota DC3 laboured in its rate of ascent, in a slow and cumbersome climb towards it's ceiling of 20 000 feet. Once airborne, Andy and his team settled in with their kit at their feet ready for attachment. The team had long since come to know that a parachute is an uncomfortable appendage at best, and having ten days of supplies and equipment clipped to it and resting on one's legs while seated on an uncomfortable bench made it almost unbearable.

At 15 000 feet they rigged their personal equipment containers to their harnesses. As the Dak droned on towards the drop zone, they started to make use of the oxygen canisters as breathing apparatus in the unpressurised cabin.

When the team got the action stations order, they gratefully stood up and got some of the circulation back into their limbs, once again checking each other's parachute and equipment. The soft red glow of the cabin nightlight, portrayed them in an eerie form of ghostlike apparitions floating on air.

They gathered one pace from the door, in a multi-exit formation, steadying themselves against the turbulence of the plane's oscillating motion. The red light above the door came on, and the dispatcher called out *'In the door'.*

Bunched together with a firm grip on each other's harnesses, they shuffled to the door with their loads, looking and feeling like a group of Michelin men. The green light blinked on. Above the wind and the roar of engines, the dispatcher shouted *'GO!'* and they tumbled out into the darkness. As they went, they let go of each other and stabilised themselves individually in their descent, evenly spreading arms and legs in a swallow position.

Vern had the shoulder strobe and they focused on him, riding the cushion of air beneath them like body surfers on an invisible wave, resting easily against the wind resistance as they plummeted earthward.

Andy kept his eyes on the twin altimeters attached to his reserve chute, watching the dials turning: 15 000 feet, 12 000, 8 000, 5 000. At two and a half he tucked his arms in, took a firm grip of the cord handle, and pulled. The chute came out with a loud *thwap* and he felt his descent slowed by the drag of the deploying canopy. He heard the other chutes deploying and looked around to find the strobe. There it was, forty feet below him and to his right. He released his equipment so that it dangled beneath him and held steady, straining his eyes in a quest to see something of the ground coming up to meet him.

Beneath the parachute canopy (invisible in the night sky) there was absolute silence. The motion, with a gentle upward breeze, induced in Andy a dreamlike state. It was unreal, like floating on an imaginary cloud, descending slowly in the warm night air.

The spell was abruptly broken. He heard his equipment harness crashing into bush below him, and he braced himself, legs tight together, toggles to stall, and without seeing a thing he was on the ground, amongst a tangle of Jesse bush.

He quickly unclipped one side of the canopy and removed his rifle from the constraints of the parachute harness, and then he lay still—following the drill of an operational night jump. They lay there listening for noises around them, not making any sounds themselves. They held their positions for fifteen minutes in total silence. Nothing moved. There was not even the rustle of wind through the trees. Satisfied that they were safe, Andy stood up and released himself from the confining straps of the parachute. Then, in a hoarse whisper, he called out to the others:

'Everyone okay?'

'One okay,' 'Two okay,' 'Three okay,' came the replies in the same hoarse whispers. They'd landed within a 50 metre radius of each other and were all safely on the ground.

Untangling their chutes from the bushes they folded them into tight bundles, and stacked them together at the base of a Mopane tree. At first light they would find a place to hide and camouflage them.

Talk was kept to a minimum and in low whispers. As planned, they would stay on their DZ for the night, get the lay of the land while holding a listening post for the whole of the next day, and then move in on their objective in the evening twilight. They weren't sure how far off their target they were, but they'd have to wait until daylight to take their bearings and orientate themselves on the map.

They spread out over a fifty-metre area, got out their bedrolls and slept. Their state of mind and discipline were such that the merest change in the direction of the wind would bring them wide awake and alert.

The dawn broke with the intense beauty of the African bush. There was a refreshing chill in the silent air and the sky was pale turquoise, with tiny clouds painted crimson by the sun that lay, as yet, below the horizon. Against the sky, the trees and scrub were etched in black.

The sun made its rapid ascent, the sky turned to a deeper blue and the crimson faded from the sparse clouds. The bark of baboons echoed off the hills and a hyena cackled in the distance, while all around were the chatter and hum of awakening birds and insects.

The wonder of it enthralled Andy, as it always did. Mystique, sanctity, elation. It was a wonderland. The birth of each new day in this forested wilderness was, to him, a kind of narcotic. And each time he witnessed it, the intoxication grew.

He shook himself from his reverie. He signalled to the others, and the four of them moved in extended line through the thick forest to a position 500 metres east of where they'd slept.

Again they spread themselves out, keeping a distance of about twenty metres between each other. They unpacked their Hexi cookers and put on a brew, and Andy gratefully lit a cigarette.

He got out his map and compass and pinpointed their position. Stuart set up the radio and they reported their position and progress to base. They were eight km away from the point where they would set up their OP, a walk of about three and a half hours by Andy's reckoning. He guessed that they could be in a lay-up position within an hour's march of their target by eight that night, if they moved out with the five o' clock shadows. The last one or two km would be in the dark, and they'd have to allow extra time for that.

They had their breakfast of tea and wheat biscuits, packed up their gear, and gathered together. In soft whispers, they decided the order of march and the route, taking into account the thickness of the bush and the undulating ground that they'd have to negotiate on the way.

Rob and Vern went down to where they'd left their chutes to find a place where they could be stored without fear of detection. There was so much thick bush that they had no difficulty with their task, and were back within the hour.

The day passed uneventfully. Around midday they heard an elephant trumpeting in the distance. In the early afternoon a small herd of impala, followed by two bachelor zebra, wandered unsuspectingly past their position, but they detected no other movement. By all accounts, their presence was unknown to anyone but themselves. Clouds started to build up as the afternoon progressed, and it seemed they'd get some rain later. Probably while they were on the move that evening.

At 17h00 they picked up their kit and made a quick check to ensure that they had left no trace of their presence. They spruced up the grass where they had sat to disguise the fact that it had been disturbed, and they moved out in a staggered file on a compass bearing towards their objective. When Andy called a break at 18h00 they laid out the long co-ax antenna cable for the radio and sent their sitrep.

'Hopefully, one day someone will come up with a better way of doing this,' said Stuart as they laboriously rewound the cable and packed it into the carrier bag.

A brew of tea and tinned bully beef constituted the evening meal, and then they moved on again. By 19h45 they had reached the lower slopes of the small range of steep hills that was their target area and a soft rain had started to fall from heavy clouds above them. They still had a distance of about a kilometre to get to the top, but it had already been dark for nearly an hour so the going wasn't easy, and they decided to stay where they were for the night. The rain got heavier, soaking them to the skin through their denim fatigues, and the water cascaded off the rims of their bush hats. The four of them were all hardened to it. This was not the first time they'd sat in the bush under pouring rain and, in all probability, it wouldn't be the last.

Just before 23h00 the distinctive drone of heavy vehicles brought the small group to full alert. The noise was a long way off, but the sound was unmistakable and they tried to figure out the direction from which it was coming. The stereophonic echo of the sound distorted their judgement of distance and direction, but then Rob saw the lights. Three or possibly four vehicles—it was difficult to tell through the trees. At a guess, they figured that the convoy was about three km off to the north on a south-east heading. There must have been a road of sorts, but it didn't appear on their maps and they assumed that whatever path the vehicles were using must have been recently carved out of the bush. From the straining sound of the engines it was obvious that it was no easy ride.

'I tell you what,' said Andy, 'let's move out and get to a vantage point at the top of this hill. That way we can get an idea where those vehicles are going, and probably get a clear indicator on the camp's exact location. I can't think of any other place they could be headed at this hour.'

In the darkness, the going was slow and dangerous. The rain had stopped, but the cloud cover was still thick and it added to the impenetrable darkness of the moonless night. They walked into trees they could not see, and they tripped on rocks that appeared underfoot without warning. Trying to go quietly was impossible, but they felt cautiously confident that they were well clear of any immediate danger. They had been moving for around forty minutes and Andy guessed that they'd covered about 800 metres from the lower slopes of the hill where they had seen the lights of the vehicles. The sound of the vehicles had died away, and they weren't sure if this meant they'd stopped, or if the noise was muffled by the shape of the hill.

All these thoughts were on Andy's mind and his concentration was not entirely on their surroundings. They had stopped every hundred meters or so to listen for any hint of movement around them, but on each occasion they were surrounded by total silence.

The ear-splitting cacophony of automatic gunfire was so sudden and unexpected that a jolt like an electric shock ran through Andy, and everything seemed to go into slow motion.

Muzzle flashes from the ambush position showed it to be fifty metres ahead of him and to the left. The green tracer lit up the surroundings as clearly as a full moon, and he saw Rob go down like an unstrung puppet. Stuart had dived for cover, but he'd been stopped in his tracks as though he hit a solid wall. He was blasted backwards, striking the ground against his backpack and rolling away onto his side.

Returning fire was an instinctive reaction, but Andy had been carrying his rifle at waist level and he knew as he pulled the trigger that it was an exercise in futility. There was no thought of aiming. He fired at random in the direction of the muzzle flashes and then he, too, was going for cover.

His shoulder hit the ground heavily and he rolled away to his right. He felt the painful jar of a rock digging into his ribs as he went over, and the press of his Bergen in his back and neck, and he rolled back onto his stomach.

There was an ear-splitting crash of rounds through the bush above him and to the left, shattering the surroundings in long uncontrolled bursts of flaming fire power. It was so close that he felt the heat of the flying tracer on his face and hands. The deafening assault filled his consciousness with an immediate sense of doom.

Then, as suddenly as it had erupted, the firing stopped. The echo of the attack rolled away into the night and a deathly hush descended like a shroud. The whole action had taken no longer than a matter of seconds, but it seemed that a lifetime had gone by.

Stuart was in serious trouble. Andy could hear from his gurgled breathing that he was drowning in his own blood, and if he didn't get attention he would die.

Adrenaline pumped through his veins as the shock of the attack settled into his being and he tried to take stock of the situation. His mouth was as dry and rough as desert sand; he found he could not swallow, and he nearly choked trying. He lay absolutely still, trying to get a bead on the ambush position, straining his eyes for movement—but there was none . . . . Only a deep impenetrable darkness.

For almost an hour Andy lay there unmoving, helplessly trying to work out his options. He needed to get to Stuart with the medics kit, but there was no profit in getting himself killed or injured in an attempt to cover the thirty metres that separated them.

He remained where he was. He had heard muffled voices from the direction of the firing point, but had no way of assessing the strength of the enemy or their exact position. The agony and helplessness of his situation bore into his stiffening muscles. His conscience told him to get across and help Stuart, whose agonised groans and blood-bubbled breathing spoke of impending death, but common sense, discipline, and the probable consequences stopped him. Every minute seemed like an eternity as the time dragged by.

Then Andy heard the movement. Somebody was creeping towards him with great stealth. One slow step after another: he heard the crunch and shuffle of dead leaves underfoot as the foe advanced warily on Andy's position.

'He must know I'm here,' he reckoned. 'He's coming straight onto me.'

He had his weapon at the ready.

'This bastard's going to be the one to die first,' he thought. 'Let's worry about what happens afterwards—when afterwards arrives.'

He knew that if he fired on the stalker, the rest of the party would open up and probably tear his body to shreds, but he saw no alternative. He wasn't going out without a fight. As long as he remained quite still, the stalker didn't stand a chance. He just needed to get a glimpse of the approaching figure, for an accurate shot. To open fire wildly would only serve as a target indicator for the rest of the ambush party and nothing would be achieved.

There couldn't have been more than fifteen metres between them, and Andy was sweating profusely. The fear inside him suddenly burst from his body and when he felt the urine and faeces soiling his fatigues, he nearly cried out aloud. Then there was silence, a silence that screamed in his ears. Only the bubbling in Stuart's heaving chest broke through it.

'Move, you bastard!' he said inwardly. 'I need to know where you are.'

'He can't see me and he's as scared as I am,' he kept telling himself. 'He's shitting himself, just like me.'

The single gunshot, from where Stuart lay drowning in his own blood, came with such an unexpected impact that Andy's sanity teetered on the edge. His instinct was to cry out, but anger stopped him. He knew full well what had been done and the execution was confirmed by the silence that followed, rubbing in the death of his wounded friend. Andy's throat was filled with bile, but he had to stay focused. He moved his attention back to the lurking danger a few short metres in front of him. But he was acutely aware, too, of the shuffle of soft retreating footfalls from Stuart's position.

During the long preceding hour, Andy had slowly and noiselessly drawn the pistol he'd packed at Dawson's suggestion. He had struggled to move himself into a position from where he could reach down and draw the weapon without making any sound that would expose him.

He had slowly moved his right hand down his side to the holster on his belt. Hoops and a shallow cup on the side of the holster secured the cylindrical silencer, and he had carefully drawn it out before unclipping the webbing flap that covered the butt of the pistol.

Very slowly he had brought the items up to eye level where he could work with both hands to secure the silencer. At first he couldn't line up the threads. His hands were too unsteady, and he had bumped the two metal objects together. To him, the soft clink was alarming. He was sure that anyone within a hundred metres must have heard it as clearly as a church bell on a quiet Sunday morning, and he held still while he waited for shots to ring out and for the bullets to shred his body as they had done to Stuart and Rob.

But nothing happened and he had lain still, trying to control the spasms of fear that wracked his nerves and muscles. After a minute or so he had tried again. This time, by touch and feel, he got the two to marry and slowly twisted the silencer into the pistol barrel; and then he waited.

That had been an agonising forty minutes back, and his anger had increased tenfold at the brutal slaying of Stuart. Now, after what seemed like an awfully long time, but in reality couldn't have been more than minutes since the footfalls had gone silent, he heard the sound again. Cautiously, the man started to move, but this time away from him to his right, walking gingerly, each step taking forever.

Andy kept repeating encouragement to himself. He had to get a glimpse of his stalker; it would give him a chance of survival. He needed to take him out with the minimum of noise, leaving no room for error.

The soft slow stepping movement was still there, moving away to the right and past him. Andy the prey, and this unseen, unknown person the hunter. He lay face down, perfectly still, just his eyes moving. The sound of movement stopped again and an eerie silence descended once more.

As Andy tried to gauge the distance between himself and his hunter, the sounds of the hunt started again. This time they came from behind him and to the right, and moving closer.

Very slowly, very quietly, Andy rolled to his left so that his back was firmly pressed against his Bergen and he lay on his side, giving himself more mobility and a wider arc of vision.

He strained his eyes to pick up any sign of movement, and then he saw it.

Nothing more than a dark shadow, ghost-like, moving ever so cautiously step by cautious step, a little less than eight metres away.

He levelled the pistol with trembling hands, taking an unsteady bead on the widest part of the apparition, and—as gently as he could—he squeezed the trigger.

The weapon jarred in his fist with a thud like the sharp rap of a knuckle on a wooden door, and the shadow fell to the ground. Working purely by reflex, without conscious thought, Andy leapt from his place of refuge and was upon the man, pistol in hand. Pressing the end of the silencer into the head of the shape on the ground, he fired again. The body jerked as if hit by an electrical charge and the form gave out a soft sigh.

In that brief moment of contact, Andy felt the body go slack as if the man had been released from enormous tension and had slipped into a state of total relaxation. It had all happened in one movement, and Andy rolled away, got to his feet and took a number of stumbling strides over the rocky ground, away from the ambush site. Then he went to ground again, a few metres away.

As he hit the ground the silence was shattered once again by a long burst of automatic fire, and a stream of tracer tore through the bush over the point where he'd left the body of his stalker. But it was only one weapon firing.

Immediately there was firing from behind Andy and to his left, one short explosive burst. It could only have been Vern, returning fire with the RPD. The tracer from that unexpected source of support flew straight into the location from where the muzzle flashes and tracer were still coming, and the shattering onslaught came to an abrupt halt.

As the echo of the fire fight rolled off into the night, silence came upon them again. Andy kept his position, his senses acutely tuned to his surroundings. He now knew where Vern was, and that he was very much alive. He mentally noted the area, but he was listening for other sounds, other movement.

The tension pulled at his nerves and muscles. He could feel the ache of it in the nape of his neck and in his shoulders. A nauseating tightness in his guts threatened to erupt and spew out his suppressed panic in a demented scream. His heart was pounding and he felt the perspiration on his face and down his back and in his groin, where it mingled with the sticky mess of his evacuated bowels. He lay perfectly still except for the involuntary trembling of his nerves, and he listened. An eternity went by but there was nothing. No return fire had gone down on Vern's position; there was no scurrying for cover, no sound at all.

'There can only have been the two of them,' thought Andy in disbelief. 'And that trigger happy bastard must have panicked when he heard the sound of the pistol.'

With adrenaline coursing through his veins, and through the fear and the barely suppressed panic, Andy took stock. He realised that they had not walked into a large pre-planned ambush party. This can only have been a couple of strays that had opened fire spontaneously at the sound of their movement. They probably didn't even know what they were shooting at.

The whole bizarre chain of events and its effects boiled up inside him. He felt a combination of relief, sadness and anger, like a kaleidoscope of emotions. It brought his tears to the surface, and he stifled an audible sob. 'God, what a waste!' he thought. 'What an almighty balls-up.'

From inside him, the wreckage of his resolve and his helplessness welled up. It rose up from a place so deep he'd never even known it was there.

He was angry, and he felt shame for not having had the courage to get up and go to Stuart. The horrors of the night clung to him as if mocking and scorning him, and he felt afraid for what might still come to pass.

It was a racing certainty that an enemy patrol was on its way, and probably pretty close by now. It had been well over an hour since the first volley of gunfire and a patrol would certainly be coming to investigate.

'Shit! If we'd come in by chopper and done the three-day walk in, we wouldn't have been anywhere near this place,' he thought. 'We'd still be bloody miles away and Rob and Stuart would still be alive.'

'Hey, Andy,' came Vern's whispered voice from somewhere that seemed far away, and Mason was surprised when he looked up and the dark form of his saviour was right there beside him. 'You alright?'

'Rob and Stuart are dead,' he whispered back, choked and unsteady.

'Yeah. No doubt about that,' replied Vern in his soft New Zealand drawl. 'Shit! Stuart had a bad time of it! But that bastard had no right to do what he did. He won't be doing it again though.'

'We're going to have to get them up and get the hell out of here, Vern,' said Andy. 'We can hide them down the hill and get the Air Force in at first light to blast whatever it is we're supposed to have come to look at. Then we can recover the bodies.'

'Right,' whispered Vern. 'Let's get to work. How many grenades you got?'

'Just two, standard kit. And you?'

'Same,' said Vern. 'Should be enough to set booby traps in their packs. That should keep the gooks occupied when they arrive. Jesus! Something smells like shit!'

'That's me,' responded Andy. 'I'd rather not talk about it. Let's get to work.' He paused, and then said 'Keep your grenades. We might still want them. Rob and Stuart won't need theirs, though.'

Andy moved cautiously towards where Stuart lay. In the pitch darkness he nearly fell over the body when he got to it. He bent and felt for any sign of life, knowing that his friend was dead but going through the motions of wishful thinking.

Stuart's shirt was a sticky jelly of drying blood that had saturated the fabric and spilled onto the ground to form a dark pool around him. In the darkness, Andy could not see the extent of his wounds but judging by the amount of blood that had been lost, whatever had hit him must have torn half his chest away. The *coup de grace* had left an angry circular abrasion on the side of Stuart's skull, from where a stream of dark blood continued to run. He moved on to where he'd seen Rob go down. Vern was already there.

'He'd got wings before he hit the ground,' said Vern. 'Look at that.' He pointed to the side of Rob's head, and Andy bent down close.

It was as if the head had been opened with a crowbar and emptied of its contents. White fragments of shattered skull and trails of cranium flesh, still attached from inside a gaping hole in Rob's head, were spread out in a broad pool of blood. His left eye had been torn from the socket, leaving a grotesque sightless hole that exposed temporal bone along the side of his head. Even in the darkness, Andy was nearly sick at the sight of it.

'God's truth!' he whispered, 'what were those bastards using for ammo? Explosives?'

There was no time to waste. Andy got out his medic pack, and after pressing the exposed spongy mass of rubbery organ flesh back into the ghastly wound in Rob's head, he swathed a crepe bandage around it, trying to keep as much as possible of the gory mess inside the bandage.

They rolled him over and removed his Bergen. They took out two radio batteries, and Andy transferred most of his rations into Rob's bag, leaving himself with enough to eat for two days. He didn't think he'd need more than that. By the following night they'd be back at Deka, or dead. Either way, they didn't need the weight of ten days' rations slowing them down—and the ration tins left behind would add to the flying shrapnel if the booby traps were triggered. Vern had gone across to where Stuart lay and had taken out the radio, and put his own rations into the bag in its place. Then he called softly across to Andy:

'Let's bring the bad guys into play,' he said. 'They're not likely to be needed for anything else.'

More by feel than by vision, they found the second guerrilla. He had taken a full burst of four rounds in the chest and the blood that poured from his wounds as they lifted him made a sound like water being poured onto hard ground from a dish.

Then they made another discovery. A third man lay dead with a bullet wound to the head a few meters from the man that Vern had killed. It can only have been that Andy's random firing from the hip at the outset of the attack had not been entirely in vane. So there had been three of them.

They dragged the bodies back to where they'd left Rob and Stuart and placed them and the stalker into what they hoped looked like sleeping positions between two trees.

They leaned the two Bergens against the trees, roughly three metres apart, and Andy opened the pins of the hand grenades that he'd taken from Stuart's pouches.

Working by touch and feel, he tied both grenades to the tree with a length of para cord so that the pin rings were facing outward. He drew the pins to a point where they were barely holding the release levers and tied them together, then carefully threaded the other end of the cord through the straps of the Bergen, leaving no more than an inch of slack between the grenades and the bag. Vern had done the same with Rob's Bergen, but had removed the lid from the landmine inside the rucksack and placed the open canister hard against the front end, leaving only a thin canvas barrier between the grenades and eight kilograms of high explosives.

'That should make their eyes water,' he said.

Andy took a length of fishing line from the small survival kit on his belt and carefully ran it between the two packs, pulling it up as tightly as he dared. He tied the ends to the para cord triggers between the grenades and Bergens. Even if it was suspected that the packs were booby trapped and thus left alone, he hoped that the decoy of their three dead adversaries would draw someone into the trip wire. With that amount of explosives, it would flatten everything inside of a fifty metre radius.

They then removed the working parts from Rob's and Stuart's rifles, and placing the barrels in the fork of a tree Vern put all his weight against them, so that the breach alignment shifted and rendered them unserviceable. They did the same to the weapons they'd found on the dead guerrillas.

The two of them worked feverishly. Vern and Andy both knew that each of them was fighting down the fear and apprehension. Twenty minutes had passed since they'd come to the realisation that they were alone for the time being, and they had no idea how long it would be before they had unwelcome, hostile company. They just knew that it would come.

Andy got hold of Stuart by the belt and shirt collar, and heaved him up against a tree. His hands slipped on the sticky congealing blood as he tried to get a purchase on Stuart's shirt, and he had to change his grip and get under his armpits. He then dipped his shoulder under Stuart's body and let him fall forward so that he had him in a fireman's lift. Blood that felt like the white of a half-cooked egg oozed from the body and down Andy's back, mingling with the grime and sweat and faeces that stuck to his flesh, and he had to steel himself against the revulsion. Vern had lifted Rob with relative ease, though the wound, haemorrhaging through the bandage, made a sucking noise with the movement.

They cautiously started to make their way down the hill. They'd come up it not even two hours earlier. *God! Was it only two hours?* A whole lifetime seemed to have gone by, and two vibrant and gallant friends had not made it. What else awaited them before this night was over? Andy didn't want to think about it.

Sorrow, shame, anger, fear, hatred. Andy was screaming inwardly:

*How many emotions can the soul accommodate at one time, Doc Morrison? Can you tell me that? And which one takes priority in the control line?*

The weight of Stuart on Andy's shoulders, in addition to what was left in his pack and the awkward hold he had on his rifle, made progress slow and unsteady. The darkness didn't help and twice Andy fell over unseen roots or rocks, onto the wet ground underfoot, and he struggled to get Stuart back up on his shoulders.

Vern seemed to be having fewer problems, but Andy could hear from his heavy breathing that he was taking strain. They had to reach a safe lay-up position before first light, but they also needed to rest and set up the radio. Getting through to base was top priority—to let them know what had happened, and get a recovery team in to fetch them.

Their last sitrep had gone in at 18h00 and they'd reported good progress, an easy ride and good spirits. At that stage they had been confident that they'd get into position, do the job and get out again, just as they'd done so many times before.

Well! God had made other plans, and He'd certainly chosen a very distinct way of showing it.

They'd been on the move for half an hour, and had covered no more than four or five hundred metres. Both Andy and Vern were exhausted, and they had to take a rest.

'You know what?' whispered Vern as they sat with their gruesome loads propped up next to them against a small rocky outcrop.

'What?' Andy whispered back.

'We're actually fretting over nothing. I've been thinking. If that camp is where it's supposed to be, there's a distance of about two kilometres from where we got held up. Those guys who spoilt our evening could possibly have been there as aircraft spotters or an early warning lookout post, which just happened to be where we stumbled into them, but they had no radio or other comms with them which makes that unlikely.

'So, Andy, the more probable pitch is, maybe were just a threesome of assholes who got lost and were waiting out the night but were scared shitless of wild animals. Or maybe deserters thinking they'd been busted. Who knows?

'One thing is certain,' continued Vern, 'if it had been a planned ambush there'd sure as hell have been more than just the three of them, and you and I would both be sitting in the queue at the Pearly Gates beside Stuart and Rob here. The gooks in the camp will have heard our fire fight, but no way could they even begin to pinpoint the location. You know what sound does at night.

'Another thing—they've got the same problems as us. They can't see shit beyond about two or three metres, so how are they going to find us tonight if we just stay put right here? Think about it, if they don't break camp and all fuck off in different directions, as they've been known to do when the shooting starts, they probably won't even send a patrol out until morning, by which time . . . ,' and he put his hands together and looked upward, '. . . . please God, this place should be crawling with good guys.'

'You make a lot of sense, Vern,' whispered Andy. 'Let's get that radio set up.'

With stumbling fingers they felt their way through the assembly of the antenna, and after what seemed like far too long they breathed a sigh of relief as the power light on the set came dimly to life.

In a voice barely above a whisper, Andy called, 'Zero, this is two zero; do you read?'

There was a long pause, and he could imagine the duty signaller back at base, dozing with his head down on the desk in front of his set with the comic he'd been reading spread out next to him. He called again.

'Zero, this is two zero. Do you read?'

When he came up, the signaller sounded startled and in a quick, sleepy voice responded:

'This is zero, reading you fives two zero, go ahead.'

'Contact. I repeat—contact close to objective. Two deceased. Request earliest uplift. Over.'

'Standby two zero. Out.'

The set went silent and they waited. Five minutes went by.

'Two zero, this is Sunray at zero, over.' It was Dawson.

'Go ahead zero.'

'What are your co-ordinates? Over.'

'Two zero, difficult to say for sure, but about three K southeast of our last sitrep. Over.'

'Roger two zero. Who are the deceased? Over.'

'Stuart and Rob. Over.'

'Are bodies recovered? Over.'

'Affirmative. Over.'

'Roger that. Stay open, we'll be in touch. Over.'

'Roger; out.'

'Well, at least the cavalry's on the way,' said Vern, leaning back against the bole of a tree.

The exhaustion from the night's horrors was overwhelming and they craved release. The unrelenting anxiety sat in Andy's guts like an indigestible lump of dough. Every slight sound, a rustle of wind through the trees, the scuttling of nocturnal insects or the distant hoot of an owl, scratched at his senses and had him jumping nervously. The sticky mess of dried blood and faeces that clung down his back, down his denims between buttocks and inner thighs, did nothing to relieve the tension.

Leaving the bodies of their dead comrades where they were, Vern and Andy moved away about ten metres to either side and lay down, leaving the radio ready to use. Andy didn't even take out his bedroll. He just lay on the ground and fell into fitful sleep.

# CHAPTER 7

Andy and Vern were jerked awake by a massive explosion, accompanied by the screams of terrified men. It sounded absurdly close. Despite the wet undergrowth, the fireball of high explosive had ignited the bush and a curtain of flame was spreading towards them through the trees. Uncontrolled bursts of automatic fire, spitting long lines of green tracer, raked the foliage. It was high and not directed towards them, but Andy and Vern instinctively took cover facing the pandemonium.

'I think they found our calling card,' whispered Vern grimly.

'I think we're in big shit! answered Andy. 'Christ! Nothing like being woken up with a bang.'

The rush of adrenaline had a calming effect although both men's senses were on a razor edge. The knot in Andy's stomach had dissolved into that chemical rush, as it had evidently done with Vern. They were within touching distance of each other, Vern with the RPD ready holding a fully loaded belt, and Andy with his R4 rifle through which he had fired more rounds over the years than he cared to think about.

The fire was their biggest threat for the moment. They would have to move Rob and Stuart or they'd be prematurely cremated, but Andy was concerned about being exposed by the light of the flames.

The appalling screams of men up on the hill continued to reach them through the darkness, and Andy figured that they'd inflicted mortal wounds upon the patrol, who'd probably lost limbs or received ruptured stomachs and burns from the explosion.

He knew from follow-ups after countless previous contacts that the guerrillas were issued with scant medical supplies and that they were either careless when packing or were mostly issued with the wrong stuff. It was rare to find morphine, Sossegon or other analgesic drugs amongst their medical supplies.

'Keep your ears open,' said Andy, reaching for the radio microphone. In the softest of whispers he called: 'Zero, this is two zero,' and without hesitating, 'do not, I say again do not respond by voice. Give me a click signal. Over.'

Almost immediately there was a distinct double click through the soft static of the set.

'Roger. We are under attack and a fire is moving towards us. We are going to hide deceased and move location. Click confirmation, over.'

Two more clicks. 'Roger, get that backup force ready to move. Out.'

'Click, click'.

Andy immediately started dismantling the radio, but did not disconnect nor roll up the antennae. Instead, he shoved them into the bag, bundling them up on top of the set and shrugged into the shoulder straps so that it sat low on his back.

He touched Vern on the shoulder and pointed to the corpses.

'Leave your kit,' he said. 'Water bottles, radio and ammo only. By the time the gooks get here it will all be ash anyway.'

Andy pulled the medics pack from his Bergen and strapped it to the outside of the radio pouch. Then he pocketed a single tin of bully beef, leaving the rest of what he'd kept of his rations to be consumed by the fire.

'Right, let's get out of here!' Andy bent and lifted Stuart, and as he did so there was a loud extended fart, expelling the built up gases in the corpse's stomach, and his open bowels spilled out through his denims into Andy's shirt and down his neck and back with the stench of rotting flesh. Andy gagged at the foulness of it, and was all of a sudden aware again of the intense anxiety. It crept back up his spine and into his guts with the adrenaline come down, and he felt like a drunk who needed another drink to evade the hangover.

The two frightened souls with their grisly loads turned away from the fire that now burned furiously no more than a hundred metres from them, flames licking high into the air. They felt the heat of it on their faces and the whoosh and crackle of damp burning foliage was terrifyingly loud and close. They would have to stay far enough away from the glare of the fire to ensure that they remained unseen in the darkness.

The bush was thick and the fire covered the sound of their withdrawal, but both Andy and Vern were acutely aware that the dawn was not far off and that their progress would soon be visible by the shifting bushes as they moved through the undergrowth. At first light, they'd have to go to ground and stay silent and motionless. But they needed to get good distance between themselves and the search party that would undoubtedly be launched with the coming of day.

They had covered about three hundred metres when an outbreak of firing erupted ahead of them. A long burst was followed by two shorter, and then silence. The shots were in the distance, maybe a kilometre in front of them, and the sound echoed away into the night like rolling thunder.

But that was ridiculous! They knew that they were the only friendly forces on the ground. As far as Andy was aware, the camp was confined to an area roughly five kilometres behind them. So who was ahead? And what were they shooting at? By now their presence would be well known, although the enemy had no way of knowing that they were only two fatigued soldiers carrying two dead comrades. But, in any event, it was a certainty that they were now being chased. Could it be that they were being surrounded and that the firing was coming from a stop group? But how did the enemy get to be that far from the camp?

These thoughts haunted Andy. Everything was guesswork and that was not how he liked his options.

When silence returned, they started moving again. They'd reached the bottom of the hill, close to the point from where they had seen the vehicle lights earlier, roughly where Andy had made the fatal mistake of deciding to move upwards in the pitch darkness.

The ground had flattened out, but the terrain was still uneven underfoot and the bush was thick, snagging on their clothes and clutching at the bodies that they shouldered. The clouds had cleared and stars shone brightly above the canopy of trees, giving the worn-out duo a shadowy view of shapes and forms around them.

They could hear the crackling of the fire at their rear and it was still burning furiously, but its advance had moderated and it seemed to have contained itself in a line about three hundred metres behind them, where it was devouring everything in its path.

The two plodded forward, and then Vern stopped. Turning to Andy, he pointed out what appeared, in the faint starlight, to be a wide flaw behind a natural alcove in the side of a rocky outcrop. From what they could see, it seemed like a suitable place to hide the bodies. From there they'd be able to move on with greater effect and vigilance, unimpeded by their oppressive burdens. They moved into the recess and, with sighs of relief, deposited their encumbrances.

The putrescent and bitter stench that flowed from the bodies was sickening. That, and the slimy mess of excretion, sweat and blood that covered Andy, would draw a tracker toward them like iron filings to a magnet. But they needed rest, even if only for a few minutes. They dragged the corpses deeper into the outcrop, and covered them with what they could find in the way of fallen brushwood and leaves.

They sat behind the screen of rock, and rested. For the moment, given the circumstances, they were satisfied.

Andy craved a cigarette. He hadn't had one since their meal of bully beef and rice the evening before when they'd sent their last sitrep. He knew full well, though, that the smell of cigarette smoke could lead to discovery and death—and, having cheated the grim reaper once that night, he pushed aside the thought of lighting up.

'I don't want to sound pessimistic,' he whispered to Vern as they sat beside the rocks, 'but I remember a story that my grandfather used to tell me about the First World War. He said he was out on patrol one night when they came under fire. He was always very detailed about how they were two against a hundred. And then he'd finish the story by saying "By God! Did we give those two buggers a hiding!" I kind of sympathise with that pair.'

'All I know about sympathy,' said Vern, 'is that it comes in the dictionary somewhere between shit and syphilis. What I do know well is what I vow to myself: to outlive my enemies.'

'I wonder how many of them there are this time?' reflected Andy.

'More than two, that's for sure!'

Vern's words were barely out when they both froze. From the same direction as they'd heard the firing, someone had coughed, and the sound was not more than twenty metres away. It was a muffled sound, but unmistakable.

Andy heard it like a blow to the stomach. The blood drained from his face as the adrenaline kicked in again. He and Vern slunk down lower beneath the cover of the rock formation, bringing their weapons to bear in a silent movement. They were too close together, something that should have been avoided and which was a departure from ingrained and elementary bush-craft training, but their fatigue and the belief that they were relatively safe for the moment had allowed them to be careless.

Almost on top of one another and fearful of moving, they held their breath with their ears pricked. Then, close at hand, they heard movement.

The sound was like what Andy had listened to for so long earlier in the night. A soft rustling underfoot. But there were a lot more than one set of footfalls.

A soft grey light had started to show in the east, just touching the edge of the darkness at the base of the surrounding forest, and they both knew that the refuge of night would soon desert them.

From the sound of the footfalls they surmised that there was a group who were well spread out, but moving with less caution than the stalker who had tormented Andy earlier in the night. Nonetheless, they were close by and threatening.

Andy and Vern lay motionless, trying to see through the remains of the darkness. Andy's nerves were betraying him again. He felt the involuntary trembling of his muscles and he forced himself to concentrate on attack rather than defence.

He speculated that although he and Vern were clearly the reason for the ongoing activity, the guerrillas could not possibly know their location or even if they were still in the vicinity, nor for that matter how many of them to expect. It followed that their discovery would come as an unexpected event to their hunters. This would keep the element of surprise on the side of Vern and himself. They would have at least a second or two to engage their foes first, which could be the difference between life and death. At least they now had the advantage of knowing the whereabouts of their adversaries.

As he pondered on his calculations, mulling over their situation, there was a footfall no more than an arm's length away, betrayed by a twig that snapped. In the silence and tension it sounded like the crack of a bullwhip. Another rush of adrenaline-charged horror hit Andy's stomach, and he froze in amazement. In the soft half-light, a booted foot appeared beside the rocks, only inches from the barrels of their weapons and all Andy's calculations turned to mist.

In his frozen state he was aware of a spring-like movement beside him. Vern leaped from their cover with the speed of a striking cobra, and with only a whisper of sound he had the man around the neck in an arm lock. A violent jerk of his massive shoulders and powerful arms, the grinding of tendon and muscle and a crack like a dry branch, and the guerrilla's neck snapped under the pressure of Vern's grip and twist. As silently as a cat he dropped back into the undergrowth with his victim, sinking to the ground and holding the man's body down beneath his strong limbs.

The action was a blur of precision, speed and timing, executed in the murky light of early dawn, and in a matter of seconds Vern was back at his weapon. The dead guerrilla was tossed beside him like a discarded sandbag, with a gush of scarlet arterial blood pouring from his flat, wide nostrils and a stare of astonishment frozen into his swollen eyes.

Unsuspecting, the patrol continued towards the raging fire. They moved in an extended sweep line that stretched away from

Andy and Vern, and though it was not yet light enough to count the party they guessed that there were five more men.

Andy realised the predicament. It wouldn't be long before it was noticed that the patrol had lost one of its members, and the search would be concentrated in the direction of the dead man's last position. Added to that, the patrol could not go much further before being driven back by the fire and they would restart their search from their turning point.

The dawn light in the east was strengthening and soon it would be clear enough for Andy and Vern to be visible, and even if by some fluke they could hide themselves, their tracks would be picked up and they would have lost what little opportunity of escape they had. The movement of the group towards the fire, which continued to spread across the duo's flank two hundred metres away, inspired an idea and he touched Vern's arm, pointing a finger in the direction of the flames, and then silently signalled for them to move out across and behind the extended line of the patrol.

With the skills learned and practised over and over again with monotonous repetition on their sniper course, very few visible targets would survive an attack by Andy and Vern, operating together, on single shot—but Vern's RPD only fired on automatic. Although it could be fired from the shoulder, the full automatic function made snap shooting an uncertainty. Even so, Andy was confident of taking out three of the patrol if they could retain the benefit of surprise, and he had no reason to doubt Vern's ability with the RPD on the other two. Communicating with hand signals, and pointing back and forth between them with a show of fingers, Andy indicated his plan and Vern nodded his understanding.

Gingerly they stood up, and as furtively as leopards stalking a herd of impala, the two moved away from their place of refuge to position themselves behind the line of enemy soldiers.

Andy's reckoning was that the men he and Vern were now setting up in a trap were advancing towards the fire and their eyes would be accustomed to the glare ahead of them, and the enemy would be silhouetted against the flames. Even allowing for a slow shot, the enemy would be virtually blind when turning and unable to see them against the fading darkness.

They moved across the back of the advancing line, and the dark shapes of their quarry could be as clearly seen as cut-outs, although their movement was erratic. The mass of trees and scrub through which they moved made it unlikely that a clear shot could be had at more than one of them at a time.

A split second glimpse was all that a trained sniper needed, but this did not apply to multiple targets moving in semi-darkness in and out of sight across a space of fifty metres. They would have to take out what they could and then go to ground using as defence the poor light and their advantage of surprise.

Andy held his rifle in one hand and moved forward. The tension tore at every nerve and his guts felt like they were in turmoil. Vern was ten metres behind him, and as they gazed across the rear breadth of the line, furtively surveying the scene in front of them, two targets slightly to Andy's left showed up clearly and simultaneously against the flames. In a split second he put his rifle to the shoulder and sighted through the rear aperture. It was a practised and fluid movement.

He fired at the first figure and, without hesitation, moved his aim to the second and fired again.

The shots went off in such quick succession that they seemed to be as one. The aftershock of the discharges reverberated through the dawn and echoed off the surrounding hills. In the speed of shifting his aim, Andy had not seen the first man go down—but the second one fell limply to the ground and by that he knew that his first shot had been true.

He rose up from his firing position, moved rapidly away to his left, went to ground in an easy roll and was back up on one knee, looking for a third target. Vern had opened fire with two short bursts from the RPD, and Andy was as sure as he could be that the volleys would have accounted for another two.

Where was the last one? He scoured the area, searching for movement that would expose his quarry, but other than the leaping shadows thrown back at him from the fire there was nothing. A trickle of confidence crept up through him, easing off the tension.

Then Andy let out an involuntary cry. On their right flank and to their rear came an eruption of rifle and machine gun fire. Andy threw himself forward, and rolled away whimpering into the cover of the surrounding scrub. The full horror, the fear, was back. He crawled on his elbows and knees, like a mortally wounded animal, towards the bole of a nearby baobab. There, he pulled himself up into a sitting position against the giant trunk.

He breathed heavily, more from shock and terror than exertion, and he pressed himself against the tree with his eyes closed in a silent prayer.

His pulse calmed down and he checked his magazine. He was sure that he'd only used the rifle for the two shots he'd just fired, but his mind was agitated and he changed the magazine to a full load.

The firing continued for what seemed like an eternity and he heard the thunderous devastation being inflicted upon the bush around him, but it was clear that the shooters had no specific target. They were simply raking the ground from where they'd heard the shots fired by Andy and Vern.

The filth and stench from his body, mingling with the outpouring of sweat that ran down his back and chest and into his groin, was an all-consuming cocktail of horror. He felt the dirty stubble of two days' growth on his face and noticed for the first time that the front of his shirt had been ripped. His exposed flesh was covered in runnels of dried excretion from Stuart's bowels and mixed with black camouflage cream and dried blood.

Suddenly the disgusting condition of his person and his helplessness erupted in an involuntary discharge of projectile vomit that spewed out and spattered the ground beside him. It left the acid taste of bile in his throat.

He carefully unscrewed the cap of his water bottle and put it to his mouth in an attempt to wash away the bitterness. He could easily have emptied the bottle and begged for more, but he was acutely aware that the fluid could be his life blood later on—if he lived that long. He forced himself to be conservative.

Daylight was strengthening and the colour returning to the landscape, and he knew that he had little time in which to conceal himself. He wondered where Vern had gone to ground.

The two of them had been only metres apart when the surprise counter attack had erupted from behind, and if Vern had survived he couldn't be far away. The radio had been left behind the rocky outcrop which was within sight about thirty metres away. But it could as well have been thirty miles

The bush fire raged on, but the morning breeze was enticing it into a westerly direction, away from him. He idly looked at his watch. 05h10 was the time, and it occurred to him that he'd had practically no sleep in the past twenty-four hours.

The time between putting his head down and being bludgeoned awake by the blast of their booby trap was unclear, but it can't have been more than ten or maybe twenty minutes. The stress and violence of the aftermath had left an unrelenting chill within him and a dryness in his mouth that was not helped by the taste of bile. The foulness of it had not been relieved by the sip of water. The tension that, for the past six hours, had kept his nerves keyed up like violin strings, the roller coaster of emotions, sapped his mental and physical reserves. The burden was close to intolerable.

Andy hid behind the baobab for what seemed like forever, but in reality it was less than five minutes. For most of that time, in the wake of the unexpected gunfire, total silence prevailed. He replaced his water bottle in its pouch and ventured a furtive glance around the side of his tree, pressing his back firmly against the protection of it. He could see nothing in the rapidly strengthening light other than a mass of intertwined scrub. Then, as his eyes cast across the forest floor, he stopped.

There! Not fifteen metres away he saw a heap of filthy clothing and the unmistakable shape of an RPD barrel protruding from the undergrowth. He couldn't see any definite human feature in the pile, but he knew it was Vern. It couldn't possibly be anyone else. But what startled Andy was that he was looking at a corpse—and the impact of it triggered a whimper of dismay.

He withdrew back behind the tree trunk in despair. The thin line that separates fear and the unimaginable state of unrestrained dementia loomed over him like a gloating, long toothed demon and he clenched his teeth against the need to scream away the horrors that threatened to possess him. He stared upwards through the canopy of trees to the glowing promise of a beautiful day in Africa, and as he did so the terror subsided. It gave way to a dull and reluctant sense that he'd never leave this place.

Maybe they'd find his dead and mutilated body. They would take it back for burial or cremation. There'd be a grand funeral, where they'd say a whole bunch of nice things, and they'd insist that nothing in the defence of liberty was in vain. There'd be the twenty-one gun salute and the last post, which would bring on the inevitable tears, and then they'd all retire to the mess and have a wake where everyone would get pissed. The next day the war would go on, as would life everywhere else. But Andy Mason, the person, the spirit, the soul? No! He would stay here. This would be his resting ground, and they would no longer be able to frighten him, and they could shoot and bomb and mortar him as much as they liked, but they wouldn't be able to hurt him ever again.

It was now a matter of how many of the enemy he could kill before they killed him. He giggled stupidly to himself.

'I've always tried to get to know people well before I make up my mind whether or not I would like to associate with them,' he mused through another giggle. 'Now here I am planning to kill people I've never even met.' The thought lingered for a time, and he gave off a private little guffaw. 'Seem to have been doing that for a while now, haven't I?' He stifled another giggle. 'Pretty bloody good at it I am, as well. Probably about two hundred not out at this stage. Giggle! Hah! But then . . . they're all trying to kill me, aren't they? Silly bastards should learn to shoot straight! Why would they want to do that? They don't even know who I am! Silly fucking game this. I think I'll tell them all I want to go home now.' and he giggled again, but without any sound or mirth.

Andrew Mason shook himself in an involuntary shiver. He had been drifting off into a state of mental rambling. God, but he was tired! 'Stay alert! Think! I'm alive, damn it!' He forced his mind back into focus.

Help was on the way. That was one thing he could count on, but it would be a long time coming.

Dawson had said that they'd scramble a fixed wing aircraft to provide overhead cover in an emergency, but no one had anticipated three out of four men killed. Even when help arrived, Andy had no way of communicating his position to them, nor to let them know that the problem on the ground was much bigger than a little transit camp.

It was now obvious to him that there were many more occupants than a couple of night stoppers on their way to the Rhodesian border. The place was crawling with guerrilla patrols that popped up all over the place, and this indicated that the base was spread over a wide area.

There were surely communication facilities between the various concentrations, and what had been reported through intelligence and subsequently confirmed by aerial photography was merely the tip of a very large iceberg.

The march from their DZ the previous evening must have taken them through areas that had gooks falling from the rafters, and he now found himself mildly surprised by the fact that they had not been seen and attacked earlier.

He'd have to be half-witted not to realise the desperate danger that he was in. The volley of shooting that had chased him into cover and killed Vern had come from close by, and as far as he could make out nobody had yet left. So he was back where he'd been six hours ago, waiting for that final oblivion.

Idly he wondered if the stories of the grim reaper's list were true. 'When your name's on the list, you're history, no matter what you do to try and avoid it.' That's how the story went. Well, if the name of Andy Mason was on the list this night, the man with the hood and the scythe had missed him once—and maybe now he was coming back to get him.

'He must be a persistent sonofabitch,' thought Andy dispassionately. His thoughts were starting to wander again. Then suddenly his mind came alive and fully alert, and he shook of his mental state like a Labrador emerging from a lake. He started to think positively.

Vern had one of the A60s in his webbing pouch, and he'd kept that with him. Andy had stowed the other small means in his Bergen which he'd left to the mercy of the fire. If backup support was on the way, he needed to have comms with them. The A60s hadn't been required until now, and they'd remained turned off. It was a compact two-way VHF radio, with a roll-up spring-steel antenna. It had limited ground-to-ground range, but was perfect for ground-to-air over comparatively long distances. Just what he would need to make contact with his incoming rescuers.

Vern was lying fifteen metres away, the bush was thick, and he figured he could get there and back if he was very careful. The grey light of dawn was still soft and shadowy, and he had no choice but to risk it. He turned slowly from his sitting position onto his hands and knees.

Holding his rifle just off the ground in his right hand, a filthy wretch of a man, looking like the sole survivor of an unspeakable cataclysm, he cautiously moved around the side of the tree and scanned the immediate surroundings. Nothing moved and no sound could be heard. Acrid smoke from the fire hung in the air like a thick blanket, mingled with the lingering smell of burnt cordite.

Andy moved slowly away, with the stealth of a snake, from the tree's refuge. Filled to the throat with tension, he made his way to where Vern lay. Each metre was like a milestone in a marathon and it took him a full five minutes to cover the fifteen metre distance. Vern lay prone on his stomach; his left hand was clasped over the butt of his weapon, his right hand around the pistol grip and his index finger around the trigger.

Andy stared. This isn't how a dead man would have fallen! As he reached over to touch the prone body, it turned its head imperceptibly and in a course whisper, barely audible, said 'Piss off, Sarge. You stink. I'm trying to stay alive.'

The surprise almost made Andy cry out, and he sank down feebly alongside Vern. The relief made him feel pale and weak.

Nothing further needed to be said. After a few minutes, having rebuilt his resolve, Andy slowly withdrew back in the direction of his baobab, and he signalled for Vern to follow.

Back behind the cover of the tree, he sat in confusion. He had closed his mind to any likelihood of companionship or respite. He'd been convinced that Vern had died in the volley of gunfire. The fact that he was alive and apparently well was an indescribable relief, but Andy still wondered how long they would enjoy that status.

He looked at his watch. 05h30. He looked again and then checked to see that the second hand was ticking. He couldn't believe that only twenty minutes had elapsed since he had last checked, and most of those had been taken up getting to and from Vern. Time seemed to have stood still for at least an hour.

A movement to his left caught his eye, and he froze. He distinctly felt his heart stop, and then pick up again from the surge of adrenaline. Barely five metres away, in the undergrowth, was a man.

His eyes were starkly white and wide against the contrast of his black face, and clearly he was as terrified as Andy, if not more so. As Andy stared at the figure, time seemed to enter into a vacuum. The pistol was in Andy's holster, but he had removed the silencer and replaced it in its pouch. Firing with the R1 would draw attention, which he could not afford as it would mean that he and Vern would have to split up again. Neither of them would know where the other had taken fresh refuge.

For seconds, but what seemed like forever, Andy stared at the form on the ground in front of him. Then he sprang forward, reversing his rifle as he did so, and brought the butt down upon the man's head with every ounce of strength he could muster.

The guerrilla had seen the movement and tried to roll away, but he was a split second too slow. The rifle butt caught him on the cheek, and there was the crunch of shattered bone. The flesh was split, and a long gash of white bloodless tissue from beside the right eye to the line of his jaw was exposed beneath the black skin.

The terrorist continued his roll and made an attempt to scamper to his feet, but the movement was lethargic and he stumbled, losing his footing. Andy went after him, rising to his feet and bringing the rifle butt down again into the nape of the man's neck.

The bone snapped under the blow with a sound like boxwood struck by a heavy mallet and Andy immediately went to ground beside the man. His eyes were fixed in the clearly identifiable stare of death.

Andy rolled away to take cover, convinced that there would be others. But there weren't. Then he realised that the man didn't have a weapon of any sort, and his astonishment grew. The whole incident had lasted no longer than a matter of seconds and Andy was bemused and shaken, wondering why on earth this man would have been crawling around unarmed and all alone.

It struck him then that this must have been the man that they had missed when they attacked the patrol from behind. He guessed that the man had dropped his weapon in his dash for cover and was too afraid to retrace his steps to retrieve it. He was probably trying to get back to his comrades.

'Well,' thought Andy indifferently, 'you should have stayed where you were.'

As he pondered this, moving cautiously back across the short distance to the refuge of the baobab, he heard the aircraft. Or was it? He strained his ears, holding his breath so as not to inhibit his hearing. Yes, definitely. It was a Lynx spotter plane, very high and some distance away, but he knew the sound.

\*　　\*　　\*

Major Greg Dawson sat in the co-pilot's seat of the converted Cessna 337,—fondly known as "The Lynx"—9,000 feet above the area where aerial photography had been captured only a few days previously.

From the height at which they were flying, he and the pilot had seen the sun rise above the horizon ten minutes earlier, but the ground immediately below them remained in deep shadow. They had tried three times to raise Sergeant Mason on the small means but had got no response, and Dawson was worried. The last transmission they'd received just before four that morning had not been encouraging and anything could have happened since.

If Mason and Dempsey had run into more trouble and ended up getting themselves captured or killed, it would result in the prisoners or bodies being put on public display for the international press to feast on. Not only would that be enormously demoralising to other troops and the Rhodesian

71

public as a whole, but the cross-border op would spark an international incident that would reverberate off the walls in the corridors of power from Washington to Beijing. The thought filled him with dread. It was his patrol, sent out on his orders, and he felt responsible for the outcome.

This job had lost its status of reconnaissance patrol and was now a search and rescue mission. Nobody wanted it to become search and recovery.

Dawson could see the extent of the fire and the spread of flames that still licked about the edges of a huge blackened area like an infantile attempt at drawing a circle on the ground. He scanned the untamed bush beyond it through a pair of Zeiss 10x50 binoculars. There were scant paths that were more likely to be game trails than access roads. To the south-west was the silver snake of the Zambezi River where it ran south through Zambia from its source in Angola. The bush stretched out below them like a massive undulating carpet of broccoli. As far as he could see, the area was devoid of any sign of life.

'I can't believe that there's nobody home so quickly,' he said to Darryl Walters, the pilot, through the microphone mask that covered his nose and mouth. 'There has to be something down there. The group that shot up Mason's crowd didn't appear from nowhere.'

His search for signs of movement seemed more and more futile. He felt the onset of the despondent frustration that goes alongside knowledge without proof. Then there was a sudden split-second gleam of light—like that of a photographer's flash bulb—from beneath the canopy of trees, and he shifted in his seat with excitement, trying to pinpoint its source and get a second look—but to no avail. He turned to Darryl:

'Can you come around on the same bearing and try a re-run on the course we've been following? There's something down there with a shiny surface. It could be one of the lads flashing a heliograph at us, or maybe a vehicle windscreen, but it's definitely something.'

Darryl Walters dropped the left wing of the small aircraft, rolling into a 180 degree turn, brought it back into level flight in a little more than three times the width of the plane's wingspan, and they were headed back the way they'd come.

They flew for just over two minutes and Darryl repeated the manoeuvre, bringing the aircraft back onto the approximate flight path of their previous run.

Dawson's eyes were glued to the binocular lenses, frantically scouring the undergrowth for a repeat of what he was sure he had seen. They flew on, way past the position where the flash had come from, but there was no repeat performance.

'Well, I know I didn't imagine it, Darryl,' said Dawson into his intercom mask. 'Take us down. Let's get a closer look.'

Darryl closed the throttle and gently pushed the stick forward, bringing the aircraft around and into a 30 degree descent, while turning the plane back again in the direction from which they had come. He rolled out of the turn and kept the aircraft in a semi-dive heading ground-ward at increasing speed.

Darryl realised that they would overshoot the position where they'd been when Dawson had called his attention to the flash, and he levelled out at 4 000 feet, flying level for a bit more than a minute. Then he turned the Cessna again and resumed his angle of descent.

Suddenly, from below the canopy of trees and scrub ahead of them, they saw the instantly recognizable line of red tracer. It floated upwards in what at first appeared to be an idle movement, but as it neared them it seemed to increase in velocity with the alarming energy of an accelerating spacecraft.

Darryl had completed nearly 10 000 hours of flying time and this was not the first occasion that he'd witnessed tracer. With a competence that appeared relaxed, he pushed the stick forward and pressed the little aeroplane further into its dive, while simultaneously rolling left at full throttle and turning the aircraft away and short of the path of the oncoming projectiles. He then rolled right and raised the nose of the plane, bringing the stick gently back toward him and manoeuvring the aircraft into a level, tight, right-hand turn.

'Shall we give them a squirt?' he asked. An overtly nonchalant grin hovered about his lips.

'They started it,' replied Dawson. 'They know we're here. We might as well let them understand why.'

Darryl kicked left rudder, bringing the aircraft out of its right-hand attitude and into an opposite turn dropping the left wing and pushing the stick forward, taking the small plane into a spiralling dive.

The gunner on the ground had adjusted his aim and was tracking the aircraft as the pilot manoeuvred his sights into position for the attack. Suddenly there was fire coming from three other positions on the ground, but it was inaccurate and clumsy as if the gunners were on the training range for the first time.

Darryl thumbed the safety cap away from the top of his firing button. He had sighted the first gun position and he pressed the electronic trigger, causing the small aircraft to shudder violently from the impact of the weapons discharging their heavy calibre loads. The tracer from the weapons over the wings of the aeroplane sailed away dramatically in four converging lines like searching beams of laser, screaming toward the target while Darryl kept the aircraft in a steep dive on a collision course with the ground, now less than a thousand feet below them.

An explosion of light from the barely visible gun position gave them a whoop of joy as Darryl drew the stick slowly back towards his chest and brought the plane through the nadir of its loop-da-loop manoeuvre at less than a hundred feet from the ground, and into a shuddering climb.

*   *   *

Andy heard the aircraft engine alter pitch, turning and moving away. He needed to make comms with them, let them know what was happening on the ground. He wondered if Vern had made his move to get across the short distance to join him here where he felt relatively safe.

From where he was, Andy could keep an eye on his surroundings for 180 degrees. The huge tree that had become his place of temporary retreat blocked him off from the rest of the circle, but what he needed most, now, was the reassurance that a rescue party knew of their whereabouts—even if only to clear the area with fire power from overhead and give them a chance of getting to a more accessible pick-up point.

He shifted carefully and took a furtive peek around the edge of the massive tree, toward where he had left Vern. The pile of soiled, putrid clothing and the RPD barrel were no longer there. He felt as though he'd been hit by a stun gun. He stretched his neck out as far as he dared to see where his surviving team mate had gone, but there was no sign.

He felt betrayed. Vern had nodded his understanding when Andy had indicated his intention of withdrawing back to the tree, and Andy had expected him to follow. Together they had a fighting chance, but separated they would be uncoordinated and could end up shooting at each other. That was the last thing they needed. The A60 radio in Vern's pouch was their most vital possession and a crucial means of survival, and Andy's stomach hopped like a child on hot coals with the agitation of wanting to get onto the thing.

'Where the devil is he?'

The aircraft engine's tone had changed again, and the plane was returning. Still very high.

Andy wondered idly how much they could see from up there, but he knew as sure as a bet on life itself that they couldn't see him, which is what he badly wanted them to do.

The plane was off to the north-west, in the direction of what was thought to be the camp, and Andy and Vern were the only ones who could warn them that what they were looking at wasn't really worth the effort.

'Where *is* Vern?'

Frustration and anger swirled up from Andy's kaleidoscope of emotions.

He rarely became angry; he hardly ever had cause to. Generally, he could see the merits or demerits of a situation and, by adapting to the circumstance, he'd quickly make a decision as to whether he would control it, participate in it or walk away from it.

He was now abandoned, for what seemed like an eternity, in a turbulence of indecision. With Vern having made his own arrangements, leaving him guessing, he began to feel a fizz of frustration—like bicarbonate on battery acid. It added to the gamut of uncertainties that seemed to package him in utter helplessness.

The distant tone of the plane's engine altered again, and a high-pitched whine emerged which rapidly grew to a screech. This gained in momentum for all of half of a seemingly endless minute, before it wound down and returned to the normal sound of a plane in level flight. It sounded like an aerobat entertaining the crowds at an air show.

'Whatever are they doing?'

Then he heard the eruption of heavy and rapid gunfire. Long straggling bursts, unmistakeably from a Russian-made 14.7mm anti-aircraft gun. The quick-firing thud of the gun mingled with the changing tone of the aircraft engine, and this was followed almost immediately with what he recognised as the bark of 20 mm Browning air-to-ground fire.

'Shit! They've got a contact going!' Then the crescendo of ground fire increased and the significance of the ack-ack dawned on Andy.

He was stricken with fresh anxiety.

'What's so important about this so-called transit camp that makes it necessary to bring in anti-aircraft weaponry and ammunition to defend it?'

'And where the hell is Vern?'

Suddenly there was a burst of automatic small-arms fire only metres away from Andy's place of refuge, and his unrelenting state of nervous tension was drawn to a new high.

There was only one short burst, and Andy identified the sound of the RPD.

He threw himself flat, rifle at the ready, and crawled an inch forward on his stomach to see around the base of the tree in the direction from which the firing had come.

Vern was on his feet and running towards him in a crouch, with the TR48 radio bag slung over his shoulder. In one hand he carried the light machine gun by the pistol grip, and he dodged from left to right as he ran.

Andy leaped to his feet against the huge tree trunk, scouring the surroundings, desperately trying to find the immediate source of danger.

It can only have been Vern who had loosed off that volley. Short accurate bursts were his trademark. Andy knew him well enough to know he would not have fired unless it was absolutely necessary, nor without a clear target, and it could be taken as a certainty that he would have hit whatever it was that he'd shot at.

From behind a tangle of Jesse bush, Andy saw movement. A guerrilla emerged, in blue civilian denim jeans and a khaki tee-shirt, with chest webbing strapped across his front. The man had an AK47 levelled and aimed at Vern, but in a swift and controlled movement Andy had his weapon up and fired a double tap into the man before he had a chance to squeeze the trigger.

The terrorist had made the fatal mistake of showing himself and hesitating while trying to get an accurate shot at his moving target.

Vern tumbled in at Andy's feet, and quickly rolled over so that he was on one knee, facing the way he'd come with his other foot firmly on the ground in front of him. He dropped the radio on the ground beside him and had the butt of his weapon at his shoulder ready to be used.

'There were three of them!' Vern gasped at Andy. 'Thirty metres, three o' clock of those rocks. It must have been them shooting at us earlier.'

Vern had left the spot where Andy had found him earlier and had stealthily crept back to where he'd left the radio. He'd got there undetected and then, about to crawl back, he'd seen the small group of enemy. It was obvious to him that he hadn't been spotted, but he couldn't take the chance of crawling back to Andy with his back to the group which he now knew were keeping watch.

He had decided to take a chance and had dispatched the clearest target, getting the heads of the others down, and then he made the unpredictable dash, anticipating that Andy would react as he did.

'There'll be more,' said Andy. 'I took out one, which means there's still one more to come from that group. Can you get a fix on him?'

They were still whispering, although their location was no longer a secret.

'Unless he's taken off, he must be in that copse where your boy fell.'

"Rake it, Vern. And then let's find another spot.'

Vern raised the RPD and let loose a long burst into the area where the group had taken cover, roughly forty metres away. A man stood up, screaming, with his hands high in the air, waving them together and apart in an attitude of surrender above his head.

Vern held his fire, and Andy gestured for the man to come towards them. He was a youngster, probably no more than seventeen. He was dressed in olive green military style fatigues, with the fighter's trade mark of magazine-filled chest webbing pouches strapped across his torso. On his head was a floppy green jungle hat, common among the guerrilla forces, and on his face was a look of impassioned terror. He hesitated, and Andy called to him:

'Come here! Keep your hands raised!'

The tension in the air was like the static of live electricity and each second seemed like infinity. Their vulnerability became greater as each of those long seconds ticked by.

Andy repeated his command, and reinforced it by waving the man towards them.

The man continued to stand where he was, staring blankly, either not having understood the command and gesture, or reluctant to respond. He started to go down, bending his knees and dropping his hands to his sides, and Vern shot him. The short burst from the RPD blew away the hat and shattered the man's head in an explosion of bone splinters and blood. It was like a ripe pomegranate being struck squarely with the swing of a baseball bat.

'The quick and the dead is all we have time for today, my friend,' said Vern impassively as he bent to retrieve the radio.

'Shall we go?' he quietly suggested to Andy.

It had occurred to Andy that the dead man could have been a useful source of information, which was sorely needed right then, but he said nothing to Vern.

He had been quite right to shoot. Neither of them could afford to take any chances if they were to live through this day, and the man's movements had left a measure of doubt as to his intentions.

'Let's break out the small means, Vern,' said Andy softly. 'We need to chat to the guys in that aircraft—and we've got nowhere safer to go—not until we have some back-up. We might as well hang in here and wait.'

His voice betrayed exhaustion and nausea. A nausea that permeated the soul and not the stomach. He was no stranger to violent death, or to fear—he had conquered both more times than he could remember (including the events of the past twelve hours), but he now felt an unaccustomed weakness, born of fatigue and strain.

The ground-to-air contact in the distance had abated although the thump, thump of 14,7mm anti-aircraft fire continued intermittently. The Lynx was still in the air and it could be heard from the pitch of the engines that it was now climbing with all its available power, racing to get out of range of the heavy calibre guns.

By now it was fully light, and they could get a proper perspective on their surroundings for the first time since the previous evening—when life had still seemed relatively simple.

They could see the rocky outcrop where they'd left the bodies of Rob and Stuart, and it appeared that their camouflage job had been reasonable given the circumstances.

The bush around them was a mass of trees and scrub. They could move on foot through the dense foliage, but bringing in a helicopter was out of the question. Once the choppers got here, they'd have to get out by hot extraction. But first the choppers would have to find them, and as things were, they couldn't give them an accurate map reference.

The dense trees and bushes obscured any features of the landscape from which to take a bearing, so they'd have to use smoke. Andy's gaze was cast upward and he sighed inwardly— there was so much smoke in the air already, that unless it was coloured smoke this too could be a problem. In their haste to get away from their earlier refuge and to secure the bodies of Stuart and Rob, the two smoke grenades in the side pocket of his Bergen had been abandoned.

Vern took the A60 from his pouch and inspected the dial. It was set on channel 40, the standard unrestricted communication channel. They did not have a call sign for incoming traffic, but they knew that there'd be a listening post on that channel. Vern called, still in a rasping whisper:

'This is two zero to Lynx, do you read? Over.'

There was a short pause, and then Dawson came up:

'This is Lynx on Bravo two zero, read you fives two zero. Go ahead.'

There was an audible note of relief, almost jubilation, in Dawson's voice.

'Roger. Bravo two zero, we have a problem. Base far larger than anticipated, possible heavy resistance to be expected. Over.'

'Roger that, two zero. We've already been welcomed. Do you have co-ordinates? Over.'

'Negative that, bravo two zero. No visible features. How far out uplift? Over.'

'Figures two zero minutes. Over.'

'Roger, bravo two zero, we have aircraft audible, you are due north our position on far side of fire area. Do you copy?'

'Roger that. Are deceased secure? Over?'

'Affirmative. Over.'

'Roger, headed your location now. Guide us in. Over.'

'Roger that.'

They heard the aircraft's engine tone alter slightly as it went into a turn and then start towards them. They still could not see the plane, and they waited apprehensively for it to close on them. It was too far west by the sound of it, and Vern got back on.

. 'Bravo two zero, this is two zero. Copy?'

'Go ahead, two zero.'

'You are too far west. Turn half left. Over.'

'Roger.'

The engine tone altered again, and the sound drew closer. The tension was unbearable. Although there were no visible signs of the enemy on the ground, there was no doubt in the minds of Andy and Vern that there were elements close by in large numbers. The stress of keeping out of sight while having to talk the aircraft in, with the likelihood of another contact with the enemy, was pulling at their nerves.

The plane had reached the top of its climb and had levelled out way out of reach of the ground-to-air fire power. It would be difficult enough to see from that height, but having to guide it in by sound under a heavy canopy of trees and bushes made it almost impossible.

To add to their state of nerves, the delay made them yet more vulnerable to an attack. The prickle of fear and tension made the likely onslaught more of a pending reality than a potential threat. The shots that had been fired only minutes before would have attracted attention, and they anticipated the arrival of a retaliatory force.

The choppers were twenty minutes out. That could as well be twenty years if the two of them came under attack now, and the pressure on both of them was becoming unbearable as their mental and physical resilience wore down.

Without the need of speech, Vern and Andy moved apart so that they were barely in sight of one another which meant, in their dense surroundings, a little over ten metres. Andy's eyes and ears were peeled while Vern carried on talking to Dawson.

'Indistinct location your side,' he was saying 'Aircraft heard, not seen. Over.'

'Dropping flare. Over,' came Dawson's reassurance, and there was a moment of silence. 'Figures—seconds—five, four . . . now!'

The sudden emergence of a bright fireball, with white smoke trailing behind it, so high that without it neither Vern nor Andy would have identified the aircraft's whereabouts, provided an exact location of the pinpoint in the sky.

'Roger!' said Vern. 'Seen. Circle this area. You are still west; stand by.'

As Andy watched through the entwined undergrowth, he saw Vern pulling at his lower left leg. Vern released the drawstring that strapped his denims tightly to the top of his boot. The purpose of that string was to block out the multitude of insects that could crawl into the skin and take up residence in the groin or the anus. Lifting the bottom hem of his fatigues, Vern removed two Velcro straps from around his ankle. To Andy's amazement, he had in his hand a small cylindrical smoke canister. Attention to detail was something ingrained in training, and survival was an intricate part of it. Nonetheless this was the first time Andy had known that anyone walked around with a smoke grenade strapped to his ankle.

Despite his exhaustion, he could have whooped with delight. He silently applauded the professional foresight of his comrade.

'Bravo two zero, do you copy?' asked Vern into the handset.

'Go ahead, two zero.'

'Roger. Have orange smoke. Can you guide helos over?'

'Affirmative. Wait. Out.'

The transmission was interrupted as Dawson changed channels. Within a minute, he was up again:

'Two zero, do you copy? Over.'

'Go ahead,' said Vern.

'All elements on channel two niner, lead whirly on call sign Alpha one zero. You have priority. Do you copy?'

'Affirmative! Waiting. Out.'

Vern changed channels to 29 and called:

'Alpha one zero, this is two zero. Do you copy?'

A static disturbance followed, and for a while Vern's call remained unanswered. The tension grew. Vern was about to call again when they came up:

'Two zero, this is Alpha one zero.' The words came in the unexcited simplicity and apparent carelessness associated with pilots, and Andy wondered, not for the first time, whether or not they had to undergo voice modulation instruction before they were allowed to fly, or if it just came to them naturally.

'I read you, three/five and approaching. Over.'

'Roger that, Alpha ten. Area not secure. I say again, area not secure. Confirm with Bravo two zero your approach. Over.'

'Roger. We have some nasty people on board, keen to help. Over.'

'Better make them angry,' said Vern absently. 'Over.'

There was a brief chuckle from the pilot and the comms were cut.

Vern gestured toward Andy with a shrug of the shoulders, and held up the grenade. Andy smiled weakly and shook his head in wonder. 'Top marks, Vern,' he thought, reflecting on his own meticulous operational preparation procedures. Vern had probably carried that grenade with him on a hundred ops without anyone ever knowing, never really thinking that such a precaution could make the difference between salvation and death.

'Not in my book of stupid,' thought Andy. 'Not today, anyway.'

Ten minutes went by, and the two of them sat under the bushes in the increasing heat of the sun. It had risen into a cloudless sky. The dawn had come with all the magnificence that Andy loved so much, but in present circumstances it had gone unnoticed.

The whine of the circling Lynx was now audible, high in the sky, and this brought a measure of reassurance. There had been no further comms from them since Vern had spoken to the helicopter. There was no reason to break the silence, but now in the distance they could hear the sound of approaching helicopters and Vern picked up the handset.

'Bravo two zero, this is two zero. Do you copy?'

'Go ahead, two zero,' came Dawson's immediately reply.

'Have helos audible, am putting up smoke in figures three zero seconds. Over.'

'Roger that, two zero.'

The clatter of the chopper rotors with the distinctive whine of the turbos was still in the distance, and Vern and Andy could tell that their approach was too far east of their position.

Vern stood up and removed the firing restrainer of the smoke canister, and with an almighty heave threw the missile through a gap in the overhead canopy of cover. They watched it as it spiralled upwards and outwards. There was a loud *pop* followed by a fizzing sound, and they saw the thick emission of orange smoke pouring from the flying grenade as it reached the zenith of its arc and began to fall. Vern picked up the radio handset again:

'Bravo two zero, this is two zero. Smoke gone. Over.'

'Seen,' came the immediate reply. 'Helos approaching your loc. Over.'

There was a distinctive change in the clatter of the rotors as they turned in towards the billowing orange cloud.

'Roger,' said Vern, and immediately started talking to the helicopter pilot.

'Alpha one zero, this is two zero. Do you copy?'

'Affirmative, two zero. We have your smoke visual. Over.'

'Roger that, Alpha one zero. High alert. I say again, high alert. Come through low and at speed. Area hostile. I say again, area hostile. Over.'

'Copied,' came the relaxed response from the pilot.

The four G-car troop-carrying helicopters, supported by a gunship K-car, swooped in at full throttle, mere inches above the tree tops, and did a pass directly overhead. Then they fell into single file, and then spread out into a fan formation above the carpet of undergrowth.

There were troops, balanced precariously in abseiling crouches, on the narrow rungs on either side of the fuselages. They clung to the descent ropes which were secured to winches inside the aircraft. The gunners behind the twin 7.62 Browning machine guns, which protruded from the rear portside of each of the 'copters, looked menacing and ready for action. Taking up the rear of the formation was the K-car gunship and the thirty millimetre cannon that protruded from the rear portside door was an additional comfort.

The two men on the ground heard the aircraft circling once about a kilometre beyond their position, their horsefly shapes banking almost to ninety degrees as they rolled around with a loud wind-beating clatter of rotor blades, and back onto the position held by Andy and Vern.

The lead helicopter flared dramatically, like a charging stallion being brought up short from a gallop, and the four soldiers sailed out into space and rapidly descended to the ground. In seconds the backup were spreading out, while the nose of the hovering craft dipped and the helicopter moved forward again in a tight turn as the ropes were reeled in.

The other helicopters had mimicked the manoeuvre with simultaneous precision, the downward rush of the rotor draft blowing up a storm of loose leaves and pressing at the trees, so that they rocked and fought against the lashing wind.

In less than twenty seconds of the high-speed approach, Andy and Vern were in the company of sixteen men, whose professionalism descended on them like an aura. These were their comrades, men they had rehearsed with in training and fought alongside dozens of times. Their presence grasped Andy in a throat-constricting grip of excitement. The rush of relief was a huge load lifted, not only from their shoulders but from within. The release of tension wanted to make him laugh and weep.

Andy moved in a low crouch to where he'd seen Lieutenant Mike Bryant taking cover, and dived in beside him. The filth and stench of his presence contrasted sharply with the fresh clothing and recently washed body of the officer.

'Welcome aboard, sir!' said Andy. 'I'm not sure you're going to enjoy the ride, though.'

'Looks like you guys had it a bit tough, recently,' replied Mike with a familiar grin.

'There seem to be gooks everywhere,' Andy responded. 'They keep popping up. We need to get Rob and Stuart moved and onto the choppers.'

'That's what we've come for,' said Mike breezily. 'You and Vern go along with them. We'll settle things here and come out later. We've dropped fuel drums about fifty clicks out, so you'll have a pit-stop on the way back.'

'Sounds good to me,' said Andy. 'We've hidden the bodies in that rock flaw over there.' He pointed towards the location, and for the first time he noticed the swarm of huge, ugly green-back flies that buzzed noisily around the branches covering the bodies of his dead friends.

As they approached the site, Vern came up beside them and started to remove the branches and scrub covering the bodies. The flies swarmed out angrily in a humming cloud, and Vern shooed them away with branches, but once the bodies were exposed they were horrified to see that a colony of ants had invaded this temporary resting place and covered the corpses from head to foot. The ants had made an angry mass of tiny bites and larger suppurating ulcers on the exposed skin of their hands and faces, like an ugly red rash of chronic acne that stood out starkly against the yellow-grey pallor of death.

Andy reached into the recess and lifted first Stuart and then Rob and laid them out on the flat ground, while Vern and Mike frantically brushed away the invading insects.

All around, the bush remained quiet. There was no conspicuous sign of the enemy. With eighteen men now on the ground and five helicopters circling the area, scouring the surroundings for a threatening presence, the controlled panic had subsided. Andy's confidence began to return.

Two combat medics who had come in took over at the side of the bodies and rigged them onto makeshift stretchers, and Mike got on the radio to one of the choppers while Vern and Andy strode off to gather what was left of their kit beside the baobab tree.

'Alpha two zero, this is Charlie two zero. Do you copy?' called Mike.

Alpha two zero reading you fives, go ahead. Over.'

'Deceased ready for uplift. Approach. Over.'

"Roger, approaching now. Over.'

The helicopter broke formation from the other circling craft and passed overhead in a rush of wind and screaming rotors. With a rolling turn, it settled into a hover above the point where Mike held aloft a folded white map. The stretchers were linked to a hook that spiralled down from the aircraft at the end of an abseil rope, and seconds later they were hoisted aloft and disappeared into the gaping fuselage of the hovering helicopter. The pilot engaged forward motion and the craft tilted slightly and was away, falling back into the circling formation with the others.

'Alpha three zero,' said Mike into the radio handset, 'approach for personnel uplift. Over.'

'Roger. Approaching.'

Andy and Vern were back beneath the baobab that had been their refuge and they grinned in triumph as the second helicopter made its approach in a hovering flare a hundred metres away, tail rotor in a downward attitude moving slowly toward the pick-up.

Then it happened—a sudden distinct crack from behind where Andy was standing with Vern, followed immediately by a whoosh of sound that all the troops on the ground recognised instantly as a rocket leaving the tube of an RPG-7 launcher.

'Rocket!' screamed a confusion of voices from half a dozen men, and there was a mad scramble for cover.

The helicopter pilot had seen the launch of the missile and frantically took evasive action, but the rocket, trailing its feather of flame, screamed towards the hovering Allouette with deadly speed.

It smashed into the chopper just below the rotor blades in a shattering explosion. The fuel tanks were ignited in a sheet of flame and a pall of billowing oily brown smoke, and it plummeted to earth in a fireball. The tangled and crippled blades spun helplessly as if in a death throe, seeking purchase on the flaming air.

The twisted craft hit the ground in a fury of flame. There were the maniacal screams of the pilot and his gunner as they burned inside the stricken shell, and with that came a cacophony of automatic rifle fire. The shooting seemed to erupt from all around the defensive circle formed by Vern's and Andy's rescuers. It sounded like being inside a small corrugated iron shack while a hundred tormentors ran broomsticks back and forth across the exterior.

Nobody had been directly beneath the falling aircraft, but the heat scorched and blistered the skin and hair of those nearby. The soldiers scrambled to identify the positions from where the attack was coming. The circling helicopters broke formation like an erupting bombshell and spread into a widened circle, guns blazing at the terrain in an expanding periphery below them.

Andy and Vern, who'd expected to be safe aboard the helicopter and headed for home, had taken cover when they heard the launch of the rocket from the tube. It was a sound with which they were both familiar, as were all the men around them.

The two had been on their feet. They ran outward and away from the hovering helicopter and dived for cover, opening their mouths and covering their heads. Andy hoped on hope that the rocket would go wide or high, and he'd turned his head upward in an attitude of prayer, willing the rocket to miss. But even as he did so, he heard the sickening impact and saw the dreadful spectacle of the explosion and the burning helicopter falling to the ground.

The horrifying demonstration of violent death unfolded in fine detail, as in a well-modulated slow-motion scene from a horror movie, and Andy had seen the terrified expressions on the crews' faces as they were engulfed in the inferno. He watched them screaming in anguish, with the skin on their bodies ablaze and peeling off their scalps and faces in bursting blisters and bubbles of blood and mucus.

He raised himself to move forward, away from the heat of the burning helicopter, and to get abreast of the others who defended their wide circle. The burning trees threatened to rage out of control, as had the fire started by their booby trap earlier that day. The sound of gunfire was deafening. All around, tracer flew like sparks from a Catherine Wheel. It was difficult to tell from the total confusion whether there was any point or direction to it all.

The sound of the diving Lynx was drowned out by the din of what seemed like a hundred rifles on the practice range, responding to a 'fire at will' order.

High above in the Lynx, Dawson had seen the flash of the RPG-7 and the disintegration of the ill-fated helicopter, and he pinpointed the firing location. He also saw the muzzle flashes of small-arms fire in the same vicinity, amongst the trees in the early morning light, and he guided Darryl Waters onto the area.

They were in comms with the circling helicopters and between them they co-ordinated an air-to-ground assault. The gunner in the K-car, manning the thirty millimetre, had brought his weapon to bear, and in faultless co-ordination with the pilot he raked the bush from an angle well out in a hover so low that the undercarriage of the helicopter touched the upper leaves on the trees, making it difficult for the guerrillas on the ground to get a fix on the target. The gunner's strike rate was disorientating the enemy, and it forced them to take cover where the ground troops could advance and over-run them.

Andy had fallen into the skirmish line which worked in groups of two. It was an automatic and well-rehearsed action that came naturally, like a well-oiled machine. He and his partner gave covering fire as their comrades on either side of him moved forward. They went to ground fifteen metres ahead and Andy and the man he'd teamed with rose to follow and then go ahead of them, while the primary team covered their advance.

The bullet took Andy just above the right hip and spun him around in an involuntary pirouette as if he'd run full tilt into an invisible concrete pillar.

It was the sensation of a white hot poker being rammed through his lower abdomen. He didn't at first comprehend that he'd been hit. The suddenness of the blow left him completely bewildered. Disoriented, he half recovered from his staggering rotation, and then he fell face down with a thump, like a drunken man. He tried to pick himself up, but his right leg would not respond. Under the habit of his training, he rolled away, straight-legged, from his prone position. 'Never lie still in the open under fire.'

He tried again to pick himself up and the jarring agony took his breath away. Only then did it strike home. 'Shit! I'm hit!' he heard himself say, aloud or otherwise he could not tell.

He rolled away again, this time in the other direction, and the torn muscle and flesh protested with such pain that he thought he would lose consciousness.

He put his hand down to where he thought the wound was, and then he looked at it. The filthy combination of blood, faecal waste, sweat and cammo cream on his clothing and hands and through the rend where his shirt had been torn was so disgusting that his first thought was 'I need a bath'.

Lying on his back, fearful of moving again, he felt the warm trickle of blood as it emerged from the wound. It ran from his stomach in a rivulet, and down his side to accumulate in a pool at his back. He knew that there'd be a wound in his back as well, larger and more profuse in its letting of blood.

And then the pain hit him. It came in rolling waves like an angry, living beast inside him that became bigger, stronger and more angry with every laboured breath that he took. All around him the battle raged on, but the sound of it was changing in Andy's mind and it seemed to recede and rush back at him before drifting away again, as if it took place somewhere else. The pain felt as though the downed helicopter had somehow found its way into his soul and was venting, inside him, all the fury of its flaming demise.

Then there were hands on him, turning him over. He felt his shirt being ripped away and then the soft texture of cloth applied to his wound. He felt the sharp jab of a needle which pierced his arm just below the elbow as the plastic cannular was inserted. He was conscious enough to realise that the medics were there, putting up a drip and trying to staunch the blood coming from the wound. He could hear them around him, talking in soft animated voices, reassuring him that he was fine:

'A little scratch like that shouldn't keep you down for long, Andy my boy. I've seen a guy do more damage shaving.'

The fire inside him felt as though it was being fanned by a bellows. It flared up in agony that made him want to scream, and then as quickly it started to subside. The pain swam slowly away, as if it was moving out to sit beside him rather than inside, and his mind registered the effects of morphine before he drifted off into an all-engulfing cloud.

Vern, further up the sweep line, had seen Andy go down. He rose up on one knee with the RPD at his shoulder. He fired three short bursts into the attacking enemy's position, and then turned briefly to look towards his stricken friend. In what seemed like a distorted optical illusion, his head suddenly changed shape as an AK47 round smashed into him just behind the ear and emerged beneath his right eye, blowing away half his handsome face and leaving a grotesque gaping hole in the side of it. As had been the case earlier with Rob, Vern died without knowing what had hit him.

Beside him, as Mike Bryant rose to move forward in the sweep line, his chest exploded in a mass of shattered bone and blood that sprayed the ground around him as if his upper body had burst from internal pressure. Lieutenant Bryant collapsed to the ground in a heap with his arms trapped beneath his lifeless body and his face pressed hard against the stony ground, eyes wide and staring.

Andrew Mason had seen neither of his friends die in the fierce firefight—a battle that had emerged from what began as a simple intelligence-gathering op.

# CHAPTER 8

WHEN ANDY SAT UP, HE WAS ALONE. The pain in his side was a nagging ache, as if he'd pulled a muscle while exercising. He did not recognise the place that they'd brought him to, but it was cool and the light around him was of a strange quality.

There were uneven rows of small trees in a field of golden brown wheat-grass that swayed in unison, like a troupe of perfectly co-ordinated dancers flowing in a side-to-side motion that fascinated and enchanted him. He wondered why they had brought him here, and then wondered where exactly 'here' was. It had a vaguely familiar appearance to it, as if he'd visited the place in a dream at some previous time, and he tried to concentrate on the significance of the familiarity. He stared out over the field, mesmerised by the constant flowing motion of the grass.

The sound of the helicopter rose suddenly above him and he frowned, curious that he had not heard it approach. He looked up. The aircraft had an unusual appearance about it. It was neither an Alouette nor a Bell 206. He'd never seen one like it before and he turned in his sitting position, one knee pulled up to his chest, resting with one hand on the ground at his side and the other raised to shade his eyes against the light that seemed to have grown brighter with the arrival of the chopper.

Suddenly the dimensions of the helicopter began to alter. Its sides began to bloat as if it were a balloon being rapidly inflated under the pressure of a giant pump. Andy stared up at it, in curiosity more than surprise, trying to work out why that would be happening. He grinned in disbelief as if a joke were being played on him, and his grin turned to a broad smile as he realised that that's what it was. A joke! He laughed, wondering how the guys had done it.

As he watched in fascination, the swelling sides of the machine exploded in a billowing cloud of black and orange flame. The flame rushed at him in an all-consuming billow of scorching horror.

The abrupt change filled him with terror and he screamed as he turned and scrambled to his feet, trying to run. But his legs had no strength in them and the fireball overtook him, setting his clothes alight and spreading through the grass in an inferno. He fell forward onto his knees, screaming hysterically as the fire licked at his face and burned his hair and eyebrows and the dirty stubble of his beard.

Then he found strength in his legs and started to run, but he was grabbed from behind. He turned to shake off the firm grip that pressed into his shoulder. Stuart stood behind him, one hand grasping his shoulder like a bench vice and the other flung casually around Rob as if in a photographic pose. Andy struggled to free himself from Stuart's grip.

'Let me go, Stuart!' he yelled. 'I'm burning! Can't you see I'm burning? Let me go!'

Stuart grinned and looked towards Rob, gesturing with a sideways tilt of his head as if mockingly acknowledging something that was already well known. 'We're all burning, Andy,' he said calmly. 'But that's because you let us burn.' And then they both laughed as if they'd caught him in a practical joke.

As their laughter echoed through the flames, Rob's and Stuart's features began to change. Gradually, as if by trick photography integration. they became the helicopter pilot and his gunner. As Andy tried to absorb this bizarre shift, their faces burst into flame, burning and blistering their flesh with oozing yellow milky puss and watery blood that mingled and ran like molten lava. Their features distorted again to present grotesque eyeless creatures, like melting rubber men in an animated movie.

'I'm burning!' screamed Andy. 'Please let me go! I'm burning!'

There was a mocking laugh from behind the repulsive mask. It sounded like a tape recording being played backwards very slowly. Andy screamed again in terror, and as he did so the wound in his stomach burst with such agony that his vision blurred and the perspiration ran down his forehead and neck. He was still being held, but now he was on his back with strong, invisible hands holding both his shoulders.

As he fought to free himself he looked up and saw Rob and Stuart. They were laughing, and they had their arms around each other's shoulders. They were walking away with a jaunty swagger, and then they faded as they floated through the flames. Andy tried to call after them, but he had no voice. They vanished through the swelling wall of smoke and flame which roared like the flow of a waterfall.

'Sergeant Mason? Can you hear me? It's alright, Andy. Everything is alright! Can you hear me?'

'Voices! Where are the voices coming from? Who are these people talking to me? Where's the fire? God, it's hot! Of course it's hot! I'm burning!'

'Sergeant Mason, can you open your eyes?'

'Silly bloody question! My eyes are open!'

A flash of light brought him awake and he looked up into the eyes of a man and a woman dressed in white clothing and wearing surgical masks. They were on either side of him, their heads almost touching as they stood over him looking down.

Confused, he looked away from them to his surroundings. He was aware of discomfort around and inside his nose, and his throat felt as though he'd swallowed a lump of molten rock. There was a strong odour of antiseptic. Alongside the woman was a hooked stand with a bag of liquid, and from it ran a tube that disappeared into the back end of a needle lodged in his arm. On his naked chest were a number of small circular suction caps with wires and tubes running from them to a monitor that he could not see, but which emitted a regular rhythmical beep.

Realisation dawned. He was in a hospital ward.

The sun streamed in through a tall sash window with tied-back white sun-filter curtains. The curtains fluttered in a gentle breeze. A constant reverberation, like the roar of rolling thunder, came from beyond the window and he tried to recall why it sounded so familiar.

'Welcome back, sergeant!' said the man. 'How are you feeling?'

It took Andy a while to grasp the question. He stared blankly at the pair, unsure where he was or what to say. In the end, he rasped cautiously:

'Like I've had my throat slit and been kicked very hard in the guts.'

The man stifled a laugh. 'I suppose you could call it that. Your throat's sore because of the anaesthetic tube that was inserted during the operation.'

Andy was incredulous. 'What operation?'

'You're lucky. You took a round in the lower abdomen. It tore through the peritoneum and did a bit of intestinal damage, but we've patched it up. You're going to be uncomfortable for a while but it's nothing that can't be fixed by TLC and monitoring. You've had a bad dream. Anaesthetic does that sometimes.'

Andy was silent for a while, and then his attention was drawn to the sound beyond the window. He frowned.

'What's that noise,' he asked. 'That rushing sort of roar?'

'It's Victoria Falls,' replied the man. 'You're a temporary guest at our hospital.'

'That's it!' thought Andy 'The Falls.' He gathered his wits as best he could. 'Define temporary,' he demanded.

'Well—we had to do emergency surgery. But we'll get you to Salisbury's Andrew Fleming as soon as we can. Probably tomorrow morning.'

'What day is it?" asked Andy.

'It's Wednesday, same as when you were brought in.'

'Wednesday. Only Wednesday?'

On Monday morning they'd been briefed on this little look-see' job that turned out to be anything but. It was Tuesday night—last night—when they'd walked into the ambush. This very morning, then, all hell broke loose and the chopper was shot down. God! It seemed like a lifetime ago.

'Are you sure?' asked Andy

'Unless I've lost track of time, I'm absolutely sure.'

'What time is it?'

The doctor consulted his watch. 'Four thirty.'

'Are any of the others hurt?' asked Andy. And then, as an afterthought, 'Any of them here?'

'You were the only one we had to keep. One or two burn cases that have already been casevacked to Salisbury—and some chaps that didn't make it, I'm afraid.'

'Didn't make it?' Andy's stomach heaved with apprehension.

'You'd better talk to your CO about that,' replied the doctor. 'He said he'd come in later. He'll fill you in. Meanwhile you need to rest. If there's anything you need, just ring.'

The doctor and nurse turned to leave, but Andy called them back.

'May I know your names?' he asked. Reality seemed to have slipped away. He wanted to get a handle on it.

'Of course! I'm sorry. I'm Dr John Tafner, and the prettier one is Sister Jean Struthers.' The nurse blushed, but she smiled at the doctor and at Andy.

'Thank you,' said Andy. 'Thank you. Both of you.' And then he closed his eyes.

The burning pain in his abdomen was like an electric iron inside him and he ground his teeth. But he was alive; he'd live.

He wondered who hadn't made it. Rob and Stuart, he supposed. He knew about them. But, even so, the release of tension and the image of those two brought an uncontrollable sob. His eyes brimmed over, and then he wept openly.

*   *   *

'VERN AND MIKE,' SAID GREG DAWSON. 'They got taken out just after you went down. I'm sorry to be the one to break it to you.'

Andy nodded, and looked out of the window. *Not just Rob and Stuart!*

The sun was going down and they'd moved his bed so that he had a clear view of the river above the falls. The spray rose from the gorges like a thin bridal veil that concealed the full beauty of the image behind it. The orange ball that Andy remembered so well, the image tattooed in his mind so many years before, was drifting towards the throat of the great flow of water. It turned the river to the deep rich colour of honey, and the wild bush on its banks was a dark silhouette against the curtain of fire.

He said nothing. He dared not. He wouldn't be able to control his emotions.

His thoughts went back twenty-four hours.

Around this time they were putting out their evening sitrep and breaking out their bully beef and rice rations. Rob, Stuart and Vern were alive and vibrant, without the slightest idea of what awaited them. Vern this morning, running crouched over, having successfully retrieved the radio and taken the enemy so much by surprise that they'd faltered long enough for their position to be neutralised. The image of the huge shoulders tweaking the neck of the terrorist who would probably have exposed them in the soft pre-dawn light, and the smug grin that he'd cast Andy's way as he produced the orange smoke canister. How could he be dead?

And Mike? Andy had worked with him on dozens of ops. A brilliant young officer, only about 24 or 25. As a cadet, he'd won the sword of honour at the School of Infantry. He had a quiet efficiency about him that made everything seem easy. He'd led the rescue party in, and had been first on the ground.

God! He can't have been there for more than ten minutes on this op and now he was gone, never to lead again. Never to stand or sit or laugh again. He'd become just another statistic in what Andy suddenly realised was an utterly futile war. Just another cloud in the wind.

'Andy, you were right about the base.' Dawson, aware of Andy's thoughts, changed the subject. 'We've known for some time that ZIPRA have been trying to congregate a force big enough to launch a conventional attack, which they thought would catch us napping.

'We had no idea where it was, and now we do. We've already launched air strikes over the area. They gave themselves away with their anti-aircraft fire. If the bugger behind the gun hadn't been so keen to shoot at us we'd probably have missed it.'

Dawson then changed his tone: 'There's no point in apologising for sending you in with only four men, Andy. It goes with the territory. And besides, it wouldn't change anything. We'll lose more men before this war is over and each one of them will be a good man. And the way it is, either we take that chance and accept the consequences or we put up our hands and say "enough".'

He paused and followed Andy's stare—out of the window to where the sunset was in its full glory.

'The thing is, though,' he continued, 'we aren't going to do that. Ever. It would mean that all those who have died and those who have been injured were for nothing. Men get killed in wars, Andy. You know that as well as anyone, and its right to mourn them, but we can't just not go on because our friends have made the ultimate sacrifice. Believe me, hardships affect different people in different ways in all walks of life. But you can't let them drag you down. We've got to get over it and move on.'

'Yeah, well,' said Andy, having regained some of his composure. 'We both know that I'm no stranger to it. As you say, it's not the first time. And it won't be the last.

'But something happened out there last night, sir. Don't ask me to explain it, but I've always boasted that my butterflies fly in formation.

'Last night they broke that formation and I was scared shitless. I was terrified. I guess mostly from not knowing what we . . . .' He paused. 'Or more accurately, what *I* was up against. But my confidence went for a ball of chalk and I expected to die, and in the end I didn't give a damn. I've never been incontinent from fear before. I've never vomited from shock before. I'm a mean sonofabitch. But last night the curtain came down, and what scares me most is I don't know if I can pull it up again.'

Dawson was pensive. He got up from his chair and strolled over to the window. He leaned with both hands against the sill, one foot a stride forward of the other, and he stared out at the fading beauty of the sunset. Then he turned:

'Andy, you're one of the best field operators we've got. The men respect you. They're comfortable working with you. But I think you need to come off ops for a while.'

Despite himself, and despite the pain in his stomach and his heart, Andy felt the blow. It struck him like a tactful reprimand.

'Is that because I lost an entire patrol on an OP job?' he asked.

'You can't be blamed for that, Andy.' Dawson's voice was terse. 'No matter who led the patrol on the information we had, the same thing would have happened. But right now I don't think you'll be any good to yourself or those around you. You need a break.'

'Let's take it as it comes, sir,' said Andy. 'This hole in my guts isn't going to go away overnight. It'll be a few weeks before it's fixed. I'll have time to regroup.'

'Okay, Andy,' said the major. 'We'll talk about it later. Meanwhile, when you're back on your feet, there's work to be done in military intelligence—your security clearance will get you in. I think we'll put you there for a while.' He looked at his watch. 'I've got to get going. I'll be in touch. Cheers.' And he left the ward without looking back.

Andy watched him go through the swing doors. He was left alone with his thoughts.

'How many friends have been taken in this damn war? Who'll be next?'

He bit down hard on his lower lip. 'You're losing it, Mason,' he told himself. He blew his nose and wiped his eyes. 'You're not as tough as you thought.'

The friends he'd lost in action were good guys. Some he had held in his arms, comforting them while their life slipped away. He'd been hard enough to stay calm while in front of him those who had lost limbs or eyes or had been burned screamed in agony. He had the power of giving comfort, even in the heat of battle, when he knew that a comrade would never see or walk again or was dying. But he'd never had to confront his own mortality. He'd never bothered about it.

He wasn't ignorant of the reputation that had grown around him: 'Andy the cool; Andy the unshakable.' Even as a child he'd been fascinated with danger and adventure, and he was excited by recklessness. The adrenalin rush left him breathless and energized. Under fire, he'd acquired the ability to remain calm and focused despite the possibility of sudden death looming as the potential outcome.

But the intensity of the past twenty-four hours, the unprecedented fear which he felt as the hunted, had brought him face to face with the reality of death. Up to now, he had treated mortality with the same contempt as he would an alienated bastard brother. Now this unwanted relative had visited him, and it exposed his vulnerability. For the first time, it struck him that life was a valuable commodity and that he was unprepared for a violent and premature death. His confidence had been shaken, and the outer shell of well concealed indifference had been cracked.

When he'd left Allison's apartment on the Avenues early on Sunday morning, he'd floated easily on a cloud of contentment. The euphoria stayed with him as he was driven out to Kabrit, where he'd collected his kit. He was still awash with it when he hitched a ride in the duty Landrover across to New Sarum Airbase, for the flight to Wankie. Happy-go-lucky Andy Mason. The warmth of it was still with him when he'd strode down to the Ops Room for briefing by Dawson, and even when he had leaped, along with Rob, Stuart and Vern, from the aircraft at the start of this ill-fated operation.

But now he felt exposed and rattled. He had to come to terms with a depth of fear that he'd never before experienced, and it irked him that Dawson had recognized his vulnerability. He was exhausted, too. His mind drifted.

He dozed off among a thousand thoughts, and he found himself being drawn back to the bizarre sequence of events that had brought him into this war. It all seemed so long, long ago and so far away.

.

# CHAPTER 9

## Johannesburg
## *June 1974*

T HE EXQUISITE BALLROOM AT THE JOHANNESBURG COUNTRY CLUB was crowded with men and women elegantly dressed in tuxedos and evening gowns. The lavish ambience of the venue radiated wealth and success; as did the occasion—the annual Results dinner of Highgate & Savage, Merchant Bankers.

The soft flowing melody of a Strauss waltz mingled unobtrusively with the drone of a hundred conversations, interspersed with short outbursts of confident laughter and the tinkling of ice cubes in glasses.

The circular dance floor, on which couples swirled to the rhythm of the waltz, was an island of polished wood within a sea of expensive carpeting. Tables draped in white linen, laid out with silver and crystal glass, lined the walls. At one end was an ornate bar, made of solid oak, its mirrored alcoves reflecting the many-coloured bottles and the shining glasses. Tall Regency-styled windows, ornamented with velvet curtaining, ran along the length of the ballroom as a formal backdrop to the coloured ball gowns and the crisp black-and-white of the men.

Highgate & Savage held their Results dinner every June, and in attendance were the senior executives from an array of multinational corporations, and their wives or partners.

Andrew Mason stood at the bar chatting idly to Gary Chalmers, his immediate superior in the line of middle management within the banking group. He cast a casual eye around the assemblage, recognising important personalities from the mining conglomerates and construction giants with whom they transacted millions of Rands worth of business each year. Many of these had their names writ large in the 'whose who' columns of *Finance Week* and *The Economist*.

He surveyed the crowded room, and his face lit up when he saw the unmistakable and gorgeous rear end of Merryl Sherbourn. She was secretary to James Bailey, the Managing Director of Robust Construction. Andy had introduced Robust Construction to the bank after getting into a play-off for "the most golf" with their financial director at a charity golf day, and sharing the prize (a bottle of Johnnie Walker Red) with him. All of Robust's banking was soon transferred to Highgate & Savage, which is how Andy and Merryl had met.

There was instant and passionate chemistry, but it only lasted six months. Despite her very evident personal attractions, Merryl carried a cocktail of emotional and physical scars—She was a young widow who had lost her husband, Craig, when they had been involved in a collision with a buffalo near her home town of Fort Victoria in Rhodesia. She'd been seven months pregnant at the time of the tragedy and she had given premature birth to her daughter Charmaign, while still in a coma in the intensive care unit of the Andrew Flemming hospital in Salisbury.

Merryl had been a magnificent looking young woman, with a luminous head of thick flowing blond hair, a pair of deep aquamarine eyes with a body and pair of legs that would make a blind man stare. The hair, the eyes, the body and legs were all still superbly intact, but flying glass from the accident had left her face badly scarred and the disfigurement stood out like malicious razor slashes across an artist's masterpiece

She was fun to be with and a passionate lover, but while she managed in public to minimise the scars with cosmetics and the pain of loss with strength of character, in private she remained troubled—unable, as yet, to commit to a permanent relationship. She was the first woman Andy had fallen truly in love with, and the sudden break-up left him bewildered.

Andy had his own rugged good looks, a great career ahead of him in merchant banking, and he'd quickly got over his bewilderment. His sexual and emotional philosophy was simple and effective: 'why buy a book when you can join a library? Nothing is forever.'

He and Merryl were mature enough to remain friends and there was no animosity between them. He was young with time and talent enough for him to move on.

Standing at the bar with Gary, one hand in his pocket and the other nursing a glass of beer, he rested his eyes on Merryl. From across the room, she felt it. She turned, their eyes met, and a smile of pleasure lit up her scarred face. She excused herself from the people around her and crossed the room.

'Want to buy an old friend a drink?' she asked as she approached. She kissed Andy's cheek and glanced at Gary with a glint of mischief.

'Gary Chalmers, meet Merryl Sherbourn,' said Andy. 'The most remarkable girl in the room. How've you been, you gorgeous creature?" and then before she answered; "What would you like to drink?'

'You can get me a Gin and tonic, thank you, Mr Mason.' She held out her hand to Gary.

'I like the "Mr Mason",' grinned Andy. 'Are you bowing to your superiors or just trying to impress me?'

'Only keeping you at arm's length,' she laughed. 'Gary, this man's a monster at close range. Absolutely no respect for a lady's virtue.'

'Ladies with virtues that need respecting are snobs and pains in the ass,' retorted Andy. 'And I know better than to think of you as either.'

He turned to the barman and ordered Merryl's drink. 'How's Charmaine?'

'She's fine as ever, and a handful. The grandparents have been visiting so she's still in happily spoilt mode.'

'How are your folks? Are they still up in Rhodesia?'

'Yes, they are—and they're fine too,' said Merryl. 'But I worry about them with all the trouble going on. While they were down here, the terrorists attacked a game lodge near the farm. They were worried about going back. These days, you never know what's waiting for you.'

Gary joined in. 'What's the take on the real situation there, Merryl? Apart from what the press tells us.'

'It's open warfare,' she said. 'Guerrilla warfare. It's been like that for over two years. My folks live behind high security fencing. They never go anywhere without a rifle. The Agric-Alert radio system is their lifeline.'

'Why don't they pack it in and come down here?' Gary frowned. 'That's an awful way to live.'

'You don't know Rhodesians,' said Merryl with a chuckle. 'They're stubborn. Firstly, most of them are convinced that South Africa's on the same downhill path. They reckon it's inevitable. But basically they can't afford to leave. If you emigrate, the reserve bank only lets you take out a thousand Rhodesian dollars. How do you start a new life with that? And leave behind all your fixed assets, the stuff you've built up over a lifetime?'

'A thousand dollars!'

'Yes. Besides, my folks and most of their friends are too old to think of starting up again. They'll bite the bullet. They'll make sure that their guns are loaded, keep the high voltage alive in the security fences, and soldier on. You won't believe what a festive life they live. Their motto is "Let's wait and see". Despite it all, Rhodesia's a wonderful place and most people don't want to leave.'

'Scary stuff,' said Gary glancing up. 'Excuse me—I see old man Barret trying to attract my attention. See you later.'

Lloyd Barret was a senior general manager at H&S and part of his portfolio included ultimate control over asset-based finance projects. He was a stern, hard-faced man with a shock of white hair and thick bushy eyebrows that met above the bridge of his nose, giving him the appearance of one with a permanent scowl. He obviously had something important on his mind, as he and Gary disappeared through a side door.

'Are you seeing anyone new?' Andy asked Merryl apprehensively, not wanting to hear the affirmative. 'Any rich playboys in the wings?'

'I should get that lucky,' Merryl retorted. 'There's a guy who lives in my apartment block—I think you might have met him—also an ex-Rhodie. We sometimes go to movies or dinner. No fireworks. No debauched lust. I actually think he might be gay, and that kind of suits me. I still think about you Andy, but let's not go there. How about you?'

There seemed to be a trace of malice in Merryl's voice, which Andy hoped he was imagining.

'Playing the field,' he said. 'Keeping my chastity intact for the woman I marry.'

Merryl made a choking sound and laughed. 'Christ! Mason, you're a bullshitter. How can you say that with a straight face?'

'It's the truth,' protested Andy, and they both laughed. 'Have another drink. It's really very good to see you.' He allowed his gaze to stray down over her perfectly shaped breasts and trim waistline. 'Where are you seated for dinner? You think we could work it so that I can stroke your leg under the table?'

'In your dreams, lover-boy! I'm at the captain's table with my boss and his wife so get a cold shower and forget'

'Spoilsport,' retorted Andy. He noticed that a buxom woman was signalling to Merryl across the ballroom.

'The boss's wife,' she said. She rolled her eyes and shrugged. 'She's like a mother hen. I'd better go and say my shaloms.'

'Enjoy,' said Andy. 'I'll see you later.'

They moved away from each other, but the vibe lingered. Andy suffered a pang of regret—all that they might have had was now reduced to mere chitchat.

He felt a hand on his elbow. Looking around, he saw Hamish McDonald beside him and he held out his hand in greeting.

'Nice to see you, Andy.' Hamish was the financial director of Anglo Cape Enterprises, producers and exporters of fine wines and fruits that graced tables in restaurants and hotels all over the world. 'Listen, I hate to bring this up here,' he said, 'but we need to push progress on the Mozambique project. Can we get together? I want to show you the feasibility reports.'

Anglo Cape's head office was in Cape Town, close to the rich winelands and orchards of Ceres and Franschhoek, but they had an administrative office on Commissioner Street in Johannesburg. The project Hamish spoke of involved the financing of agricultural capital equipment for a programme of expansion into Mozambique. Anglo Cape planned to put a small fortune into cashew nuts.

Despite his readiness to take risks, Andy had reservations about this. He thought about the political climate in Mozambique where, in the north of the country, the Frelimo guerrilla movement were in daily skirmishes with Portuguese troops. Was there a long-term future for investment in plantations?

The feasibility studies seemed satisfactory. The project had the blessing and financial guarantees of the Portuguese government. Given the financial strength of Anglo Cape itself, Andy felt that it was worth pursuing. The commitment of H&S could be confined to a maximum of three years. Anyway, the project was in the far south of the country where the Portuguese were still very much in control and it seemed far from likely that this would change within the following three years. Andy pushed away his reservations.

Andy Mason was young, confident, and assertive. His career with Highgate & Savage, the South African arm of an international finance empire, was only starting but he'd already made his mark.

After leaving school, he'd done nine months of compulsory military service and taken the hard route by volunteering for training as a paratrooper. Then he'd secured a junior position in the post-discounting department of Highgate & Savage, and at the same time begun a diploma in business and financial administration. By day, he got to grips with the complexities of merchant banking. By night, he studied.

On-the-job training in the many divisions of the bank opened up his imagination and his talents. He was inspired by the high-pressure world he moved in, and captivated by the flow of millions of Rands in daily transactions. He showed an aptitude for project co-ordination and logistical planning. Working in the competitive and specialised field of asset-based financial projects, he surprised and impressed his superiors by his grasp of things. He was quick to identify the strengths and weaknesses within proposals. Deals that looked untenable were given a new dimension through his ability to see beyond face value and to restructure from within, while keeping risks down to an acceptable level.

On occasions, though, it was a high-risk business. He had been fearful of losing his job the first time he had brought forward a proposal based on his own insights. It was for a multi-million rand hydraulic plant deal that cut across just about every rule in the book.

He had been chastised for wasting valuable time on an unwanted and unworkable business proposal that had the potential for nothing but failure. He had been told how rules were there to be obeyed, and that there was no room for gamblers. He had quietly listened to the roasting dished out by the panel of dinosaurs to which he had presented the proposal, and when they were done, he asked if he could take up half an hour of their time.

Within that half hour, drawing on research that he'd done outside of standard procedures, he had pointed out every positive aspect of the deal and challenged the conservatism of the panel. Reluctantly, and only after two weeks of verification of Andy's projections, they agreed to go ahead, but firmly pointed out that Mason's head was on the block. The transaction turned out a huge success for both the bank and the client, and men twenty years senior to Andy started taking notice of him.

They then sent him to the London office on a six-month Group orientation programme where he gained valuable insights into the European and Far Eastern markets. In between all this, and his part-time studies, there were also the ongoing military camps (three weeks each year) which he tolerated, although he regarded them as a waste of time and taxpayers' money.

He thrived at H&S. New aspects of the business emerged as the bank and their competitors became more innovative. More complicated and exciting projects were presented on an ever-increasing scale. After four years, having completed his diploma in business management and with a wealth of in-house experience, he was promoted to the position of project development analyst. His research and his reports carried strategic importance for the bank's credit panel's decision-making.

All in all, Andy Mason rode a wave of youthful exuberance. At twenty-five, he had rugged good looks. He had a strong square jaw line, broad shoulders and a good head of neatly trimmed light brown hair. He was physically fit, with a regular gym routine and a run of five kilometres every morning. Well-being and self-confidence radiated from his bright hazel eyes. He had an interesting and well-paid job; he owned a late model car and a half-share in a speedboat which he used most week-ends for water-skiing. He owned a well-appointed apartment in an upmarket suburb of Johannesburg and he was a member of a noted sports club where he used the gym and played squash three times a week. He was on the up, with an active life.

*　　*　　*

THEY SPENT THE BEST PART OF THE MORNING PORING OVER HAMISH'S NOTES.

'We'd like to take this offshore, Andy,' said Hamish. He put down his pen and leaned back. 'I think the tax benefits, doing it that way, would be good for both of us. Besides we rather hope that once this deal is moving and the Porks are suitably impressed, we can get a bit of action in their port-wine business—on a reciprocal trade for our wines. We'll need an offshore facility then anyway. If we get it all in place now, on a revolving offshore account, we won't have to suffer the heartache of the Reserve Bank's scrutiny later on.'

'Sounds alright to me,' said Andy, 'but we'd have to deal through London and that could be expensive. It'll be easier and less costly to set up the foreign exchange facility in our name. I'd just have to check it with the nursery. The offshore purchases could be done against that and shipped via yourselves, and you could then claim the export incentives by moving the equipment through your own asset register. We can start working on the offshore facility through our foreign investment division. Then it'll all be in place by the time the port deal is ready'

'What's the nursery?' asked Hamish.

'It's what we call treasury department. They're the protective matrons of the bank's money. They keep it tucked away in an incubator and they only let it out into a germ-free environment.'

Hamish chuckled.

They spent another hour working through options and possibilities, until Hamish looked at the time. He was due to fly back to Cape Town that evening and it was already almost three o'clock.

'I have to get going,' he said. 'Can you come down to the Cape early next week? We'll go through the whole structure. We need to get this ball rolling.'

Andy agreed. They shook hands and parted.

Over the next two weeks, work on the Mozambique project took up a large portion of Andy's working day. In this time he finalised the approvals through the treasury department, confirmed the supply and delivery dates of the equipment, and arranged to have the goods inspected and reported upon with all necessary serial and identification numbers. He completed the piles of paperwork that would need resolutions and signatures from the directors of Anglo Cape. The shippers confirmed the manifests with the necessary clearance from customs on both sides, and the project was reaching closure.

Each week, with absolute regularity, there was a meeting of the management team in asset finance. At these meetings, new business, pending projects and work in progress were discussed and minuted. The meetings were always attended by Lloyd Barret, who cast his eye over everything and retained it all in his remarkable memory. Without taking notes, he could recall every detail of each meeting that he presided over—with what appeared to be a permanent expression of disapproval. During the meeting that followed Andy's work on the Anglo Cape deal, Barret looked up and, in his dry voice, addressed Andy:

'Well, Mr Mason, thank you.' Barret never used first names. 'It seems you've done an excellent job on this. When will we effect payout?'

'I'm flying to Lourenco Marques on Monday next, to do the onsite asset inspection.' he answered. 'If that's fine, there shouldn't be any hold-up. I'd say we should be able to issue our drafts by Thursday next week.'

Andy noticed a slight change in Barret's demeanour at the mention of his flight to Mozambique.

'Why should it be necessary for you to do the onsite inspection? Don't you think that's a waste of money? Surely we can get someone up there to do it. Flying around the continent to tick off items that are already stated and confirmed on the shipping documents seems a bit extreme.'

Andy was taken aback. Asset inspections were relevant to all deals involving imported items financed by H&S.

'It's standard procedure, Mr Barret,' he said. 'We always do it for local deals. I think it's even more important considering that the equipment's beyond our borders.'

Barret thought for a moment. Then he responded: 'I'd rather we got someone up there to inspect the goods.'

'Mr Barret,' replied Andy, 'our mandates are quite clear. In fact, if my memory serves me correctly, the instruction was signed by you. "*Once delivered, all goods should be inspected by an authorised member of Highgate & Savage personnel.*" I've been involved in this deal from the start and I'm an authorised staff member.'

'Seems like an unnecessary expense to me,' muttered Barret, but he left it there.

Andy was puzzled. It was unlike Barret to question the necessity to follow procedure, and although this was an unusual case it did not change the principle.

When Andy entered his office a few days later there was a note on his desk from Gary. It asked him to call as soon as he got in. He picked up the phone and dialled the extension. Gary answered on the first ring.

'Can you come down to my office, Andy? Something's come up.'

The tone in Gary's voice rang an alarm bell in Andy's head, though he could think of nothing that he should be alarmed about. There were no outstanding issues that hadn't been discussed and taken in hand, and Andy felt comfortably on top of everything in his charge. But when he walked into Gary's office, his gut told him that trouble was brewing.

Sitting opposite Gary was Lloyd Barret, looking as stern and annoyed as ever. Gary waved Andy to a chair.

'What's up?' he asked, casually.

Barret spoke:

'You were in Cape Town last week, with Anglo Cape Wineries?'

'That's right,' said Andy. 'What of it?'

'It appears that you've been working on the Mozambique project in association with Industrial and Commercial.'

Industrial & Commercial Finance Ltd was Highgate & Savage's biggest local competitor in the field of asset-based finance. They were an aggressive rival and their management team at board level was made up of young university graduates and adventurous entrepreneurs. There was a tendency for them to cut across the ethics of old school traditions in the financial industry, often leaving a trail of disbelief in the structuring of deals.

Andy was dumbstruck. 'I've been doing what?'

'We have a report from Gordon Chatsworth at Anglo Cape that you were seen lunching with Brian Jefferson in Stellenbosch on Thursday last week. Do you deny that?'

'Absolutely not,' said Andy. 'Brian's an old friend of mine.'

Andy had met Brian Jefferson on the cricket and rugby fields at school. He had attended Pretoria College, the traditional sporting rivals of Andy's school. They'd both played at centre in rugby and excelled at cricket. They'd come through the age groups together from under-thirteen A to the first teams. Brian had gone on to university and studied as a chartered accountant and by pure coincidence he and Andy had ended up in the same line of business, though Brian flew higher than Andy did.

'We played rugby and cricket against each other at school and we've been acquaintances for years. What's the problem?'

'The problem is,' said Barret, 'that when one of our junior executives is seen in a small town that happens to house a big client, in the company of an executive of a major competitor, and these two are paging through documents that clearly relate to the business that our boy is there to attend to, there is cause for us to consider a serious breach of confidence.'

'Perhaps you'd like to tell me what documents I was paging through with Brian.' Andy was starting to feel uncomfortable—and annoyed.

'Our source suggests that it was a copy of Anglo Cape's balance sheet.'

'With respect to you, Mr Barret,' replied Andy, 'your source—and I don't give a damn who it is—is a bloody liar! Brian Jefferson happened to be on the same flight to Cape Town as I was, and we arranged to meet for lunch. We hadn't seen each other for months. There's no harm in that!'

'What was he doing in Cape Town?' demanded Barret.

Andy laughed. A short laugh of disbelief.

'I have no idea,' he said, 'and frankly I didn't bother to ask. He mentioned something about one of the distilleries in Stellenbosch, but we weren't talking business. We talked rugby, politics and sex. That's what friends do over casual lunches. Christ! I can't believe I'm hearing this. Why not bring your *source,*' Andy spat the word, 'and let's ask him or her some leading questions. I feel as though I'm on trial here with a bloody lynch mob as my accusers! I would like to speak to your source, Mr Barret, and until that happens I don't want to hear any more of this.' He got up to leave.

'Sit down, Mr Mason,' said Barret. 'We're not finished here.'

'Oh yes we are,' said Andy. 'If you have anything more to say, put it in writing.'

He stormed out, resisting the temptation to slam the door, and found that he was shaking. He could not remember ever being so angry. The indignation and rage welled up inside him as he went back down the passage to his own small office. He sat down behind his desk and put his face in his hands.

'Shit!' he swore bitterly to himself, and slammed his clenched fist down on the desk top, lifting papers and pens from the surface with the force of it.

The note from Barret arrived less than half an hour later.

*Dear Mr Mason,*

> *In the light of our discussion this morning, and in consideration of your refusal to assist in addressing this very serious matter, I am left with no alternative but to demand that you vacate your office with immediate effect pending a full investigation by the board into allegations that you have wilfully breached the confidence to which you are bound and entrusted in terms of your letter of appointment.*
>
> *You are hereby suspended and instructed to deliver, without delay, all files and company documentation in your possession to Mr Gary Chalmers, and to leave the building within the hour.*
>
> *You are further instructed to leave a contact telephone number with Mr Chalmers, and to ensure that you are available to attend a board of enquiry into this unfortunate matter.*

> *Yours faithfully*
> *Lloyd G. Barret.*

Andy read the letter through, and then read it again. He idly wondered what the *G* stood for. 'Surely not George.' He put the memo down on his desk and stared out of the window.

This wasn't happening. This had to be some kind of a bad dream. On the basis of hearsay by some unknown *source* who had conspired to tell a pack of lies, he was under suspicion of unethical conduct—and he'd been tried and convicted without the least bit of constructive evidence.

As he thought about it, it became more and more apparent to him that this had to be some kind of set up. There was no other explanation. But who would want him out of the way? And why?

Without conscious thought, and by his very nature, he'd always stayed in favour with everybody he worked with. As far as he knew, he had no enemies either in or out of the office.

So what the hell was this all about? Was there something he was working on, where his analysis of a deal would turn up something questionable? So many questions. This was ridiculous. His record was spotless; his presentation of work was meticulous. Christ! They'd paid for him to spend six months in London, and had chosen him above a whole bunch of other potential candidates—and in spite of it all, they were going to trash him without taking it to a level of proper discussion or giving him a chance to confront his accuser.

*Barret!* It came to Andy in a flash. He started to think, putting the events together.

'*It can only be Barret.*' Everyone knows that he's a cantankerous old bastard, but wouldn't he tend to err more on the side of fair play and caution if something like this was genuine? Surely he'd get his facts straight before flying off at a tangent? Unless *he* was the one who needed to have his fat arse covered by removing the person who was worrying him?

'If so, he must be desperate—clutching at straws. The truth must come out eventually, and when it does, not only will he have egg all over his face but he could be liable to a law suit on defamation charges. I wonder who else knows about this morning's meeting and this letter.'

The thoughts spun around in Andy's head. How could he find out where, in his work, what it was that threatened Barret? Something that needed to be covered up? 'That's the only possible explanation,' he said to himself. 'But where does it take me? It's delicate ground. For some reason, Anglo Cape is scratching him. Maybe that's it?'

It occurred to Andy how Barret had tensed up when he reported that he'd be going to Mozambique for the goods inspection. And Barret's objections, which were completely out of character and against protocol. 'Is there any significance in that?'

He was wasting time. He opened his filing cabinet and took out the files of the five major deals that he was researching, including Anglo Cape. Leaving alone most of the documentation that he'd secured on the deals, he took from the files the proposal submissions and balance sheets, copies of management accounts and schedules of deliveries and shipping documents, some of which he hadn't yet felt the need to look at.

He put them into a sequence and bound each bundle with an elastic band. Then he put the files back into the cabinet and went out of his office with the papers he'd taken and gave them to Gail Saunders. She was a young college student who studied part-time and worked as a general secretary for Andy and two others during the day.

'Gail,' he said, smiling at her, 'I need these copied—like yesterday. Do you think you could drop whatever you're doing and get this done for me?'

'Sure,' she said, returning his warm smile. 'How soon is yesterday?'

'The day before will do just fine. Put the copies into envelopes and drop them on my desk. I'm just going to see Gary.'

He couldn't afford to have Gary come to see how he was doing or ask for the files, as he was sure he would have been instructed to do. He wanted to keep him busy in his own office.

'Gary,' he sat down opposite his boss, 'you were very quiet while the judge persecuted me! Do you think I've been selling us down the river to I&C?'

'Hell, Andy, I don't know what to think. This was all laid on me the day after our meeting the other day. Barret called me in to tell me what he'd heard.'

Andy, incredulous, stared at Gary:

'He called you in, to tell you that I'd been double dealing? And right after he'd showered me with niceties for the way in which I'd handled the deal? Let me tell you what I think, Gary! Something smells on this. I didn't get to be one of the best damn analysts in this company by being stupid. Something is dirty here and I'm being used to filter the dirt. That's where the dirt is sticking, but it's not where it belongs.

'You know, or at least you should bloody well know, that I'm not the kind of guy who'd get involved in duplicity. It seems somebody wants it to look that way, though. I can only imagine that it's being done to shift the focus from another person's activities onto me.'

He paused and looked Gary in the eye for a long moment:

'I hope you're not part of whatever this is, Gary. Although you're my boss I like to think of you as a friend. It would really piss me off if you turned out to be one of the executioners in this fake trial.'

He didn't give Gary a chance to respond. He changed tack:

'I take it you've seen a copy of Barret's note to me?'

'I saw the note,' answered Gary. 'I read it. That's as much as I know. I'm not any more involved in this than you are Andy, but I've got a wife and two kids and all the trimmings that go with that. So I do as I'm told and I don't ask questions. I'll support you as much as I can, but don't ask me to compromise on my family's well-being. There I draw the line.'

'Well, Gary,' said Andy bitterly, with sharpness in his voice, 'I hope that one day when your kids grow up, they appreciate the fact that their father was prepared to stand by and watch while an innocent colleague was fried at the altar of dishonesty because you didn't have the guts to feel a bit of heat on your fingers. That is what I see happening here, Gary! You know it's a set up. You might not know why, but you'll walk away and close your eyes without caring—in case you're next. That's being part of the problem, Gary. I'd sort of hoped you'd have the balls to be part of the solution. Goodbye. I'll see you at the lynching.'

He got up and turned to go, and then paused.

'Oh! By the way, you'll find all the files that Barret wants, in my cabinet. It's not locked.'

Walking out of Gary's office in a rage was becoming a habit. This was the second time he had done it that morning.

Andy walked back into his office, and found that the copies he'd asked for were all in a large manila envelope on his desk with the originals neatly stacked in their rubber bands.

He quickly replaced all the documents in their respective files and then scrawled his own name on the envelope under which he wrote 'c/o Ground Floor Security'.

He walked down the passage to the mailing room and dumped the envelope nonchalantly onto the internal mail trolley. He returned to his office, took his jacket off the hanger behind his door, picked up his briefcase and walked out.

As he strode toward the elevator, he was approached by two security guards, one black, and one white. He knew them both by name. They were tenth floor 'executive suite' personnel. "Good morning, Eric, Phineas,' he said as they reached him. 'How are you guys today?'

'Mr Mason?' Eric ignored the niceties. 'We have instructions to remove the contents of your briefcase and search your pockets before we can allow you to leave the building.'

Andy grinned. This was a first. He'd been walking in and out of this building every day for nearly four and a half years, and had never attracted anything other than friendly greetings from those he passed.

'Whose instructions might those be?' he asked innocently. 'And why would they want you to do that?'

'It comes from the tenth floor, Mr Mason,' said Eric apologetically. 'We're just doing our job. We can't answer your questions because we don't know the answers.'

'Fine,' said Andy. 'And how are you going to recognise what you are looking for if you find it?'

'Company files and documents are all we've been told to look for.'

'Just a minute,' said Andy. He opened his briefcase and removed his diary and a Parker pen set. Other than that there was a flat folder with a blank examination pad and his plastic lunch box with his uneaten sandwiches still inside it.

'I'll tell you what,' he said, 'take the briefcase up to Mr Barret. I don't need it. Tell him from me to shove it up his fat arse. Would you like to look through the diary?'

'We're sorry, Mr Mason,' said Eric, clearly feeling uncomfortable. 'Like I said, we're just doing our job. You understand, don't you?' The end of it sounded like a plea.

'Yeah, whatever. Just sign for the contents and it's yours.'

He rapidly scribbled a receipt in his diary on the day's page, handed it to Eric for signature and then turned to Phineas.

'Sign as witness, will you, Phineas?'

Phineas looked dubiously at Eric, who nodded. Phineas signed.

'Right, gentlemen,' said Andy pleasantly, 'I think that concludes our business. Have a good day.'

He turned, pressed the down button and waited for the elevator.

Andy walked across the street to a coffee shop and ordered. He took out his cigarettes and lit one, watching the smoke trail up to the ceiling. He pondered over the events of the morning, still trying to come to terms with his situation.

He'd walked into his office less than two hours earlier, with his usual exuberance and excitement, and now here he was with his job in jeopardy on the grounds of some trumped up allegation that he couldn't fathom. He was angry. The indignation burned in the pit of his stomach like undigested chilli, and it rose up in a wave of hot anger.

He waited half an hour, then wandered back across the street and strolled up to security in the foyer of the building.

'There's an envelope for me, I believe? Andrew Mason.'

The desk clerk looked through items in a tray, brought out the envelope and handed it to Andy. 'There you are, sir. Just sign this for me.' She handed him a slip with his name and the description written on it.

'1 x brown envelope.' He scribbled his signature on the line, handed back the receipt book with a charming smile, turned and walked out.

'One step ahead of you, Mr Lloyd G. Barret,' he said bitterly as he left the building.

# CHAPTER 10

Sam Cohen, Singer & Associates was a respected firm of financial investigative brokers. Andy had used them on dozens of occasions to dig up details of a company's history when he'd felt uncomfortable with sketchy information that begged verification. He now wanted them to look into a transaction that he'd not only felt comfortable with, but for which he'd leapt into the air with fist raised, whooping, when he'd steered it to its final stages.

Andy telephoned Sam Cohen and asked if he could pinch half an hour of his time on a personal matter, and Sam agreed.

Sam's suite of offices in central Johannesburg was on the fortieth floor of the Carlton Centre, the tallest office block in Africa.

Towering over the city, the skyscraper offered a magnificent 360-degree panorama across the Witwatersrand.

Beyond the city proper sprawled a landscape dotted with yellow mine dumps which, for almost a century since the discovery of gold, grew larger every year. Mineshaft headgear and factory complexes dotted the skyline of the industrial areas close to the city. These then gave way to far-reaching suburbs and townships, dominated by a vast, varied mass of trees that formed what was reputed to be the largest man-made forest on earth.

From Sam's own office the view was northward, taking in the city skyline of lesser high-rise buildings that spread outward for a mile. There lay the railway station and its massive east-west network of tracks that split the city from the commercial centre of Braamfontein. Abruptly beyond Braamfontein Ridge came the mansions, villas and woodlands of the northern residential suburbs. On a clear day the Magaliesburg mountain range, a hundred kilometres distant, was visible shimmering and rising on the horizon like a mass of angry thunder-heads.

Cohen's domain was decorated with a thick pile olive green carpet that complemented soft water colours of African scenes hanging on the beige walls. Neat indoor shrubs in terracotta pots stood like guardsmen on either side of an enormous mahogany desk. This item faced the awe-inspiring vista, which was visible through floor-to-ceiling armour-glass windows.

Sam wore only the most expensive suits and, because of his height, which was little more than five foot five, he had them tailor-made. Andy guessed that he was in his early fifties, but his rotund shape and thick neck concealed the solid muscle of a former amateur wrestler. He was still regarded as a top amateur coach, and he gave up much of his spare time imparting his knowledge and skills upon children from disadvantaged backgrounds. His gold cufflinks glittered on white shirtsleeves that protruded discreetly from his pinstriped charcoal jacket.

Andy was ushered into Sam's office by the young receptionist, Sarah Goldstein. She had huge breasts, wide hips and bottle-blonde hair.

He was convinced, both now and from previous visits to these enchanting offices, that she would have enthusiastically provided him with the rumoured seven years' good luck associated with her gender and faith, if he gave her the slightest encouragement. He fastidiously resisted doing so.

The little man rose, or rather hopped down, from his high-backed executive chair and came around his huge desk, hand outstretched.

'Andy, my boy!' He spoke as though charmed by the unexpected appearance of a long-lost friend. 'Wonderful to see you! Have a seat. Can I get you coffee? Tea?'

Andy had never seen Sam without an expensive cigar stuck between the fingers of his right hand. He'd also never seen him smoking it. Sam clenched the stubby weed between his teeth as he held out his hand in greeting.

Andy declined the offer of refreshment and Sam gestured cordially towards an easy chair beside a low coffee table. He didn't want to take up any more of Sam's time than necessary, so he came straight to the purpose of his visit.

'Sam, I'd like you to look at a deal that I've all but finalised. I think that I'm missing something.'

They went through the needful assurances of confidentiality, and then Andy put Sam in the picture. He outlined the details of the deal with Anglo Cape and told him the story of his unceremonious exit from H&S. He spoke of his concern about Barret's reaction to the onsite inspection. He explained the thought, crazy as it seemed, that Barret was trying to cover something up.

Sam listened intently. When Andy had finished, he got up and strolled around the office with his hands clasped behind his back, twiddling the cigar between his fingers. He came back to stare out of the window, fitting the description of someone deep in thought. After a while, he turned back to Andy:

'Dealing in finance anywhere in Africa these days is a risky business, Andy. But having said that, I wouldn't look so closely at Mozambique for my risk evaluation in a case like this, because I'd be confusing the woods with the trees.'

Andy raised his eyebrows.

'I'd be looking at Mother Portugal. I don't need to tell you that Mozambique is a disputed Portuguese colony at war with itself. Selling cashew nuts out of Mozambique into the markets of Europe and the Far East is about as easy as it would be to sell sunshine and warmth to Eskimos, except the market is a whole lot bigger.

'If the shit hits the fan and things go sour in that sort of deal it will be for political reasons only—and Portugal's where that would happen. Keeping their colonies alive is costing Portugal more than they can afford.

'The so-called Prime Minister Dr Caetano is cast in the same mould as Salazar before him. He's a bloody dictator. He's not personally affected by the state of the country's economy so he doesn't give a damn. All he sees is empire, and he likes that. It is my guess that in the not too distant future, he will be removed either by a civil revolution or by heavyweights in the military who are losing men in action on a daily basis for a lost and irretrievable cause.

'It's been going on since the early sixties and it's sucking out around forty percent of the country's annual GDP. Given the hardship that their little southern African wars are causing at home, anyone with brains would give up Mozambique and Angola and be delighted by the shedding of them.

'If, or rather when, that happens your guarantees are not going to be worth the paper they're typed on because Frelimo will be the new government in Mozambique, and whoever takes over in Portugal will undoubtedly disassociate themselves from the responsibility of any guarantees issued by the Caetano dictatorship.

'If those facts are clear to me, Andy, they should be just as clear to anyone else who has their eyes open and an ear to the ground.'

'Okay,' said Andy slowly.

'So, let's build the scenario.

'Someone at Anglo Cape put the plan together based on market demand and the high quality of the Mozambique crop, both of which factors would excite the most conservative sceptic. That person puts his proposal to the board, who collectively get a dose of the smarts and decide that they can capitalise on their ready-made international markets by adding cashew nuts from Mozambique to their already impressive list of quality fruit and wine exports from the Cape. So they do all their homework and feasibility studies with dollar signs blurring their vision, they find a plantation that's already in production but needs development funding and new equipment for it to reach its full potential, and they buy a stake in it. This much we know to be fact. It was in the *Farmers Weekly* and the *Financial Mail* six months ago. You probably saw the articles.' Sam looked at Andy speculatively.

'From here, we are guessing—but let's just build a story on what we have for the sake of the exercise.'

Sam paced up and down as he elaborated his ideas:

'We'll say that it was all systems go. The share transaction for the plantation was finalised, probably through an irrevocable and unconditional share swap on an agreed scale rather than by cash. The equipment requirements were studied, agreed upon and ordered. The finance was arranged and the overseas markets that hold Anglo Cape in high esteem had been alerted and were buzzing. Then someone woke up, wiped his eyes and saw the realities of the political situation and what it could mean.

'Taking that snippet of news from the real world and putting it onto the table for the enthusiastic directors to chew on must have burst bubbles and rattled teeth. My belief is that, in those circumstances, the whole project would have been put under wraps and laid up in the freezer.

'But let's say the enormity of what they've embarked upon comes home to roost. Anglo Cape are committed to a large piece of real estate which has cost them big time and which is situated in a place where the future is likely to be decided upon by the law of the jungle. They've got themselves some new partners who probably saw the writing on the wall before their own rude awakening, and did the deal on the plantation for just that reason. They've got expensive equipment on the water destined for a port that may be in the wrong hands by the time it gets there. They've spread the good news far and wide about this enterprising expansion programme. They're facing a potential shareholder revolt and some high profile jobs, with all the accompanying prestige, are on the line. They need a way out, so they decide to use a bit of creative accounting.

'Here I have a problem, Andy,' continued Sam. 'These guys are not amateurs. Why would a group of successful and astute businessmen with a history of making rational and intelligent decisions want to invest in a deal involving millions of Rands in a country with a limited and uncertain future? To me that sounds pretty damn odd. It just doesn't add up. My money says it didn't happen that way. But it seems that elements of the deal are going ahead, and clearly there are forces at work that are hell bent in their determination to keep you away from doing your inspection in Mozambique. Your analysis of risk and reward is usually pretty good, Andy. What's your take on it?'

'I'm not sure,' replied Andy. 'Anglo Cape are high fliers and big enough to take a knock and survive. But I'm more concerned about how H&S fall into the picture. Obviously Barret knows something, otherwise I'd be in my office right now—planning my trip to Mozambique instead of sitting here playing with scenarios.'

'Have you checked with the suppliers to establish shipment dates and destination?'

'That's all on the manifests and pro-forma shipping documents. No, I haven't gone back and spoken to anyone directly. I didn't see the necessity until now.'

'Who else other than Hamish McDonald have you met with at Anglo Cape, on this deal?'

'Nobody,' replied Andy. 'From day one, it's only been Hamish. As far as I know he's had regular meetings with the rest of the board, but I've not been invited.'

'How long has this proposal been floating around on your desk, Andy?' asked Sam.

'Since late April. That's when they first asked us to look at preparing a facility for the project. They gave us scanty detail to work with at first and it wasn't until about three weeks ago that Hamish started pushing me on it, and the fine detail that's in these files has only become available since then.'

'Okay, so what have we got?' Sam started to pace the office again. 'We have assumed that there are corrupt elements in high office at H&S. Let's not forget, Andy, that everything so far is an assumption based on your sudden fall from favour, and just when you thought things were going swimmingly. But our assumptions have a strong basis for validity. Barret is obviously in on it, but he would have to be doing it in collaboration with a person or persons at Anglo Cape—and the only person so far identifiable there is McDonald. How much sway does he carry?'

'I'd say probably carte blanche on everything he does,' said Andy.

Sam stood staring out of the window at the inspiring view that probably cost him three times the worth of the floor space of his offices. After a while, he turned. He came back to his seat and leaned forward eagerly.

'Okay!' he said. 'Let's rethink this thing.

'I think this makes more sense. The proposal to the board of Anglo Cape that they should be growing cashew nuts in Mozambique is looked at, and thought to be good. They do everything that good businessmen do—feasibilities, costing, market reviews, the works—until all their ducks are in a row and they've reached decision time. By that stage they've all had a rethink, and based on the undercurrent of political activity in Portugal and its imminent effect on Mozambique (and by extension their investment), they decide that the risk is too high, and they shelve the project.

'At that juncture they would have advised H&S that the deal was off. They would have cancelled any orders for the equipment, if they had ever been placed, and you by rights should have been one of the first to know about the change of plan. But what happens if their financial director and the chief operator from the bank have seen a gap through which they can exploit the situation and cover the bases until the winds of change have blown the Portuguese back to Portugal?

'Those originals, which should have been scrapped, are still sitting in the official file, which gives it the appearance of legitimacy. But if, and I say it again, *if* our assumptions are correct, that file should have been closed and relegated to the not-taken-up section where it belongs. The fact that this has not happened, means that someone wants it to look as though the deal is still alive—in order to take eyes off alternative documents, in a separate file, hidden in a drawer somewhere.

'So an ulterior motive is being worked behind the scenes, and the only reason would be that someone with the authority to do so is trying to make sure that the payout goes through anyway. This means one thing only: the person concerned would be in a position to benefit from the deal. So you have to ask yourself the question "who and how?"

'Could it be that Barret and McDonald, between themselves, have structured it in such a way as to divert the funds into an account that has been set up on the pretext that it belongs to the purported supplier, but is in reality a dormant numbered account that can't be traced?

'In such a case,' continued Sam, 'the supplier would know nothing about it because as far as they are concerned the orders have been cancelled and the file is already closed.'

Sam stopped and leaned back in his chair. There was an enthusiasm in his manner as though he'd just cracked the safe code for Fort Knox. 'Who is shown as the payout beneficiary?' he asked.

Andy took the documents from the envelope he'd collected from the security desk and paged through them. He knew that they'd been given a banking account in Switzerland on behalf of the German company who had quoted on the equipment and who had originally agreed to ship it. Those documents appeared to be authentic, but it now seemed that what he was looking at was a pile of papers that were no longer of any relevance.

'You see, Andy,' Sam continued, 'what I'm thinking here, is that you say the deal is worth five and a bit million Rand? At the current exchange rate you're looking at close on four million US dollars. That's one hell of a lot of money in anybody's language.

'If it's been established beyond reasonable doubt that something is brewing in Portugal that is to change the shape of things as they are in Mozambique, which in my opinion would be good thinking, then that money could be paid away into an account that has nothing to do with the supplier, and kept there. Then the equipment that doesn't exist could conveniently get lost in the political outcome.

'Frelimo is armed, financed and fed by the Russians and as we both know the Reds get their pay-back from Africa by looting the countries that have enjoyed their support. Their modus operandi, as has been witnessed throughout the continent, is to nationalise everything down to the shoes on your feet. If that happens, Highgate and Savage despite all its international muscle would have to sing for whatever assets are tied up there. But if those assets were never there in the first place, no-one would ever know. Now if the record can show that the assets were in fact delivered and paid for against a finance agreement underwritten by H&S, who are conveniently covered against such an eventuality by a special risks insurance policy . . . ?'

Sam shrugged, leaving the sentence unfinished. Then he said:

'What a wonderful way for someone to get very rich very quickly. The problem, of course, is that if Mr Andrew Mason goes to Mozambique to inspect the assets that are not there, he's going to tell someone, isn't he? Now that would be most inconvenient!'

'You have a devious mind, Sam,' said Andy grinning. 'That's a feasible explanation. But the risk would be enormous. What happens if Caetano is not in any danger of getting his butt kicked out of the hot seat? What if things in Mozambique keep going for another five years?'

'You're bright for a young Yok, Andy,' said Sam. 'But you've got a lot to learn. These are areas you should concentrate your research on when dealing offshore, particularly in Africa.

'Like I've said, Portugal can't afford to keep twenty thousand troops tied up in Mozambique and Angola, and my guess is that sooner rather than later something will have to give—either by negotiation or by capitulation. Even if Caetano stays in power, and I don't give that another six months, those colonies are doomed to the trash heap of African politics.

'As soon as that happens, Frelimo (together with their Ruskie mates) will be in there picking up everything down to yesterday's garbage. Any thought of private ownership, particularly when it comes to expensive equipment, will be like autumn leaves in the wind.

'As long as the two trusted and highly regarded executives can keep the ball bouncing between themselves until Barret reports a successful claim against the insurers, which will have left the bank unscathed at the same time as letting Anglo Cape off the hook, they could probably get away with it. But with this wise-guy called Andy Mason hanging around in the wings trying to make sure everything is done according to the rules, it becomes a little scary—so they trump up a reason to get rid of him. That's my cynical view of what you have here, Andy.

'With the tense political climate the way it is all over southern Africa, including here in our temple of white supremacy where, believe me, the black power movement is stronger than ever although only functional underground, the temptation to get serious offshore money stashed away may be too hard for some people to resist. And this could be the perfect way to do it, as long as they can keep the "equipment" under wraps long enough. Why don't you get on the phone to the suppliers in Germany and find out if the equipment has actually been shipped—and what the status of the order is?'

'I think I'll do that, Sam,' said Andy. 'But it puzzles me. These guys have been with their respective companies for eons, they practically are the companies, and they have reputations that are worth protecting. Why would they suddenly want to get their fingers dirty on some shady deal?'

'Andy, I'm only drawing pictures for you,' said Sam. 'I'm not saying that the scenario we are playing with is for real. Remember, these are all assumptions. But I've been in this game since before your father's sperm reached the womb and I've seen some pretty weird stuff go down. What would a man like Barret or Macdonald earn? Eighty-five, maybe ninety thousand a year? Add the fancy car and one or two other perks and you've got what? Maybe a hundred grand. Let's just pretend that the two of them have done some kind of deal and that they will share and share alike. That's two and a half million apiece with a little bit of change.

'It would take them twenty-five years at their present income to earn that money. To have it all in one place at the same time would mean that they would have to toil through the years and not spend a cent. We know that doesn't happen. If we could earn without spending, there would be no point in earning. They must both be getting toward retirement age anyway, maybe another five or six years at most?

'No, Andy! Don't ever underestimate the power of greed. Some people will do anything for wealth, and one never knows who those people may be. Some of the wealthiest people on this planet got that way by cheating others—and others don't necessarily have to be competitors.'

Sam raised an eyebrow and cocked his head sideways. 'Did you ever hear the story about the supermarket chain that opened a hyper-store on the north coast near Durban?

'The guy they put in charge of the whole project had been with them since he left school, something like twenty or twenty-five years. He was trusted implicitly and given a blank chequebook to build his dream store within the parameters of the group's image.

'The store was a massive success, and his management superb. The plans provided for seventy-five cash register check-out points. He put in seventy-six and nobody ever noticed. The only thing that caused the slightest concern was that shrinkage at the store was a bit higher than the budget allowed for, like about one and a half percent. The fella made a huge show of bringing in loss adjustment experts, he put in closed circuit TV cameras, he organised random searches of staff, he put floor-walkers in-store—the works—to show that he was trying to nail the culprits that were pushing up his shrinkage figures.

'When he retired—in fact, the month after he retired—the shrinkage dropped to point zero two percent. There was a lot of head scratching, and it took them another year to work out that they had been operating seventy-six tills for over ten years, and only collecting from seventy five of them. I think they stopped counting their losses when the figure hit six million. In the meantime, the honest Joe who had engineered the whole thing and whose farewell party had probably cost the firm the equivalent of a month's shrinkage and which was dispassionately paid for out of overall profits in gratitude for a lifetime of dedicated service, had said he was retiring to Australia and probably went to Canada.

'The story goes that he was never found. Other stories say that it was such an embarrassment to the group that they didn't want to find him, and wrote off the losses to save their dignity. That guy also had a reputation to protect. Like I say, Andy, don't underestimate the power of greed, nor the lengths to which some people will go when it grabs them.'

Andy left Sam's offices deep in thought. He had known since his meeting with Gary and Barret that he had been put in this situation as a fall guy to cover someone else. Now he had the makings of a motive, though he still felt sceptical and reluctant to go back and face Gary or Barret with what was on his mind. He wanted to be sure that he had more solid ground to stand on before confronting anyone on the subject.

He went home to his apartment and booked a call through the international exchange to the number he had for the German suppliers in Hamburg. The call took an hour and a half to come through and he was answered by a woman who could not speak English, at the other end of a poor connection. It was another ten minutes before he was able to speak to the overseas sales division and a further five before he was finally speaking to Herr Heinrich Bortmann, the export consultant who had dealt with the Anglo Cape transaction.

Bortmann answered in heavily accented English.

'Herr Bortmann,' Andy said, 'my name is Andrew Mason from Highgate & Savage in Johannesburg, South Africa.' He spoke loudly and slowly in reaction to the bad line and the man's obviously poor grasp of English. 'I am enquiring about the shipment date for the goods covered under order number HG/AC58981. The bill of lading number that I have here is CUNRD8898/74. Can you tell me what the latest position on that shipment is?'

'Please hold,' Bortmann replied tersely.

Andy looked at his watch. His average monthly telephone account amounted to not much more than fifty or sixty rand. This single call must have cost him close to that already and he hadn't got anywhere yet. Another five minutes went by.

'*Ja*, Mr Mason?' There was another voice on the line, not quite as deeply accented as Bortmann, and Andy frowned. Who could this be?

'Herr Bortmann?' he said enquiringly.

'*Nein*. One moment, please.'

Another minute passed, and finally Bortmann was back.

'It seems that the documents that you have are out of date, Herr Mason. There have been many instructions for changes in this matter. What is your authority to make these enquiries?'

Andy's heart was racing. Could Sam have hit it so squarely on the button?

'I am preparing drafts for the transfer of funds against a facility to finance this equipment,' lied Andy. 'I need this information for my requisitions.'

'Have you not received our amended documents?' asked Bortmann

'It is possible that they have arrived, but have not yet reached me. I will check with our mailing department, but can you give me the most recent details while I'm talking to you so that I can update my file?'

There was a pause, and Andy thought for a moment that he'd lost the connection.

'Hello?' he said.

'A moment!' The man sounded irritated, but spoke again a few seconds later.

'The order number from Anglo Cape Enterprises remains unchanged, but the shipping destination is now Durban, South Africa and not Lourenco Marques in Mozambique, as was the original, and we have been instructed that final destination is to Seaside Cashews (Pty) Ltd at Kosi Bay, South Africa. Our guarantees are confirmed by Highgate & Savage International, Threadneedle Street, London. The shipping documents were sent by courier to Highgate & Savage Johannesburg as per your instructions, for the personal attention of Mr L. G. Barret, two weeks ago.'

'When were these amended shipping instructions received?' asked Andy.

The man paused and it was obvious that he was consulting his documents. 'Three weeks ago.'

It was three weeks since Andy had been at the meeting with Hamish McDonald, after Hamish had expressed his urgency, at the results dinner, to get the deal finalised.

So McDonald knew then that there'd been a deviation from the original instructions. Andy's meetings during his trips to Cape Town had revolved around the agreed format and structures that were relevant to the original proposal. The fact that the changes weren't mentioned clearly implicated Hamish. But who the hell were Seaside Cashews?

Andy thanked Bortmann, and replaced the handset.

He sat down and looked at his watch again. It was four pm. 'Not too early for a cold beer,' he thought.

He crossed to the bar and took a can from the drinks fridge beneath the counter. He poured the beer into a glass and returned to his seat beside the small dining table. He drew the telephone towards him and dialled Sam's number.

Sarah picked up at the other end. 'Cohen & Singer Finance,' she answered in a professional no-nonsense tone.

'With a voice like that, you should be on radio,' said Andy flirtatiously. 'You'd have an audience of a million guys tuning in just to hear the sound of it.'

Sarah laughed delightedly. 'You're an outrageous tease, Andy! But don't let me discourage you.'

Andy chuckled. 'Is Sam available?'

When he came on, Andy told Sam about the change of shipping instructions and asked him if he could do a run on Seaside Cashews.

'I'd like to know who they are,' he said. 'What their relationship is, if any, to Anglo Cape, who their directors are, and if possible their latest trading results. There's something very smelly about this.'

Sam said he would get onto it the following day. He was about to leave his office for the wrestling gym and wouldn't be able to do anything until the morning anyway.

Andy was tempted to phone Gary and fill him in on what he'd found, but decided against it. He didn't want to play open cards with anyone at H&S until he had all the information he was looking for.

He battled against an attack of frustration. He was uncomfortable and angry with being unemployed. Even more so, he was angry at the circumstances where he'd been side-lined to facilitate what seemed to be emerging as breach of authority— or, more accurately, fraudulent conduct on the part of senior executive staff. There was no other feasible explanation and he wasn't going to let it rest until the truth was out.

Andy's telephone rang shortly before eleven the following morning. Sam was on the line.

'You're not going to believe it, Andy. I've pulled out all the stops on this, because I'm almost as curious as you are. Guess what?'

'Let's not waste time with games, Sam,' said Andy. 'I'm not in a guessing mood. Tell me.'

'Okay,' laughed Sam, 'but hold on to your hat. This is one hell of a ride.

'Seaside Cashews is privately owned by two women, who by coincidence happen to bear the names Beatrice Margaret Barret and Maria Goncalves McDonald. The shareholding in the company is split down the middle and that, along with the plantation, was registered as a going concern four years ago—but they are not the registered owners of the land. They lease it. Seaside Cashews, who are the lessees, is managed by one Carlos Goncalves whose sister Maria is, by further coincidence, married to a Scot by the name of Hamish McDonald. What is more interesting is that Mrs Beatrice Barret was Miss Beatrice McDonald up until about thirty years ago when she married a Mr Lloyd Graham Barret.

'The land, measuring one thousand hectares in extent, was acquired by the registered owner eight years ago. That registered owner is an obscure trust that was set up when the land was bought. I'm working on who the trustees are, but there are no prizes for guessing what'll come out of there. What's also interesting is that Carlos and Maria have a brother, who just happens to be the Mozambican Trade Commissioner through whom all Mozambican imports and exports must be channelled. Now isn't this all just cosy?'

'Whoa, Sam!' said Andy. 'You're going too fast for this young Yok. You're saying that Barret and McDonald are brothers-in-law and that their wives are in partnership on Seaside Cashews, which is where the agricultural equipment that forms the subject of the deal I've been working on for them is headed. In addition, McDonald has a Portuguese wife whose brother pulls all the strings on imports?'

'Keep going,' said Sam. 'I think you're getting it.'

'So the happy family gets hold of a piece of ground mere kilometres from the Mozambique border,' said Andy, 'turns it into a cashew plantation, and then uses a deal between H&S and Anglo Cape to finance the whole thing once their trees start to produce. Bearing in mind that the deal with the Mozambique plantation is unlikely to produce anything, but if things go wrong and the truth comes out, there can be this wonderful story of how foresight saved the equipment from being seized due to quick thinking by Carlos who spirited everything back across the border before Frelimo could seal it off. But if everything goes according to their plans, they record the loss of the equipment and claim on the insurance and still walk away smelling like roses?'

'So you're not such a dumb Yok after all!' laughed Sam. 'What are you going to do?'

'Reporting what we now know to Barret is only going to scare him,' said Andy. 'But maybe a quiet word in the MD's ear would rattle some cages. I wonder if Gary Chalmers is in on this little scam.'

'You know what I'd do, Andy? I'd speak to Barret very quietly, showing him copies of all the facts that we have, and let him make the next move. You never know what might turn up.'

'I might turn up dead if these guys have Portuguese connections in high places,' said Andy with a chuckle.

Andy drove into town, parked in the basement at the Carlton Centre and caught the elevator up to the fortieth floor and Sam's office. Sarah smiled delightedly as he entered the reception area and adjusted her blouse to enhance the already clear view of her cleavage.

'Hi Andy,' she said, fluttering her eyelashes. 'We're certainly getting to see a lot of you.'

'Not as much as I'm seeing of you,' thought Andy with a wicked grin.

'I'm attracted by the receptionist here,' he said aloud. 'I can't stay away.'

Sarah seemed unsure as to whether or not that was a come on, and her smile slipped slightly before she recovered: 'Well, you don't have to come here to see her. She has a home, you know.'

'Whoops,' thought Andy. 'Let's not go there.' He gave a friendly laugh. 'You'll have to tell me where that is, some time.'

He moved on quickly to discourage further intimacies. 'Sam's expecting me. Can I go through?'

She looked disappointed, but she put her smile back on. 'Sure, he's waiting.'

Without getting up, Sam waved Andy to a chair. He had a large manila envelope on his desk, which he slid across to Andy's side.

'It's all in there, Andy. I'd normally charge someone about five hundred rand for what's in that envelope, but I'm in a good mood. You owe me lunch.'

'It'll be a pleasure, Sam. You name the time and the restaurant.'

'And stop teasing my receptionist!' added Sam. 'Either take her out and shag her, or let her know that you're not interested.'

Andy was taken aback,

'Hey, I'm not the teaser here, Sam," he said with an embarrassed chuckle. 'But either way I'd be lying. To say I'd never is a lie, and if I went ahead and made her day I'd be committing myself to the impossible. It's a tough call.'

Sam laughed. 'Ah, what it is to be young. But I agree with Oscar Wilde—"Youth is wasted on the young". You kids don't know how to deal with it.'

Andy used Sam's office phone to call Hamish McDonald at Anglo Cape offices in Cape Town.

'Hi there Hamish,' he said. 'It's Andy Mason.' There was an audible intake of breath from the other end, and Andy wondered what had been discussed between Hamish and Barret.

'Hello, Andy,' said Hamish. 'What's happening? I heard that you've had some trouble at H&S.'

It was a little over twenty-four hours since Andy's meeting with Barret, and he wondered how Hamish could have had access to that information.

'News travels fast. How did you know that?'

'I called to speak to you yesterday, and I was put through to Gary Chalmers who said you'd be out of circulation for a while.' Hamish's words were easy, but his tone was not convincing. Andy thought he detected a slight hesitation in his voice.

'Well—I'm doing a bit of private work. On a project for a company called Seaside Cashews in Kosi Bay, and Barret thought there may be a conflict of interests. I've taken leave of absence until the job is completed.' Andy waited for Hamish's response.

The pause became a pregnant silence, so Andy went on. 'You see, it seems that it might be connected in some way with our Mozambique deal. You wouldn't happen to know anything about it, would you?'

'I'm not connected with anything in the Kosi Bay area, Andy. Why would I know anything about it?'

'The cat's out, Hamish,' said Andy. 'You guys have taken me to the cleaners. You're using me as a fall guy. I'm more than just a little pissed off about it.'

'Andy,' said Hamish solicitously, 'you've got no idea what you're dealing with here. Walk away from it. Believe me, that's all you can do.'

'I don't think so, Hamish. I'm not going to stand by and watch my integrity go down the tubes because a couple of hot shots decide to get long fingers at my expense. You may need to come up here if you want to defend yourself in this, because I'm going to blow it open.'

He replaced the receiver and then phoned Highgate & Savage and asked for Lloyd Barret.

'Mr Barret?' he enquired when he was put through. 'It's Andrew Mason here. I've got some information that you might be interested in. I'm going to be setting up a meeting with James Sinclair, where I'd like to talk about Seaside Cashews and its shareholding. I'd like to hear from you and Hamish McDonald, whom I've also contacted, about certain equipment being financed by H&S on behalf of Anglo Cape. Would you like to set the venue for our meeting, or shall I ask Mr Sinclair to do that?'

James Sinclair was the Chief Executive Officer of Highgate & Savage. He was endowed with the ability to get things done while maintaining a hands-off management style. As long as profits remained on the increase he felt that his job, whatever it may be, was done. He was, however, one of the most approachable of the senior management team in the bank, and Andy had no doubt that he would allow protocol to be waived under special circumstances. Andy had made no such approach to Sinclair but he wanted Barret to think that he had done.

'Mr Mason, I have no idea what you are talking about.' Barret spoke without a trace of apprehension or surprise. 'And I'll thank you to remain within the bounds of laid down reporting structures. For as long as your suspension remains in place, you are neither invited to comment upon, nor become involved in, pending transactions. In future, kindly ask Mr Chalmers's secretary to set up your appointments with him and ask him to report to me, as is laid down in standing instructions. I really don't have time for this!'

The line went dead.

'*Sonofabitch!*' Andy swore to himself. 'That guy's a natural con artist.'

He couldn't believe that Barret did not so much as hesitate nor allow his voice to yield the slightest sign of a man who should be rattled. He turned to Sam who had been listening while he pretended to browse through a pile of documents on his desk.

'The man's as cool as they come,' said Andy. 'Sam, are you sure that your information is correct? I thought he might at least show signs of nervousness.'

'McDonald did,' said Sam. 'What you should do now is leave a message with Barret's secretary for him to contact you. I think the call will come in, but don't give him this number. Take it at home.'

'If I want to keep my nose clean,' said Andy, 'I think I should carry this upstairs. Let Sinclair deal with it. I don't want to be seen negotiating with anyone, nor do I want to be involved. I know where you're coming from, Sam. You think I could make some slush money out of it. But I don't think that's a good idea. Once my fingers get dirty, there'll be no cleaning them.'

'Good on you, Andy,' said Sam with a satisfied smile. 'I hoped you'd take that attitude. You're a good man. We really don't need thieves in this business and I'm glad to know that you're on the right side.'

The response that Andy got for his pains was far from what he expected.

He put a call through to James Sinclair's office and was told that he would not be in for the rest of the day. He was asked in what connection his call was, and he explained to the secretary that if he wanted to discuss it with her, he would not have asked for Sinclair personally. She in turn told him that Mr Sinclair was extremely busy—which Andy knew was not the truth—and that only calls of real importance would be referred to him.

'Tell him it's important,' said Andy. 'He's got a thief under his nose.'

It was a comment he would live to regret.

The following morning, after a bad night of insomnia, Andy went for a longer than usual run, trying to release the anxiety. By the time he returned to his apartment, it was after seven. At that hour he was normally in his office. The fact that he could not go there was tearing him apart, largely because he felt so cheated. If he'd been on leave, he would have gone out water skiing or parasailing on one of the many dams within an hour's drive of Johannesburg. Instead, he paced up and down his apartment like a caged animal.

The call from Sinclair came through shortly after ten, and the aggression in it was far from what Andy had anticipated.

'Andrew,' he said without preamble, 'I understand that you have taken company documents off these premises, and had an outside party scrutinise them for the purpose of trying to justify what I believe to have been an earlier breach of confidence. You have also made an attempt to blackmail senior management within this company, and that of a major client. That is a dismissible offence.'

Andy was floored. It took him a moment to digest what Sinclair had said.

'Mr Sinclair,' he said, with less confidence than he felt was his due, 'you seem to have been misinformed. I was sent off the premises by Mr Barret so as to cover up what has clearly emerged as a conspiracy to defraud Highgate & Savage.'

'That should be dealt with through available channels, Andrew,' said Sinclair. 'Documentation processed within this bank is privileged information, and not for general consumption.

You know that as well as I do. I don't know what it is that you are attempting to achieve by your conduct, but your actions are totally unacceptable.'

Andy was speechless. He was taken completely off guard. At the very least he'd expected a hearing, from which he could arrange a meeting with Sinclair and explain the situation. It seemed that he'd been pre-empted. It was now obvious that he was painted as the villain.

'I don't think you understand, Mr Sinclair,' he said awkwardly. 'I have evidence that I've been set up. I've been suspended in order to cover up a deal that shouldn't be on our books.'

'The decision as to what should and should not be on our books does not rest within your scope of responsibility, Andrew,' said Sinclair. 'Your job is to report on research gained within the bounds of laid down procedures. You have exceeded that authority and have given information to outsiders that should not have been available to anybody outside of this building. If this company was a country, you'd be facing treason charges.'

'Mr Sinclair,' said Andy incredulously, 'I have been trying to protect the company, not betray it! For God's sake, can't you see that? You don't even know what I've unearthed and already I'm the bad guy. Let me come and see you, sir. I promise you'll be intrigued.'

'Tell me, Andrew,' said Sinclair, 'did you or did you not take the entire documentation of a deal, including permits from local government, to be looked at by someone who has a good working relationship with most of our competitors?'

'With good reason, Mr Sinclair, yes,' said Andy. 'That's the reason why I need to see you urgently.'

'I can't imagine why that would need to happen. We know about an indiscretion on the part of a certain executive of this bank, and that will be dealt with in accordance with laid down company policy. You, however, have breached the confidence to which you are bound and I don't think I need to repeat what that means.'

'I find it hard to accept what I'm hearing, Mr Sinclair,' said Andy. 'I've heard of blind justice, but I was never aware of the true meaning of the term until now. Maybe I should take what I've got to the Institute of Banking. Perhaps they'd listen.'

'Andrew!' rapped Sinclair, 'don't be foolish enough to threaten me. I know what you're sitting on. I think I had it all on my desk sometime before you made your move. The appropriate action is being taken. But that does not detract from the fact that you have, without authorisation, taken confidential company property and made it available to unauthorised parties. You could have come to me, as you now have, but you chose to exceed your authority.'

'How do you know that, Mr Sinclair?' Andy was suddenly alert to the fact that he hadn't made any mention of the information that he had, or to whom he'd imparted it.

'There is nothing that I do not know about in this business, Andrew,' said Sinclair. 'That is what they pay me for. I admire what you've done, but I cannot condone it. One day, you will understand what I'm talking about. But, in your own interests, don't go rocking any boats that are resting peacefully at the quayside. In this business you can go with the flow, ride the rapids and reap the rewards or you can fight against the current and drown. I thought you'd already learned those basic lessons.'

It suddenly occurred to Andy that he might, all the time, have been unwittingly at the lower levels of an unscrupulous industry. He found himself wondering if everyone at the top were corrupt and covering each other's backs.

Up to that point he had considered his role in a banking career as one of dignified reliability—the very image that the bank put out to its clients. He was now suspicious of everything, even of his own involvement. He realised with anger that he was nothing more than a pawn in a game of deceit. He was using investors' money to satisfy the selfish ends of those to whom the money had been entrusted.

'So, what are you telling me, Mr Sinclair?' he asked. 'That I'm a liability because I'm too naïve to be dishonest?'

'Do you consider illegally removing documents containing privileged information from within the confines of what is expected to be a bastion of confidentiality as being honest?' said

Sinclair, in a tone of incredulity. 'Come on, Andrew. Even you know better than that.'

'Mr Sinclair,' said Andy, revealing his rising anger, 'my motives were entirely legitimate and honourable. The fact that you have chosen to make them appear otherwise is a disgrace, and I do not intend to let the matter rest here.'

'Andrew,' said Sinclair patiently, 'you have broken the rules. You came across a matter that involved an indiscretion by a senior executive of this bank, and instead of reporting that matter through the correct channels, you took things into your own hands and acted unprofessionally. That is what we are talking about.

'Now I don't really give a damn who you wish to share that bit of poor judgement with, but make sure it's someone who cares, because I don't. My decision to replace you stands. There are other financial institutions, and I will not discourage you from approaching them if that is what you wish to do. I will also not do or say anything that may discourage them from employing you. You have committed a dismissible offence in the corridors of Highgate & Savage, and you are therefore dismissed.

'I have given instructions to personnel as to how you are to be remunerated. I think you should consider the package generous, Goodbye.'

And with that the line went dead.

Andy stared at the receiver in disbelief, resisting the temptation to pick up the telephone and hurl it across the room.

It had been agreed that his pension contribution and outstanding leave pay would be paid to him, together with three months' salary in lieu of notice, but none of this was of any consolation. He felt cheated and disillusioned. No way could he agree that he deserved the treatment he'd received.

He slumped down on the sofa in his lounge, and wondered who had spread the word of his visit to Sam—but it took no great intellect to work out that it was either Sam himself, which he doubted, or Sarah. 'Why would she do that?' he wondered.

He sat quietly for over an hour, wondering what to do. The sense of powerlessness held him in confusion.

Eventually, having resolved nothing, he rose and put on his running gear. He went out onto the road at a fast trot, oblivious as to how his life was to be further disrupted.

# CHAPTER 11

I T WAS TWO DAYS LATER. He had lodged an appeal in the form of a letter addressed to the board of Highgate and Savage. He had delivered the letter by hand to Security on the ground floor, but it hadn't been acknowledged.

Frustration and vexation consumed him. He wandered around aimlessly, hoping upon hope that someone would contact him and give him the chance to exonerate himself—but the call didn't come.

On the third night, he was awakened from a deep sleep by the incessant ringing of his phone. He hauled himself awake and looked at his bedside clock. It was three am.

'Who the hell can this be?' He stumbled through to the living room to answer it.

Hello?' His voice expressed sleepy annoyance.

'Andy! It's me, Merryl. I'm sorry—I didn't know who else to call. It's . . . . It's my folks.'

Andy heard the anguish in Merryl's voice, and dread crawled up his spine.

'What is it? What's happened?'

'They've been attacked on the farm! They've taken Dad to Fort Vic, but I can't get any word about Mom. Andy! I don't know what to do!'

'Sit tight,' said Andy. 'I'm coming.'

He replaced the receiver, dashed through to his bedroom and threw on a track suit and a pair of running shoes, and then ran down to the basement where his car was parked. The distance from Andy's apartment to Merryl's on the Berea ridge, north-east of the city, was just under ten kilometres and Andy was there in seven minutes, stopping only briefly at red traffic lights and then speeding on through the deserted streets.

He charged up the stairs to Merryl's lodgings on the third floor of the block, and she was waiting for him. She threw her arms around his neck.

'Andy!' she sobbed. 'Thank you!' She paused, and she hiccupped. 'I don't know what to do!'

'Sit down,' said Andy. 'I'll make tea and then we'll get on the phone. I'm sure everything will be alright.'

But he wasn't sure at all. He'd taken a great interest in the Rhodesian bush war. He carried fond memories of the country from his schoolboy days, but he'd read reports of atrocious farm attacks and the ruthlessness of the guerrillas who perpetrated them.

He made tea and poured for her. He took her hand. 'Right! Where do we start? Who phoned you with the news?'

'The hospital at Fort Vic,' she said unsteadily. 'They must have got my number from Dad. But they couldn't tell me anything about Mom, and I'm scared.'

'Did they leave a number to call back on?'

'Yes.' Merryl crossed to the phone table and picked up a message pad.

Andy rose and took the pad from her and then picked up the phone and dialled the international exchange.

The phone rang in the ear-piece for so long that he thought that nobody would answer.

'Damn it!' he thought. 'It's supposed to be a twenty-four hour service. They surely can't be so busy at this time of night that it takes this long to pick up a call.'

He was about to hang up, when a tired female Afrikaans voice on the other end answered.

'*Kan ek u help? Dis Internasionale.*'—Can I help you?—This is International.

'Thank God.' Andy, responding in Afrikaans to ensure maximum co-operation, gave the number in Fort Victoria and explained the urgency.

'*Bliksemse terroriste!*'—damn terrorists—agreed the voice, and gave the assurance that she'd get the call through as soon as possible. Andy hung up and they waited. Ten minutes later the phone rang, and Andy snatched it from the cradle.

'*Jou oproep, meneer. Jy's deur*'—Your call, sir. You're through.

'Fort Victoria exchange,' came an English-speaking woman's voice on a clear line.

Once again Andy explained the purpose of his call, and was immediately connected to the casualty section of the hospital.

'Good morning,' said Andy as calmly as he could. 'My name's Andrew Mason. I'm calling from Johannesburg, and I'm looking for information on the status of Mr and Mrs Sherbourn."

'Not Sherbourn!' whispered Merryl. 'That's my married name. My parents are Carlisle.'

Andy had never given a thought to that. 'Such a basic thing!' he thought. 'How little I know about her.'

He corrected himself and waited.

'Are you a relative?' enquired the voice a few minutes later.

'I'm with their daughter. I'm a friend. We're desperate to know what's happened. Please help me out.'

'I'm sorry,' said the woman, 'but the news isn't good. Mrs Carlisle died on the way in. She was shot, and then she was beaten and raped. Mr Carlisle has multiple gunshot wounds which could be life-threatening. Hold the line, please. The doctor's here.'

Andy was devastated. The news was given in so matter-of-fact a way, so clinically, that it shook him to the core.

'This is Dr Whitely. How can I help you?' The baritone voice was incisive.

'I'm enquiring about the Carlisle family. I think I've heard all I need. Are matters serious enough to warrant that their daughter goes up there?'

Andy was thinking on his feet. He didn't want Merryl to pick up the news through hearing a one-sided conversation.

'Goes without saying,' said the doctor. 'And I suggest that it be done with some urgency.'

'Thank you. We'll arrangement it. Goodbye.'

Andy replaced the receiver and turned to Merryl, who stared at him with a look of expectant dread in her beautiful eyes.

'Come here,' he said, and walked towards her. She rose from her chair and Andy held her in a gentle embrace.

'Do you have flight times for Rhodesian-bound airlines?' he asked. 'We need to get you there, ASAP.'

'What's happened, Andy? Tell me!'

Andy took a deep breath. He didn't know what to say. This was something he'd never had to deal with before. He hesitated for a few seconds, during which time a thousand thoughts and images raced through his mind. He gave her the bald facts, gently and quietly.

'Your mom's dead, Merryl. And your dad's critically ill. You've got to get there.'

Merryl held tightly to Andy, but he felt her go limp in his arms. 'No! No! No!' Please God, don't do this to me! Not again!'

And then she cried her despair, beating at the air around her with her fists.

Andy stooped and lifted her as he would a child. He walked over to the sofa and laid her down. She hung onto his neck with a tight grip and he wondered if he should call a doctor to administer a sedative. Glancing at his watch, he saw that it was nearly four in the morning. Should he take her down to Johannesburg General—not far away?

He turned, and he saw Charmaine. The child stood under the archway between the bedrooms and the living room.

She stood in her little girl's pyjamas and bare feet, with her thick blonde hair tangled in an unkempt mass, wiping sleepy eyes with the back of one hand and holding a brown teddy bear in the other.

'What's the matter with Mommy?' she asked in her drowsy voice.

Andy went across and picked her up, cuddling her head to his shoulder, and kissed her forehead gently.

'Mommy's had bad news, sweetheart,' he said. 'But we're going to fix it so that everything will be fine. Let me take you back to bed and we'll tell you all about it in the morning.'

'Why can't you tell me now?'

'Well—we don't know ourselves how bad it is,' said Andy gently. 'It might be nothing. But if you go back to bed, we'll find out and tell you. How's that?'

'I want to stay with Mommy,' said the child.

Andy was out of his depth. Brushing away her tears, Merryl managed to take control:

'Come to mommy, darling. I'll try to explain.' She sat up on the couch and Andy took the child across and placed her in her mother's arms.

'Let me get you a drink, Merryl,' said Andy, not knowing what else to do. He went to the wall cabinet where he knew she kept a supply of liquor, although she drank very little herself. He poured a double measure of brandy into a glass and added a splash of soda. He handed the drink to her and she took a swallow and then pulled a face of disgust.

'God! That's awful stuff!' She handed the glass back to Andy. With Charmaine on her lap, she was more composed.

'Look . . . .' said Andy. He faltered. He was unaccustomed to domestic arrangements. 'I'll try to get details of flights to Salisbury. Have they got a service from there to Fort Vic? Or would you have to go by road?'

'I don't know,' said Merryl. 'Andy—I'm not going to cope with this.'

She held Charmaine tightly and started to weep again.

'It's so unfair! Why do these things have to happen? I can't handle it again, Andy.'

Craig's death was still raw in Merryl's memory.

Nobody close to Andy had ever died suddenly or tragically. His grandparents were all dead, but that was to be expected. They'd lived long and fruitful lives and all their journeys had ended in old age. Trying to deal with Merryl's grief was like nothing he'd ever had to confront before. It made him feel helpless and uncomfortable.

'Hey!' he said gently, going down on one knee beside her. 'For what it's worth, I'll be at your side every step of the way. I'm not sure what to do, but let's work it through together. We'll go forward, Merryl, and we'll do it at your pace. But first we've got to work out how to reach your dad. Let me handle that. Okay?'

She tried to smile but it came out as a grimace. She raised a hand to his face, and stroked his cheek with the palm of her hand. 'Thank you, Andy. You're a good friend.'

It struck him that there should be an all-night number for flight information at Jan Smuts International, the largest and busiest airport on the continent, and he went to fetch the telephone directory. He found an after-hours number for the airport and dialled.

After an interminable wait, the phone was answered—but the information wasn't good. There were only three flights a week from Johannesburg to Salisbury. They'd cut them down because of reduced demand and for fear of terrorist attacks on civilian aircraft. The flights all left at eight pm so as to be in Rhodesian air space after dark and the next one was not until the following evening—effectively two days' time.

'Well,' thought Andy, 'that's out.' His next thought was the Rhodesian High Commission in Pretoria. 'Surely they can help?'

He found an after-hours number in the Pretoria directory and called. The phone was answered on the second ring by a man who sounded awake and efficient. Andy briefly laid out his problem and asked for the man's advice.

'What I suggest,' said the official, 'is that you go by road. It's only 260 kilometres from Beit Bridge, and there's an armed police convoy that travels the route twice a day escorting visitors. The convoys leave at 7 a.m. and 1 pm. You'll have the protection of three armoured vehicles which are spread out over the length of the convoy. So far we've had no trouble from the terrs on that bit of road. It's actually pretty safe.'

Andy thanked the man and hung up. He turned to Merryl.

She was absently rocking backwards and forwards on the sofa, with Charmaine's head tucked neatly into her neck and shoulder. The peculiar, faraway look in her eyes startled him. She seemed to be in some sort of hypnotic trance, witnessing in her mind's eye a horror that could drive her over the edge of sanity.

'Hey!' he said. 'Let's get you packed. We're driving to Rhodesia.' He said it without conscious thought, and the enormity of it only struck him when Merryl snapped out of her rumination and demanded loudly, 'We're what?'

His mind was made up.

'You heard me. We're driving to Fort Vic to see your dad. Let's go. I'm going home to get some clothes. I'll be back in an hour. If we can get away from here by six, we'll be at the border well before one.'

'You're bloody mad, Mason!' yelled Merryl. 'That road is crawling with murderous bloody terrorists who kill women for kicks. I'm not going there, and sure as hell I'm not taking my daughter up that route.'

Andy repeated what he'd been told by the man at the High Commission.

'We could be there by tonight, Merryl. If you wait for the next plane you'll only get away from here tomorrow night, and then you've still got to find a way of coming down the road for the same distance from Salisbury.

'I'm not going to push it. It's not my dad lying up there in hospital. But I'll be back in an hour. If you're ready, we'll go. Otherwise we'll try to think of something else—but I think my way is the quickest. It's five hours from here to Beit Bridge, which means we can be there in plenty of time to join the one o' clock convoy, and then it's three hours under the protection of the convoy to Fort Vic and your folks. Think about it.'

He turned and strode from the apartment, but as soon as he was in the corridor, heading to the stairwell, he started having doubts. The issues at Highgate & Savage were far from resolved, although he had no reason to think that they would improve. Rushing off to war-torn Rhodesia to help out an ex-girlfriend seemed a bit impulsive.

'What the hell,' he thought. 'Whatever the outcome, I'll be back in a week—and the break will do me good.'

Andy got back to his apartment shortly after five. The late winter sun was still below the horizon, throwing up streaks of red against sparse thin cloud. From the wall safe inside his bedroom cupboard, he took his passport and a bundle of cash. He put into a hold-all a suit and a variety of shorts, tee-shirts and jeans, underwear and socks. He then called his parents.

His father answered with the same irritation that Andy had expressed two hours earlier when he'd answered Merryl's call.

'Sorry to wake you, old man,' he said cheerfully, 'but the sun's almost up and so should you be.'

'What do you want, Andrew?' grumbled his father. 'It's the middle of the night.'

'It's dawn, dad, and a beautiful one at that. I'm popping off to Rhodesia for a few days. I thought I'd let you know.'

There was silence on the line. Then his father spoke:

'I'm trying to think of a clever response, but it's a bit early for repartee. Now what do you really want?'

'Just to let you know where I'll be for the next few days.'

He sketched to his father what had happened. He explained about the convoy escort and the urgency of getting up to Fort Vic.

Andrew's father had been born in Livingstone, Northern Rhodesia, and had spent most of his youth growing up in Bulawayo. He knew the country intimately and still spoke fondly of his experiences there. But he followed the news and he had his own pessimistic opinion, usually expressed with the dourness of a Jeremiah, about events in the region.

'You're mad, Andrew! Let the girl wait until tomorrow night when she can fly to Salisbury. And, if your judgement has to be clouded by lust disguised as chivalry, pay for her to get a bus down from Salisbury to Fort Vic. Tearing off into a war zone as a civilian—especially anywhere in Africa where the bastards will cut out, roast and eat your balls while you watch—is a very dumb idea.'

'Dad, relax,' said Andy. 'You've been watching too many African Missionary movies. I'll see you in a week. Love to mom. I've got to get going. Cheers.' He hung up and left his apartment.

When he got back to Merryl's apartment at five to six, she had packed a suitcase for herself and Charmaine. She sat on the sofa in a state of indifference.

'I don't think it's a good idea, Andy. I know I need to get up there, but I also think we're taking a hell of a chance.'

'Merryl,' he said patiently, 'it's up to you—but people travel by road to Rhodesia all the time. The tourist industry's in trouble up there. It's in their interests to make sure that visitors are safe— that's why they run the convoys. My one concern is to get you to your father's bedside, and it can't wait. He's seriously injured. And, believe me, I'm no more interested in getting shot at by a bunch of renegades than you are—but I don't think that will happen.'

'I know the danger's not that serious,' said Merryl. 'But I can't help feeling worried. Let's phone the hospital again. I'd like to get an update before we do anything stupid.'

It was after seven by the time that they had a connection and Andy was concerned about being in time to catch the one o' clock convoy at Beit Bridge. This time Merryl spoke to the doctor. When she got off the phone, she simply said 'Let's go.'

# CHAPTER 12

D riving through Johannesburg's early morning traffic was frustrating, and it was already eight by the time they reached the northern highway to Pretoria and Pietersburg. Andy gunned his Datsun *SSS* as fast as he dared, given the strictly enforced speed limits. These were a national fuel-saving measure in the wake of the OPEC-initiated oil crisis of the previous year.

Andy and Merryl maintained an uneasy silence. How to lighten the mood, without sounding frivolous? With nothing to say, they said nothing. Andy thought it best to leave Merryl with her thoughts and her grief. Charmaine eased the tension with her endless questions about the things that she saw in the fields on either side of the highway. She was strapped in, on the rear seat, with her toys, until she became restless and Merryl sat the child on her lap. Answering Charmaine's questions took Merryl's mind off the anguish.

Near Warmbaths, a small resort town 160 kilometres north of Johannesburg, the three-lane highway narrowed to a single lane. Slow-moving heavy transport vehicles with Rhodesian—bound goods on board reduced their progress to a tame average of less than sixty kilometres per hour, and Andy grew anxious. He kept looking at his watch—at this rate, they'd miss their connection with the armoured convoy at Beit Bridge.

It was nearly one when they reached the frontier town of Messina, sixteen kilometres south of the border. They would not make the one o' clock convoy on the other side of the border. Andy knew that it was pointless to try. He pulled his car into a travel lodge and checked in for the night.

The Limpopo Inn was a scattered collection of thatched rondavels set in an extensive bushveld estate. Each small circular chalet had a single bedroom and an en-suite bathroom. They stood in a wide horseshoe configuration, separated but linked by shale pathways. At the centre of the horseshoe were the reception, bar and dining area. The paths were lined by colourful gardens with tropical shrubs, and a swimming pool—built into a natural rock formation—sparkled invitingly. There were clusters of outdoor chairs and tables decorated with tablecloths and sunshades that bore the logos of South African Breweries products: Lion Lager, Castle Lager and Black Label.

Andy felt the awkwardness of the situation. He and Merryl had said very little to each other since leaving Johannesburg and the silence was uncomfortable. So, after checking in and settling Charmaine and Merryl in their chalet, he dumped his hold-all in his own room and headed for the bar.

Half an hour later, Merryl joined him. He was on his second beer. He looked up and smiled at her, noticing her sombre features.

'Let me get you a drink,' he volunteered. 'Where's Charmaine?'

'She's beat,' said Merryl. 'I laid her down on the bed and she went out like a light.' She paused for a moment. 'I'd just like a Coke please, Andy.'

Andy called the barman and ordered.

The front of the bar room was a wide French window. The sliding glass doors led out onto the patio and provided a scenic view.

'Can we sit outside?' asked Merryl. 'I need to talk to you, Andy. There's a lot that I've wanted to explain to you for ages—but I didn't have the courage.'

They moved out to the deserted patio area where they sat at a table facing each other.

'I'm all ears,' he said good-naturedly. 'Shoot.'

'I've thought about this for so long, Andy. I've run it through my mind so many times. I'm scared of sounding foolish. Please try to understand where I'm coming from.'

She paused.

Andy waited. Anticipation, mixed with the fear of another let-down or anti-climax. Then she spoke, and Andy was surprised at the intensity in her voice.

'When Craig died,' she began, 'it was as if the whole world stopped. I wanted to die with him so that I didn't have to be apart from him. I think a big piece of me did die, Andy, like I'd lost an arm or a leg—but mostly my heart. It's hard to explain, but harder to live with—because nobody really knows. How can they? The truth is, nobody really understands—or even cares.

'All the good intentions of the nice people who tell you they know how you feel—it's just a pain in the ass. No matter how much moral support you have, you still stand by yourself on hollow stumps. It's personal and it's lonely.'

Merryl paused. She composed herself and went on:

'We met when we were at school. I was in standard six and all of thirteen years old. He was sixteen and in standard eight and I loved him from the moment we met. It was inconceivable that there could be anyone else. What surprised me, even as a pubescent child, was that he loved me back and made no secret of it, even among his teasing friends.'

Merryl smiled at the memory.

'You know what it's like with kids at dating age. It sounds stupid, but we just fitted together like a dovetail joint. Sunshine in a clear sky. Puppy love. Both our parents tried to discourage it because we were so young, but our bond just grew stronger.

'I was twenty when we got married. It was soon after his twenty-third birthday and the year after he had finished university. Sometimes, after making love, we joked that we'd died and gone to Heaven together "'cause nothing else could be so perfect". I don't think an angry word ever passed between us.

'When I fell pregnant it was like being in Eden. They haven't invented the words to describe our happiness. It was irreplaceable.'

Merryl paused. She was on the verge of tears, Andy was sorely tempted to reach out and embrace her, but he waited.

'I'll never forget the look he gave me the last time I saw him,' continued Merryl. Her tears now flowed.

'We were on our way to the farm. I could feel Charmaine kicking inside me. It was such a wonderful sensation and I reached across and took his hand off the wheel to put it on my stomach so that he could share. He took his eyes off the road and looked at me with a smile, but it was a sad smile, like nothing I'd ever seen before. The look in his eyes astonished me. He held my gaze for maybe a second longer than he should have done and when we looked away from each other, we both saw the buffalo standing in the middle of the road. That's the last thing I remember—and I never saw Craig again."

Merryl raised her hands to cover her face. Softly, through the tears she said, 'They buried him without me even knowing about it. All I wanted to do was to dig myself into the ground to be with him. He was only twenty-five.'

Andy's resolve broke. Tears brimmed in his eyes and he reached out to hold her, but she resisted him gently. She held up her hand, in a gesture that said 'please wait'.

'I left Rhodesia and came to South Africa with Charmaine. I couldn't bear being reminded every day of what I'd lost.

But when I met you, Andy, something happened—as if, in a strange way, part of him had been returned to me.

'Andy, you're so much like him in many ways—but you aren't him. I felt as though I was cheating on both of you. When you and I made love, I was with Craig. There's never been anyone other than you and Craig, and I wanted to fall in love with you the way I did with him—but I knew it wasn't possible.

'I was totally confused. I couldn't begin to explain to you. It seemed that my only way out was to go back to the ghost of Craig, and push you away—so as not to confuse or hurt either of you.'

Now I've got to go through all that again with mom.

'It's different but the pain's just as intense—and I don't want to be alone anymore.'

Her words ran into wordless tears, and she reached her arms around Andy's neck. He felt her tears, warm and abundant, running off her cheeks and onto his own.

For a long time they sat like that, awkwardly entwined in each other's arms, sitting sideways on the plastic chairs in the hot afternoon sun.

Andy tried to gather his own emotions. He had been more offended than hurt when Merryl had broken off their wild relationship. He remembered the day well enough, and he'd never made sense of it.

Since that moment, and other than the Highgate & Savage dinner, they'd not seen nor spoken to each other.

'So,' said Andy eventually, 'where does that leave us? Are you saying that you can put it all behind you now, and move forward?' He paused, deep in thought. He spoke again:

'I'm not sure, Merryl. I can't bring Craig back. And I refuse to be a substitute for someone else. I'm not good at this sort of thing. I'm not much good at matters of the heart.'

He hesitated. He wasn't sure how deeply he was prepared to go in this. Then, throwing caution to the wind, he said:

'I missed you terribly. But life goes on. You can't look back when you're trying to go forwards. It's like taking your eyes off the road.'

Merryl said nothing. Instead, she turned her head so that her mouth found his. She parted her lips and squeezed him tighter, pressing her tongue against his closed mouth until he responded and they were embroiled in a kiss of such passionate wanting that Andy was aroused, surprised and breathless.

'Make love to me, Andy,' she whispered. 'I want you now . . . please! . . . I need you. It's you I want. Not a ghost.'

They rose, leaving their unfinished drinks on the table. They stumbled arm-in-arm to Andy's chalet

They entered and closed the door.

Their wanting was obsessive. They groped at each other's clothing in a deep, adoring embrace and when Merryl's open blouse exposed her breasts he took her nipples into his mouth, first one and then the other. He lifted his mouth back to hers. In a state of wild desire he lifted her to the bed. They tumbled onto it with Merryl pulling at his belt and releasing his jeans.

She moved her hand down beneath his underwear and held tightly to his explosively erect penis, then slid down and took him into her mouth, while he pulled off her blouse so that she was naked from the waist up.

He placed both hands on her breasts, gently holding her back where he could look into her eyes.

She stared at him for only a moment and then crushed her mouth against his. She pulled his tee-shirt off over his head and rolled on top of him so that her breasts were soft and warm against his naked chest. The feel of them took him to a new height of arousal.

Merryl raised herself and pulled his open jeans down over his knees and away from his feet so that he lay naked and enormously erect below her. For a moment she kneeled over him, admiring his physique, and Andy reached up to unclip her skirt.

He cast it aside, exposing her firm thighs and a pair of scanty white lace panties that scarcely covered her pubis. The sight of her swollen mound almost brought him to a shuddering climax, but he controlled it and pulled her down to him, smothering her with kisses as he slid his hand under the lace. He felt the warmth and dampness and the urgency of want from her vagina beneath the tangled curls of soft pubic hair.

'Take me, Andy!' she whispered breathlessly. 'Take me now! Make love to me! I can't wait. I want you in me so much.'

They rolled together on the bed so that she lay beneath him, wet and wanting, and he went into her easily, silencing her impassioned pleas and her groans of ecstasy with deep, loving and heartfelt kisses.

They climaxed together in a rush of passion so deep that it seemed to erupt from far below. It mingled into a spiralling and tangible thing, carrying them high. It devoured them in mindless beauty—a sensation that neither of them had words to describe.

They lay breathless in each other's arms, still deeply coupled and holding tight, as if fearful of the other slipping away. In the midst of the passion a vice-like bond had taken hold of them like none that Andy'd ever known. His mind exploded like a fireworks display, and the sensation thrilled and excited him.

Without withdrawing, they moved together in unison. They made love slowly and patiently, whispering to each other in strangely inadequate and garbled sounds. They took turns to be on top, rolling over without losing the intense coupling. Words came and they spoke of fantasies of love. What had, before, been simple lust was now a total bond.

Wild and uninhibited desire was now blossoming into something like divine happiness.

When they came to orgasm the second time, it was as intense as the first. They guided each other to it so that they reached their climax together again, and the small room was filled with nothing but shared sensation—an emotional explosion of body and spirit that defied reality.

\*     \*     \*

Shortly after sunset, they dined on the patio outside the bar. The orange and gold lowveld sky brought back memories—Andy's trip to Northern Rhodesia when he was a schoolboy, in the years before that country had been renamed Zambia.

The air was still and warm and despite Merryl's obvious anxiety about her parents, her mood had lightened in the wake of their afternoon love-making. The atmosphere was contented. Their speech was light and easy, between companionable silences in which their thoughts and dreams took shape.

Charmaine had woken up at four, when Merryl went in to check on her, and they'd all gone for a walk around the grounds of the lodge, before returning for a drink under the fading sun.

After putting Charmaine to bed, Andy and Merryl returned to the patio for a nightcap and then went back to Andy's room where they made love again with renewed intensity and passion. Andy did not want to let her go but, shortly after eleven, she kissed him and spoke:

'It's an early start in the morning Andy. I must get back to Charmaine in case she wakes up and worries about where I am.'

Andy, lying on his bed naked and mellow with sexual contentment, gazed at her as she dressed. He wondered at her graceful form and revelled in the sensation of their coupling. She turned and looked at him with deep affectionate eyes. It seemed as if her scarred face was lit up with a burst of dazzling tropical sunshine.

'This might sound totally inappropriate,' she said. 'Even ridiculous. But I haven't been this happy in a long, long time. I feel that I'll cope a lot better this time with you by my side. Life will go on and become happy again. Forgive me, but I now know that I love you.'

She bent quickly and kissed him on the forehead, then turned and rushed from the room as if what she had just said might get up and bite her.

'I know exactly how you feel,' said Andy quietly to himself as the door closed behind her. 'I love you too.'

# CHAPTER 13

## Rhodesia 1974

They met outside the reception area at five thirty in the morning. Together, they marvelled at the beauty of the rising sun, heralded by a curtain of orange that spread across the eastern sky.

They stood together contentedly, listening to the bushveld sounds of insects and birds—the growing chorus of welcome for the new day. They heard the call of a fish eagle in flight and the faraway bark of baboons. An elephant trumpeted in the distance and there came the cackling laugh of hyena close by. Nothing of the moment was designed or planned, but Andy was struck by an intoxicating sense of unbridled freedom, a drink from the cup of Providence.

They completed the border formalities on the South African side, drove across the narrow bridge that spanned the dry bed of the Limpopo River, and entered into Rhodesia through the customs and immigration hall at Beit Bridge.

They were directed to the convoy assembly point outside the Peter's Motel and Andy was drawn into the clutches of nostalgia.

He vividly recalled coming through this dusty little rural town by train. Little had changed in ten years, other than the ominous presence of sandbags piled up around the border post and police station and the attendance of armed soldiers in camouflage fatigues.

Before departing the assembly point, the convoy commander, his army-issue shirt bearing the badges and flashes of the police reserve, summoned the civilian drivers in his charge to a briefing.

'The lead vehicle will travel at a speed of 100 kilometres per hour,' he said, in a monotone that suggested tedious regularity of explanation. 'It is recommended that you maintain a distance of approximately thirty meters between each car.

'In the event of a breakdown, pull your vehicle off the road so as not to obstruct those behind you, and wait there. The rear guard vehicle will render whatever assistance possible, but we are not equipped nor trained to deal with mechanical failure.

'In such an event you will be required to travel on the escort vehicle and leave your vehicle where it stops. It will be up to you to make arrangements for its recovery.

'We do not carry spare fuel. There is no fuel rationing here at Beit Bridge, so make sure that your tank is full or you may have to leave your vehicle at the roadside. This convoy is run for your protection and you are therefore under my command until we reach our destination.

'Now . . . ,' the officer paused for effect, and then continued, 'if we are shot at—which I can assure you is highly unlikely—our vehicles will pull over and return the fire. You will accelerate and drive like the clappers. Do not attempt to overtake vehicles in front of you; that will only lead to chaos. Therefore, vehicles with higher speed capacity should travel up front.

'If your vehicle is disabled, get out and run for cover. There is plenty of bush and we will be keeping the terrs occupied, so you'll be safe enough. Let me repeat—this is highly unlikely.

'Are there any questions?'

The briefing had been given with an air of nonchalance and boredom, almost as if the convoy was an unnecessary inconvenience imposed upon the men who ran it.

'They're territorial guys, Andy,' said Merryl when he returned to the car and repeated it all to her. 'They spend six weeks trying to hold down a civilian job and then get called away to do this for the next six weeks—and so it goes. You can hardly expect them to be enthusiastic.

'But they know that protecting tourists keeps the industry going despite the war; and tourist revenue is important—so it's a showpiece for them and an adventure for us.

'The guys you see manning those dangerous-looking guns on the escort vehicles have probably never seen a shot fired in anger in all the time they've been doing this job.'

Merryl's attitude towards the danger of the trip had eased considerably since Andy'd first suggested it.

'That's encouraging,' responded Andy in a dry tone as he started the car. 'How would they react if we do get shot at?'

Merryl laughed. 'They'd probably run like hell. But it won't happen—trust me.'

Then abruptly her attitude changed and a streak of pure bitterness emerged in her tone. 'The terrs are shit scared of anything military—it's only lonely farms and old people that they feel comfortable attacking.'

Suddenly she was crying, as the reason and reality of their journey re-emerged.

'God, I hate them!' she said bitterly through her tears. 'This was the most wonderful country in the world when I was a child. There was no malice or anger between the races, everyone just accepted who they were and got on with it. Then a bunch of pseudo-educated bloody savages with lots of brawn and no bloody brain started all this!' She made a noise in her throat and shook herself theatrically.

The convoy consisted of twenty-two civilian cars and pick-up trucks, some of which towed boats or caravans, plus the three open-backed escort Land Rovers.

Each of the escort vehicles was equipped with twin Browning belt-fed 7.62 machine guns that protruded through an embrasure in a semi-circular armoured turret mounted on a swivel base. One-inch armoured glass panels protected the driver in the cab. What seemed absurd to Andy, considering the protective armour given to the escorts, was the fact that these vehicles had no doors. The escorts took their places in the procession, travelling front, middle and rear. Andy slipped in directly behind the vehicle holding centre protection.

The drive took the party up the Salisbury road from Beit Bridge, and they travelled at a steady pace in serenity through the unspoilt and beautiful Rhodesian wilderness. The road was a surprisingly good two-way tarmac strip that had been carved through the virgin African bush. Recent rains had left puddles at the roadside and washed the landscape with fresh green intensity.

They stopped at a country lodge near Bubi River, 120 kilometres north of the border, where they stretched their legs and bought refreshments.

Andy continued to revel in the sense of liberty that he'd felt that morning—reinforced by the broad expanse of virgin bush. He felt light hearted. His elation was a blend of deepened love for Merryl, and the beauty of his surroundings. The bird and insect life was prolific, and the animation within the bush echoed his feelings. Small blue-headed lizards scampered amongst the rocky outcrops surrounding the lodge while two resident giraffes grazed idly from the tops of the acacia trees.

After a half hour's leg-stretching and chatter amongst the members of the convoy, they resumed the journey north towards Fort Victoria.

The exhilaration in Andy made him want to burst into song, but he was sensitive to Merryl's sombre mood which deepened as they got closer to their destination. They'd had no contact with the hospital at Fort Vic since the call from Merryl's apartment the previous morning, and Andy felt her apprehension. He reached out and took her hand and put it to his lips, giving her a reassuring smile. Charmaine saw the gesture from the back seat, and in a possessive scramble she came between the front seats to sit on her mother's lap. Andy laughed and ruffled her hair. He took her hand and kissed it.

In the next instant all changed, utterly, for ever.

There was a thunderous bellow like the sound of a runaway steam train and the car's windshield burst and shattered into a thousand splinters of flying glass.

It took Andy only a second to identify the noise. He'd heard it last on an army shooting range. There came a rapid succession of hammer blows to the passenger side of the car as the rear windows were smashed and the upholstery ripped to shreds. He heard a brief scream from Merryl, which was cut short.

A front tyre burst and he lost control of the car. It veered to the right and careered off the far side of the road, through a ditch, smashing the sump and snapping the CV joints. The Datsun bounced, wheels in the air. Then it came down to earth, hit a solid concrete milestone, cartwheeled, and landed on its side among the thick thorn bushes.

From start to finish, the incident had taken less than five seconds. The truth of it sank in to Andy's shaken mind—machine gun fire.

Merryl lay on top of him, knocked from her passenger seat, with Charmaine on her lap. The car, overturned onto its right side, was immobile. Through the daze of disbelief and shock, Andy felt pain in his right shoulder. He realised that he bled from wounds to his forehead and face, caused by flying glass. Merryl? Charmaine? He tried to control his voice:

'Are you alright?'

There was no answer. Andy felt what he thought was warm engine oil dribbling onto his face. He shifted and looked sideways, and saw the angry open wound at the side of Merryl's glorious head of blonde hair, from which a torrent of blood poured like red wine from a poorly corked decanter.

He began to scream. He was seeing death at close quarters for the first time in his life. Merryl's eyes stared at him, lifeless and unseeing.

With an expression that summed up all his shock, horror, and loss he screamed again.

He tried to lift her weight off him, but he was restricted with Charmaine wedged between them. He then saw that the child's head was turned at an impossible angle, as if she was looking too far back over her shoulder. Her tongue protruded limp and grotesque from a slack and sagging jaw, and her pretty young eyes seemed to have grown huge in their sockets. She was as lifeless as her mother.

'NO! NO! NO!' bellowed Andy, over and over again, as he struggled to get free so that he could lift them out of the car and seek help.

On the road behind them he heard speeding vehicles tearing past as other panicked members of the convoy scrambled to get clear. There were long heavy bursts of machine gun fire, which Andy realised was outgoing from the police escort vehicles.

Andy's senses were enhanced by a rush of adrenaline. Horror and fear descended vividly upon him. Emotions he had never encountered before raced through his mind. He found strength through denying the truth of what he faced, and he heaved the two bodies off him—the dead weight of the two he'd come to love. They rolled gracelessly into the rear of the car and slumped there like a pile of laundry. He eased himself out from behind the steering wheel and crawled through the shattered windshield and its vestiges of broken glass.

'Get down!' he heard someone yell. 'Get under cover, away from your vehicle!'

'Like hell!' shouted Andy as he emerged.

He immediately started trying to right the Datsun so that he could get in and help Merryl and Charmaine.

The car would not budge, and someone continued to shout at him: 'Get down, you bloody fool! Get under cover!'

Andy turned and saw a helmeted man in camouflage fatigues who cowered behind the armoured protection of the Land Rover. His comrade fired long, extravagant, and uncontrolled bursts towards a point on a nearby hillside. Tracer from the weapons on the other two vehicles was being directed into the same location. The armoured trucks were 500 metres up and down the road from Andy's position, while the centre vehicle, behind which he had been travelling, was off the road fifty metres from where his car had come to rest. They were all concentrating their retaliatory fire into the same area.

'There are injured people in this car!' screamed Andy. He dared not say dead people. They couldn't be dead! What he'd seen in the car must have been an illusion created by his state of panic—everything would be alright. Merryl was alive and so was Charmaine. They just needed to be helped from the car and have their wounds attended to.

'Come and help me!' It was a bellow filled with desperation from the depths of his soul, and more sincere than he'd ever been before in his life. 'Now!' he yelled and pleaded. 'PLEASE!'

There was no more incoming fire and Andy, even as a novice with no combat experience wondered why these people kept on wasting valuable ammunition on an unseen and silent enemy instead of coming to help him—to help *his* woman and *his* child in the car.

He kept heaving and pulling at the vehicle, trying to push it back onto its wheels, and eventually, after what seemed like an age, he heard running feet across the tarred road. The two men who came across were youngsters, probably not long out of school, but they were tanned, strong, healthy looking young men who now put their shoulders to the upturned car and shoved it over, back onto its wheels.

Andy grabbed at the rear door and tugged violently but the door was jammed. He dashed to the other side and found that the door opened with ease. He reached into the car and, as gently as he could, put his arms under Merryl's shoulders from behind and eased her out, laying her down delicately on the ground. Then he went back in and lifted Charmaine.

Both of them had their eyes open in a sightless stare and, as Andy looked at them, the realisation struck. It burned into him like a branding iron, and he bellowed to the sky like an injured bull elephant.

'Take it easy, sir,' said one of the troopers who'd come to help. 'We'll get our medics to attend to them.'

Andy wanted to grab the man by the throat and strangle him.

'What are the medics going to do?' he demanded loudly. 'Bring them back?'

Then he turned as the lead vehicle returned to the scene and came to a halt at the roadside. A man bearing sergeant's stripes and a red cross on a white armband on the sleeve of his camouflage jacket leaped from the Land Rover, carrying a canvass bag. The man hurried across to where Merryl and Charmaine lay. He took a short sorrowful look at them and then bent over them one by one and, with thumb and forefinger, gently closed their eyes. He straightened and said simply to Andy, 'I'm sorry. There's nothing I can do.'

Andy knew it, but the confirmation welled up in him like a raging torrent. He leaned against his wrecked car and sank slowly to a sitting position. He covered his face with his hands, his elbows on his knees, and wept like a child.

'You look in a terrible mess, sir,' continued the medic kindly. His voice sounded as though it came from a long way off down an open pipe. 'Let me clean up those cuts. You're bleeding like mad.'

Andy hadn't even thought of his injuries. He felt no pain other than the jar to his shoulder. Although he didn't realise it, the blood on his face, both his own and Merryl's, made him look as though he had been mortally wounded.

He took his hands away from his face and saw that they were covered in warm sticky blood. He allowed the medic to apply cotton wool swabs, with a burning antiseptic fluid, to the abrasions.

The convoy commander, who had briefed them only two hours previously, had been talking on the two-way radio. He now came out of his vehicle. He leaned down and touched Andy's shoulder.

'We can't stay here, sir,' he said gently. 'We'll have to get along. We'll load the deceased onto one of the trucks and get you to Fort Vic. We've alerted Fire Force and they'll have a few choppers here within an hour with troops to track those bastards down. I'm sorry—but we must get going.'

'*Load the deceased*,' thought Andy bitterly. '*Load the bloody deceased!* He makes it sound like a second-hand furniture removal.' But he said nothing. He just let his anger simmer while they led him to the waiting vehicle. Before long, it would mature into full-blown hate.

*   *   *

AT THE REQUEST OF RELATIVES THEY BURIED MERRYL AND CHARMAINE, THREE DAYS LATER, IN A SINGLE COFFIN. They laid them to rest together in a grave alongside that of Craig Sherbourn. The event was made all the more painful by the fact that the ceremony was combined with the funeral service for Merryl's mother.

In her will, Merryl's mother had expressed the wish to be cremated, so her coffin remained behind in the church while the procession carrying Merryl's and Charmaine's remains drove slowly to the cemetery.

Whilst Andy was probably the person closest to Merryl and Charmaine when they died, both physically and emotionally, he was an outsider among the people of her past. They did not know him and they knew nothing of the love that had lain dormant for so many months—a love that was allowed to bloom for a mere few hours.

The grief and the anger bubbled inside him like a witch's brew. His helplessness turned his anger into uncontrollable frustration. Then he thought of Merryl's father—and he wondered what horrors might be eating at that man's mind.

It made news headlines throughout Southern Africa: two acts of atrocity perpetrated against the same family, in totally different incidents and under the most unlikely circumstances.


The day after his arrival at Fort Victoria, and after telephoning his parents with the news of his ordeal, Andy went to see Merryl's father in the hospital.

He came away feeling more depressed than before. Merryl had told him that her father had been a vibrant, talkative and attentive man, who had worked hard at everything he did. He had been admired by others. He'd kept faith in the future of Rhodesia—if only the political parties could get their collective acts together and work towards a common goal of harmony and equality.

The man that Andy met was vague and, for most of the time, incoherent. He was gaunt and pale in the face with eyes that seemed to have receded into their sockets for fear of seeing what was going on around him.

Anthony Carlisle had been told of the ambush and the death of Merryl and Charmaine, but he didn't seem to understand. He kept asking Andy what time he expected them to arrive. He also kept referring to his wife, saying that he expected her to visit soon, given the fact that they had been married for nearly thirty years. Then he broke down and asked why they'd killed her, and he announced that, in consequence, Merryl would have to come back to Rhodesia to help him run the farm.

Andy left him with his illusions. He had no idea how to respond, and he was forced to conclude, clinically, that it wasn't his problem. There was nothing he could do—and he chose to leave it that way.

After the funeral, Andy exchanged pleasantries with the mourners. He got the impression that some of them sensed that he and Merryl were friends, but little more than that.

He extracted himself as soon as he could and left the cemetery on foot. He had nothing to say to these people. Nothing that would make them understand who he was, why he was with Merryl and Charmaine, or what there was between them. He walked from the cemetery to the Meikles Hotel and went straight into the bar.

There was a crowd of soldiers in camouflage fatigues, sitting around a low table in the corner. They noisily but good-naturedly berated one of the group over what sounded like a romantic adventure with one of the local girls.

'We should nickname her Mtoko Road,' said one. 'The ugliest piece of scenery in Rhodesia but almost every bugger in the army has been on it at some or other stage.'

There was a hoot of laughter.

'You losers are just jealous!' retorted the subject of their badgering. 'Just because I beat you all to it. Truth is, none of you've got my charm. I'd love to know what you'd be saying if I'd left the door open to one of you lot"

'It wouldn't be "thank you", that's for sure,' responded one of the others amidst another outburst of laughter.

Andy sat at the bar and ordered a beer which he poured into a glass and sipped thoughtfully. The exchanges between the soldiers went on, with the chiding comments becoming more and more amusing and the laughter filling the bar room.

'Tell you what, Johnny boy, if it weren't for the fact that I saw her move I'd have mistaken her for a scarecrow. It looks like her face caught alight when she was a kid and her mother put the fire out with an ice pick.'

Listening in, Andy couldn't help grinning. But he was surprised when one of them rose up and came across to him:

'Well I'm damned if it's not Andrew bloody Mason! What the hell are you doing here?'

Andy looked up and was astonished to see his old school chum, Alec Bradford, standing beside him.

'Alec!' he cried in delight. Standing up, he grasped his old friend by the shoulders. 'What a surprise! What am I doing here? What the hell are *you* doing here?'

'I'm on Fire Force duty,' replied Alec. 'We've been out on a follow-up exercise after a convoy attack.'

Andy was astonished.

'Was that the one four days ago? About forty K out on the Beit Bridge road?' he asked.

'What do you know about that?' asked Alec.

'Hell, Alec, surely everyone in the country knows about it. I was the only survivor in the vehicle that was hit.'

Alec stared at Andy. His face expressed disbelief, horror and sympathy.

'My God, Andy! I'm sorry! The funeral was this morning. Is that where you've been?'

'Yep,' said Andy. He paused while his emotions rose in his throat, and his eyes started to water. He composed himself, cleared his throat and continued:

'I had to get away from there, Alec. I'm still in shock. Nobody ever got murdered in front of me before.'

Press reports on the incident had varied so vastly and out of proportion that Andy had lost faith in anything that he had ever read in the papers. It had emerged that two of the ambush party had been killed in a fire fight during the follow-up operation and a left wing British tabloid had twisted the story, screaming allegations of atrocity on the part of the Rhodesian troops:

### Another Rhodesian Atrocity

*In yet another despicable act of barbarism perpetrated by Rhodesian security forces, two freedom fighters of the*

*ZANLA liberation movement were yesterday brutally murdered while attempting to assist a stranded family of tourists whose car had left the road in a remote area near Fort Victoria. It is reported that the Rhodesian soldiers opened fire indiscriminately when coming upon the scene, killing the two guerrillas as well as a white woman tourist and her four-year-old child. Undisciplined actions of this nature are not uncommon amongst Rhodesian soldiers, to whom life appears to be possessed of a bargain basement price tag.*

Every newspaper that ran the story seemed to have their own version of events, none of which were accurate except for the *Rhodesian Herald* and the *Bulawayo Chronicle*. Both printed the same account that reported:

### Convoy Ambushed

*The police-protected tourist convoy between Beit Bridge and Fort Victoria was ambushed by terrorists shortly before ten o' clock yesterday morning. Ms Merryl Sherbourn and her four-year-old daughter Charmaine, both from Fort Victoria but recently living in South Africa, were killed in the attack. The incident is made so much more tragic by the fact that the party were travelling in Rhodesia to attend the funeral of Ms Sherbourn's mother, Mrs Margaret Carlisle, who had been killed by terrorist action on her farm two days previously.*

*This latest terrorist attack is bound to have an effect on the lucrative tourist trade from South Africa.*

*A Fire Force follow-up has accounted for two of the terrorist gang involved in the attack, and operations are continuing.*

'What can I say, Andy?' asked Alec. 'We live with it all the time here now. Although I must confess that I haven't been that close to it. I've seen the reports, but we don't believe anything we read in the papers. We generally just ignore them, but this one could be seriously damaging. We rely heavily on tourism and an event like this will keep 100,000 visitors away this season.'

Andy realised that Alec, like the mourners at the funeral, could have no idea of the personal depth of feeling, the intimacy that lay behind it all for him.

Thankfully, Alec changed the topic. He went on to talk about events since they had last seen each other, seven years back, on the day that they'd left school.

'It's been a long time, Andy. But, hell it's good to see you! What have you been doing with yourself?'

Andy sketched his activities and finished by telling him of his recent suspension from H&S, and the saga behind it.

'And you?' he asked. 'What's kept you busy?'

'I came down from Zambia with my folks in '68,' said Alec, 'the year after we left school. I went to varsity here. I studied engineering, but by the time I'd finished, the war was on. I put engineering on ice and went into uniform. Because of my degree they gave me a commission. I'd have spent more time on call-up than working, anyway, so I figured that I may as well make a career keeping the Commies out.

'After what happened in Zambia,' Alec added, 'it made good sense. My old man saw it all coming. It didn't take long after independence before the mines and factories were nationalised and the whole place ceased to function efficiently. Things changed rapidly and life up there became impossible.'

'What are your folks doing now?' asked Andy.

"My dad bought into a private gold mining operation in Shamva about 60 Ks outside Salisbury. Personally I think it was a mistake. He should have kept going, and gone to South Africa or Australia where the real mining happens. This place won't last much longer and we'll all be packing up and moving again. I don't think the Rhodesian forces have ever lost a battle, but we'll end up losing the war because it's economically unsustainable. It's just a matter of time before we're forced to capitulate—but we fight on. Hopefully some kind of settlement will be worked out and we can all get back to our lives. Anyway, enough of that. Come and meet the guys who took out your attackers.'

Alec guided Andy across and introduced him to the others in his party.

'This is the man who got us all down here, lads,' he said light-heartedly. 'He's the one who the gooks shot up.'

The group welcomed Andy with nods of sympathy and a warm hospitality that reminded him of the people that he'd met, as a schoolboy, on the Copper Belt. He was gripped by a surge of emotional nostalgia. But despite their friendliness, it was difficult for him to join in their banter and revelry. His heart wasn't in it. More, he felt out of place amongst this close-knit group of comrades, who obviously enjoyed an unrestrained rapport with one another.

'You must be pretty bloody bitter about what happened,' said one of Alec's companions who had been introduced as Eric. 'Hell, if it was me, I'd be baying for the bastards' blood!'

'I'm still trying to come to terms with it,' said Andy. 'But, yeah, I'm pissed off. I'd like to get my hands around one or two throats. But from what I gather, you guys seem to have done that for me.'

There was a general chuckle, and then one of them said:

'Did you do military service down south?'

Andy raised an eyebrow. 'Doesn't everyone?' he replied, grinning. 'Yeah, I did my nine months, and I still do a stint once a year. We're a peacetime army and mostly we just get shunted around. The army calls it retraining. I call it a waste of time.'

'What outfit are you attached to?' asked Eric.

Andy hesitated. There was a natural reluctance among the Parabats to reveal their elite status. Sometimes, to say that one belonged to that unit brought glances of scepticism. Every second-rate national serviceman had dreams of being in the battalion, and many who hadn't got past the first five minutes of the PT course tended to self-elect themselves to permanent membership for the sake their egos. 'Ah, what the hell,' thought Andy. 'These guys are different.'

'I'm with the parachute battalion,' he said.

'Hell! That's a coincidence!' came the reply. 'I've just come back from a three-week para course in Bloemfontein. Part of the support we get from South Africa includes the use of your training facilities. You've got some tough bedfellows.'

From there the conversation took flight, about the personalities and connections within the elite world of airborne infantry. Andy relaxed. These men were good for him. They had things in common.

Then Alec butted in. 'Seeing that you're out of a job and you've got time on your hands, why not join the regular army? I can tell you, they'd welcome you with open arms up here. We're thin on the ground, particularly amongst us regulars. It would give you a chance to get your hands around some throats. But, more than that, it's a hell of a life, Andy. Despite the hostilities we get a lot of fun. You won't believe how keen the girls are to save the troops from celibacy.'

'It's never crossed my mind,' replied Andy. 'I've been too busy trying to build a career in Civvy Street. My achievements have all been in finance—not in the army. Besides, the career soldiers I've come across in the SA Defence Force aren't my kind of bloke. Different worlds entirely. Different backgrounds.'

'The army down south and the army up here are on different planets,' said Eric. 'I know what you mean about some of the career soldiers with the South African military. We're almost entirely dependent upon South Africa for supplies of weaponry and ammunition. Like I said, cross-training facilities exist between us, so we come into close contact with your regulars. You've got some good men, but the training methods for your civilian forces are rudimentary.'

'I wouldn't know,' said Andy. 'I just do as I'm told when I put on the uniform. That way I stay out of trouble. My active military exposure has been confined to the rifle range and the drill square and a few war games on manoeuvres. Crawling around the veld, carrying a rifle loaded with blank ammo, is about my bundle. We're all there in the dispassionate belief that those giving the orders know what they're doing. Frankly, I've stopped believing it.'

'That will change,' said Alec. 'I think it was pretty much the same here until the gooks started taking their dream of Black Power so seriously. Once that happens down south—and it will happen—the training you get, especially in units like the Parabats, will kick up a few gears.

'We've got chaps with us in the RLI,' continued Alec, 'who've been around since Korea. They tell some wonderful stories of how casual it was before this war started. Now we've got outfits like ourselves, who train and gain by experience every day. We've learned from day-to-day survival how important the basics are. Then there are units like the SAS, whose training is designed to take them one over the top. They're said to be up with the best in the world for the work they do. They're very selective as to who they let in, but those who make it have the benefit of specialised training that is unmatched—certainly anywhere in Africa.'

The conversation was becoming too intense, and Andy felt as though he was spoiling a good afternoon of drinking and laughter amongst Alec and his friends. The discussion drifted back towards light banter and Andy felt again like an intruder. He found an excuse to leave.

He exchanged contact details with Alec, shook hands all round, and left the bar room. With a heavy heart he strolled down to the Victoria hotel and found himself a quiet seat in the corner of the bar, where he stayed until well after dark.

Early the following morning, nursing a hangover of gigantic proportions, Andy went to the police depot, from where the convoys were controlled. The convoy commander who had brought him in from the ambush site had suggested that he could arrange for Andy to travel to Salisbury with a military supply convoy, from where he could get a commercial flight back to Johannesburg.

'So you're the guy that got shot up in the convoy,' said the corporal driver of the Mercedes four-ton truck. They trundled northwards from Fort Victoria to Salisbury as part of a convoy of military vehicles.

'Sorry about your family,' continued the corporal. 'We don't need this sort of thing. It wouldn't be so bad if the gooks attacked military objectives, but they don't do that—only soft targets, easy to run away from. That's their style. I hear you were right behind the centre escort vehicle. Bad place to be. Nobody ever taught those bloody cowards how to shoot. They were probably aiming for the armoured vehicle, but didn't aim off to allow for the speed—and you drove straight into their fire power. Bloody horrible.'

'*Talkative prick*,' thought Andy. He wanted to tell him to shut the hell up. The corporal spoke so matter-of-factly that one could have been forgiven for thinking he was doing a rugby game post-mortem amongst friends.

Andy was in no mood to listen to the diatribe of a self-proclaimed expert with verbal diarrhoea, but he was grateful for the fact that he'd been given the ride—and he tolerated the man. He tried to discourage the ongoing verbal assault by responding only occasionally, and then with barely audible monosyllabic grunts.

# CHAPTER 14

Andy's parents were at Jan Smuts International to meet him. They raced across the arrivals hall to embrace him.

He had been dropped off at Cranbourne barracks in Salisbury and had taken a taxi from there to the airport, where he had waited for five hours until the scheduled departure time for the Air Rhodesia Viscount Sky Coach that flew, twice a week, the Salisbury-to-Johannesburg route.

'Andy!' exclaimed his mother. 'We've been so worried! We heard the news about the attack before you phoned us, but we thought you'd got there safely the day before. It must have been ghastly!' It was obvious from her strained looks that she'd been beside herself with anxiety.

On the drive home, Andy described the events of his fateful journey as he had done to no-one else. He told them of his relationship with Merryl, whom they'd never met, and about the state in which he'd met Merryl's father, and how senseless it all seemed. He told them of his meeting with Alec and the strange set of circumstances that unfolded, almost as if destiny had a hand in events.

'If it wasn't for the crazy situation at the office,' brooded Andy, 'I'd have been in Mozambique when Merryl phoned. She would have had to wait for the plane or make another plan, but none of us would have been where we were at the time—and none of this would have happened! If we hadn't delayed before leaving, we would have avoided the early morning traffic in Johannesburg—we'd have been in time to travel with the earlier convoy. "if . . . if . . . if . . . !!"' It seemed almost as though the hand of fate had contrived to set him up.

His mood was gloomy. He'd heard that mourning came in four distinct stages. First denial, then anger, followed by grief and finally acceptance. He had nothing to deny. He'd been there and seen the bodies and he had been at the funeral. No!! There was nothing to deny! But the anger and grief had hit him together with the force of a hurricane. The turmoil and strength of those emotions were far from subsiding into any form of acceptance.

Cold blooded murder was totally unacceptable, no matter what the circumstances. He had every intention of nurturing his grief to keep the anger alive. Never before had he harboured such feelings of pure malice and vindictive rage, and they were sensations that made him uncomfortable. But he couldn't shake it off, and he began to feel that some dormant monster had been awakened and was viciously eating away at his good nature. A monster like a barbarian at a primitive orgy.

Andy's car insurance didn't cover acts of war on foreign territory. This was a factor that hadn't occurred to him until he attempted to lodge his claim against the written-off Datsun. There was an almost audible chuckle from the claims assessor when Andy told the story relating to his claim. The car had been taken to Fort Victoria where it nestled in a scrap yard and all Andy had was a receipt for its delivery, which was of no interest to his insurers. His claim was repudiated and he had to use some of his hard-earned savings to pick up a car from a second-hand dealer of doubtful repute, where he found the best of a bad set of options within the limitations of his means.

He found unexpected difficulty in adjusting to his new existence. Everything had changed. It was ten days since he had been called to Gary Chalmers's office to face Barret's accusations of misconduct—and from there, it seemed, had begun a downward spiral. It was a week since Merryl had called with her terrible news. The subsequent and rapid flow of events, the rush of extraordinary misfortune, seemed like something out of a bad dream.

Through a mix of frustration, boredom, grief and burning anger, Andy had started drinking during the day. It was something he'd never done before—with the exception of the occasional Saturday when he played squash at the club and would settle down at the bar after the game and share some laughs with other members over a few beers. But here he was, in mid-week, on his own in his apartment, trying to wash away his misery and anger with double shots of raw spirits.

He knew it couldn't go on this way. He yearned to be back at his desk, filling his days with the distractions of work. He realised that was unlikely to happen—he'd ruffled far too many feathers at H&S for them to ever take him back. Reflecting on the injustice of it added to his frustration. He began to get an urge to yell, and to hurl things around in his room. Things were brewing up inside him.

He kept thinking about Alec's absurd suggestion that he offer his services to the Rhodesian army—and the thought started to take on a certain appeal. He had no job, he had no real commitments, and he was consumed by the rustic beauty and mystique of Rhodesia. On top of that, he found the people there kind and generous. And at the same time he was being devoured by the loss of Merryl and Charmaine—over the ruthless actions of terrorists who randomly shot and killed innocent civilians.

There was a seductive and rebellious charm in the idea of casting to the wind his ambitions in the international financial industry and becoming a regular soldier in the Rhodesian army—where he could join in with the straight-talking, honest guys such as he'd met in the company of Alec.

The stimulus of excitement and adventure in the beautiful Rhodesian bush, backed up by the professional training that Alec had alluded to, grew more and more appealing. In fact, it held out to him a glamorous and romantic charm.

It also spoke of another side of things. His fury over the recent events was becoming a tangible thing. It festered inside him like an untreated septic wound and, somewhere deep down, he harboured a desire to take out his vengeance on the insurgents in Rhodesia. He started to feel as though he had a moral duty to get back at the bastards who killed Merryl and Charmaine.

Andy wasn't consciously aware of the fact that he had learned to hate. This was a sensation that had never been a part of his emotional make-up, but through his anger and grief he suddenly woke up to the fact that he wanted to become a killing machine. He wanted to be part of a campaign to hurt and destroy those who'd brought about the loathing that was now upon him.

\*     \*     \*

# CHAPTER 15

## Rhodesia
## August 1974

Andy's appointment at the Rhodesian High Commission in Pretoria was inconclusive.

"What you're suggesting of course" said the military attaché who interviewed him, "is that we recruit you in a sort of mercenary roll, so you can become just another international terrorist, killing for money. We don't actually run that type of recruitment operation here, or anywhere else in the world. What we do have is a professional army and if one complies with the necessary immigration requirements, we would obviously consider their application to join the army as a means of employment. That doesn't necessarily mean you would be successful."

"I'm prepared to take my chances," said Andy, "I can't think of a reason why I should not be successful. I'm fit and healthy, plus I'm a trained paratrooper. I have my mind set on joining the S.A.S."

"You're clearly misinformed Mr. Mason" said the attaché, with a cynical grin. "One does not just pop in and ask the S.A.S. if they want one or two new recruits and then move in. I'm not sure that the experience you have at national service level would be sufficient to qualify as previous military experience, and even if it does they tend to be rather selective as to who they will accept into their training programme"

"I'm still prepared to take my chances," said Andy. "How do I proceed?"

"Well", said the official, "you'd have to complete your immigration formalities first. Once that has been accepted, . . . and we're assuming that there are no obstacles in that process, you'd be at liberty to put an application to the army for consideration. I must point out however, that simply because you have had military training here in South Africa, does not mean that you would qualify. As for your S.A.S aspirations' . . . he paused for a few moments looking at Andy intently . . . , "The medical and fitness requirements are such that you could be rejected for having ingrown toenails, so don't get your hopes up. I can tell you that in a recent intake of personnel, two men out of a starting line up of over three hundred managed to complete the selection course and enter the ranks of the S.A.S. It is a highly specialised unit, and not even I have the slightest idea as to what they do or why the selection criteria are so strict."

"Thank you," said Andy, "where do I find the immigration section in this building?"

*    *    *

A month later, Andy arrived at Salisbury Airport, his residence permit carefully packed away in a folder alongside his military record. His mood was very different from the last time he'd been there, when he flew out after the funeral of Merryl and Charmaine.

He landed at night, but the darkness did not detract from his enthusiasm and his sense of the warmth, the homeliness, of the place. 'Sunshine City,' it said, on a large circular yellow billboard with painted red flames and an animated smile. He smiled back. Andy Mason, immigrant to Rhodesia, a man on a mission, seeking a new life.

He caught a cab to the Ambassador Hotel in the centre of town and dumped his single suitcase. Then he wandered out into the city to get the atmosphere of the night life. He had tried to telephone Alec, but was told that he would be out of town indefinitely. He left a message for him to respond to the hotel's post box.

Next day, Andy ate a hearty hotel breakfast. Then he went out again, to explore the streets of the city.

He was impressed. The atmosphere was fresh and breezy, warm and positive. He was reminded of his brief stopover in Bulawayo as a schoolboy en route to his holiday with Alec. The streets of Salisbury were wide and clean, and bustling with activity. The people, going about their everyday business, presented a sense of focused purpose.

The vehicle traffic, however, seemed to be caught in a time warp—there were no new cars, no recent models, in evidence. Andy was to learn that vehicle imports were at the bottom of the list of priorities in this country. Trade and industry were carefully managed in the face of economic sanctions, imposed for over a decade already by the United Nations. Most of the cars on the road were Peugeot 404 and 504 station wagons and small Renault 4 sedans which, in South Africa, would long since have found their way to the scrap heap.

The people moved with a sense of purpose, and their informality of dress implied a no-nonsense efficiency. Among them was a startling number of young people in military fatigues, evidence of hostilities—but in other respects the general atmosphere made it seem unbelievable that this was a country at war with itself.

Andy walked the streets for over an hour, and every impression that he received reinforced his belief that he'd been right to come here. He congratulated himself on his decision. He made his way to the Forces Recruitment Office where he handed over his residence certificate and the letter that he'd brought from the High Commission in Pretoria.

A brief question-and-answer session was conducted by a young sergeant dressed in camouflage fatigues, after which he was given a ream of forms to complete.

An army Land Rover then transported Andy to the hospital at KG VI Barracks, where he was examined and declared fit for service.

He hadn't doubted that he'd pass the test, but that was just the start.

He returned to the Recruitment Office with the medical clearance and he told the orderly that he now wanted to apply for training with the Special Air Services. He was given a wry grin and another set of forms, and he was instructed to report back at 08h00 the following morning.

He was tested again, this time with a marathon examination that probed everything from stress-and-rest ECG to the strength of his toenails. After several hours, he was passed as fit, and sent back to the recruitment office.

Next day, Andy reported to the adjutant at the nondescript barracks complex that housed the SAS training troop. He handed over his papers and was taken to a barrack block in the compound where he was allocated a bunk and a locker in the long dormitory-like building. He was shown where to go to be issued with essential kit and told cursorily, to keep himself busy until the following Monday when a basic selection process of trainees from other units was due to be conducted.

Over the days that intervened, new recruits arrived continuously at the compound, and the number grew to over 500.

Early on the Monday morning the recruits were called to assemble on a field beside an obstacle course behind the barracks. There, they were addressed by an officer bearing captain's insignia on his epaulettes and clad in battle fatigues. He wore the distinctive sand-coloured beret and blue stable-belt of the SAS.

'Good morning, gentlemen,' he began. 'My name is Captain Evans. I am officer in charge of training and for the foreseeable future some of you will be under my command." He paused and cast a sceptical eye over the assembled troops. "You may have heard rumours." he continued grinning, "that to qualify as a member of the SAS you are expected to border on the superhuman. Well, let me put your minds at rest. They're not rumours.'

There was a murmur of nervous laughter:

'The operational SAS' Evans went on, 'is a small elite unit of highly trained and skilled individuals. Training and selection is a long, gruelling process. Many of you simply won't have what it takes to be a part of this outfit—but those of you who go the distance will have received the most intense and professional military training available anywhere in Africa.

'Your training starts today. But, before we commence, I'd like to introduce to you our squadron PTI and light weapons instructor, Sergeant Nel.'

A tall and well-built man came forward. He wore a vest, and denim fatigues tucked neatly into a pair of combat boots. His chiselled features, broad shoulders and sinewy arms were tanned to a golden bronze. He appeared to be in his mid to late twenties. His thick blond hair was neatly trimmed and he had an easy smile that dimpled his cheeks. He radiated carefree self-assurance.

'Good morning, men,' he began in a clear baritone. 'I'm Sergeant Nel. You've all volunteered to join us, and undergo training. As Captain Evans has pointed out this is not a walk in the park and unfortunately many of you will not meet the minimum basic requirements. The physical tests that we'll conduct this morning are pretty basic and will determine which of you meet those standards.

They were formed into ten squads of 50 men each and told to stay in their groups.

"Right guys" called Nel once the squads were ready, "here we go. Please follow me and do your best to keep up."

With that he turned and set a steady pace on a long road run that lasted almost an hour. An instructor had been assigned to each squad to run alongside them and keep them in their formations as the run progressed.

Upon their return to the base, the groups were already smaller than when they started out. They were then spread out and taken through dozens of strenuous physical exercises with Sergeant Nel and his aides helpfully walking between the men showing them the correct use of each. Another run ensued, this time much shorter but the pace had been picked up, and that led them to the start of a daunting obstacle course.

They followed the sergeant up and over gantries, pulling themselves up on the dangling ropes, swinging across from the top of one to descend by another, climbing over A-frames on commando netting, crawling on their stomachs through a trench one metre deep and thirty metres long under a mesh of barbed wire, out of the exit side, up and over a two-metre wall, through the tyre gauntlet, across a shallow ravine by way of an over-and-under rope bridge that swung from side to side as they held on.

It seemed to go on for ever. Over and over they came up against the same obstacles, sometimes from different directions as the sequence of crossings was alternated.

Sergeant Nel led them all the way, at first showing them techniques to simplify the crossing of an obstacle, but not slowing the pace, and then letting them get by on their own while he kept up the pace from the front.

He tore through the obstacles with an appearance of consummate ease, hardly breaking a sweat, while the volunteers who had been so enthusiastic earlier started to drop out one by one to sit out or lie down at the side of the course, totally spent. After every third passage through the course Nel broke away and led the recruits at a brisk pace across an adjacent field, around its perimeter, and back onto the obstacles.

After an hour and a half, and countless circuits, there were less than a hundred men still trying to keep up. Andy was one of them. His limbs felt like lumps of lead, he had no strength left in his arms or hands from the repetitive rope climbing, and his legs shook like jelly. His chest felt as though it could explode. His ears rang with the mounting pressure in his head, which ached and throbbed to the beat of his racing heart. His clothing was soaked in sweat and he started to feel cramps in his shoulders and hips and rising waves of nausea in his guts. He felt that he could not go on—he had to rest. The prospect of yet another circuit filled him with dread, and he doubted his ability to complete it.

He realised that he had pushed himself to his physical limit and that this was beyond him. He was going to give up, and join the guys who lay beside the field, recovering from their ordeal. His decision was made and he was on the point of dropping out.

He was about to turn away and join the ones who failed to stay the distance, when Nel called a halt.

Andy was barely aware of his surroundings. He stood on weak and shaking legs, quite sure that if he tried one more step, they'd give in. His heaving chest ached as he tried to regulate his breathing. He felt as though he'd throw up if he didn't keep trying to swallow.

'Right!' called Nel. 'You chaps still on your feet, take a break over there.' He pointed toward a patch of lush grass under the shade of a line of trees. 'We'll carry on tomorrow.'

'The rest of you,' Nel smiled his easy smile as he approached the group who had dropped out, sitting at the edge of the field, 'thanks for coming along—but you won't be invited to join us for further training. Fall into ranks, and Corporal Grant will see you out.'

Andy watched the crestfallen collection of tired, limping troops as they were marched away from the obstacle course.

*How close he had come to being one of them,* he thought. Would he be on his way down that road by this time tomorrow? At that stage, he really didn't care.

'Congratulations, men,' said Nel. 'You did well. Now we can get down to proper training.'

*    *    *

The following eight months were taken up with training of such intensity that Andy barely had time to think about anything else. He was determined that he was not going to be sent off to some infantry regiment outside of this elite unit, and he threw himself into the task.

They were trained in weaponry, signals, explosives, fieldcraft and map-reading, first aid, infiltration and withdrawal tactics, self-defence and unarmed combat.

At the end of each week, they were tested and as the weeks went by, fewer and fewer recruits remained on the course.

Andy's enthusiasm to reach the ultimate goal of this training was fired by anger, grief and determination, and he put his heart and soul into his efforts to stay at the top of the squad. He far exceeded the minimum requirements in every task and each day his determination burned deeper as his strength, fitness and mental alertness took on new meaning at levels he had never dreamed achievable.

Competitions were held to strip down and reassemble a wide range of weaponry while blindfolded and hooded. Weapons placed upon a table would have to be identified by feel and then stripped, reassembled and reloaded within a time limit set against the complexity of the weapon in question. The process would then be reversed, having to identify a different weapon by feeling its stripped-down components, assembling, loading and then dismantling.

Fitness was a high priority and exhausting physical training sessions took up three hours of each day commencing at 05h00 until 07h00 and then again after the day's activities from 17h00 until 18h00.

Night exercises were regular and intense.

The enemy's political structures and guerrilla warfare phases were lectured upon by experts in the field. The men learned the lines of command within ZIPRA and ZANLA, and identification of individual commanders.

By the end of the third month the recruits had dwindled to less than fifty. These were sent to the advanced training camp at an abandoned chrome mine in the north-west of the country where tactics and techniques were taught. They were taught boating skills, river crossings, rock climbing, abseiling, helicopter drills, night attack disciplines, tracking and anti-tracking, demolitions, foreign weapons, survival skills, bushcraft, enemy tactics, combat discipline and aircraft identification.

They were instructed in the use of weapons from crossbows to anti-aircraft guns and mortars. The pace was intense and repetitive. Proficiency rapidly became second nature.

After a further three months they were transported to survival camp in a remote part of the country a short distance from the Mozambique border. The barracks were huts built on concrete slabs, roughly roofed with thatch supported by gum tree poles. Instead of walls, they were enclosed with sandbags up to the height of a metre, and then with lengths of fly-screening stretched between the gum-poles. Each of these structures was five metres wide by twenty long, and they stood in identical rows five abreast on either side of a dusty parade ground.

The mess hall that doubled as a lecture room, and the field kitchen—equipped with gas stoves and paraffin refrigerators—were similarly constructed. On the opposite side of the parade square was the transport depot, which was housed under sagging sheets of khaki shade netting, supported by evenly-spaced rows of gum-poles. Parked beneath the netting were two open Land Rovers and twelve three-ton Mercedes trucks, all painted in a drab military green.

Around the entire perimeter of the camp was a two-metre barbed wire fence, with five-metre-tall sentry towers evenly spaced to cover 360-degree fields of fire around the base.

The region had, for nearly five years, suffered in the grip of a devastating drought and the sparse vegetation showed signs of encroaching desert. A water hole from a natural spring a hundred metres from the perimeter provided water, pumped hot and putrid to a green metal tank on top of a scaffold frame.

The spring was the only source of nourishment for the dry earth, and a belt of green foliage around the hole stood out like an oasis. Outside of that rough circle of greenery, the bush was a drab greyish green that brought to mind the association of a sick and dying old man.

About four kilometres from the camp was a tribal village, serviced by a derelict trading post. A double row of old whitewashed buildings with corrugated iron verandas, adorned with fading posters advertising OMO and Coca-Cola were the only brick structures. A creaky steel windmill stood behind the store and seemed to beg for a wind and some lubrication, so as to do its job. If the blades could turn, they'd feed lime-corrupted borehole water to a rusty old square tank perched on a steel framework.

It was in these lack-lustre surroundings, on a hot dusty Saturday morning, that Andy witnessed for the first time the brutal reality of the war to which he had committed himself.

He was sitting on the barrack room step, cleaning his rifle and chatting idly with his mates, when an elderly black man came at a limping run up the dusty road from the trading post.

He was dressed in a tattered cast-off tee-shirt and filthy ill-fitting shorts, and his feet were bare. His bony frame was clear evidence of poor diet and lack of hygiene. Above all this, he was hysterical. He was so visibly shaken that his eyes seemed to be bursting from their sockets and he screamed incoherently from a mouth that exposed a handful of rotting yellow teeth.

'Bring the army!' he yelled. 'Bring soldiers!'

Alan Duke leaped to his feet. Alan, one of Andy's comrades, came from a farming background near the small town of Rusape. He had grown up around black people, and he recognised the urgency of this terrified man.

'There's trouble,' he said to Andy, and he dashed across to intercept the old man.

'Whoa, Baba,' he said in Shona. 'What's the trouble?'

The man turned to Alan, a maniacal frenzy on his face. A stream of spittle dribbled from the corner of his mouth.

'ZANLA!' he shouted. 'ZANLA!' He grabbed Alan's forearm in a vice grip born of fear, and pointed back in the direction of the trading post. Then his shoulders sagged and he put both grubby hands to his face and began a high-pitched wail.

ZANLA's ruthless brutality towards anyone suspected of co-operating with the Rhodesian security forces was legendary. Stories had emerged of the most vicious savagery perpetrated by members of the movement.

The training commander, Captain Evans, sprinted across from his billet and Alan turned toward the officer.

'What's going on?' demanded Evans.

'He says there are ZANLA gooks at the trading post,' replied Alan.

Evans's reaction was immediate and resolute. Within a minute he had mustered the camp. He pointed toward the old man, who was now crying unashamedly.

This man has come to report the presence of ZANLA terrorists at the trading post. Equip yourselves with light webbing, mess tins and water bottles, and then report to the

Motor Depot. We'll issue ammunition, rations and radios at the vehicles. You have five minutes, men!'

A co-ordinated scramble ensued. Nobody had expected anything like this, but the months of training swung them into action like a well-oiled machine as they prepared for deployment. Some had seen action before, while others such as Andy were trained for it but had not yet tasted battle. Emotions were mixed—anxiety, excitement or habituated indifference.

The old man, bewildered by the rush of activity, sat on the ground beside the mess hall as the troops scrambled towards the waiting vehicles.

The trucks pulled off the road into the bush 500 meters from the trading post and the troops deployed themselves in an extended line, well spread as they advanced on the settlement, each of them on a knife-edge of anticipation, expecting to be fired on at any moment.

No sign was found of the guerrilla infiltrators, but in the dusty street of the trading post a donkey cart was pulled over in the scant shade of a dilapidated building. On the cart were the mutilated bodies of two women and a child.

The child was an infant of less than eighteen months old, and he had been repeatedly bayoneted. The flesh of his belly was torn in jagged slashes and his swollen face bore the marks of a severe beating. The two women's genitals had been violated in the most ghastly manner. The tearing and bruising indicating the use of bayonets as well as the bruising caused by rifle butts. Where one woman's dress had been pulled up and tied by a friend or relative in an attempt to cover her, the drenching blood stains and torn flesh made it obvious that one of her breasts had been cut off. Both women had been severely beaten about the face and back. Death had not come simply or quickly.

There were three other women and an elderly man beside the cart, also severely beaten and bleeding, and the look of despair on their faces was the picture of tragedy.

'Why were these people not brought directly to our base?' demanded Evans of one of the local tribespeople, who stood dumfounded, looking on in shocked horror at the mutilated bodies.

There was no response and it seemed that everyone had been struck blind, deaf and dumb. The villagers simply stood back in horrified fascination.

It took half an hour of coaxing, during which the injured were given water and basic treatment, before one of the tribesmen spoke up. All the others distanced themselves and dispersed. To talk to soldiers was an invitation for more of the same.

The ZANLA group had arrived in the early hours of the morning from across the Mozambique border. They had forced the villagers from their huts and accused them of being sell-outs and colluding with security forces.

The mutilations and torture had been carried out systematically on random victims as a warning that ZANLA would not tolerate the tribespeople of the area having anything to do with the Rhodesian troops. When the ZANLA invaders had left, they'd taken with them all the young men and women who were considered of fighting age, leaving behind them a fear and anguish that would ensure compliance with their cause.

Andy stood quietly, observing the evidence of inhumanity.

Merryl and Charmaine came into his mind, and their images fuelled his anger. He had heard stories of the brutality meted out by the guerrilla forces but he'd paid little heed to them. He'd considered them to be hugely exaggerated. There was no exaggeration, though, in what lay before him. It seemed to him beyond words—the appalling ruthlessness of the attack on innocent and defenceless peasants.

A Fire Force alert had gone out, and within an hour helicopters had arrive on the scene with medics and combat tracker troops and Andy and his group returned to their base.

Later that day, Evans called a debriefing. The incident was a lesson in what could be expected in time to come he told them.

'You have witnessed the methods of jungle justice,' Evans said to the assembled trainees. 'Nothing that I could say explains more clearly what we're fighting against. There is no form of inbred evolution amongst these so-called freedom fighters. There is only barbaric savagery. These animals have no respect for human life or human dignity and if they can do to their own people what we witnessed today, imagine what they will do to you and your mothers and sisters, even your grandparents, if they get half the chance.

'This, gentlemen, is what this war's about,' he continued. 'It's not about white supremacy or the preservation of privilege. It's about the preservation of civilized norms. Today's events clearly illustrate the justification of our efforts.'

The next day, training recommenced as though the incident had never occurred—but there was a heightened sense of purpose among the trainees, and the desire to be done with the basics and get into action was palpable.

\*    \*    \*

By the time they returned to Salisbury, Andy and his fellow trainees were a formidable group. They had learned the art of silent killing, how to blow bridges, and set booby traps. They'd learned how to blend with their surroundings, how to travel at night using the stars as their guide. They could strip, assemble and fire an extensive range of weapons with speed and accuracy. Their bodies were hard and toned; their minds sharp and focussed.

But it still wasn't over. Final selection was yet to come and that was a gruelling ten-day survival mission preceded by thirty-six hours of unwavering physical activity

Throughout the first day, through the night and for the whole of the following day, they were pushed with little respite. From beginning to end no food was issued, and water was a scarce commodity. By the time the thirty-six hours came to an end, their numbers had fallen to eighteen exhausted men.

They were then taken into the bush and dropped in groups of two with hardly any rations, a single water bottle, a wrist compass of doubtful value and a tourist map. They were given rendezvous points at distances of between fifteen and twenty kilometres apart, over some of the roughest terrain in the country, and given ridiculously short time periods within which to reach them.

By the end of the ten days, only twelve remained out of the original aspirant training group of nearly 500. The camaraderie that had been forged between them was a bond akin to brotherhood.

They returned to the SAS barracks transformed. From raw recruits they had become highly trained specialists, eager to put their skills to use in the field of combat. What Andy did not know was that although he was now highly capable in the academic art of war, the functional aspects still to come would leave him dismally unprepared for the reality of it.

\*   \*   \*

'Five years ago,' thought Andy. 'All those memories. All the experiences and all those guys who lost their lives.'

He lay in the Victoria Falls hospital. He was alone with his thoughts and the pain in his guts, with the desperate need for sleep. It seemed so long ago and far away. A world apart where the optimistic glamour of elitism had degenerated into an existence of gunfire, burning villages, death, destruction and fear.

Finally, he slept.

# CHAPTER 16

HE WAS ON A DESERTED BEACH. The sand beneath him was virginal white. The waves broke in long, perfect lines of white foam at the margin of an indigo-blue sea. Tall date palms, swaying gently in a light breeze, framed the view. Behind the palms, blending into their surroundings, were clusters of thatched bungalows surrounded by emerald-green lawns and beds of brightly-coloured flowers.

The sun was going down on the horizon, and the orange glow suffused the western sky. It flecked the white breakers with gold as they tumbled in a hushed murmur onto the shore.

He wasn't sure how he had got there, or why, but the seclusion and tranquillity gave him no reason to want to question his presence. The air was warm and still, creating within him a sense of mild euphoria. He smiled and lay back on the sand, watching the waves as they rolled towards him with their golden shimmer.

Suddenly, like the shadow of a cloud that crossed the sun, there came a change. As he watched, the sea turned from its consummate blue to a dirty grey, and the water grew rapidly darker. Then the sun flared up in a ball of fire, turning it abruptly from grey to red, and the waves were transformed into a dancing mass of flames.

He sat up, both curious and alarmed, as he realised that the sea was on fire. The water had become a rolling inferno of liquid flame and it rose up in swells and crashed ever closer to him.

He got to his feet and began to run towards the bungalows, but as he approached he saw a fearsome change—in place of the flower beds there were bastions of sandbags, and from these protruded the barrels of rifles and machine guns. He couldn't see the faces of the men silhouetted behind the sandbags, only their shapes—and he paused, unsure who these people were.

But beyond them, standing at the door to one of the bungalows, he saw Alyson waving frantically at him, calling his name and telling him repeatedly to go back. But then her appeals seemed to change and it sounded as though she was calling 'come back'.

He looked over his shoulder at the ocean and gave a cry of anguish. It was now burning under a thick pall of black smoke that rushed towards him, flames licking as if trying to engulf him. He was sweating profusely and his nerves were on edge. He had no idea what was happening, and his fear was heightened by the shocking speed at which conditions had changed—mere seconds, from contentment to horror.

He looked again to where he'd seen Alyson, but she was gone. He needed to make up his mind which way to go, either towards the sandbags or along the beach.

As he turned toward the bungalows, one of them changed in shape and astonishingly a set of rotor blades emerged from the roof which immediately started spinning, with the clatter and roar of the blades beating the air. Then the thing lifted off and tilted forward, flying directly towards him. Simultaneously, all the weapons behind the sandbag ramparts opened fire at him and a combination of coloured tracer, like speeding shards from the inside of a burst kaleidoscope bellowed in his direction, kicking up the sand at his feet and shattering the palm trees in a frightening display of splintering destruction as he dived for cover.

He rolled away, instinctively groping for a weapon, but there was none. He cried out as the sand in front of him exploded under a hail of automatic rifle fire, covering him in fine grit that stung his face and hands, and he rolled away again. As he did so he saw the oddly-shaped flying bungalow above him burst into flame, and his anguish rose as it hurtled directly down towards where he lay with his arms covering his head. He tried to roll away again, but he was trapped by some unseen force and he struggled in frustration to free himself.

Suddenly he was engulfed in hot liquid from the burning sea that cooled and stuck to him like salt on Lot's wife. He seemed to have become instantly petrified and he stared up from the embracing cocoon of solid lava as Stuart and Rob appeared out of the inferno of the flying bungalow, which seemed to shrink and fade as if drawn into an invisible vortex.

They hovered above him under parachute canopies, side by side as though held in a thermal. They both wore their SAS colours, blue belts, sand berets and distinctive para wings on the shoulder of the right arm. He struggled to free himself. He had to get up, had to get away. He didn't know what these guys wanted, or why they had come to wreck the comfort of his reverie on this beach.

All of a sudden the parachutes holding Rob and Stuart aloft disappeared and the two of them hurtled downwards in a tumble of flailing arms and legs, hitting the ground in grotesque heaps on either side of him, and he recognised the pose in which he'd last seen them. In their filthy bloodied fatigues, with huge green flies and ants crawling in and out of their mouths, eye sockets and nostrils.

He started to yell again and as he did so he saw an enormous wave of flame that had rushed up the beach to break down upon him. An instant before it engulfed him, he felt a flush of warm fluid spreading over his body and he tried to call out, but his voice failed him.

Then he heard another voice.

*'Andy! Come on . . . . It's okay . . . . Come back to me!'* it was calling.

All of a sudden he was awake, lying in a bed, with someone standing over him and sponging him down with a towel soaked in warm water. The perspiration rolled off him as though he'd just emerged from a sauna, and the gentle strokes of the wet towel did nothing to stem it.

He stared at the figure beside the bed. She had a familiarity about her, from some remote past. Beside her stood a man wearing the uniform and colours of the RLI and bearing the rank insignia of a major. Andy stared blankly at the pair, straining his memory through the clouds of terrifying disorientation, and then—suddenly—came recognition.

'Andy,' said the woman softly, her eyes brimming with tears.

Andy was still incoherent and it took him a few seconds to realise where he was; and then he came fully awake as the major spoke for the first time.

'You do realise, of course, sergeant, that we cannot allow these outbursts?' He smiled. 'They tend to disrupt the repose and well-being of other patients.'

'Piss off Alec,' he said weakly, his mind beginning to clear. 'What are you doing here?'

'I was in the ops room when the sitrep on your little "accident" came through,' said Alec, 'So I got hold of Alyson here and brought her to see you.'

Although he was still smiling, Alec showed what Andy, in his semi-comatose frame of mind, thought was mild awkwardness, but he went on breezily:

'You shouldn't shoot up on that shit they give you. It makes you have strange dreams.'

Alec and Andy had renewed their friendship after the completion of Andy's selection course, and they saw each other socially on infrequent occasions. Alec's roll in the RLI as a Commando 2IC kept him away in the bush as frequently as Andy was away on external ops and they were rarely in Salisbury at the same time. With those limitations, in addition to the wide disparity in their rank, their contact with each other was sporadic.

Alec had got married a year previously to a well-placed ordinance clerk in the police special branch, named Geraldine Sheldon. Andy had introduced them to Alyson on one of the rare social occasions and the two of them had taken to her from the outset as if they were old friends. She seemed to share an easy-going understanding with Alec, while she and Geraldine had begun calling each other and meeting occasionally for drinks or lunch.

Alec turned and smiled at Alyson, and then punched Andy lightly against the side of the head. 'Chin up buddy, you'll get over it.' Then he turned and left, reaching out to Alyson as he went and gently ruffling her hair.

'Dammit, Mason!' said Alyson in mock reprimand as Alec left. 'Can't I leave you alone for a bloody minute without you getting yourself into trouble?'

They'd moved Andy from Vic Falls early that morning. Dr. Tafner had pronounced him fit to travel and he was now in the 'army injured' convalescent ward at Andrew Fleming Hospital. He had been gently loaded into an army ambulance and transported to the small Spray View airstrip at the Falls, where a transport Dakota had been offloading supplies and was ready for the return trip to Salisbury.

He'd slept fitfully on the plane, strapped to the stretcher that had been fastened to the metal floor by retaining clamps. He'd had brief and unclear glimpses back into the recurring nightmare of fire and flame, with the same appearance of Stuart and Rob and the helicopter crew. And fire! Always fire. It was beginning to haunt him every time he drifted into sleep. The assault on his mind that he'd just woken from had been clear and terrifying.

Alyson stepped closer to the bedside and placed the towel she'd been holding into the wide stainless steel bowl of warm water. The concern displayed in her eyes behind the now light-hearted teasing demeanour was clearly visible, and merely seeing her brought a swell of passionate adoration from deep inside him, and a lump to his throat.

She was not a stunningly beautiful woman who would turn heads in a crowd. In fact, in many ways, she was quite plain— but she exuded an imperceptible chemistry that attracted and aroused Andy as no other person ever had.

Her soft, wavy, light brown hair was kept short, just covering her ears and tucked neatly in the nape of her neck. She was an outdoor girl who loved the wide open spaces, and her skin bore the signature of the African sun. The spread of light freckles on her nose and cheeks was offset by a pair of eyes the colour of the morning sky on a clear summer day. She had a luxuriously inviting mouth that revealed one slightly crooked tooth when she smiled, and she was dressed in a pair of faded blue denim jeans that fitted tightly around her narrow waist, and a pink V-neck tee-shirt that drew attention to firm, unrestrained breasts, showing enough cleavage to attract, but not enough to tease.

'Those guys play rough sometimes,' he croaked with a weak smile. The pain from his injury was no longer localised, but had spread though his entire torso as though he'd been pulled apart and put back together again with the incorrect parts. Every muscle and bone ached with an intensity that kept him breathless.

Alyson bent and kissed him on the mouth and then on the forehead and he felt the warm wetness of tears on his face as she put an arm up and around his head and rested her cheek against his.

'I was so scared,' she choked, and Andy was surprised to realise that she was crying. 'After you left on Sunday, I had this weird premonition that I might never see you again, and I spent the day in panic. When Alec phoned me from the base it was so unexpected and I thought he was going to tell me you were dead—and I died a silent death of my own. Andy, I was so scared!'

'Hey, steady on,' said Andy in a weak attempt at heartiness. 'I always told you those pricks can't shoot straight.'

But the lump in his throat now threatened his composure. The emotional stress that he had been under, and the warmth of her tears on his face, nearly pushed him too far. He had to restrain himself from joining her in a flood of tears. He'd had no idea that Alyson's emotions were so intense. But there was no doubt that they were contagious.

'If you promise not to tell,' he continued, struggling to control his voice, 'let me say that I got a little scared myself. I thought we'd be out for a whole ten days and I wouldn't see you, so I fixed it to get back here. This silly wound is self-inflicted and nothing to worry about.'

Alyson started to laugh and cry without control of either.

'Andy,' she wept, 'you stupid man, please don't ever go away again! I don't think I could bear it. I love you.'

Andy was mentally shaken at the words. The passion and emotions between them left little room for doubt of their feelings for each other, but it was the first time that the word 'love' had been used between them—and it came as a shock to him. Lust he knew about and their activities, when alone, left no uncertainty in his mind that they were in common accord on that. Although probably deeply felt, the acknowledgement of love had been left out on the fringes—for fear of spoiling what they had in passion.

After completion of his access training to the SAS and in the wake of losing Merryl, Andy had gone on a spree of wanton, meaningless sexual escapades when he was not on operational deployments, and love didn't enter into any of them. He would always refer to love as a four-letter word, and he facetiously explained its origin:

'It was defined by the Philistines in primitive research of human emotions. When they called their pubescent, masturbating youth to council, the kids would be asked what they felt. Was it Lust, Obsession, Virility or Excitement? And the general consensus was "all of these". So they started calling sexual arousal L-O-V-E. Hence this word, that isn't actually part of the English language, defines our affection and our relationships. It's all bullshit of course, and it doesn't last anyway.'

It was a frivolous response, used in conversations on the subject of love, and it usually raised a guffaw from the company he was with, but he'd never really given much thought to its reality.

He had been happy to concede that the words from his self-made acronym applied to him, but he'd never been able to make the word itself a commitment. Now it seemed that Cupid had found a gap, and with his emotions flying all over the compass Andy's resolve broke and he felt a surge of such emotion that he could barely control himself.

He said nothing, but the rush of deeply hidden and hitherto misunderstood feelings that he had simply taken for granted, burst to the surface. Without fully realising what had happened, he knew that he was in love. Despite the pain of his injury, it came to him with such an explosive and euphoric sense of well-being that he could barely contain himself.

Alyson pulled up the straight-backed chair that stood alongside a metal cabinet beside Andy's bed. She sat down and held his hand. For what seemed like a long time, they didn't speak—and then Andy turned his head towards her and smiled.

'Where do you feel it?' he asked, grinning. 'In the heart or the loins?'

'You're a rude sonofabitch, Mason,' she said with a chuckle, 'but to be honest—I feel it from my fingers to my toes and everywhere in between.'

Andy's memory of Merryl had faded almost entirely, but she crossed his mind now—and the thought of her did not bring the anger or the sense of bitter emptiness that it would have done five years previously. She was now a part of his distant past. She was another statistic on the long list of casualties. He had never openly acknowledged his love for her, although he'd been acutely aware of that emotion. Alyson was real and alive and she loved him . . . . Dammit! He loved her! Passionately! What more could he ask for?

Alyson had dried her eyes. She was smiling again.

'Well,' she said, with a nervous slant in her voice. 'I've got good news and good news. First, I'm pregnant—and second, that means you'll have to make an honest woman of me and marry me.'

The manner in which it was said made Andy think she was joking, but he realised almost immediately that she wasn't. The news threw a whole new meaning into his swirling emotions. It took him all of a minute before he could reply, and he was as off-hand as she had been.

'How do you know I'm the father?' he asked mockingly, but there was absolutely no doubt in his mind—and he spoke with teasing laughter.

'I don't,' replied Alyson, tossing the banter back with casual nonchalance, 'but none of the guys on the rugby team that I've been screwing really turns me on. They're mostly overweight and sweaty. I wouldn't want them anywhere near my child. You, on the other hand, drive me nuts in bed and on the floor or over the couch or on the stairs and in my heart, and you'd make a wonderful father—so I'm pinning it on you.'

Andy laughed and the pain of it blurred his vision, but he squeezed her hand and, without giving it serious thought, said: 'So when's the wedding?'

'I'm just over six weeks gone. I got confirmation from the doctor on Monday and I haven't told my parents yet. I'd kind of hoped we could do that together. I didn't think we'd have the opportunity quite this soon, though.'

Ralph Carstens was a pillar of Rhodesian culture. A member of the influential Pioneer Society and of pioneer heritage, he was a personal friend of both the Prime Minister and the Minister of Finance, as well as being an old school chum of Lieutenant General Paul Wallace the current head of Combined Military Operations.

He was a tall well-built man with a thick, immaculately-trimmed crop of brown hair, greying slightly at the temples. He had a constant air of relaxed confidence about him and Andy had never seen him in the least bit ruffled by anything.

Ralph was a successful architect, and the driving force behind the development of recently-built luxury hotels in the tourist resorts of Kariba and Vic Falls. Andy had marvelled at the tenacity of Rhodesians who, despite the war, continued to build and believe in a future that statistics and reality could simply not sustain.

Outside of his architectural activities, Ralph also held a non-executive director's seat on the board of the country's largest banking group, and he owned Golden Acres, a 10,000 hectare farm in a tobacco and citrus community in the district of Mazoe, some sixty kilometres north-east of Salisbury.

He and Andy had taken an immediate liking to one another when they'd first met, a little over a year previously, and whenever possible they'd get together for lunch or a round of golf. Andy's golf had not improved since his days with Highgate & Savage but he enjoyed Ralph Carstens' company, and although Ralph took his game more seriously than did Andy, they both enjoyed their time together on the course.

Alyson's mother Jennifer was an imposing woman whose fine features hinted at an aristocratic heritage. At their first meeting, Andy had formed the opinion from the way she conducted herself, that what she had achieved in life had come from hard work and perseverance. It struck him that she'd protect and defend it with her life if that's what it would take. He didn't think she'd be a compassionate adversary if one chose to betray her trust, but he harboured the belief that he had earned her affection and he liked to keep it that way.

She was an exceptional hostess with a reputation for her lavish dinner parties. The Carstens mixed with the cream of Rhodesian society but Jennifer exhibited no airs and graces. She possessed the rare quality of being in the same comfort zone with roughnecks as she was with royalty, and she needed little in the way of an excuse to turn up the music, open the bar and roll up the carpet to dance. Jennifer's imitation of adolescence when the mood took her was contagious, and parties that she hosted never failed to bring out abandoned merriment in her guests, even those more reserved types who tended to err on the side of social dignity.

Andy had come to consider himself entirely at home as a component of the Carstens family, and it now seemed imminent that the relationship was to become official.

The Carstens kept an apartment in Salisbury in the same block and adjacent to the one in which Alyson lived. These were on The Avenues, an upmarket tree-lined haven of well-appointed townhouses, but their home was on Golden Acres where Ralph was able to concentrate on his architectural projects and, with the assistance of his managers, attend to the day-to-day needs of running the farm.

The road to Golden Acres was dangerous and terrorist ambushes on civilian vehicles were not uncommon, but Andy and Alyson travelled the distance to the farm as often as possible during the brief spells when he could get off duty. Alyson drove, which she did like a professional at high speed, and Andy rode shotgun, holding his rifle out of the car window ready to respond to any incoming fire. It was a mere gesture and he knew it, but being armed and driving in excess of 160 kilometres an hour on good roads gave them an illusion of safety. So far their trips had been uneventful. Ralph and Jennifer did the journey as frequently as four or five times a month and they too were, as yet, unscathed.

'Have you told them that I'm stuck here in hospital?' asked Andy.

'I spoke to them straight after I heard that you'd been hurt,' said Alyson. 'They're very worried. They just happen to be in town so they'll come in and see you later on.'

Andy and Alyson remained hand in hand, chatting quietly in between companionable silences. Then, 'you look whacked,' she said. 'I'll take off and let you get some rest. I'll come back later with the folks.'

She bent and kissed him on the forehead, letting her lips linger. She moved her lips down to cover his, opening them, and pressing her tongue deep into his mouth in a passionate encounter that made his heart race.

'I love you,' she whispered. 'Stay safe. I'll see you later.' And she turned and walked away, turning back at the door to wave and blow him a kiss off the tips of her fingers.

Andy felt drained after the time he'd spent with Alyson. His mind was in turmoil and his guts were on fire. He'd refused the prescribed pain killer earlier in the day and was now starting to regret it. The mental and physical exhaustion that enveloped him did not take his mind off the recent events in his life. The failed op, the death of four friends, his emotional roller coaster ride through the horrors of the preceding three days and now the fact that he was going to be a father.

He was unsure how Ralph and Jennifer would react to the news that they had a pregnant daughter, although she was twenty-four years old and it shouldn't be their problem. He had no illusions, though, that fathers tended to be protective over their daughters chastity no matter how old they were. Of course, if they thought that he and Alyson were still at the hand-holding stage, it was time they were brought into the real world, so he didn't let his thoughts linger there.

His future with the SAS would have to be looked at, though. Three days previously, four of his friends who were alive and well were now dead and gone and he knew that given the state of the country's political turmoil, something would have to give—and those deaths together with thousands of others were probably in vain.

Events of the previous few days had driven home the fact that he too could easily become another statistic on the altar of political sacrifice. With the sudden change in his collection of responsibilities he felt the need to minimize that risk. In addition, he no longer tingled with the confidence and motivation that he'd been possessed of up until recently.

It was a dangerous frame of mind in the business of survival.

Alyson returned with her parents shortly after six in the evening and Ralph showed genuine concern at Andy's discomfort and overall condition.

'What did they do to you, son?' he asked. 'You look as though you've had a rough time of it.'

'Just a fluke,' said Andy, not feeling the nonchalance that he tried to put into his reply. 'One of the bad guys got in a lucky shot, but they tell me I'm getting over it.'

'We've been worried, Andy,' said Jennifer, 'but it's good to see you.' She seemed a little nervous, which was entirely out of character, but Andy hardly noticed. He smiled at her warmly.

'Thanks Jen,' said Andy, and then he immediately went on: 'Did Alyson tell you the good news?'

'What good news is that?' asked Ralph expectantly.

'We're going to parents,' said Andy. 'I'm afraid we must have been a little careless.'

There was a deathly hush that lasted for an interminable twenty or thirty seconds. Jennifer went pale and glanced at Alyson with a look that Andy found alarming, almost as if she'd been betrayed. Ralph's reaction was quite the opposite—and after the silence his face slowly lit up into a broad grin.

'Well,' he said, 'If I were to choose someone to be careless with my daughter, I couldn't think of a better choice! What are you two going to do?'

Jennifer had quickly regained her composure and she too was smiling, but Andy noticed that the smile didn't quite reach her eyes.

'Don't be so pushy, Ralph,' reprimanded Jennifer. 'They probably haven't even thought that far yet. Why, Andy,' she continued, 'that's wonderful news!'

She turned and glared at Alyson before almost reluctantly placing her arm around her shoulder. 'When did you find out?' she asked.

'I got confirmation on Monday,' said Alyson, looking relieved. 'I told Andy this morning. I wanted us all to be together when we told you.'

'Do I get a son-in-law from this?' asked Ralph cheerfully.

'I guess you'll have to,' said Andy. 'But I'm going to have to make a few changes. I'm not happy about getting myself shot at under the circumstances. I'll put in a transfer request just as soon as they let me out of here, and then we can start making wedding plans.'

He couldn't mention Dawson's suggestion of work in military intelligence. He'd have to come up with a story to cover any activity in that department. But for now that wasn't important. First he needed to get his ducks in a row and get more clarity on what that work involved, and how long he could keep at it.

# CHAPTER 17

A ndy was released from the hospital four days later, although he was still in a great deal of discomfort.

Alyson came to fetch him and drove him directly back to Golden Acres. It had been less than a week since they had left to go back to Salisbury at the end of Andy's leave.

On this occasion he was there to gather his wits and reflect. He spent time relaxing, and he took his mind off the war to concentrate on how his future would pan out.

The farm was a haven surrounded by beautiful scenery. The house was a magnificent rambling bungalow, built high up on a hill by Ralph Carstens' grandfather in the pioneering days of Rhodesia's birth.

From the wide veranda there was a breath-taking view of green citrus and tobacco plantations. These undulated over the surrounding countryside in neat rows, bordered by wide areas of untouched African foliage. Small herds of antelope, zebra and buffalo roamed in the stretches of bush, unperturbed by the agricultural activity around them. Around the house were rolling lawns and well-tended flower beds and rockeries. A thatched gazebo with a fully stocked bar and barbeque area was strategically positioned at a high point above a natural rockery and provided a 360-degree view of the surroundings.

Up here, the sky appeared to be so much wider and the sun seemed to shine with exaggerated warmth—as if it were smiling down upon this transformation of the African wilderness.

The house consisted of eight large bedrooms, each with its own en-suite bathroom and dressing room. The dining room was like a banquet hall, housing a heavy mahogany table and chairs that could seat twenty-four dinner guests. Suspended from the high pressed-steel ceiling was a twenty-four bulb crystal chandelier, and the floors were of polished Rhodesian teak.

Adjacent to the dining area, behind swing doors, was a kitchen of a size in which five staff could work without being in each other's way.

Ralph's study was a huge room furnished in leather and teak, walled along one side by a floor-to-ceiling cabinet that contained an extensive collection of leather-bound books. On the opposing wall ran a long wide shelf that bore the tools of his architectural profession. Wide folding doors opened onto the veranda which looked out over the garden and the panoramic view beyond.

Andy revelled in the attention paid to him by Alyson, and by the housekeeping staff. The staff wore uniforms of colourful African cloth and they went about their daily chores smiling and singing, bringing further resonance to the charm of Golden Acres.

Each morning, Andy and Alyson took long walks to build up his strength and get the exercise that his body craved.

Carrying with them the weapons, assault rifle and pistol, that had become an extension of everyone's life in the rural areas, they rose early and walked out into the sunrise along the dusty farm roads and into the fields, cherishing the beauty of the orange glow that lit up the eastern horizon, listening to the insects, birds and animals as they greeted the new day.

They watched as the sun turned the sky from scarlet to turquoise while puffy clouds held on to the last of the orange glow around their edges. Andy never grew tired of the splendour presented by the African dawn. Having Alyson by his side to share it filled him with a joy that went beyond his richest dreams.

In the evenings, sitting in the gazebo, they watched the sunsets and drank cold beer. The condensation frosted their beer glasses and ran off them in fine squiggly lines of precipitation.

Nothing interrupted the moment and they chatted in the effortless intimacy of young lovers.

Friday and Saturday evenings were club nights in the district. The community of farmers, driving an assortment of locally-adapted armoured vehicles, mostly converted Land Rovers or Toyota Land Cruisers, braved the risk of a guerrilla ambush and converged on the club house. This rustic venue, whose grounds boasted three tennis courts, an Olympic-scale swimming pool and a bowling green, formed the centre of their social lives.

The weekly parties at the club were festive affairs where the revellers danced to blaring music for all age groups from speakers attached to an old Bang & Olofsen hi-fi set behind the bar. There were frequent and enthusiastic sing-along evenings with the accompaniment of an ancient but finely-tuned grand piano. It was a happy-go-lucky source of escape from the ever-present knowledge that an attack could take place at any time. The weapons that stood in wooden gun racks along the walls and under the bar counter gave testimony to the reality of that threat, but life went on blissfully despite the danger—and Andy never failed to marvel at the contrasts and courage that existed in this war-ravaged but beautiful land.

Despite all this, the reality was not entirely ignored—though it was held, purposefully, just below the surface.

Andy was reminded of this, one afternoon. He was sitting on the veranda, reading, when Ralph came out through the doors of his study and strolled across.

'You're looking mighty healthy for a victim of war, son,' he said cheerfully. He pulled up a chair opposite Andy and sat down.

'And getting better all the time, thanks to my surroundings,' said Andy, marking his place and putting the book down on the coffee table beside him. 'I love it out here, Ralph. It's so peaceful. You'd never believe that there was a bloody war raging all around us.'

Ralph chuckled wryly. He looked across at Andy's rifle that leaned against the wall within easy reach and he stroked the sidearm that was holstered to his belt.

'It's absurd, isn't it, Andy? Here we sit in the most beautiful surroundings, bearing weapons wherever we go just in case we are attacked by a marauding mob of terrorists. I never fail to be amazed at the contradiction in our lives.'

Ralph sat silent for a while and Andy did not interrupt his thoughts. Then he roused himself and continued:

'It's bloody sad though, son. Because the truth is, we're actually in a lot of trouble. I know you get to see what goes on in the field—and, my God, I admire you and your fellow soldiers for what you have to endure. But we're going to lose this war, Andy. No matter how good you guys are, or how many battles you win, we're up against a hiding to nothing. We simply can't sustain the cost to keep on fighting, and there isn't a country in the world that will support us. Even South Africa is demanding that we capitulate.'

He looked out across the security fencing that bordered the magnificent garden, and over the vast plantations beyond. He shook his head.

'In meetings with my banking colleagues,' he went on, 'we have endless discussions about how to preserve what's been built here. This lifestyle that we've come to love. But there's nothing that will stop the march of tyranny that threatens to destroy it all. International politics will see to it that we are brought to our knees in the name of what they call democracy, and within ten years everything that we and our fathers before us have built and fought to uphold will have been reduced to naught.'

Andy's mind was taken back to the day when he'd sat on a veranda similar to this one, while Jed Bradford spelled out his views on the future of Northern Rhodesia. Jed's portrayal hadn't been far off the mark.

'We have to accept,' Ralph continued, 'that the days of Rhodesia are numbered. In the not too distant future it will be renamed Zimbabwe and we will be ruled by an elite group of bitter, angry rebels who claim that their right to this land is fair repatriation of stolen property.

'In a thousand years, the bastards did nothing to develop or improve what was here.

'In a short ninety years, we've turned a barren wilderness into a paradise with the sweat off our backs, and despite all the efforts of our critics to isolate and destroy us, this country has become the breadbasket of Africa.

'That's no coincidence, Andy. It's come about through good management, honest governance and incredible people. Now, as a condition to stop the terrorism, they want everything that has been achieved by us—the so-called settlers—to be handed over. And there is nothing, short of burning it all, that we can do to prevent it.'

He paused pensively, and then went on.

'Shit, Andy, I was born on this farm and so was my father. My grandfather came here as a penniless immigrant and with the barren piece of land given to him for his part in the march of pioneers he built this house and a lot of what you see out there.'

He cast an arm across in a broad sweep, indicating the citrus and tobacco plantations.

'We have carried that on as a family and have built an empire. We're Africans, Andy, born and bred here. I speak Shona with the fluency of a native, but I hold my western values near to my heart and trying to integrate those with African customs and cultures would be like trying to mix oil and water. An exercise in futility.

'This is our land and we have a right to defend what we have here, Andy, but that right will not be recognised by anyone who has the power to make the least bit of difference. We'll lose it all because of a bunch of hypocritical politicians who find it politically expedient to ignore the truth.

'But the reality is no secret, Andy. What is now a vibrant, productive and well-managed economy providing employment and structured administration for all population groups will become the personal counting house for a handful of prominent black politicians who send ignorant women and children into the field of battle as cannon fodder—in the name of what they advertise as liberation and freedom.

'What our critics ignore is that the freedom that these poor suckers are encouraged to fight and die for, will be nothing more than the accomplishment of the personal dreams of a handful of power-hungry politically privileged whose understanding of freedom is the ability to randomly abuse their power and to subjugate and exploit their subjects. Liberating the cash register is all that they've really got in their hearts.

'That, Andy, is the African way,' he continued. 'And the world not only lets them get away with it, they even lend them money to carry on after everything worthwhile has been stolen or destroyed. Its bloody madness!'

Andy listened to Ralph's increasingly angry analysis, and he thought about the futility of it all—the futile effort to defend their rights and to preserve a lifestyle in what he still perceived to be God's own country.

He thought of all the death and destruction that he had witnessed, all the political rhetoric that had been spewed forth— in failed attempts to resolve the issues that lay beneath this guerrilla war. There had been dozens of abortive attempts at solving things, including a recent desperate attempt at internal settlement, a compromise between moderate black politicians and the white Rhodesian government that sought, thereby, international recognition and support. All that this had done was to spur the guerrilla leaders to greater efforts, and the war continued on an ever-increasing scale of intensity.

Andy remembered clearly the day Jed Bradford had cried silently while talking about the imminent demise of what had then been Northern Rhodesia, the country he loved—and how accurate had been his prediction of the future for that country. The possessive conflict over the right to govern Southern Rhodesia had been a longer, harder and more bitter struggle for all concerned, but the end result seemed imminent and, inevitably, the same.

'We could have shared it, you know, Ralph,' said Andy, knowing he was skating on thin ice in the face of Ralph's opinions, but he went on quickly to make his point:

'I firmly believe in our right to protect and defend what has been achieved here, but it goes a bit deeper than that—because it's a two way street. The belief on the other side is that they have a right to be part of the wealth and privilege that has been created, and to have at least their share of the spoils.

Withholding that right is what got us into this mess in the first place. I don't agree with the methods that have been used to claim that share, nor will I ever support those methods, but in hindsight sharing would be better than losing it all.'

Ralph stared at Andy calmly for what seemed like an age, and Andy held his gaze.

'Don't think I'm not on your side here, Ralph,' said Andy, anxious to fill the uneasy silence. 'I am. But I had this conversation with a mining engineer in Zambia when I was a kid. It was still Northern Rhodesia then, and I think he got it right.

'He seemed to understand the complexities of the African problem as it applies to the race issues, and I can't help agreeing with his idea that by turning the indigenous people into servants is what ultimately turned them into enemies. It could have been different, but no-one saw it. We're just paying for mistakes of the past—and the bill is getting bigger all the time.'

Ralph continued to look intently at Andy, and he felt uncomfortable. He felt that maybe he should have kept his mouth shut and his ideas to himself. But then Ralph smiled and shook his head sadly, as if in disbelief.

'I have over 200 staff on this farm, Andy,' he said. His voice was calm and even, but the undercurrent of controlled anger in his tone was unmistakable. 'I know every one of them by name and I know each of their wives by name. I know their children's names; I know their ailments, their strengths, weaknesses and the marks they achieve in the school that I built for them.

'They know that they can come to me every time they have a problem and that something will be done about it. From the oldest pensioner in the compound to a baby that was born this morning named Mpho, I am their adopted father and I have never let them down.

'Collectively, over 2000 local people are dependent on me. Most of them are descendants of men and women who worked for my grandfather. All but very few have lived here since the day they were born and they have shared our lives and this land in more ways than you can imagine.

'There is not an empty belly among them, Andy, and as long as I draw breath there never will be. I'm not unique in what I do—that is the way of the Rhodesian farmer. That is the way of Rhodesia. Do you think for one second that those privileges will be extended to them by a black master once this country has been turned over to the management of the political terrorists that we're fighting?

'If this land and all the other farms in the country are confiscated and redistributed as per the promises dished out by Mr Robert Mugabe and his ilk, do you think that the redistribution will be for the benefit of anyone outside the inner circle of power? If you do, you're just bloody naïve and we have the rest of Africa to prove it.

'Let me tell you, Andy,' he continued with restrained annoyance, 'that if land redistribution becomes a reality under a government led by Mugabe or Nkomo, the people who have worked the land under the conditions of today will be lucky if they are allowed to keep a roof over their heads. And the land will not be put in the hands of the masses, but in the hands of an elite few. Whether or not they have the aptitude to harvest any crops from the land they'll steal is a question that no one has ever bothered to ask.

'But the truth will emerge, you mark my words. Not immediately like it was in Mozambique and Angola or any number of other African dictatorships, but I foresee a steady decline with corruption, dishonesty and tyranny gradually rising to the surface and consuming us like a dark cloud of poison gas.'

Ralph paused thoughtfully and then continued:

'Just in case you were unsure, Andy,' he said, 'you and your fellow soldiers put your lives up for grabs in the line of duty as much to protect and preserve the rights of the black labourer in this country as you do to protect and preserve the lifestyle and investment of us so called *settlers*. We're not fighting for white supremacy, Andy; we're fighting against a system that will destroy everything that nearly a hundred years of honest hard work has achieved. I think that is worth thinking about. My God, there are more black soldiers in our army than there are whites. That should tell you something.'

Ralph rose and looked out over his domain. Then, without a word, he strolled away towards his study.

Andy watched him go, feeling as though the point he'd tried to make had missed its mark, but nonetheless experiencing a sense of deja vu. It was like listening to Jed Bradford all over again. Except on this occasion he was struck by a premonition of impending personal loss—and the intensity of it made him shudder.

By the tenth day at Golden Acres, Andy had started going for short runs after his morning walk with Alyson, leaving her behind to share time with Jennifer. After two weeks of rest and relaxation he felt as though he had fully recovered, although the ache in his abdomen resurfaced periodically and caused bouts of discomfort.

He had begun to feel the frustration of inactivity. Sitting around for most of the day, with nothing to do other than read and admire his surroundings, was starting to disturb him. He felt detached and he yearned to get back.

# CHAPTER 18

ALYSON DROVE ANDY BACK TO SALISBURY THREE WEEKS AFTER HIS DISCHARGE FROM THE HOSPITAL and dropped him at the barracks the morning after their return to the city.

Here he could, at least, feel as though he was not entirely isolated from reality. He was feeling far stronger and the pain in his abdomen had all but gone.

Traditionally, the walking wounded who returned to base after having been hospitalised due to combat injuries were expected to appear in the mess and propose a toast to those who had not been as lucky.

The tradition dictated that on the return of the lucky—no matter how unlucky their luck had left them (some came back in wheelchairs, some sightless or limbless and the luckier ones just on crutches but alive)—they would pay for the drinks until the first of the uninjured and healthy either left the mess or passed out.

It was an expensive way to recuperate, and the parties were invariably wild and raucous, but when Andy arrived there was hardly anyone at the barracks as most of the active troops were away on operational deployment. The up-coming night in the mess promised to be relatively tame.

Hostilities in the rural areas had intensified to the point where rest and recreation leave for the troops was becoming infrequent. All three squadrons were practically on full-time deployment, back to back, in their external operations to disrupt and quell the infiltration of guerrillas.

The barracks had an eerie silence about it, but ops backup troops were mulling around on camp duties and Greg Dawson was in the ops room.

'Well, look what the wind blew in!' he said cheerfully, as Andy stuck his head around the door. 'We were starting to think that you'd had your sick leave sheet switched with some poor bugger who actually needed a rest. How's the gut?'

Andy smiled. 'They tell me I'll get over it sir. How're things here?'

'Hotting up daily,' said Dawson. 'Farm attacks up twenty-two percent, rural village burnings up forty-three percent, civilian ambushes up fifty-two percent. Cattle rustling is also becoming a much bigger problem that it has been in the past. Thousands of head have been taken over recent months. The bastards are putting the pressure on. But have you seen a newspaper lately?'

'Not one that I've sat down and read,' replied Andy, 'but I've heard odd bits of news on the radio. It seems another effort's underway to bring the politicians together.'

'This morning's *Herald* tells us that the Patriotic Front has agreed to talk,' said Dawson. 'So I guess that means they're feeling the pinch as much as we are. I'd think that their sponsors are getting pretty tired of paying out, and I can't imagine that their host countries can keep them as guests for much longer. It's too much of a burden.'

Dawson sat back in his chair and frowned, then went on:

'I'd lay odds that the heat is about to be turned up a few more notches, Andy. All the players in this game will want to concentrate their efforts on getting a military advantage ahead of whatever date they set to get their talks underway, and the gloves are going to come off. If you think we've seen blood and guts so far, think again—this is where things get nasty.

'It should be an interesting bunfight, though. All the manipulators in one big room trying to convince each other that their way is the only way, while the tools of destruction, like you and I, try to prove who's got the most muscle. Well, let's see how it pans out, but in the meantime I've arranged some work for you to do in MI.'

Andy had given a lot of thought to what Dawson had said about work in Military Intelligence, and with the change in his circumstances the idea had started to sound appealing. Logistics and planning, at the same time as having an inside track on overall operations, sounded like a good way to recuperate and keep himself busy and off the operational list.

'ZANLA as always are making more noise on the international stage,' continued Dawson, 'and we need to weaken their leadership ahead of the talks. What we really need is to get some of their top brass military commanders out of the way, guys like Josiah Tongogara, Rex Nongo and Edgar Tekere. Those are the buggers who hold the rabble together. Without them, ZANLA would fall apart. There'd be no military leadership.'

He paused, unsure whether to say more, and then added:

'The brass at Com-ops wants someone to build dossier profiles on a selection of the heavyweights that we know about, so that we can plan their demise ahead of the talks. Mugabe, of course, would be first prize but unfortunately he's a difficult bastard to get close to. We might have to leave him alone for now, but we need to continue interrogating the snatches that we've brought in. I've arranged that you will be seconded on temporary transfer to assist in that department.'

'Why don't we just send a flying hit squad into Maputo and take Mugabe out?' asked Andy. 'Surely that would make the problem go away?'

'You may not be aware of this, Andy,' said Dawson, 'but we've tried a dozen times and we've never got close to him. That guy even has his food tasted by some poor sucker before he'll take up a knife and fork, or his fingers, or whatever it is that he uses to eat with. He never opens his own mail, he has five decoy cars, all identical down to the licence plates with blackened windows so no-one can see in, and when ho goes out of his fortress he randomly chooses which car he'll travel in only seconds before he leaves—and that is from behind a screened off area that's impenetrable from outside.

'Sometimes he gets into one car and then stops the convoy as they start to move and gets into another. Only he knows where he's going, and he only gives his driver instructions once they've been moving for a few kilometres. Meanwhile all the cars in the convoy separate and head in different directions. Unless someone can pin a homing device to his shirttails it's almost impossible to corner him.

'No, Andy,' continued the major, 'what we need is to get a fix on when he plans to travel to one of the camps, and then we wait for his arrival. We've all done our time sitting on O.P's watching and waiting for something to happen, and that's what we may have to do again. We need to know which camps he's visited recently because we can take those off the list. The only one that may be worth keeping on the list is Chimoio—he's been there recently, but we know that's one camp he visits regularly.'

*Chimoio!!* The name rang in Andy's mind with the clarity of a bell.

Andy had visited that camp several times on reconnaissance and intelligence gathering jobs, and he'd been there in the forefront of the attack force when they'd launched the most intense raid of the war.

It was during that operation that he had been awarded his Chested Wings, the highest award for gallantry that an SAS member below commissioned officer rank could earn.

Andy's mind drifted back to the events leading up to the Chimoio operation, almost two years back, and to the carnage that was wrought.

It had been obvious that something important was brewing, because for no apparent reason all ops were put on hold and the entire complement of SAS personnel were in barracks at the same time on retraining and refitting.

Para drops and skirmishing training through the thick bush in their training quarter were followed by days on the firing range. Medics were put on intensive retraining courses, with gunshot trauma being covered over and over again as a priority.

Mortar-men spent days on the range perfecting missile trajectories. Chopper drills were repeated, from embarking and disembarking by hot extraction methods to abseiling descents.

Call-sign interaction and emergency evacuation were rehearsed endlessly as was house clearing and mission co-ordination. Nobody other than the planners knew what the rehearsals and training were in aid of, but everyone knew that something big was about to happen.

Finally, one windy November afternoon after two and a half weeks of intensive training activity, the squadron was given stand-to orders at 16h00, and the entire complement of 120 men were transported by vehicle to a high-security area at New Sarum airbase. The area had been entirely cordoned off and military police patrolled its perimeter. The MPs would have known less about the frantic activity than those who were inside the cordon, but their orders were that no-one was to leave, irrespective of rank or status.

The briefing that was given shortly after their arrival behind the cordon had been more detailed and intensive than any that Andy had attended before, with a huge papier-mâché model adorning the centre of a hangar floor surrounded by spectator bleachers.

The model was meticulously built from information gleaned during aerial photography and close reconnaissance operations, which had taken place over a period of nearly a year. Andy had been on more than one of these recce operations and on each occasion when they returned had handed in his reports, together with photographs and route maps that had been drawn from activity on the ground. Until now, though, nobody had any idea what the information that the call-signs had provided would be used for.

He was surprised to see a small group of RLI soldiers and several members of the air force who represented all branches from choppers to jets and whom he recognised from ops where they'd worked in unison. He'd always thought that the air force were only briefed by their own flight commanders, but it seemed that this job had broader implications. Evidently they needed to be in close touch with what the ground troops were tasked with, and how they'd have to interact. The RLI contingent, it appeared, had been seconded to the squadron in order to swell the numbers.

'Gentlemen,' began Lieutenant General Paul Wallace, the head of Combined Operations, 'this is the most significant and probably the boldest attack upon ZANLA that has been planned to date. We believe that we may well be able to destroy their entire hierarchy and, with it, the spirit of the movement as a whole. We know that most of the military heavyweights of the movement are in attendance at the camp and we want to do everything possible to ensure that they stay there after we leave.'

The general paused for a moment and then grinned mischievously as he went on:

'Well! We'd like their bodies to stay. Where *they* go really doesn't merit any long-term concern. Hell would be nice.'

There was a chuckle of polite laughter throughout the gathering, and the general continued:

'We will attack the camp on four fronts. It will be noticed from the model, which is built in scale of approximately five million to one, that the camp is split into five sections, spread over a twelve kilometre radius. The central area is the admin and command component with parade ground and lecture facilities, and built on this watercourse, which is about waist deep at its centre.'

He placed a pointer on the model to make his point.

'The air force will neutralise that section of the camp by Hunter strike. The other areas provide accommodation, dining, ablution and armoury facilities for each section. Every morning the combatants leave their accommodation and converge upon the central admin area for roll call and indoctrination periods, after which they are split into training groups.

'Our first air strike will go in at 08h00, which is when the parade ground is at its busiest, and that has been calculated to be one minute and thirty seconds ahead of the para Dakotas that will follow, dropping troops by static line onto the four outer areas, plus a contingent to sweep through the command area. Helicopter-borne troops will be landed simultaneously to the para drop to cut off escape from the outer sections.

'There is likely to be chaos on the ground and gooks will be running everywhere.

'Your orders are to shoot to kill and ask no questions. Bear in mind that we will have neither the personnel nor the facilities to accommodate prisoners, and cannot afford to mess around. Those who get away could regroup and turn the tables on us.

'This base, gentlemen, houses 3000 fully armed and trained terrorists who all think they will be alive tomorrow night. We'd like to change those plans for as many of them as we can.

'We believe that the air strikes over the command stronghold will account for several hundred, but those who don't get it will be running like hell to escape. Stop groups surrounding the four outer camps are to move through those areas destroying whatever is there. These groups will take up positions to block the exit of terrs running from the central command area.'

The general laid his pointer on the subject areas of his oratory as he spoke.

'If you look around this hall, gentlemen,' he continued, 'You will notice that the numbers are not in our favour. There are 144 ground troops in this audience, just in case you were wondering—but air cover will neutralise the odds considerably.

'We'll have total surprise on our side and the bad guys will have no idea how many of us there are. They'll see what will seem like hundreds of parachutes in the air with helicopters, jet bombers and Lynxes sustaining high rates of fire power, which will be sufficient to confuse and disorientate even the most level-headed of their officers. We believe that we will cause total panic, and your jobs will be that much easier—but don't think of it as a cake walk.'

'Are there any questions at this point?'

Rob Southey raised his hand: 'Would you consider a leave application inappropriate if I were to put it in at this late stage, sir?'

There was a buzz of nervous laughter from those seated on the bleachers.

'Sit down, Southey,' said the General with a chuckle.

'Now—somewhere in the camp (and with the best will in the world we've not been able to find out where) there is a storage depot with enough fuel and ammunition to sustain an ongoing offensive by ZANLA for a long time to come. We know it's there somewhere because Chimoio supplies all arms and ammunition for insurgency along the entire Beira corridor. We've not been able to locate it, so it's obviously well hidden—but we don't want to leave without destroying those supplies. Other than the despatch of as many as possible of their commanders, that ammo dump is top priority.'

The General closed the briefing with more question time and the traditional 'Happy Landings' signature.

The plan was executed with the fine precision that had come to be expected from the commanders of what was considered the most professional military unit in Africa.

Helicopters began lifting off at 05h00 at twelve minute intervals, and split into groups, all seemingly headed in different directions so as not to raise speculation by the civilians living near the air base. Following circuitous routes, the helicopters converged for refuelling at Grand Reef airbase outside the border town of Umtali. The Dakotas with paratroops on board took off at 07h10. Andy's call-sign was in the lead aircraft, which was due to attack the admin and command base, and the tension was at fever pitch.

Twice in the night since the briefing Andy'd woken with churning in his guts and he headed for the makeshift toilets, only to find soldiers with similar problems queuing up ahead of him. Any attempt at humour had been weak and without conviction. Here had been a collection of very nervous men. The prospect of 144 men attacking a base of 3000 armed and trained enemy troops seemed ludicrous. The air power was an enormous factor in favour of the Rhodesians, but nonetheless the task was daunting and a high casualty count was, without question, an upcoming reality. Every one of the attack force was acutely aware of the fact that he could be amongst those.

The twenty nervous troops on Andy's plane were seated on benches fixed along the length of the aircraft, waiting for the order to stand up and check equipment. They were clad in full Rhodesian camouflage fatigues, so as to leave no doubt to friend or foe as to positive identification. Their parachutes were securely strapped on and their weapons were clipped under their harnesses, helmets firmly fastened beneath chins.

Andy looked at his watch, counting down the minutes to H hour. It was five minutes before eight and they were twenty kilometres from target.

Glancing across the narrow aisle through the small porthole windows behind the troops opposite him, Andy saw two Hawker Hunter jets scream by on their approach to the target area. Simultaneously the command from the dispatchers came, shouted over the engine noise and the wind from the aircraft's open hatch: *'Stand up! Hook Up! Check equipment!'*

The command was familiar enough. They'd all heard it a thousand times. But on this occasion it had a daunting, almost fatal, ring to it and they responded mechanically, rising clumsily from their seats and hooking their static lines to the overhead cable.

They carried out the equipment checks on each other, ensuring that there were no possible snags that could encumber the static line, that the reserve chute was firmly in place and that the hook up was in sequence of their place in the line.

*'Action Stations!'* yelled the dispatcher, listening intently to the instructions that came from the pilot through his intercom headset.

The line shuffled aft toward the gaping exit hatch, keeping the left foot forward and dragging the right upward and repeating the manoeuvre until the first jumper was a single pace from the door.

The dispatcher took a firm hold on the front man's harness, steadying him against the rocking of the aircraft which battled the turbulence at a height of only 500 feet above the hostile terrain.

The red light above the door blinked on. The command was bellowed, *'Stand in the door!'*

The line shuffled forward by a single pace, and waited, the front man with the left toe of his boot protruding over the edge of the drop. The atmosphere was electric. The tension hung like a tangible shroud in the confines of the aircraft.

The green light came on and the command *'Go!'* sent the men bailing out. They jumped in such rapid succession that the boots of one man almost touched the helmet of the man in front of him, as they leaped out into space and were whipped away into the slipstream of the aircraft.

Andy's canopy flared and took shape, and he looked around to orientate himself.

He was met with the spectacle of a sky filled with parachutes as the aircraft disgorged their loads of fighting men. Five Hawker Hunter jets in a V formation, flying at a height of 200 feet, were showering bombs and rockets onto a crowded parade ground, the strikes throwing up clouds of debris and human remains. A group of ageing Vampire jets, relics of the Korean War (and which had been a feature of the Rhodesian Air Force ever since) followed through with under-wing machine guns blazing.

There was no time to take in the full extent of the carnage meted out on the thousands of guerrillas on the huge parade square. Andy had to negotiate his landing through thick undergrowth and trees. They tugged at his canopy and caught him dangling three metres off the ground, suspended like a toy that bounced up and down on a rubber band.

Frantically, he detached one side of his harness from the canopy, and swung precariously across to where he was able to gain purchase against a branch of one of the trees that had snagged his chute. He released the other side and let the rigging lines swing free.

The descent had taken no longer than thirty seconds and his clambering with the harness another five. To his astonishment, as he looked down, he saw a group of ZANLA fighters—a mere 200 metres distant—men and women, all dressed in ZANLA combat fatigues. They tore, screaming, through the dense vegetation directly towards the attack force.

Andy's rifle was firmly strapped under his parachute harness and there was no chance of him getting that off until he was on the ground. Instead, perched as he was on a tree branch, he withdrew his pistol and let them approach.

The group was more of a mob than a formation. They were in a state of hysteria, unaware of the troops that awaited them, and they hadn't spotted Andy in his tree. He took advantage of the situation by firing carefully controlled shots at those who were carrying weapons. Other members of his jump group had reached the ground, and they were firing into the oncoming mass of escapees.

None of the guerrillas appeared to want a fight—they simply threw up their arms up in surrender—but the odds were too great to take chances and no mercy was shown.

These were trained enemy soldiers. Any sign of weakness or show of sympathy for this horde could easily turn the tables. Too often, in the past, a group that surrendered became a Trojan horse for a surprise attack. The relatively small group of Rhodesian soldiers would lose the advantage of surprise and would have to withdraw into defence. Such a consequence would make it impossible to push home their attack and achieve their objective, and so they pressed on.

Andy leaped down from the tree and, hitting the quick release on his harness, released his rifle and went to ground. He rapidly took in his surroundings and tried to assess the whereabouts of the others in his group.

Nobody had anticipated fleeing guerrillas to be under them when they landed. It had been expected that the men on the ground would at least have time to organise themselves. It was an exercise they had rehearsed with nauseating repetition and normally took no longer than twenty seconds once they had their harnesses off—but this was abnormal.

Troops were firing with side arms while still trying to get out of their chutes, and nobody seemed to be firing back. The air was filled with the roar of jet aircraft and helicopters, accompanied by the continuous firing of heavy machine guns and rifles. The acrid smell of burnt cordite hung like a shroud over the valley and the noise of battle echoed off the surrounding hills.

Once all the men were out of their harnesses, it took only seconds to co-ordinate the attack sweep line, but the line was transformed at once into a stop group. Coming at them was a running mass of disorientated men and women, more like a football crowd escaping a burning stadium than fighters.

Over the sights of his rifle, Andy stared in disbelief—the surge of humanity ran into rifle fire from the ground, and a barrage of small-calibre shells from the helicopters hovering above. It was carnage, and it went on for what seemed to be an eternity. Andy wanted to scream at the oncoming mass to go back, to stop coming at them like cattle to the slaughter.

The message must have got through at last. The decimation tapered off. Fewer and fewer of the guerrillas now came at them. They'd hardly fired a shot. Clearly, they'd been so taken by surprise that they'd lost their wits, running mindlessly into the waiting guns. Andy felt ill. He felt as though they'd come on a mission of mass murder—in which case, it seemed as if they'd achieved their objective.

He had to thrust away these feelings. Once on the ground, he told himself, the small Rhodesian force had no choice but to follow through and press their advantage. If not, they'd quickly become the defenders. The situation would be reversed.

During this initial engagement there'd been no radio communications between the call-signs. Once the carnage subsided and the immediate threat was neutralised, the lines started to buzz. Sitreps came in from the call sign commanders, and the advance onto the main camp area was given shape.

The lack of resistance was a shock to Andy and his comrades. They'd expected active resistance. They'd expected days, if not longer, to take over the base—even with the help of continuous air cover. Instead, the experience seemed surreal and nightmarish. These were hardened and highly-trained special forces, and yet each of them felt sick to the stomach.

Even so, they knew full well that the work could not now be stopped without putting every man on the ground at risk of being killed. Training, battle-sense, took over: *'Let the bastards on the other side die for their cause!'* The words rose up in Andy's mind, and they stayed there, ringing in his ears, and the significance of them took charge.

The attacking force took cover. They waited for over an hour before launching their advance on the camp.

The bodies of the enemy lay strewn between them and their main objective in their hundreds, and within minutes of the ceasefire swarms of grotesque green flies emerged to feed on the blood and sweat of the dead. It was understandable to wonder where they came from and how they anticipated this carnage. The horrid creatures settled on the filth and sweat, the sodden and bleeding corpses of the enemy, like bees to a honey pot and they buzzed in their thousands around the faces and eyes of the soldiers.

The administration camp was about three kilometres away through dense undergrowth and rough terrain. The invading force had to get there before they could feel confident that they had taken control and neutralised the base, and the threat of hidden pockets of resistance in the thick scrub remained very real. Under the scourge of the flies and the rising heat they waited, each man feeling the tension in his guts.

Had they really deactivated this vast camp so easily? Would there be a counter-attack? But there was not a sign from the enemy, and after what seemed like an eternity the order was given to start moving forward.

It took over four hours to cover the distance that lay between the drop zone and the command camp, and the route was littered with the bullet-ridden corpses of guerrillas.

Above the small advancing force there was the constant clatter of rotor blades from the circling helicopters, and from a distance came bursts of automatic fire—the sound of skirmishing between other attack groups on the ground, and the occupants of the spread-out camps. Andy and his comrades moved on warily, weapons held at the ready. They could not let those other sounds, other events, distract them from their immediate surroundings.

On the move again, on the alert, Andy pushed away all thought of the unequal slaughter, the mowing down of the fleeing ZANLA mob. War and death were synonymous. He'd seen it all before, more times than he cared to remember.

If he and his mates had the leisure to think it through, they'd have reasoned that those dead terrs were the same ones who'd attacked farms and mines, showing scant respect for innocent rural lives. The same ones, who brutally attacked and burned the villages of simple African tribes people for the slightest suspicion of co-operation with the Rhodesian authorities.

Even so, as a soldier, it troubled him that they'd not put up a fight. Did they really understand their purpose? Their cause? Or were they—and this was an entrenched suspicion in Andy's mind—mere pawns in the game of political power, men and women who'd been abducted by the guerrillas and coerced into being there? "Cannon fodder for the greater good of the liberation struggle."

They advanced through the dense forest, towards the main camp. They crested a ridge from where the ground sloped downward to the banks of a lazily meandering river. On the farther bank, 600 metres distant, was a collection of old and ramshackle farm buildings. There was a long barn with rusty corrugated iron roofing, and beside it lay the skeleton of a long-discarded tractor and other rusted agricultural implements—relics of the time when Portuguese colonials had run lucrative farming empires in the region. Now reduced to ruin.

Through his binoculars, Andy surveyed the landscape.

Beyond the barn the ground was sparsely covered by scrub and camel thorn bushes. It rose away from the river in a gentle slope of some 500 metres, toward the remains of a dusty and barren village of grass huts. Beyond that there was a wide but sparsely-cultivated maize field and, on the far side of the field, lay their objective: the central administrative camp.

The camp was made up of a rambling brick bungalows surrounded by a dozen flat-roofed shacks. These were set back from the perimeter of the parade square that Andy had seen from the air during the brief parachute descent. The parade square was strewn with bodies—those who had been caught in the initial air strike. From this distance, it seemed that there must have been hundreds of them. Smoke rose from burning debris in the wake of fires that had been started by the bombs. It was a waste land of destruction, scattered with the blackened skeletons, the charred and smouldering remains, of grass huts.

From where Andy and his group of men crouched on the brow of the hill, the natural scrub had been cleared to knee height all the way down to the river bank. It provided very little cover. From the camp's remaining buildings there'd be a 180-degree arc of clear visibility. Instinctively the entire body of soldiers went to ground. They spread farther apart, took advantage of what little cover was to be had, and scoured the area for enemy movement.

The river below them was about fifty metres wide, flowing across their path from left to right. About 300 metres downstream, the lazy motion of the current broke up into rapids. In midstream were small islands of papyrus reed, offering some shelter to the north bank.

The river had been pointed out at the previous night's briefing and had been suggested as a feature that could place the attackers in a position of weakness.

'Keep your eyes wide open here,' the general had said, laying his pointer on the spot on the scaled papier-mâché model. 'If the gooks are going to put up a last-ditch defence, this is a very likely place.'

A sense of tension, palpable as a bad odour, hung in the air over the men as they lay silently on their bellies, under the rising heat of the day, searching out the far bank. Sweat poured off their foreheads and down their necks, the camouflage cream on their faces ran in streaks and their soaking shirts clung like wet rags to their perspiring bodies, compounding the discomfort from the weight of their packs.

The islands of reeds seemed a patent source of danger. They'd be ideal hiding places for an ambush party—a real threat to the Rhodesian soldiers as they waded, chest-deep and vulnerable, across the river.

Andy unclipped his radio microphone and spoke softly into it. 'Zero, this is two one. Copy?'

There was a short crackle of static and then the reply: 'This is zero. Go ahead, two one. Over.'

'We need mortar fire into the river area. Over.'

'Roger that, two one. Provide target indication. Over.'

'Affirmative. Fire one. Over,' said Andy into the mouthpiece.

There was a pause of several minutes while the mortar crews adjusted the base plate and tube, and the time seemed to drag out forever. Then the waiting troops heard the distinctive thump of the first bomb striking the firing pin at the base of the mortar tube 800 metres behind them. The wait seemed interminable as the missile flew through its trajectory. It landed, but it exploded harmlessly in the river twenty metres to the right and thirty metres long of the nearest reed outcrop, raising a plume of white water high into the air. From that strike, Andy could direct the mortar teams onto the identifiable targets.

Andy once again spoke into the radio mike:

'Fire two. Sweep twenty left, thirty short. Over.'

The seconds ticked by and another tube thump was heard, but this time the bomb landed with a loud explosion at the edge of the island, throwing muddy debris and reed stalks in the air in a tumbling mess of shredded foliage, stones and clods of wet earth.

'Come left fifteen,' instructed Andy, again speaking softly into the hand-set.

The third bomb exploded in the centre of the target area. It cleared the island, leaving behind only shredded stalks of papyrus.

'Bull's eye,' said Andy, 'but no sign of life in there.' He paused for a moment, eyeing the remnants of the old barn, then spoke into the radio again.

'There's an old derelict farm building ninety metres long of the river on the same line as your last drop,' he said. 'I don't think it'll hurt to shake that out as well. Over.'

'Roger that, two one. Wait. Firing one.'

Fifteen seconds later, a bomb crashed through the roof of the old barn. The explosion was thunderous. It transformed the building into a fireball of proportions way beyond the capabilities of a single 81mm mortar. The building erupted from its base and burst outwards and upwards in slow motion, sending tons of debris skyward in a mushrooming cloud of black smoke and orange flame. The heat came at them across the river in an invisible and scorching wave of air that sucked at the lungs of the men on the ground as if they'd been plunged into a volcano.

'Holy shit!' exclaimed Andy, who like all the others had instinctively buried his head beneath folded arms. 'What the hell was in there?'

But he'd already guessed the answer. This had to be the hidden ammo and fuel dump, and they'd stumbled on quite by chance.

The pall of smoke spread like a impenetrable thundercloud over the ruins of the barn and flames licked high into the air, blocking out the sun and casting an eerie shadow. Huge bits of burning debris, flung like feathers in the wind under the power of the explosion set fire to the surrounding bush and Andy recognised the possibility of them being cut off from their objective. They had to move.

The barn had carried all the hallmarks of a possible ambush site and they could have been tied down for hours in a fire fight trying to flush out the enemy.—but any life that may have been within the confines of the structure would have been instantly incinerated. Now it posed a threat of a different kind. They would have to get beyond it before the fires isolated them from the admin area of the camp.

Still shaken up by the explosion, Andy and his group rapidly made their way down the slope towards the river. The sweep line was spread wide across the open ground and they were running. The newly presented circumstance of urgency created dangers for which they had not been prepared. None of them were unaware of the possibility that trip wires and booby traps could have been laid by the guerrilla forces on the approach to the river and could easily go undetected in their haste, resulting in the loss of limbs and life. The anxiety of the situation was tangible and nerves screamed silently under the strain.

The assault group closed in on the river bank, and as half of them went to ground to cover the crossing, the others tentatively waded inwards, soaking their boots and denim fatigues holding their rifles high and walking waist-deep through the flow of water.

A volley of automatic fire suddenly erupted from the cover of a previously ignored dense clump of reeds on the far bank a hundred metres distant. The bullets churned up the shining surface of the river like a frenzy of feeding fish but the strikes were short of the crossing Rhodesians. The troops in the water sank to their necks, bringing rifles to bear and returning fire across the flowing surface, while the covering force on the bank opened up into the site of the attack. A helicopter circling above swooped low over the reeds, twin Browning machine guns blazing, and quickly neutralised the source of gunfire. The group moved on, and emerged drenched and nervous on the camp-side of the river to give cover to the men crossing behind them.

The barren earth around the barn afforded a passage where fires had not taken hold but the heat and thick smoke was potentially life threatening.

Removing his bush hat, Andy drenched it in the river and signalled to his men to do the same. Then with it pressed hard against his mouth and nose he bolted through the gap and up the path towards the maize field, followed closely by his 20 comrades. Eyes stinging and gasping for breath, they emerged beyond the smoke, their hair scorched from the heat, but they were through. Spreading out, they went to ground heaving for breath and choking on the odour of gaseous air. It was almost an hour before they moved forward again.

Parts of the camp were still burning as they approached its perimeter across the maize field. This, sparsely cultivated as it was, had become more barren under the torrent of bombs and machine gun fire that had raged down upon the area

The field gave grim and sickening testimony to the day's warfare. Scattered amongst burning forage, cattle lay bellowing in their death throes. Some had been hurt by the bombing. Many had their guts ripped out, and the ever-present grotesque green flies buzzed loudly about the open wounds and the spilt entrails. Some lay immobile and screamed their defiance and pain to the world. These dying animals were despatched by the soldiers as they passed, with short bursts of rifle fire. A group of mangy and unkempt dogs tore at the innards of a bellowing heifer, and they were scattered by another burst of automatic fire from one of Andy's callsign.

Andy cautiously approached the smouldering ruin of a hut. It lay at the farther edge of the field where the camp's modest and scanty dwellings were located. Under the watchful eyes of his troops, he peered in.

A woman, clad in shreds, lay face down. Her clothes had been ripped off by the blast of bombs. Her spine and rib cage were exposed through the torn flesh, and her swollen but lifeless lungs showed through a congealing mass of blood. Beneath her lay a small child whose legs were nothing more than shattered and distorted shafts of flesh. Half of one foot was missing and the other non-existent. The child groaned, almost as if in a contented sleep, as its lungs rasped at the putrid air.

Andy raised his rifle and, with the nausea rising, put an end to the child's ungodly suffering. He had seen more than enough in the business of death to know that a world-class surgeon with the best equipment would make no difference to the child's destiny. He quickly surveyed the mutilated humanity in the hut, and then turned away. He beckoned his men to continue.

The sweep line moved on silently and with caution, spread out in extended line, checking each remaining structure as they went. Any documentation, papers, files, or weapons that they came across they removed and set aside for later collection. The silence that hung over the area was deafening—the eerie stillness was enough to send chills up the spines of even these hardened soldiers. It pulled at their nerves.

The air was heavy with the stench of decomposing bodies and the pungent smell of burnt cordite. Russian and Chinese weaponry lay carelessly scattered among the dead guerrillas, whose bodies were spread in unbelievable numbers upon the parade square and around the huts. They looked like rag dolls carelessly thrown, in a tantrum, from a child's playpen.

The sweep line moved on, every man on edge. With each step they expected the silence to be torn apart by renewed gunfire.

The camp lay in a flat basin within a series of clearings that had been carved out of the surrounding bush. To the north was a high ridge of craggy cliffs that sloped down sharply to the east and then curved in a gradual slope to the south, embracing the camp in a horseshoe of high ground. The western side was open to the river and wide expanses of tropical foliage. The silence seemed to rebound eerily off those features, coming back to mock the men who made their stealthy way through this bed of destruction.

Then it erupted—anticipated, and yet strangely unexpected. With abrupt and terrifying effect, the ghostly silence was shattered by the thunderous roar of automatic machine gun fire. It struck the hard dry ground with explosive impact.

In an involuntary but totally conscious movement, Andy went to ground. He'd been inside a brick-and-plaster building, checking for resistance and for documents. He rolled backwards towards the cover of its wall. He scanned the area, seeking out the positions of his men and the origin of the attack. He noted the swift action of the troops as they dived into cover, moving into independent positions, to defend against the sudden fire. All was done in seconds, as if by instinct—the fruits of training and experience.

'It's coming from the eastern ridge!' yelled someone nearby. The firepower of the small force was unleashed in free volleys in that direction.

Andy grabbed the handset of his A60 radio:

'Zero alpha, this is two one. Do you copy?' As always in these tense situations, he was mildly surprised at the calmness in his voice.

A mortar bomb exploded with a roar fifty metres to his left and shrapnel screamed overhead. He ducked and raised an arm to cover his face as the chunks of steel slammed into the walls around him.

'This is zero alpha—go ahead, two one,' he heard through the crackling static of his radio.

'Bring mortars to bear in blanket fire across east ridge,' he replied. 'That should get their heads down and we can get up there.'

Zero alpha, at the rear command base, responded:

'Do we have casualties? Over.'

Andy was senior callsign commander of this sector of the attack force, and they were well spread out. For purposes of communication the call-signs were two one through to two five, and he transmitted to these in sequence:

'All call-signs in two sector respond at will. Over.'

'Two two, we have two gunshot wounded. Medics attending. Over.'

'Two three negative. Over.'

'Two four, one deceased, brought under cover. Over.'

'Two five, shrapnel wound, nothing serious. Over.'

Andy wondered briefly which of his comrades had been killed, but nothing could be done about that. They needed to neutralise the resistance in the hills around them. He scanned the area from which the onslaught continued to come. The mortars and the machine gun fire exploded around them, pinning them down and filling the air with smoke and the reek of cordite. The deafening crashes, the intensity of the explosions, and the flying debris were terrifying.

His radio crackled again and a voice demanded:

'Two one, this is zero alpha. Do you read?'

Again unclipping the handset from his chest webbing, Andy responded to the static-interrupted call:

'Read you fives zero alpha. Go ahead.'

'Roger, two one. Do you think you could get your callsign onto the northern ridge and take out that position?'

Andy looked across a hundred metres of open ground between his position and the surrounding mass of jungle. He figured that they needed thirty seconds to cover the distance before they gained any form of cover. In between they'd be vulnerable, but the need to neutralise the mortar and machine gun positions was obvious.

'This is two one,' he yelled over the roar of another mortar explosion and the ongoing chatter of heavy fire.

'Where are all the choppers?' he shouted. 'I'm not sure if we can cover ten metres of open ground. Over.'

'Two choppers down with running repairs, others occupied in surrounding sectors. They're busy. Over,' came the terse response.

'Roger that, zero alpha,' shouted Andy. 'But I'll need covering fire a-plenty. Can you give us rapid mortar and so much small arms as to make the sponsors feel ill? If you can keep their heads down we'll do what we can.'

'Roger, two one. Give me a countdown of three when ready. Over.'

'Roger. Out.'

He gestured for the other three in his immediate team to come forward, and drew in the other callsign commanders subordinate to him. They scampered toward him one at a time, doubled over under fire, and each one skidded into the protection of the wall from which Andy observed events.

'We're going to get onto the northern ridge,' he told the men. 'Once we have a height advantage, we should be able to either guide assistance in, or take out that position. Get on your running shoes,' he quipped. 'We've got ground to cover.'

He raised the handset to his ear and called. 'Zero alpha, this is two one. Do you read?'

'Go ahead, two one,' came the immediate reply, barely audible over the hammer and thud of the ongoing contact.

'Ready, counting . . . . Three . . . . Two . . . . One! Moving!'

'Happy landings! Out.' Andy barely heard the brief reply as he clipped the handset back in place against his chest.

As the countdown was shouted, every weapon on the ground came to life, firing intensely into the thick bush cover on the hostile east ridge.

Andy and his three comrades rose and sprinted from their cover out across the open ground. They ran for the perceived safety of the thick mass of bush surrounding the base. Every sprinted step seemed to take an age, and the one hundred metres of space ahead was like an endless plain.

The earth at his feet suddenly erupted, as a burst of small arms fire was directed at the small group of running men. He heard an anguished cry from behind and to his right, and he turned to see Colin Bramwell, his 2IC, going down clasping at his abdomen. He broke his stride and turned, and with the ease of the strength lent to him by pumping adrenaline, he hoisted Colin over his shoulder in a fireman's lift. He turned again and continued to run for cover.

Colin's rifle had dropped to the ground with a clatter as he'd fallen, and the Bakelite stock had splintered into a thousand pieces. Andy reflected through his rising panic and adrenaline-fuelled elation just how close he'd come to being hit. He tried to increase his pace but he was hampered by Colin's weight.

He staggered forward, his lungs bursting under the strain, his heartbeat pounding in his ears.

Thirty metres, fifteen metres. Again, the ground erupted with bullets. Five metres! Sobbing with relief, he made it into cover and he dashed behind the bole of a Mopane tree. The others eagerly lifted Colin off Andy's shoulders and laid him down gently, and Andy collapsed to his knees. Gasping for breath, barely able to move, he turned and ripped open Colin's shirt.

He glanced briefly at the wound and saw that bullet had struck him high in the left abdomen, just below the ribs. It had penetrated cleanly through the fleshy upper region near the stomach.

The first thought in Andy's mind was the possibility of the rupture of a major artery. He allayed that concern—if it was so, Colin would have bled to death in seconds. He thought about the potential of infection if the stomach had been torn, but he pushed that from his mind. There wasn't enough bleeding to indicate either of those injuries. He pulled open the small personal medics kit on Colin's belt and handed the field dressing to Stuart.

'Turn him on his side,' he said, 'and hold these tightly over both wounds.'

He talked animatedly to calm Colin, and he removed the vial of Sosegon from the pouch on Colin's belt. The injured man stared at him through huge, frightened eyes.

'You'd better hit that vein first time, Sarge,' he said weakly. 'This thing hurts like hell.'

'Don't be a sissy,' said Andy in reassurance, though he knew that the injury wasn't light. 'It's just a scratch.'

He turned Colin's arm over and found a vein, into which he pressed the syringe needle. He withdrew slightly on the plunger and breathed an audible sigh of relief as the rush of crimson venous blood rushed into the bowl. He pressed down gently on the plunger, injecting the analgesic fluid into Colin's bloodstream, and almost immediately he sensed his friend's release of tension.

Stuart had prepared the Ringer's Lactate drip and handed the giving set to Andy. Again Andy looked for a vein into which he could insert the long plastic cannular, but this time he wasn't as lucky. All visible veins in Colin's arm had abruptly receded below the surface as the shock syndrome shut down the flow of blood through non-vital organs. Andy removed the army dog tags from around his neck and fashioned a tourniquet from the length of para cord to which they were attached.

All the time, the probing gunfire from the enemy position kept the tension at fever pitch, but the fire was going wide of their position and it was obvious that the troops in the camp were keeping the guerrilla forces under pressure.

Andy looped the tourniquet around Colin's upper arm and got Stuart to pull it up tight, while he rubbed vigorously up and down, intermittently using a slapping motion on the inside of the forearm. He was relieved to see a soft blue stripe emerge below Colin's skin, and he quickly pressed the venular into the site and checked for the blood rush into the feeding tube. Andy fed the cannular up into the vein and secured the drip tubing against Colin's arm and around his thumb with short strips of plaster.

Once he was satisfied that Colin was comfortable and stable, Andy got on the radio and requested an urgent casevac and the presence of a medic to take care of Colin.

We're going up the ridge,' he said into the radio. 'I'm leaving Colin here on his own and he's not armed, so get a couple of guys across here ASAP. Over.'

'Roger, copy that,' came the reply and Andy turned to Colin who lay resting in apparent comfort under the influence of the strong analgesic drug.

'You'll have company in a flash and a blur,' said Andy. 'You okay?'

'Just great,' slurred Colin dreamily. 'You guys go on ahead. Happy landings.'

The nervous tension was wound up tight in the guts of the small group and it wasn't helped by the ongoing bursts of enemy fire. These came dangerously close at times, crashing through their surroundings and making the team duck and wince.

'Let's go,' said Andy. The adrenalin held the knot in his stomach in a tight ball. He turned, and headed up the side of the hill.

It was a steep climb and they clawed at the undergrowth and trees to pull themselves up as they went.

Halfway to the summit they came under sustained fire that scattered them into surrounding cover, and Andy realised that their position had been compromised by the movement of the bush around them. Their climbing progress, using the shrubbery to gain purchase, was shaking the upper branches, attracting attention to themselves.

He did a quick assessment. He reasoned that if they headed west along the side of the ridge and got over the top further along, they could come back from the other side and get into a halfway decent position without being spotted again.

After thirty minutes of cautious and painstaking stalking over the rough terrain, the three reached the top of the ridge. Hidden behind rocky crags, they cautiously approached the apex from the north. There, they peered over the edge towards the eastern ridge where a well-organised enemy position had been set up, overlooking the camp.

From where they lay, flat on their stomachs, the position was 200 metres distant. They had a perfect view of the stronghold from where the ongoing, but now sporadic, mortaring and small-arms fire originated.

He heard the distinctive thump, thump of a 14.7mm heavy anti-aircraft machine gun being used as ground-to-ground fire, and from this vantage point he could identify its position.

Beyond and below, the camp where his comrades were still holding out was as clearly visible as an artist's canvas. He could see the positions of the scattered groups of defenders.

From the way in which the hostile position on the east ridge had been laid out, it was immediately obvious to Andy and the others that it hadn't been done at the last minute. This was an Alamo-style bastion that had been painstakingly established with attention to detail. It was neatly covered with Russian—or Chinese-issued camouflage netting that blended perfectly into its surroundings. The position was clearly set up to serve as a secondary station to which a withdrawal from the central camp could be effected, and counter-attacks launched. It was no wonder that it hadn't been picked up on aerial photography, or by the reconnaissance groups that had visited the camp clandestinely over the months during which this op had been in the planning stages.

Andy studied it carefully, and reflected. One thing was obvious—a glaring flaw. The entire structure on the east ridge was planned to be defensive, but it had no capacity for secondary defence. Although he and his small team had been detected approaching the area from the west, the guerrilla commanders had still not put out patrols to encounter them.

All of a sudden the purpose of this backup position dawned on Andy. He saw a small group of guerrillas slipping out and disappearing into the surrounding bush to the farther side, away from the admin base—and the obvious struck him. This was the command post for the hierarchy, who'd be kept out of danger. An escape route for the camp commanders!

Withdrawing into this carefully camouflaged compound the terrs could keep an attacking force busy in the camp below and provide plenty of time for the upper echelon to make good their escape—after which, the remaining combatants would gradually withdraw and disappear, eventually leaving the secondary base empty.

Because of the good camouflage it was difficult to establish numbers. However, judging by the slower rate of firing, it was clear that these had diminished significantly since the counter attack had first erupted nearly an hour before.

What puzzled Andy was why the guerrilla force manning this stronghold had chosen to expose themselves. If they had simply sat there and slipped away one by one, their escape would have been far more effective. It would have taken the Rhodesians days of intense searching to find this place if it hadn't been revealed to them. In fact, knowing nothing of its existence, they wouldn't even have undertaken a search.

He didn't have time to waste pondering on the folly of the enemy.

It was pointless, Andy realised, for him and his motley crew to make the same mistake and expose themselves to a far superior force by using their weapons. Instead he took his mortar range table from the map pocket on the leg of his denim fatigues and between the three of them they quickly worked out the exact direction and tube trajectory that his mortar crews would have to fire from. Then he got on the radio and spoke quietly into the handset.

'Zero alpha, this is two one. Do you read?'

'Go ahead, two one,' came the immediate reply.

'Roger, Zero alpha. We have clear view of well-camouflaged holding area. Terrs seem to be using it as an escape route while holding out counter-attack activity. Suggest rapid mortar on following co-ordinates. Ready to copy? Over.'

'Go ahead. Over.'

Andy gave the straight line direction from the admin camp and then the readings he'd calculated off his range chart. 'Over to you, guys. Fire at will. Over.'

Seconds later, eight mortar crews simultaneously dropped the 81mm bombs into their tubes. The indications that Andy's party had given placed the targets for the bombs to land in an area within twenty metres of each other, and each crew let go a volley of three bombs in quick succession.

It was all over within seconds, and the result was devastating. The 14.7mm gun took a direct hit from the first volley. The mangled steel was flung through the air, the gun's ammunition was detonated, and the gun team were killed outright. Other bombs fell over the entire area wiping out every living thing within a radius of 200 meters. Firing from the stronghold ceased with alarming abruptness, and a deathly hush descended over the position.

For a long time the three exhausted soldiers lay breathless and bewildered, grimly fascinated by the carnage that their efforts had wrought upon the now-defeated enemy.

They scanned the area, acutely alert for movement among the devastation on the opposite ridge, but none came. Andy suddenly became aware that an urgent voice was crackling through his radio handset, calling him:

'Two one, do you read? Over.'

He shook himself from his trance-like state.

'Go ahead,' he said quietly.

'Are all your chaps okay?' asked the voice.

'Affirmative.'

'Give us a brief sitrep. Over,' said the commander

'Seems to be total destruction. Over,' replied Andy shortly. He suddenly felt very tired.

'Roger that,' came the reply. 'Well done! Regroup your men. Sierra Bravo will be coming in to continue search. Over.'

Sierra Bravo was the phonetic description for Special Branch, a forensic section of Military Intelligence backed up by their own army of trackers and combatants.

As Andy, Stuart and Larry Dickson (the third member of the team) descended the hill they heard the distant drone of approaching helicopters, and they hastened their pace. They got back to the spot where they'd left Colin, and there were four other men standing nearby, peering anxiously across the clearing in the direction of the main camp area.

Colin lay with his eyes closed on a makeshift stretcher fashioned from two long branches, cut from a nearby tree, thrust through the in-turned sleeves of three buttoned-up combat jackets.

Andy approached his sleeping friend and knelt down beside him.

'He's dead,' said one of the four without looking around.

The words hit Andy like a physical blow.

'What?' He bent down, disbelieving, to feel for a pulse in Colin's neck. 'How, for heaven's sake? I was talking to him just over an hour ago and he seemed fine.'

'That's what I thought when we got here,' said the medic, turning and coming towards them. 'Then he started to gasp for breath and he died in seconds. I reckon his spleen got it. There was nothing I could do. I'm sorry.'

Andy had seen enough death in the field to know that if there'd been internal bleeding, especially from a ruptured spleen, out here in the middle of this wilderness and without the correct instruments, there was indeed nothing to be done. He looked down at the still form on the makeshift stretcher and reflected.

Colin was a young and vibrant soul. Andy had met his girlfriend Sharon several times, and she adored him. He wondered how her young life would be affected by this sudden departure of the man she loved. Colin was 22, in the prime of his life, and Andy's thoughts went to his parents. He wondered, not for the first time, what words the padre used when explaining the death of a young son to a mother.

He rose and turned away. He felt ill. The anger welled up inside him, but that was always his reaction when friends went down in action.

'You will lose friends in action,' had been Doc Morrison's words. 'And you will once again be called upon to think about your emotions. Control them. Never let your emotions control you.'

Andy took the helmet from his head and suppressed the urge to throw it to the ground and kick it. He leaned his back against the trunk of a tree and took several deep breaths. Then looked down at Colin again. He looked as though he was in a peaceful sleep. He even had a contented smile upon his lips. Andy bent down and took Colin's hand in his own.

'Adios, my friend,' he quietly said. Then he rose and turned, almost bumping into Stuart who stood behind him.

'Another one bites the dust, hey, Andy?'

'Won't be the last, Stu,' said Andy grimly as they moved away. 'Let's make sure he gets on the first chopper out of here.'

The whirr and clatter of rotor blades was overhead. Andy had to raise his voice to make himself heard. The first run of choppers were flaring for their landing in the open space in which Colin had seen the last seconds of his active young life.

The medic and his three mates lifted the makeshift stretcher and charged out across the open ground towards the nearest of the waiting aircraft, crouching double as they ran beneath the spinning rotors. They lifted Colin on board and then leaped in themselves. The noise of the rotors increased sharply and, amidst a storm of swirling dust and leaves, the chopper lifted off. It joined the formation of circling Allouettes as others came in and landed to uplift the first group of waiting troops before heading for home.

Andy, Stuart and Barry spread out and walked in extended line back towards what was left of the camp buildings and grass huts. It was getting late and clouds that had been forming in the east since early afternoon were now heavy thunderheads that hung over them like gigantic purple cauliflowers.

Bright flashes of sheet lightening and rolling thunder threatened the onset of heavy rain. This was a serious concern—it meant that the remainder of the ground forces might have to stay out overnight. The French-built troop-carrying Allouette helicopters did not possess on-board stability instruments and the pilots had to fly against the horizon, so the premature darkness of an incoming storm could hamper the airlift. None of those left on the ground cherished the thought of facing a regrouped enemy who would undoubtedly move in overnight.

The men who had been left behind to be picked up when the choppers returned were hurriedly picking up scattered files and papers, an exercise that had been abandoned when the counter attack had erupted from the hills. They were loading them into cardboard boxes that had been dropped in knock-down form by the choppers. Others were preparing explosive charges against the breeze-block buildings, while fuel was poured over what remained of the thatch of the grass huts.

The mission commander saw Andy and his team crossing toward the central area and he came forward to greet them.

'Good work, Andy,' he said solemnly. 'You guys were marvellous. Damn pity about Colin, but we saw what you did out there. It won't be forgotten.'

'Thanks, sir.' Andy spoke impassively. Then, on an impulse that came on him without knowing fully why, he asked:

'Have our chutes been recovered?'

'Yes. A back-up troop from the RLI came in behind us and collected them. What makes you ask?'

'Just a thought,' said Andy. 'This place will be swarming with reporters from newspapers all over the world by this time tomorrow. It's a racing certainty that most of them will want to make as much mileage over the attack as they can, and it just occurred to me that un-recovered parachutes will give them more to write about than they deserve.'

'You should be an officer, Sergeant,' said the commander, grinning. 'But we've got all that in hand.'

The helicopters returned an hour later, by which time the threatening rain had come. It was pouring down in a torrent of swirling sheets as though an angry God sought to wash away the carnage that had been wrought upon Chimoio. There was no shelter from the rain. For the troops awaiting uplift, being wet and cold against the onslaught of the elements was part of the job. Drenched, and up to their ankles in mud, they held their defensive cover positions ever alert against the possibility of another onslaught of enemy fire. But it never came.

The charges that had been laid were ready to be detonated. White phosphorus grenades, attached to the ring mains under the eaves of the thatch huts over which paraffin had been poured, would further ensure the total destruction of the encampment.

'This fire is going to burn hotter than the hell from which these bastards emerged,' promised the demolitions squad sergeant who'd been in charge of the fuse laying.

The helicopters landed in waves of three at a time in the open space behind the camp, the downward draft of their rotor blades swirling up the rainwater and spreading the mud puddles on the ground in a dense brown misty spray, covering the remaining troops in a coat of fine runny mud, adding to the discomfort of their sodden clothing and equipment. They clambered aboard and, as the last of them did so, the demolitions sergeant put a light from the glowing end of the cigar he had been smoking to the extremity of the safety fuse that was, in turn, attached to a cortex detonator.

The last of the choppers lifted off and turned for home. The ground receded rapidly beneath them, and at the same time the camp erupted. Despite the torrential downpour, it was transformed into an inferno as the network of explosive devices detonated.

The formation of helicopters droned homeward, and the troops reflected on the op. Despite the destruction, there was a significant failure: as far as could be established, not one of the high-ranking ZANLA officers, who were among the primary targets, had been accounted for. Andy wondered, not for the first time, if there was an early-warning bush telegraph system. Could it originate in the form of a traitor at Com-Ops in Salisbury? How else, he wondered, would they have had time to escape this meticulously planned surprise attack?

*　　*　　*

A few days after their return from the Chimoio op, Andy was summoned to the office of the squadron's commanding officer. He had spent the time granted as R and R with Alyson, and together they'd explored the mysteries of love and passion with an intensity that suggested that there would be no tomorrow.

'You've been put up for your Chested Wings,' said the CO. 'The reports of your performance during the op on Chimoio are very impressive. Com-ops have approved the recommendation. Congratulations. Your award will be presented as part of a ceremony at the officers' mess. The Prime Minister will be in attendance and will do the presentations, so in order that you can be there you've got a few more days off from ops.'

Andy and Alyson continued to make believe that there would be no tomorrow.

*　　*　　*

Dressed in full ceremonial greens, and with highly-placed dignitaries looking on, Andy stepped proudly up to the podium at the end of the long ornate dining room. He saluted the Prime Minister, who nodded his acknowledgement and pinned the coveted wings on Andy's chest. He shook Andy's hand and placed his other hand upon his shoulder.

'Thank you sergeant,' said the country's leader. 'Well done. Without young men like you, this country would have been fed to the wolves of anarchy a long time ago.'

Andy saluted again, made an abrupt about-turn, and marched off.

The citation read as follows:

> **Awarded to Andrew James Mason,**
> **The Honour of 'Wings on Chest' for gallantry in**
> **action above and beyond the call of duty.**
>
> *Whence upon the 27th day of November 1977 he risked his own life in an attempt to save that of a comrade, and thenceforth proceeded to lead a patrol and overrun an enemy position that posed life-threatening dangers to other comrades who had been pinned down by overwhelming enemy fire.*

The certificate was signed under seal of State and 'Coate'de Arms' by the Commander in Chief of Combined Operations and the Prime Minister.

'A bit over the top, isn't it, sir?' Andy asked the OC at the reception that followed. 'I tried for Colin, but the rest is really bullshit—don't you think?'

'Leave it as it lies, Andy,' replied the colonel. 'The recommendation was put forward by an officer who saw what you did and he used the words he thought appropriate.'

# CHAPTER 19

A ndy's memory of the operation two years previously and the subsequent award ceremony were clear to the last detail. He hadn't thought about these things for months—not until Chimoio had come up again in his discussion with Dawson.

'I take it they've rebuilt the place?' he said.

'Not on the same site,' replied Dawson. 'But, yes, the Chimoio base is once again functional. It's the obvious location for a command base. Nice and central, and within two days' walking distance of the border. They can get supplies and manpower in from ships docking at Beira and it's at a crossroads of well-maintained routes. The problem is that it's now a Frelimo military garrison and they are giving ZANLA sanctuary—which would put us at odds with the security forces of a sovereign state if we attacked again.

'That could get us into trouble with South Africa who are doing their darndest to keep some of our most fervent critics on-side. We can't upset our only allies, so we have to let it be. The most we can do is monitor what goes on there. The thing is, because of its importance, Mugabe visits Chimoio more regularly than he does any other facility.'

'So where do I fit in?' asked Andy.

'I've already told you. We've got some recent snatches that need a bit of subtle interrogation. You've done the course. Talk to them, listen to what they say and work out where they're lying, then extract the truth.'

'Sounds good to me,' said Andy. 'But, by the way, there's something you should know.' He paused for a moment, wondering how the revelation would rest with Dawson.

'Yes?' enquired the Major.

'Alyson is pregnant. We're planning a wedding. I think my career on active ops must be put to bed.'

He held up a hand as Dawson started to speak in protest.

'I know what you're going to say, sir—other guys out there are married, and their lives are constantly in danger. I've heard it all before. But, with respect sir, I've done my bit. If these upcoming talks amount to anything, that will change everything—and I think I owe something to what's going to be my new family.

'I need to be at home. I don't want Alyson lying awake every night with a moving baby in her tummy, wishing I was there to share that and never knowing if I'll be alive to do so. I'm happy to take on a desk job or be active in MI, and I'd be grateful if you'd support me.'

'So the war hero turns yellow?' Dawson tilted his head and raised an eyebrow.

'If that's the way you see it, sir,' said Andy, 'then that's the way it'll probably be told. I think the record may reflect differently. We aren't going to win this war, sir—not because we come up short on fighting skills, but because international politics will dictate the result. And that result will be declared over a table surrounded by half-wits who can't see the wood for the trees, and who probably don't have the time or the intelligence to work out the difference.'

Andy paused and locked eyes with Dawson.

Despite the difference in their respective ranks, Sergeant Mason and Major Dawson had learned to respect one another. Below 'Sir' and 'Sergeant' (although Dawson rarely called Andy by his rank), they'd become as close to friends as soldiers could, under the circumstances.

'There was a time, sir,' continued Andy, 'when I really believed that we had something to fight for. Otherwise, I'd probably never have got involved. I still think there's something more precious to fight for than most understand—but we are like babes in the crib. We can cry all we like and it'll be put down to colic.

'There'll be no winners in this war, sir, but as sure as hell is hot I no longer desire to be listed in ultimate statistics as a winning loser. I have a child on the way, and that's now my future. I don't see a similar future in getting my head blown to bits while the politicians decide who should get the badge. I'll give you everything I can outside of ops—and if that isn't good enough, I'll ask for a transfer to the medical training school where I can lecture troop medic students on field first aid.'

'Are you giving me an ultimatum, Andy?' asked the major. 'Because if that's what's happening here, you're finished.'

'You know me better than that, sir,' said Andy. "No! I'm trying to get across what I'm feeling—and what's now my reality. Lying in the dark on that last op, there was absolutely no doubt in my mind that I'd be dead by morning. It was pretty bloody scary and I've told you the story.

'I'm still trying to recover from the emotional impact—and I've also got a bloody hole in my guts. You know it's not the first time one of us has had that sense of doom. I turned it around, and the other fella got it instead. After that I spent seven terrifying hours dodging the grim reaper, but I lost four good friends in the process—and the guy who gave me all the support I needed to survive got taken out among them.

'I've now got good reason to keep out of death's way. If I were a religious or superstitious man, sir,' went on Andy reflectively, 'I'd be thinking that maybe the guy with the black hood and the scythe was bringing me a message. As in "I've got your mates and I'll take you any time I want, boyo, so piss off now before I change my mind". I'm not scared to go back out there, sir. I'd just rather be doing something else.'

'I'll put you down as medically unfit to undertake combat operations,' said Dawson. 'But I'm putting a condition on that. If I need you for clandestine work that does not include operational contacts but may still need an active brain to function on intelligence, or an undercover agent—internally or externally— you'll be assigned. Does that help the poor little bird with a broken wing?'

'The poor little bird with a broken wing holds the Eagle Major in high esteem,' said Andy, with an impish grin. 'But shall we get down to what is needed whilst the broken-winged mortal remains flightless?'

'I should have you done for insubordination, you prick!' But Major Dawson laughed and held out his hand to Andy. 'The guys will miss you on ops.'

'Not as much as I'll miss them,' said Andy quietly.

'Right. Let me fill you in. You will report to a man for whom I've got very little time, but he's part of the system in MI and Foreign Affairs. His name is Major Stuart Combrink. He's one of those guys with an overrated opinion of himself. He's got the unfortunate knack of pissing people off without even trying.

'He is, however, an expert on African affairs with a remarkable knowledge of the internal workings of both ZANLA and ZIPRA, and he controls a crew of clandestine informers. He also speaks both Shona and Ndebele with such fluency that if you spoke to him on the phone you would never know he was white. He could easily pass for a native of either tribe.

'He wants someone—who is now you—to update the construction of a profile that we already have on the support given by the Frontline States to ZANLA in particular, and the Patriotic Front in general. Information coming through suggests that their support base is dwindling because of the effect that this war is having on the economies of the countries concerned.

'They've long since become a risky burden to both the World Bank and the IMF, and we believe that the pressure's on from their sponsors for the Patriotic Front alliance to be agreeable to a settlement if they can get these talks underway. A political settlement to end this war is stick and carrot to both Mugabe and Nkomo, if they want to continue receiving support from outside.'

'Sounds simple enough,' said Andy. 'And pretty interesting.'

But he sensed that cracks were showing in the unquestioned confidence that his superiors had, thus far, placed in him. He'd got what he wanted, but he left the ops room feeling a great deal less than satisfied or certain.

# CHAPTER 20

ALYSON AND HER MOTHER HAD STARTED ON PLANS FOR THE WEDDING. They'd spoken to a dress designer, to caterers, to the hotel management at Meikles and to the Dean of St Michael's and All Angels Cathedral.

Andy, moving into his new role at Com-Ops headquarters in Central Salisbury, was blissfully unaware of this bustling activity. When they laid it all before him, he was astonished.

They were in the ornate lounge area of the Carstens' apartment on the Avenues. Mirrors covered the entire length and breadth of one wall, giving the room the appearance of being twice its size. The room was decorated in a modern African theme, with local paintings and hand-carved ornaments along with cowhide upholstery. The muted beige walls and thick carpeting quietly exuded warmth and success. A north-facing set of sliding glass doors led onto a spacious balcony, with a view over the groomed indigenous greenery of Monomotapa Park. The city rose up proudly in the background.

They put a beer into Andy's hand as soon as he entered, and he sipped while he listened to the arrangements with mounting irritation.

'Now, Andy,' said Jennifer, 'we need you to be in top hat and tails, and all the groomsmen to be dressed identically. We'll handle the hiring of the costumes. You just need to arrange for your guys—your entourage—to be available for fittings.'

'Excuse me,' he answered, 'but don't I have any say? For starters, I will not be wearing top hat and tails. I'll be wearing the ceremonial Greens of the Rhodesian Army. So will the only other member of my entourage, namely Alec Bradford, whom I've asked to be my best man. I've got no intention of bringing in a whole lot of additional people just to make the party look important.'

He put down his beer and squared up to Jennifer:

'Maybe I'd like to be involved in the arrangements. As an example, I'd like to be in on the choice of venue for this bash. Maybe I don't want a priest. Maybe I'd like to know the date. You know? All the usual stuff. I presume I'm invited, so why don't the two of you just slow down, and we can talk about it in an orderly and controlled fashion.'

'Andy,' said Alyson, 'we need to get this show on the road. I don't want to be showing my pregnancy when I walk down the aisle. Imagine what people will say!'

'Can you imagine what they'll say when you have a baby four months after you get married?' Andy retorted. 'These people aren't fools. The speed with which this ceremony's being arranged is going to raise eyebrows in the crystal glass society anyway. Let them think what they like. If you walk down the aisle with a nine-month-pregnant stomach on you, it's not going to make any difference to our lives. If anything, it would probably get us a whole cupboard full of free clobber for the kid, 'cause every one of your mom's mates will get out their knitting needles and start putting together booties and little baby-grow items.'

'I can't believe you're so flippant about this, Andy!' Jennifer smiled, but there was a distinctly impatient edge to her voice— something that Andy hadn't noticed in her before.

'Alyson's looked forward to her wedding day since she was a child,' spoke up Jennifer. 'We've planned it together for years, even though we had no idea who the lucky man would be. I always thought that you'd want to make it what her dreams were made of.'

Andy became aware, suddenly, of a change in attitude towards him, and he felt less than comfortable with it.

'Ladies,' he said, and his grin concealed a mounting concern, 'fairy tales are for little girls with big dreams. We are talking about two real grown-up people here, who are in love and who, from the fruit of that love, are expecting a baby. I think that's wonderful. If it happens in four months or four years, why should we be worried about what other people think? Frankly I think that Adam was a gay ape and Eve got screwed by an alien, which makes the morality of our entire existence is a little unsteady, so why are we so worried about Alyson having a bulge in her abdomen when she walks down the proverbial aisle to commit herself to a life of uninhibited sex with the man she loves? Am I missing something here?'

'We'd just like it to be a wonderful day, Andy, without silly raised eyebrows and whispers. What happens after that really doesn't matter,' said Jennifer. 'Please let us get on with it.'

Andy shrugged and put his hands up in a gesture of surrender. 'Just let me know when I'm needed.'

That night Andy dined with the Carstens' at the Royal Salisbury golf club, and despite the wrangle over wedding plans he felt a warm glow of affection for the people whose family he was to become part of.

After dinner, Ralph and Andy went out onto the terrace and strolled about smoking a cigarette. Andy thought that Ralph seemed to be pre-occupied, and he wondered what was on his mind. Then Ralph suddenly stopped and turned to face him.

'Andy,' he said, 'I'm delighted that you are the man in Alyson's life. I couldn't have wished for a more admirable son-in-law. But beware, son. I worry about what happens after the lust fades. We all think we're in love when the lust is at its peak, but what few of us realise is that lust is only the seed of love.

'If that seed germinates the love will blossom and last, which in turn will continue to feed the lust and when that's secure even tedium will keep people together.

'There's a lot of what's called romance—but if that's just a ravishing of each other's minds, bodies and souls to justify a physical need, things start to go horribly wrong when the romantic impulse fades.

'Alyson is the life blood of two people, Jen and I, who have survived our differences and who have stayed in lust with one another. That is so important. But Alyson is a spoilt child and an extension of the love that Jen and I share. You are going to have to learn to live with that Andy. She generally wants things her way and gets testy when that doesn't happen, so look after her. I'm sure she'll always be a wonderful mother to your children but believe me, I see in my daughter a demanding wife. A person who will look for what makes her happy, and even if she finds it she may not recognise it when it stares at her. She tends to be self-righteous and doesn't take to criticism easily, even if it's well meant and constructive. Finally, be aware that she will never admit to being wrong. She may know she is, her conscience will tell her that she's wrong, but she will never ever admit to it and will invariably try to pass the fault onto someone else. So you've got your work cut out, son.'

'It sounds as though you're trying to discourage me here, Ralph!' Andy wanted to laugh it off.

'Not at all,' replied Ralph. He raised his brow and cocked his head. 'You've made your bed—you'll have to lie in it. I'm just giving you some upfront inside information—an early warning— that you might need to keep in your armoury.'

'I think we can handle it, Ralph,' said Andy with an indulgent grin. 'We've been more than friends to each other for over a year without an angry word so far. I'm pretty sure we can keep that up.'

'It's over to the two of you, and I promise we won't interfere in your lives,' Ralph replied, 'but anytime either of you need to offload onto an understanding ear, just call. We'll be there for both of you.'

'Thanks Ralph. I'll keep it mind.'

They shook hands, and Andy realised that he was being obliquely but very clearly warned—about something. Something that Ralph knew all about, but which Andy was yet to learn.

There was much more that Andy had yet to learn, and this arose from his new duties at Com-Ops HQ. The problem arose with his new commanding officer.

Each day that Andy got to know Major Combrink better, he got to like him less. The Major was a constant source of irritation, who hung around like an obstinate fly. Every time Andy thought he'd got rid of the man, he'd reappear with more questions as to progress that Andy was making, and the more Combrink hung around asking questions, the less work got done. Andy developed the feeling that the man couldn't be trusted. It almost seemed as if he was obstructing progress, rather than assisting in its advance.

# CHAPTER 21

## SALISBURY 1979

THE CEREMONY MARKING THE OCCASION OF ANDY MASON'S MARRIAGE TO ALYSON CARSTENS came duly to pass, in all social perfection. It was an event on which no expense was spared. Jennifer and Alyson, with the help of the bridesmaids, had organised every detail. Andy had been kept up to speed on the arrangements, but he played very little part in these.

He arrived at the church, with Alec as his best man, both dressed in ceremonial greens. Two handsome young men who had seen it all, and looking every bit the soldiers that they were, they drew admiring stares from the assembled guests.

Andy was standing at the front of the Cathedral nave, close to the altar, when Alyson arrived. She nearly took his breath away as she walked up the aisle towards him on Ralph's arm, and his heart pounded with admiration. She looked thoroughly gorgeous in a flowing white dress that was mostly fine lace over a cotton bodice. The bodice lifted her breasts and brought stares of envy from the ladies and approval from the men.

Before the gathered company, they shared their vows. Andy invested his heart and soul into these, with such purpose and intensity that it felt like they were tattooed into his being.

The guests then walked, with the shared gaiety of the occasion, across Cecil Square from the Cathedral to the Meikles Hotel. The newlyweds were driven the short distance in Ralph's Daimler with flapping ribbons that ran from the bonnet mascot to the side windows. Andy was as happy as he could ever remember, and the passion and pride surged in his chest broadening his understanding of the love that he felt for his bride.

'You know what, Ali?' he asked during their short ride across the square.

'No, but I think you're about to tell me,' said Alyson with a mischievous grin.

'If the whole world froze over,' he whispered, 'I'd be able to warm it up again from what I feel in my heart right now. I love you.'

And he felt it in every cell of his being.


Dinner was served in the ornate ball room of Rhodesia's most renowned, most venerable hotel. The speeches were done, and the traditional throwing of garter and bouquet was performed.

Alyson and Andy retired to the honeymoon suite. Andy, according to ancient custom, carried his bride across the threshold and they fell happily into each other's arms.

'Hello Mrs Mason,' said Andy. 'Would you like to have an affair with a married man?'

'Without a doubt,' replied Alyson with a delighted giggle. 'I've never been to bed with a married man before. This'll be a first.'

They laughed. They held each other in a passionate embrace of tongues, and they giggled like school kids as they whispered erotic suggestions to each other and explored the contours of their bodies through the fabric of their clothing.

Andy undressed Alyson slowly. He removed the flowing wedding gown and caressed her gently through her undergarments. He savoured every touch of her, and their arousal for each other was immense. They finally lay naked upon the bed, and he gently stroked Alyson from her breasts to her stomach and down below her waist to fondle her vagina. They were both beside themselves with desire and their orgasms came simultaneously almost as Andy entered her.

They lay together, softly whispering words of love and of plans for the future, and then slowly they made love again, this time letting it draw out, teasing each other and smothering each other with mouth and tongue in between their sighed ecstasy.

Andy thought his entire soul was on fire with the burning love he felt.

They'd come up to the room just after ten, but it was after twelve by the time they lay happily asleep in each other's arms, the warmth of their passion within and upon them in their restfulness.

At two am the telephone on the table beside the bed jarred them awake.

"Who the hell can that be," moaned Andy as he reached his arm across to answer it. It was not unusual for him to be called at his digs at ridiculous hours, but this was his wedding night and he was on leave. No-one knew where to reach him. It occurred to him that it was probably some of the lads, having had too much to drink, calling to check on progress, and he was ready to unleash some barrack-room profanities on them.

'Mr Mason?' enquired an urgent voice at the other end.

'Who is this? Do you know what time it is?'

'I'm sorry to disturb you, sir. This is Superintendent Charles Wilcox from Salisbury Central. I'm afraid I have some rather bad news.'

Andy's immediate thoughts were that his pals had got out of hand and that he was being called to bail them out. It wouldn't have been the first time. He was about to say that the buggers could sit and rot, but Wilcox went on immediately:

'Mr And Mrs Carstens have been seriously injured in an ambush on the Mazoe road. I'm afraid neither of their conditions is promising, I think you and your wife should get across to Andrew Flemming.'

Andy was up in bed, with the phone clasped to his ear. He didn't want to believe what he was hearing.

'How did you reach us?' he asked.

'Some of the guests at your wedding were on the road, following them—going up to their farm for the weekend. They're fine—just badly shaken. They told us where to reach you.'

Ralph had told Andy that they were going to drive back to the farm after the wedding. Andy's response was that they should rather stay overnight in town—but it was a passing matter, not to be harped on. Ralph and Jennifer did the trip so often that he'd given it no more thought.

'Shit!' he swore.

'What is it, Andy?' Alyson sat up in the bed. 'What's happened?'

Andy didn't know what to say. He had given out bad news in the field a thousand times and thought nothing of it, but this was something utterly different.

'Ali,' he said at last, 'there's been an ambush and your folks are hurt. Slightly.' He hoped the lie wasn't as obvious as it felt. 'That was the police and we need to get to the hospital.'

'*Oh no! God, no!*' Something seemed to snap inside Alyson. Andy held her in his arms.

This was *deja vu,* and the long-gone memory came back at him like a whiplash—trying to console Merryl, under similar circumstances, so long back.

'Don't panic, Ali,' he said. 'I'm sure they're alright.'

They dressed in a frenzy and raced down to where Andy had left his car. It was adorned with balloons and ribbons and tin cans, with sexually suggestive slogans and images in shoe whitener plastered over just about every inch of the paintwork. They barely noticed the decorations as they leapt into the car and raced up through the deserted town to the hospital, dragging the cans and a trail of sparks behind them.

They were directed to the emergency ward. Here, in an ante-room, were the couple, Harold and Julia Fox who had been behind the ambushed vehicle. Julia rushed across to embrace Alyson, who was pale and shaking with anxiety.

'What's happened?' she demanded. Her tears were barely concealed.

Harold took the lead, and Andy thought that he probably didn't trust his wife to be adequately tactful or calm. 'Panic breeds panic,' he thought wryly.

'Alyson, your parents have both sustained several gunshot wounds. The doctors are with them and are doing what they can. I'm afraid we can only wait.'

Alyson sank into a chair. Her eyes were red and puffy, her hair in a tangle and she looked nothing like the stunning bride that had walked down the aisle toward Andy only hours earlier.

'How long have they been here?' she demanded. She raised her head and looked accusingly at Harold.

'We've been here for just over half an hour,' he replied. 'But we were out on the road for nearly three hours. There wasn't much activity, as you'll appreciate. It was ages before a police patrol vehicle came by. By then they'd both lost quite a bit of blood, and that seems to be the problem. None of the injuries is in itself terribly serious, but we couldn't stop the bleeding.'

Despite a huge effort at emotional control, Harold's voice was an octave above normal. He was holding back tears.

Alyson's head sank down into her hands. She sat there visibly shaking as if out on a cold winter night without a coat. Andy sat beside her with his arms around her shoulders, murmuring that it would be alright.

'They're in good hands, darling,' he said soothingly. 'These guys deal with gunshot wounds and trauma every day of their lives and they know what they're doing. Trust me, I know.'

Alyson said nothing. She sat and shivered and rocked from side to side like a mechanical doll.

Andy had seen it more times than he cared to remember. Soldering had taught him how to handle such situations confidently—with the kind of reassuring banter that would buoy the confidence of a downed comrade. But that was in the army— that's what they expected. This was Alyson's parents, and she'd never understand a casual comment such as 'Come on you sissy, it's a flesh wound! Dry your eyes—we'll have you out of here and back with mommy in no time'—even when it was obvious that a leg or an arm would be lost, or life itself.

The four of them kept silent vigil, hoping for word from the operating theatres. They sat, dozed, walked around, and paid numerous visits to the coin-operated coffee machine. No-one wanted to speak, and Andy walked Alyson in and out of the waiting room and around the sparsely lit gardens. The hours ticked by, and the eastern sky gradually came alive with dawn.

Andy's hope was rapidly fading. He knew how long it took to stabilise trauma patients who could be saved. Those who were either not responding or could not be kept stable for this long, invariably did not make it. He was fearful of how Alyson would react if his guesswork was correct. She had never dealt with anything like this, and her parents were the best friends she had. He'd never known such a closely-knit family.

Shortly before seven, by which time the sun had risen well above the horizon, the doors to the operating area were swung open. A sombre-looking doctor emerged, removing his surgical cap and mask as he approached.

'We lost him, I'm afraid,' he said. 'I'm sorry. He'd lost far too much blood by the time we got him in. We had him on a respirator and hoped that we could get his blood pressure up before his heart went into arrest. We did all we could—but, as is sometimes the case, I'm afraid it wasn't enough. I'm very, very sorry.' His voice was burdened with genuine distress.

Alyson rose from her chair and stared at the doctor in disbelief. The look of absolute denial was unmistakable. It was as if she knew it wasn't true—and therefore to be discounted. She simply stood and shook her head, her eyes like a woman in a hypnotic trance.

Andy gently put his arms around her, and led her back to her seat. Then he turned to the doctor:

'Can you prescribe a sedative for my wife?' I think she needs it.'

'Of course. I'll get something right away.'

As the doctor hastened down the corridor towards the dispensary, Andy heard someone call his name. He looked up to see another doctor gesturing from the door of the operating room. He rose and followed the man into the theatre area, letting the swing doors flap closed behind him.

'I'm Dr Corbet,' said the gowned surgeon. 'Miles Corbet. I'm afraid Mrs Carstens has slipped into a coma. Her chances of survival are extremely slim. Do you think you could break that to her daughter?'

Andy was devastated. Surely this was some sort of nightmare, from which he would awake and find Alyson sleeping peacefully beside him in their honeymoon bed? He knew that it wasn't so, but he wished to God that it was. Life had taken another nasty turn. He instinctively knew that the bliss and harmony he'd so looked forward to in his new life would be a long time coming.

Alyson's reaction was like one Andy had never witnessed. She started to moan like a wounded heifer, with loud mooing sounds. She pulled and snatched at her clothing. Then she screamed a blood-curdling maniacal bellow and, rising from her seat, made a dash for the operating room. Dr Corbet stopped her in his widespread arms, and she clawed at him with her finger nails.

'Let me go!' she screamed. 'Let me go!'

Her strength was that of a madwoman, and she shoved the doctor aside. Andy caught up with her. He seized her from behind, around her waist, and he lifted her from the floor. He held her aloft as she kicked and screamed her defiance, arms flailing and fists beating at the air.

Nursing staff and doctors rushed towards them, one holding a syringe with a clear fluid in the bowl, and as Andy struggled to restrain his new wife, the doctor plunged the needle into her upper arm through her sleeve. Her frenzied resistance continued, but within seconds Andy felt her weakening as the sedative took effect.

He laid her down on one of the long cushioned leather couches in the waiting room and continued to hold her as her struggles became weaker and weaker. She finally stopped struggling and lay weeping pathetically in a semi-consciousness state.

'God!' he said, looking up at the anxious doctor who'd administered the sedative, 'What can we do?'

'I think we'll have to admit her for observation,' said the doctor. 'That sort of reaction suggests symptoms of dormant dementia which could be dangerous.'

Alyson was heavily sedated and placed in an observation ward for the rest of that day and overnight. Andy remained by her side without sleep for the entire period. In her brief spells of wakefulness, he spoke soothingly to her, letting her know how much he cared, trying to get her to come to terms with the tragedy.

He knew that it wasn't an easy task, but he spoke of their future together and how he would be there for her no matter what. The promise was made, a bond of heart and of honour— but, when he made it, he had no idea just what he was sentencing himself to.

# CHAPTER 22

R alph Carstens' funeral was attended by hundreds of mourners. He had been a pillar of society. He was well respected throughout commerce and industry in Rhodesia, over and above his standing in the agricultural sector.

Jennifer had always been at his side and, together, they'd enjoyed a reputation in Salisbury society which was admired, respected and in some cases envied. But now Ralph was dead and Jennifer, in the fifth day of her coma, looked more and more like joining him in that final shared experience.

Those who had revered them in life came in multitudes to pay their last respects.

Alyson emerged from the hospital the day after her father's death, pale and haggard and in a state of pitiable grief and withdrawal. Her normal ready smile and quick humour were gone. She was mantled in a cloud of deep and dark anger that Andy hadn't believed possible in her.

The newly-weds checked out of the Meikles Hotel and moved back to Alyson's apartment on the Avenues, but Alyson insisted on spending the days at the hospital close to her mother. Andy knew that she was dying, but nonetheless he continued to encourage and reassure Alyson.

He stayed by her side, taking care of her every wish. He allowed her to snap at him without comment.

He tried getting her outdoors, to walk in the vast hospital grounds, but she had no interest or inclination to do anything other than to sit at Jennifer's bedside, staring blankly at the

IAN MACKENZIE

shrivelled figure behind the oxygen mask, with tubes and monitors protruding from a dozen locations on her body.

On the twelfth day, Jennifer died.

Andy and Alyson were at her bedside. The steady bleep of the heart monitor to which she was wired suddenly altered to a series of rapid stutter like sounds and then returned to normal. Alyson rang for the duty nurse who was already emerging from the sister's station of the intensive care unit.

As the nurse approached, Jennifer opened her eyes and raised her head. She looked around and smiled compassionately at Alyson. Then she lay back, closed her eyes again, and the monitor went blank with a single flat green line across it emitting a long uninterrupted high pitched hum. Nurses and doctors went into a flurry of activity around the bed. Andy and Alyson were rapidly escorted away and the screens around Jennifer's bed were drawn closed.

Less than five minutes later, the doctor emerged and told them that nothing more could be done.

The change in Alyson's general demeanour had been so abrupt and profound before Jennifer died that Andy was tempted to believe that she had been hiding a psychopathic identical twin sister—that she'd now surreptitiously swopped places with that person. After Jennifer's death she became worse, and Andy felt as though he was living in the presence of someone he did not know. A stranger with characteristics alien to anything related to the Alyson he fallen in love with and married.

'Darling, Andy said, a few days after Jennifer's funeral, 'sooner or later we are going to have to come to terms with this. I know that it's the worst thing that could ever happen to anyone— but it's reality and we have to face it.'

'Who's "we", Andrew?' snapped Alyson. 'They weren't your parents—they were mine. They were the most important people in my life and they've been taken away without even having time to say good bye. You have no idea what that means and you never will—so don't think you can make yourself a part of what I feel.'

Andy was stunned.

'Alyson,' he said cautiously, 'do you know what you're saying? I knew your parents well enough to be very fond of them. I'm grieving for them more than you can imagine, so don't block me out of what has happened. My God, Alyson! We're a married couple now. Your problems are mine—we're in this together for better or for worse. Don't you understand that?'

'I understand that I have to re-evaluate my life,' she replied. 'My parents have always been there and they're a huge part of who I am—and now I'm alone with . . . .'

'You're not alone, Alyson,' Andy broke in. 'I'm here. I'm with you and together we'll get through this.'

'You don't seem to understand, Andrew.' She had never called him Andrew before the wedding, but she was now making a habit of it. 'My parents were my flesh and blood. You're an outsider, who until two years ago I'd never even heard of. How are you going to replace what I've lost? You have a family of your own and they're all very much alive. I have nothing.'

Andy was startled and offended by her outburst. It felt as if she blamed him for their situation and resented the fact that it had not been his parents who'd been killed. He started to get angry. He walked across the room, taking a deep breath, before he turned back and replied:

'What do you suppose marriage is all about, Alyson? Do you suppose the baby you are carrying isn't our flesh and blood? Don't you think of us as a family? How can you separate issues between us into "yours and mine"? It is *us,* Alyson, you and me and the baby. Don't go trying to build a camp of your own that sets us apart.'

'Andrew,' she said, raising her voice, 'we've been married for exactly fourteen days. How can you possibly think of yourself as my family?'

It was a slap in the face. Those fourteen days had been long and devastating and he'd had to bite down hard on his teeth to remain calm and compassionate. He was in two minds as to whether he should walk out and leave her with her anger in the hope that she'd get over it and show some common sense and reason by the time he returned, or if he should stay and help her get through it. He did know that he had never felt as helpless or as absurdly unsure of his situation as he felt at that moment. He was very uncomfortable with it. If this was the life of a married man, he wanted none of it.

Looking at Alyson, he pondered his options. She sat in an armchair, her head back and turned to the side, eyes closed and with a clenched fist resting upon her forehead.

He made up his mind.

He crossed the room and sat on the armrest of her chair. He put his arm around her with the intention of showing affection and care, but she shrugged him off. She rose from the chair as if trying to get away from a venomous snake.

'Just leave me alone, Andrew,' she said bitterly. 'I can't stand your pawing. It makes me uncomfortable.'

The anger in Andy rose almost to the surface, but he controlled it.

'Okay, Alyson,' he said calmly. 'I'm going to leave you to get over this. I'm clearly not helping, so I'll be at Milton Buildings. You can reach me there if you need me.'

And he turned to leave.

'That's it!' shouted Alyson as he strode towards the door. 'Walk away. Leave me on my own with your illegitimate child squirming about in my belly, while I mourn the death of people you couldn't give a damn about!'

Andy was stopped in his tracks.

'Have you lost your mind?' he asked, incredulously. 'Do you expect me to stand here and be kind and loving and at the same time listen to your ludicrous insults and abuse? I think you need help, Alyson. You're not the person you were before our wedding—and you're as sure as hell not behaving like the person I fell in love with. Let's get that person back here and move forward, and work things out together—or let's acknowledge that she was an illusion and put an end to this. I love you, Alyson, and I want to help you, but you're making it almost impossible for me to do so.'

Andy was in a state of cold anger and shock. He could find no words to describe his emotions, nor could he understand the change in Alyson. He thought wryly of the legendary phrase 'Wind of Change,' reflecting that it applied as profoundly to the personalities of the people it affected as it did to the circumstances under which their lives had changed.

'This is a raging bloody storm,' he thought, as he left the apartment with Alyson yelling after him that if he went, he needn't bother to come back.

As soon as Andy got to his cubicle at Com-Ops, he phoned Squadron Headquarters. He gave his name and rank and asked to be put through to Doc Morrison.

'Sir,' he said when the doctor came on the line, 'I have a problem. Can I see you?'

'Come on over, Andy,' responded Morrison cheerfully. 'I'll put on a brew.' He hesitated momentarily and then, with a laugh in his voice, added: 'Would you like that from the fridge or the kettle?'

'Your call, sir. I just need to offload.'

On the record, Andy was still on leave. In other circumstances he would have been wrapped in the arms of passion and lust as one side of a happy honeymoon couple, but events had rotated reality from an exquisite dream to a terrifying nightmare and he knew that he was not going to cope with it unless he got outside advice.

'Dormant dementia?' Morrison reflected. I don't think so. This is typical of someone who has to face the reality of tragedy. Someone who has probably never understood the true meaning of the word, nor the fact that it happens collectively to people around the world on a daily if not hourly basis. Living within the confines of our cities in this beautiful country, where people like Alyson and most other women don't get to see the blood and guts that is being spilt out in the bush, they don't think too much about the truth of war. They're complacent and ignorant of the fact that every day people have to come to terms with what Alyson is facing. In her mind she's unique in her suffering. She doesn't feel other people's pain. So as far as she's concerned, it does not exist."

Morrison paused and looked away, creasing his brow with one eye half closed. Then he turned back to Andy:

'I can't make any promises, Andy, but I think I could try to make her understand. Do you think she'd come to trauma counselling? We have regular sessions for wives and girlfriends of the guys who return from ops in body bags. She might get a better understanding of the way things are if she were to attend and realise that she's in the company of people in the same boat.'

'I'm not sure,' said Andy. 'At this stage I get the impression that in her mind I'm to blame and if the problem's going to be fixed, the results should be immediate and the responsibility is mine.'

'She's right, Andy,' said the doctor. 'Not that you're to blame, but that you are going to have to fix the problem. If you don't, you're either going to have to live with it or leave her on her own—and that, my son, could lead to further tragedy. Bite the bullet, Andy. Help her. Understanding and sympathy are what she needs now, although she probably doesn't know it yet because she's on her own private island of grief.

'Metaphorically speaking, she can't even see the shoreline of reality from where she is, so you are going to have to swim out to her and gently coax her back.

'At the moment she's fighting off your calls across the void because psychologically you are seen as an intruder—but, nonetheless, you remain the most accessible beacon of distress to fall upon. Unfortunately, we do that. Stay with it, Andy. Be patient and allow her space and time. She'll come around, then we can deal with her trauma.'

'Doc,' said Andy, 'she's nearly three months pregnant. Morning sickness gets her throwing up after breakfast which probably doesn't help either. Do you think this trauma could affect the baby?'

'That's not really my field, Andy. A paediatrician might be a more appropriate authority to consult on that. But, yes, I'd imagine that a highly strung traumatised mother could have an effect on the health of an unborn infant.'

'Thanks, Doc,' said Andy, and he rose to leave.

The hand-written message, scribbled by one of the orderlies and left on Andy's desk from Alyson, was terse and to the point.

'Going out to the farm. I need to be alone.'

It sent a tingle of alarm up his spine, and he grabbed the telephone and called the apartment. At first he thought he'd missed her, but after what seemed like forever she answered.

'Hello!' The greeting was abrupt and angry—as if from someone who'd been unnecessarily interrupted in the middle of a difficult but important task.

'Alyson,' he said, 'don't do anything stupid. I'm on my way back and you and I need to talk and be together. Please, just stay where you are until I get there. Please!'

He heard her sigh into the phone. Then she said, quite calmly, 'Don't you dare walk out on me when I'm talking to you. If you had any guts you'd stand up and take what I have to say to you like a man.'

'I'm not your parent's murderer, Alyson,' he said. 'And if you think you can talk to me as if I were, I'm afraid you're mistaken. I will stand with you every step of the way and grieve with you and work through this terrible tragedy, but I'll not be spoken to as if it were I who pulled the triggers of those weapons. There, I walk away. Now just sit down and wait for me. I'm on my way.'

He replaced the receiver before she could respond and raced down the stairs, stopping at the security counter to sign out. It was a Saturday afternoon and what traffic there was didn't hold him up, and he drove as fast as he dared through the city streets to the apartment.

As he drove into the basement parking, Alyson was driving out. He swerved his car across the path of hers and forced her to a screeching halt.

'I asked you to wait for me!' he shouted at her as he climbed from his vehicle. 'What the hell are you trying to do? Get yourself killed as well?'

Alyson simply sat behind the wheel of her car as Andy approached. She opened the driver's door.

'Come on, Alyson,' he pleaded. 'This is getting us nowhere. Let's go down to the mess and have a few drinks. Doc Morrison says he'd like to see you.'

'Oh! So now you've got me fixed up with a bloody shrink, have you?' There was malice in her voice. 'Well, you can go to hell . . . .'

She paused, and looked up at Andy. She held his gaze for all of a long minute, during which neither of them spoke. And then, suddenly, she began to cry.

'Andy, I don't know what's happening to me,' she said through her tears. 'I think I'm going mad. Please help me.'

Andy thought his heart was going to break as he reached into the car to embrace her. 'That's what I'm trying to do darling,' he said soothingly. 'But you'll have to help me to help you'. Like I said, we're in this together.'

He gently guided her out of the car and around to the passenger seat. Then he got behind the wheel and reversed the vehicle back to her parking bay. He removed the keys and went to retrieve his own car and parked it beside hers and then gently led her up the stairs and back to the apartment. There, he poured her a drink and put her favourite ABBA audio tape into the stereo set in an attempt to draw her out.

'I can't stay here, Andy,' said Alyson some time later as he sat beside her on the small sofa in their lounge. The tension was still thick in the air between them, but Andy tried as best he could to ignore it. He listened as she went on:

'I can't stay in a country that is populated by murdering barbarians and where it's not safe to travel to one's own farm without the risk of being murdered.'

'So what do you want to do, Ali?' he asked. 'This is the country of your birth. I still have a contract with the army. You are the heiress to properties and a complicated estate that needs to be settled. It's not that easy to just pack it all in and leave. Besides, where do we go? Back to South Africa?' He looked at her with a sceptically raised eyebrow and cocked his head, as he continued.

'The political climate down there is as volatile as it was here at the beginning of the war. The heat being applied to the politicians is starting to make the kitchen a very uncomfortable place. The economy is feeling the pinch and the apartheid laws will sooner or later lead to all-out violence unless an alternative solution is found. I don't see us better off in South Africa than we are here. In fact I'd say we have the edge in this country. This war is going to come to an end soon, Ali. The intelligence coming through is that the bad guy's sponsors are getting restless and can't afford to keep it up. Frankly, neither can we.

'The South Africans, who are our only allies and support, are backing off under pressure from governments in Europe and the United States and it's an economic impossibility for Rhodesia to continue without them. It's also a reality that none of the so-called front line states can continue to support or harbour the gooks—the whole thing's becoming far too damaging for them, and those governments want to see an end to this war. So it's stalemate.

'These negotiations at Lancaster House are going to have to be conclusive and settle things one way or the other. Maybe someone should have thought of this before we started killing each other in the name of freedom—but it's near the end now.'

'And what do you suppose will happen after that, Andrew?' asked Alyson bitterly. Without waiting for a response, she went on quickly:

'None of the parties other than our present government will settle for anything less than total control and equality across all population groups, and in the African culture there are those who are more equal than others. No way will our present rulers be able to talk their opponents into letting them have any say in the future of the country. It'll make a joke of this whole sad murderous fiasco and in the wake of what's happened over the past seven years there'll be many a score to settle in the "African way"'.

'If the Congo, Mozambique, Angola and other African independence "success stories" are anything to go by, we'll probably all be raped and butchered in our beds once those savages are no longer stopped from coming into the cities.'

Andy listened as she spoke. Although he had been made acutely aware of her grief, anger and loathing over the death of her parents, he was surprised at the vehemence of her views. He was taken aback at her evident scepticism, her assumption that the inevitable black rule in the country would spell the death-knell for civilised norms.

Her perception of the future once the hostilities that had caused so much misery came to an end astounded him. They'd frequently spoken about the war and the political background to it, although there was an unspoken acceptance of classified confidentiality. Andy's involvement in operational activities had never been discussed. She never asked questions and Andy never volunteered information that would lead to speculation or more questions. He had assumed up until then that she harboured no malice or racial prejudice. On the subject of a future black government to rule the country that would inescapably have its name changed to Zimbabwe, she had expressed the same concerns as most others in the privileged white community. This outburst emerged as another uncharacteristic side of Alyson.

'We'll have to wait and see, Ali,' said Andy thoughtfully. 'If total equality is a pre-condition to a settlement, then protection of minority groups will be a counter-condition. That protection, certainly in the short term, will have to be in the form of a monitoring force made up of either British and American troops or United Nations peacekeepers. The movers and shakers of so-called World Peace certainly won't allow any of the currently hostile groups to have total control. None of those hypocritical Western politicians who have bent over backwards to see a revolutionary government in this country will want to see their predictions of prosperity for all groups go up in smoke—nor will they want the remnants of the white government here being in a position where they can cock a snoot at them and say "I told you so." They know from experience that this will probably happen if they just wash their hands after an agreement is reached. So, whatever the outcome, there's bound to be a balance of control and consequently a balance of power. I somehow can't see any agreement being reached without that being entrenched.'

'So what makes us different from the rest of Africa?' sneered Alyson. 'Where were the US and British troops or United-bloody-Nations peacekeepers when Kenya went, or Tanganyika or Mozambique or Angola? Where were all these wonderful Western benefactors keeping the scales of opportunity and power in balance?'

Then she turned and looked straight at him, and Andy was physically shaken by the look of loathing and contempt in her eyes.

'Who will bring back my parents after all this crap at Lancaster House is thrashed out and agreed upon? Can you tell me that?'

Andy stared at her for a moment, gathering his thoughts. Her prejudice ran far deeper than he'd realised. He tried to reason with her:

'Who will bring back all the civilian casualties of the Blitz or the Holocaust, Ali? They were casualties of war as much as your folks—but life goes on. Looking back doesn't take you forward.'

'At least the swine responsible for the World War II atrocities were brought to book and punished. The murdering savages in this case will be given a hero's welcome by the rest of the world when they set foot on Rhodesian soil, and our lads, yourself included, will probably have to run for their lives.'

'Ali,' said Andy patiently, 'we've been fighting a war. People get killed in wars and although we think of ourselves as the good guys in this one, that view is not universally shared. We have to accept that we have collectively killed thousands more of the bad guys than they have killed of us. There are mothers, wives and daughters from the other side who hate us as much as you hate them. Think about it. This war was caused by racial injustice and although there are cultural issues that we need to protect, there has to be a compromise sooner or later and that will be the only solution. To keep this war going is just inviting more death and destruction and eventually there will only be losers because everything we've been fighting for will go up in smoke.'

'You've been in the forefront of fighting the bloody terrorists for over five years, Andrew,' spat Alyson. 'Don't sit here and get all politically liberal with me. How can you sit there and be so damn full of excuses for them?'

'I'm not making excuses, Ali, but I'm smart enough to face reality.' Andy breathed deeply, and continued:

'I'm not fooled by the rhetorical bullshit that gets burbled forth by those who say that they resorted to violence in order to secure a better life for all and that life will go on as normal but on the basis of equal opportunity.

'I'm also not fooled by the fact that the British have pledged huge sums of money toward the reconstruction of the country.

'Believe me, once this place is handed over to Mugabe or Nkomo or whoever emerges the political victor, it will become just another African state and all the poor bastards who have given their lives in the name of an elusive "freedom" will have a big monument erected in their honour.

'Those more fortunate will be sent back to the farms or schools from where they were abducted in the first place, their sacrifice forgotten, and the hierarchy will line their pockets with the proceeds of the country's wealth.

'The more progress, the more wealth—so it will be in the interests of whoever fills the seat of government to keep the producers of that wealth comfortable for as long as they are being watched or at least until there is an alternative source of wealth or—and this is the more likely scenario—until there's no more wealth because of corruption, fraud and theft and the white man's usefulness has been outlived.

'We can stand on our heads, plan a coupe and take out whoever comes to power; we can think of a hundred things we could do, but none of it will help because none of it is reality.

'We are going to lose this war for reasons of economics and across a conference table, not on the battlefield. The outcome of that conference will be reality.

'We can hate it, we can scream "unfair", we can mourn and grieve, but at the end of the day we've got to face reality.

'As we speak, there are opposing forces out in the bush trying their darndest to come up with a way to weaken the other side and strengthen their own hand as much as possible in the futile hope that they can score some sort of advantage that will give them a trump card to play in the negotiating process. For as long as that lasts, young people and old on both sides will continue to die for their cause, while others get caught in the cross-fire.

'Once a monitoring force is in place and we are able to see where we are headed, that will be the time for us to decide what we are going to do with our lives as individuals.'

Andy finished, but he realised that Alyson had stopped listening. It was becoming increasingly obvious that she took no interest in what he said.

'Like talking to a bloody wall,' he thought. He looked at her, reflecting, and then he said:

'Ali, will you go and see Doc Morrison? They have group sessions for people who are trying to come to terms with tragedy—mostly women. I'm sure you won't regret going.'

'I don't need a shrink, Andrew!' she snapped. 'I just need time, and of that I have plenty. Why don't you go back to your war games and let me deal with what's in my heart?'

Andy felt as though his fortitude was being steadily sapped—like air escaping from an inflatable boat through a defective valve.

As the weeks went by, Alyson's apparent contempt for Andy became more intense. What he had thought was a breakthrough when he'd stopped her from travelling to the farm was nothing more than a short-lived breathing-space—as short-lived as the conversation that followed.

Any approaches towards physical contact or shows of affection were rejected with an angry shrug. When Andy tried to talk about it, she turned her back and pleaded fatigue. When Andy tried to explain that he was probably the best guy in the world to share those feelings with, she'd turn on him saying he had no idea what grief was all about.

She built a barrier around herself. Within that, she chose to live alone—and it seemed to Andy that she did this out of a need for security. Any touch of affection or compassion from outside was liable to expose a weakness that she wanted to conceal.

Andy felt as though he was on a knife edge of uncertainty, and he craved to get away. On one side was his habitual disposition—carefree and happy—that marked his life before this crisis with Alyson. On the other side lay the responsibility of his unborn child, and a growing sense that maybe his devotion to Alyson was based not on mutual interest and compatibility but on the age-old simplicity of lust.

Either way, his inbuilt loyalty and compassion kept him from leaving—along with the sense that somewhere in his soul, despite her histrionics, he loved and cherished this woman. He was stuck, and he had to work his way loose—hopefully with Alyson by his side as the happy and good-natured person he had fallen in love with.

'Maybe when the baby is born,' he told himself.

# CHAPTER 23

Andy's work at Military Intelligence under the command of Major Combrink proved to be mundane and far less than satisfying, and he was frustrated by the menial tasks that he was given.

He had set out in his new role with enthusiasm. He had believed that the work would involve in-depth operational and logistical planning, with access to well-established sources of intelligence, but he was quickly stripped of those expectations. He became disillusioned, and boredom took the place of eagerness. The circumstances were so peculiar that he began to dread each day, and he found himself loathing the activity to which he'd been assigned.

In the Squadron, he had enjoyed the privilege of access to a wide range of classified information and his security clearance level had been posted as Top Secret.

As a pre-requisite he had been required to sign the Official Secrets Act and swear allegiance to Rhodesia. He'd obtained that privilege about eighteen months after qualifying for service with the SAS, and to all intents he was anything but a security risk. Combrink, however seemed to think differently and Andy was given no background information to the work that he did. He had become a mere pen-pushing cog in the wheel. Despite his high security rating, he learned more from the newspapers about what was happening in the field and at the negotiating table at the Lancaster House conference than he did from his day-to-day activities.

Combrink treated everyone as if they were brainless, but he chose to regard Andy as a mental special case and placed him on an even lower plane. It was as if he resented Andy's past record of respect as a combatant and field NCO, and he made life in his sector as difficult and as unpleasant as possible.

Andy yearned to get out of this rut. He frequently wished that he could get back on ops.

When the opportunity presented itself, it came unexpectedly. It came under a barrage of circumstances so startling that, in due course, he'd wish he could turn back the clock—wishing to be in a position where he could guide his own destiny. It was so utterly bizarre that it haunted him, causing him to regret having asked for the reposting. If only things could have been kept as they were . . . .

He had been assigned to interviewing a snatch who'd been taken off a path at the dead of night as a member of a sixteen-man squad.

A contingent of SAS operatives had waited in ambush on a remote path known to be used by insurgents. As the infiltration party had approached, the early-warning group had clicked the transmit button on the small A60 radio—one click for each terrorist, informing the SAS troops of the numbers. The last man in the band of rebels came abreast of the assault group and he was silently disabled and swiftly removed from the area. A second ambush party, five hundred metres farther up the path, accounted for the rest of the terrorist patrol.

Andy was seated, with two assistants, in the small interview room at Com-Ops when the snatch was ushered in. One of his assistants was an interpreter and the other a witness.

Through both training and experience, Andy had developed an acute awareness of how people reacted when they tried to deceive—when they tried to cover up their actions—socially, professionally, or in a hostile environment. He knew instinctively when he was being lied to or deceived, more by what was left unsaid than by what was revealed to him. Inconsistencies and contradictions in a story were like beacons in the dark and Andy never missed them. His attention to detail and his recall of detail were invariably faultless

'I'm Sergeant Andrew Mason,' he began. 'Will you tell me your name?'

The interpreter translated and then waited.

The prisoner was wide-eyed with astonishment and fear, ever since he'd been picked up. He'd been blindfolded, hooded, and driven in to Salisbury in the back of a closed van.

It was obvious that he was terrified and unsure of his fate, which Andy took as a good sign. From his training course on the subject of field interrogation, where real snatches were used as guinea pigs, it had been noted that the frightened ones were the easiest to get information out of.

'Are you going to kill me?' whimpered the man in heavily-accented broken English.

Andy laughed. 'Not if you tell us what we want to know,' he replied.

'I am Frederick,' said the prisoner. 'Frederick Mpofu.'

'Frederick,' repeated Andy in a friendly voice, 'I'm Sergeant Mason. And I'm going to ask you some questions. It will not help you to lie to me and no harm will come to you if you co-operate. Do you understand?'

The interpreter translated and Frederick nodded in acknowledgment

'Okay, Frederick, tell me where your patrol was coming from when you were caught, and what were your orders?'

'We had been at Mapai. I do not know the orders, I was just told to follow the group until we split up.'

'Where were you going to split up?'

'I do not know.'

'So you were just following along, dressed as you are in military fatigues and heavily armed, but you did not know where you were going. Is that right?'

'Yes.'

'Who was at Mapai when you left there?'

'Many people. Mostly Mozambique soldiers.'

'Who was your camp commander?'

'A big man. I do not know him.'

'And when did you leave Mapai?'

'The same day as I was captured.'

'What were your orders?'

'To follow the group until we split up.'

'And where were you to split up?'

'At the border.'

'But you told me a minute ago that you did not know where you were to split up.'

'I do not know the border.'

'But the people leading did, is that right?'

'Yes.'

'Who was your patrol commander?'

'Comrade Big Gun.'

'That is not his proper name. Who was your patrol commander?'

'That is the name by which he was known.'

'Okay, Frederick, now tell me,' continued Andy, 'what have you been told about the talks at Lancaster House?'

'We have been told that we are to make sure that all the people in the rural areas must be aware of ZANU, and that they must be told that they will be killed if ZANU does not get their support. We know that ZANU is strong, but the people are afraid of ZAPU. We must make them more afraid of ZANU.'

'When was your president last at Mapai?' asked Andy.

'I am told it was last year.'

'Has anyone told you that he will be visiting again?'

'No!'

'Okay,' said Andy, turning to the witness. 'Take him back to his cell. We'll carry on later.' He rose from his seat and strode out of the room.

Combrink was waiting for Andy as he emerged from the interrogation room.

'What was that all about?' he demanded. 'Do you know what you're supposed to be doing? What was all that crap about who his patrol commander was, and who was at Mapai? What's that got to do with anything?'

'Absolutely nothing, sir,' said Andy calmly, 'but it's the beginning of a process. I'm sure I don't need to explain that. The man's unsure of his fate and that's the way I want it. I don't know how useful he'll be—probably very little—but while I soften him up I don't want to let him know what I want to find out. That way, I'll find out everything he knows. He'll either start to contradict himself and become inconsistent in his answers, or just spill the beans to save his own sorry arse. That's what I'm moving towards. Please let me get on with it.'

A few days later, after some gruelling sessions, Andy had been able to extract from Frederick the fact that a large contingent of men in expensive suits, supported by a platoon of bodyguards all dressed in the distinctive fatigues and red berets of the ZANLA VIP protection unit, had arrived at the Mapai base camp in a convoy of Toyota Land Cruisers two days before Frederick had left the base.

Fredrick had disclosed that these visitors had been extraordinarily active in checking on the base's defences and spent much time rearranging camp discipline.

The word had gone out that the men were from Maputo and were highly placed within the ZANU chain of command. Their presence had obviously worried the camp commanders: while the visitors had gone through the facilities, giving orders on matters of security and accommodation, the camp commanders had been abnormally attentive and subservient. The inmates of the camp had taken it for granted that something of great importance was about to happen there.

This was the first bit of work Andy had been given at Com-Ops that came anywhere close to being interesting and he threw himself into collating all the intelligence about Mapai that he could muster.

The following day was a Saturday. Andy left the apartment to go and complete his interrogation report at Com-Ops—to file his conclusions on Frederick's profile, and the information gleaned from him.

Alyson had, yet again, castigated him for leaving her alone over a week-end. This resulted in yet another argument, and he'd left for work under a cloud of unpleasantness.

He wrapped up his work quicker than he'd anticipated, and he had time on his hands. He wanted to unwind and get some recreational activity. He didn't relish going straight home—he'd let the dust settle a bit first and try to pacify Alyson later. The apartment had become an uncomfortable place to be.

Since it was a Saturday afternoon, he made up his mind to take a drive out to Squadron HQ at Kabrit to see if any of his mates were in town and to have a few beers in the mess.

As he drove in through the gates of Kabrit, and up the narrow two-kilometre stretch of tree-lined road, Andy was overcome by a rush of nostalgia. The avenue, leading to the spacious gardens and lawns that surrounded the barrack blocks and admin offices, was intensely familiar to him. He'd driven up this road more times than he could remember, and on each occasion he'd had an overwhelming sense of belonging, coupled with an intense pride in his right to feel that way.

On this occasion he felt like a visitor, and the sad reality of it made him feel cheated out of something he could not quite put his finger on—reminiscent perhaps of the emotions relating to an estranged friend.

As he pulled up outside the Winged Stagger and stepped out of the car he was pleasantly surprised to see Greg Dawson. Dawson was coming across the parade square from the office block, and Andy saluted in casual greeting.

'What brings you out here, Andy?" asked Dawson, returning the salute with a smile and extending his hand.

'I thought it was about time I paid a visit, sir,' replied Andy grinning. 'Just checking to make sure things aren't falling apart in my absence.'

Dawson chuckled briefly.

'Actually, Andy, I've been suppressing the urge to contact you. We're pretty thin on the ground for callsign commanders who've got your knowledge of central Mozambique—there're a couple of jobs that could use your skills. Would you be interested?'

'Would it get me away from that prick at Com-Ops?'

Dawson cast a cognisant glance toward Andy: 'That happens to be a senior officer you're referring to, Sergeant,' he said with a cynical grin. He paused briefly, and then added: 'Has he got up your nose as well?'

'Up my nose, down my throat and under my skin. He thinks everybody around him is brain dead.'

'Yep!' responded Dawson pensively. 'Well, you're still officially on the nominal roll out here and only on attachment to that department, so getting you back wouldn't pose much of a problem. You interested? It would only be for a couple of days.'

'What do you have in mind, sir?' asked Andy.

'Convoy ambush, initially,' replied Dawson. 'And one or two other jobs that may ripple off from there. Special Branch have had some of our agents monitoring activities in Maputo harbour and we have it on reliable feedback that there's a shipment of arms and equipment on the docks that could give Mugabe and his apes the fire power to outgun us in any situation. Not only would that put us at a huge disadvantage politically but it means we wouldn't be able to control him if he chooses to do the African thing and impose his will by force after a settlement that doesn't go his way. We can't afford to take the chance of letting any of those weapons reach their destination. We're just waiting for some intelligence on its movement. At this stage nothing is certain, but all things considered it will probably be transported by road or rail or perhaps a bit of each. Mapai would seem to be a logical destination or transit point because of the good road and rail links that still exist there. It's somewhere near Mapai that we'd want to stop them.'

Andy felt a chill creep up his spine at the mention of Mapai. He thought back to the information he gleaned from Frederick Mpofu, and the activity that Frederick had witnessed before leaving the camp.

'May I break protocol and ask a leading question, sir?' asked Andy. The habit of disclosing information on a need-to-know basis only, even where high-ranking officers were concerned, was ingrained into SAS operatives. What was learned in one area was rarely if ever passed on to another unless there was a pertinent link between the two. But in this case a sixth sense warned Andy of something sinister. He knew that Dawson probably knew everything that went on within the entire structure of the armed forces, but his security rating forbade discussion.

'I won't tell if you don't,' laughed Dawson.

Andy hesitated, double checking with himself to be sure that he wasn't about to divulge anything that might compromise his own position. He spoke:

'Have you been made aware of an impending visit to Mapai by a seriously important dignitary? Maybe even Mugabe himself?'

Dawson's grin faded and he stared at Andy with interest.

'What gives you that idea?' Dawson spoke as if he were hedging information.

Having come this far, Andy saw no point in telling Dawson only half the story. But, before answering, he ran through the events of Frederick's interrogation in his mind. Then he said:

'I came out here for a beer, sir. May I invite you as my guest into the NCOs' mess?'

'Better we go for a walk, Andy,' said Dawson. 'The rifle range sounds like a sensible place to talk. We'll have that beer later.'

The rifle range was located 800 metres from the mess, down a broad path overhung by wild creepers and shrubbery. The two of them strode off saying nothing until they reached the markers' hut at the 1000-metre firing line. The hut was a long low structure with a lean-to veranda in front of the wide range-master's window. Beneath that was a long wooden bench which ran the full length of the outer wall.

'Speak,' said Dawson, as they moved in under the shade of the veranda and sat down. 'I'm curious about what they've been teaching you at that Base Walla Paradise in town.'

Andy started at the beginning, how he'd got involved and what he'd picked up from his interrogation of Mpofu, and why it was that he thought someone at the top of the pile was about to pay a visit to Mapai. But, from what Dawson had just told him, it seemed there could be another explanation for the activity at the camp.

When Andy had finished, Dawson rose and walked slowly to the far end of the veranda. He stood there, pensive, for what seemed to be a long time. He turned and came back to where Andy sat:

'Have you given all this to Major Combrink? Does he know everything you've just told me?'

'I've put it all in my report,' replied Andy. 'I only finished the official report this morning, but I've kept him up to speed with interim reports as I've gone along—both verbally and in writing.'

'How sure are you that he's read your reports?' asked Dawson

'I'd be surprised if he hasn't. He's been hanging around me like a bad smell since I was given that interrogation job. I sort of get the idea that it slipped by him and he didn't really want me involved, but once I was on it there wasn't much he could do.'

Dawson drifted away again, wrapped in thought, and after a while he turned back to Andy:

'There's something very wrong here, Andy. I was at a security briefing this morning, a meeting that was also attended by Major Combrink. A wide variety of issues were discussed. Included was the possibility of us putting in an ambush in the vicinity of Mapai to intercept that convoy once it starts moving, but not a word was said about what you've just told me. That makes me very nervous. Why would Combrink choose not to mention it?'

'Perhaps he doesn't believe what's in my report,' offered Andy, 'or maybe he wanted to read the final report before commenting on it.'

'That's not the point, Andy. He's in possession of a preliminary report of unusual activity on marked enemy territory. That could be of vital importance, and it should have been tabled at this morning's briefing even if the source is questionable.'

'So what do you suppose his motive is?' asked Andy.

'I really have no idea—but as sure as hell is hot, I intend to find out.' Dawson turned back towards the access path, and then added over his shoulder: 'Keep your ops kit ready—I'll be in touch.'


It was after six in the evening by the time Andy got home, having gone to the mess after his talk with Dawson and spending more time there than he'd intended.

He decided to say nothing to Alyson about his visit to Kabrit, nor about the possibility that he might be called back on ops for a short period. He saw no point in creating circumstances to upset her further, until he knew for sure what was in store. But it wouldn't have mattered what he had told her—she'd obviously spent the day brooding over her circumstances and she wasn't in a pleasant state of mind when he arrived.

He let himself into the apartment and she stormed through the lounge to the entrance hall and accosted him, just as he was hanging his keys on the wall rack beside the door.

'Where the hell have you been?' Her voice was one octave below a shout.

'I met Alec for a beer at The Oasis,' he lied. 'We had a lot to talk about and got a bit shot away. Sorry I'm late. I should have called.'

'You should have stayed in the bar, Andrew!' she retorted angrily. 'I've been here on my own all bloody day. What sort of husband leaves his pregnant wife at home alone and goes off pissing it up with his mates all day on a Saturday?'

'I said I was sorry, Ali,' said Andy. He knew that he was in the wrong, but he resented the circumstances that obliged him to apologise for it. Less than two months previously the thought of lying to Alyson about where he'd been wouldn't have entered his mind. He would have phoned her and she'd happily have joined him and whoever else he was with, and added to the gaiety of the occasion. He kept having to remind himself that Alyson wasn't herself and in her present frame of mind probably unplayable, but he was convinced that things would return to normal as her grief and anger subsided. He was unprepared, though, for the onslaught that followed:

'You think you're such a big shot, Mr-Bloody-Wings-on-Chest!' she spat. 'Mr-bloody-smart-arse-Andy whose friends are so important, Mr-Bloody-Andrew-Mason trying so damn hard to impress the world that he has no time for his wife. Has anybody told you that my parents were recently murdered? Why don't you just put a bed in your fucking office and stay there?' Alyson was getting hysterical and the scorn and bitterness came spitting off her tongue like venom.

Andy was taken aback and infuriated by the outburst. He could hardly believe what he was hearing. He looked at her with incredulity and instead of simply apologising again and trying to pacify her, as he would later wish he'd done, he expanded on the lie that he'd already started to regret:

'I happen to have some rather important work to do, Alyson,' he began, on the defensive. 'And Alec just happens to be in a position to help me with it. What would you like me to do? Get out of the army and find an eight-to-four job sorting mail at the post office so that I can come back early to a home where I feel like a trespasser?'

But Alyson went on, as if Andy hadn't spoken:

'It wasn't your parents killed on your wedding night, Andrew!' she yelled. 'And they'd never have been on the road that night if it hadn't been for the wedding! How can you possibly be so damn naive as to how much I hold myself and you responsible?'

Andy felt as though he'd been hit in the chest by a cross-bow.

'Run that lot by me again,' he resisted. 'Did I really hear what you've just said?'

He moved to an armchair at the opposite side of the room and dropped heavily into it as though he'd fallen, and then he looked up, wearily.

'My God, Alyson,' he asked, 'is that what you've been harbouring? Is that what this bitterness and anger is all about?'

'You've got no idea how deep that anger runs, Andrew,' said Alyson. She turned away towards the bedroom in a flood of tears.

Guilt suddenly overwhelmed Andy—guilt at having left Alyson alone so much since the death of her parents, combined with deep regret over having indicated that he'd be available to go back on ops. He was filled with a mysterious sense of emptiness and uncertainty. He felt as though he'd been dumped on an island of helplessness in an emotional void.

He sat for what seemed an age, bemused, contemplating the situation in which he found himself. Then he rose from his chair and went down the short passage to the bedroom.

He found Alyson lying on the bed, her eyes puffy and red and her hair in a mess of tangles with her forearm resting across her forehead.

'Alyson,' he said softly, sitting down beside her on the bed, 'my love, we need to talk. We can't go on like this. We're tearing each other apart and I can't stand for us to be like this. It's not right.'

Alyson said nothing and didn't move. Andy let the silence drag out until she finally turned her head to look at him. There was emptiness in her swollen eyes and her pale complexion made her look ill. The sparkle that had been so characteristic of her before the deaths of Ralph and Jennifer was gone, and it broke Andy's heart to see her like this.

'Let me in, Ali,' he said tenderly. 'Let me help you. Don't push me away. We need to be together in this.'

'I just don't know how, Andy,' she said, starting to weep again. 'I'm just so depressed—I feel like I've fallen into a vacuum and there's just nothing around me . . . . Just emptiness.'

'Alyson,' said Andy, 'that stuff doesn't come out of a hollow soul because it's depressed. Those sort of thoughts are what cause the depression. This is something that you've been keeping inside of you instead of letting it out for us to talk about. My God, Ali, I had no idea of what your source of anger with me was—and if you want the truth, it hurts me that you haven't shared it with me. That's the way it should be. We can work this out together, Ali.'

'You'd never understand, Andrew,' she retorted. 'You've spent so much time killing people that death means nothing to you— but you've never lost anyone close to you, so how could I possibly make you understand?'

Andy remained quiet and nodded his head silently. He was absorbed in thoughts of how little this woman—his wife—knew about him. His thoughts went to Stuart and Rob and Vern and all the others (Merryl and Charmaine!) with whom he'd shared the terrifying experiences of death and fear, and the horrors of combat in dark, hostile places from where they'd been returned in body bags. Those were things that he'd never discussed—nor even thought of sharing—with Alyson, or anyone else for that matter. They were events that took place in another world, another life, and had no place outside the field of operations—or his private past.

'Maybe not,' he said softly, 'but it helps to talk, and I could be here to listen. I've done that before, you know?'

Alyson was silent again. She pushed a hand through her dishevelled hair and sighed deeply. After a while she turned to him with what he thought seemed like a softer look in her eyes.

'Let me sleep, Andy,' she said. 'We'll talk tomorrow, but for now I just want to sleep.'

Andy bent forward and kissed her gently on the forehead, then took her hand and gave it a gentle squeeze.

'Okay,' he said, sensing a spark of optimism that he might be at the first stage of bringing back the old Alyson. 'I'll be in the lounge if you want me.'

He left the room quietly, dimming the lights and closing the door softly behind him.

He went back to the lounge and thought about getting a beer from the fridge under the bar. He resisted the temptation and instead lit a cigarette and sat down on the sofa, feeling drained and depressed. As he did so, he noticed that the armchair he'd fallen into earlier was about two feet back from its usual position. Indentations on the carpet marked its usual place, and he rose to put it back. As he leaned over the chair, a scrap of cloth caught his attention—a bit of cloth that showed from beneath the chair. He went down on one knee to pick it up.

What he found puzzled him. It was a shoulder epaulette that appeared to have been torn from a shirt, bearing the rank insignia of a major. He looked at it quizzically, wondering how it had got there. The only major who had been a guest here as far as he knew was Alec, but he couldn't remember a time when Alec had visited in uniform.

'Strange!' he murmured to himself. 'I wonder where this came from.'

He straightened the chair and went back to his seat on the sofa, dropping the epaulette into an ashtray on the coffee table as he sat down. He returned to his brown study, his thoughts of how his relationship with Alyson had deteriorated—and the flicker of hope that they could patch it all up and get on with their lives.

He'd only been there a few minutes when the phone rang. He hurried to answer it, fearful that it would wake Alyson.

'Sergeant Mason?' enquired an authoritative voice, in immediate response to his greeting.

'Yes,' said Andy. 'Who is this?'

'You're wanted at Com-Ops. Right now, Sergeant,' said the voice without offering an identity.

Andy was mystified. What could be so urgent that he was being called out at seven-thirty on a Saturday evening?

'That's not going to happen,' said Andy. 'I'm at home with my wife and she's not well.'

'Sergeant Mason,' responded the caller, 'this is not a request. It's an order.'

Andy's puzzlement deepened. 'And who might be giving that order?'

'It's Major Hudson, Special Branch. This is a matter of state security and under the circumstances your wife's health is of little concern to me. Twenty minutes, Sergeant.' The line went dead.

Andy stared dumbly at the receiver, startled by the call, wondering what could be so important. He realised that whatever it was, he had no choice but to obey Hudson's order.

He crept down the passage and gently opened the bedroom door. Alyson was still fully clothed but sound asleep with the duvet partially pulled over her shoulders.

He went back to the lounge and scribbled her a note of apology, promising he wouldn't be long. He tiptoed back to leave it on the bedside pedestal, and then he left the apartment and drove to Army HQ.

When he arrived at Milton buildings there was a frenzy of activity in Combrink's office. Special Branch personnel, the most junior of whom wore the rank insignia of a captain, had filing cabinets open and were poring over files and documents that were spread across the desk. Technicians were scouring the floor, walls and ceiling light fittings with what appeared to be electronic scanning devices, and a military policeman with the rank of Sergeant Major stood rigidly at the door.

'What's going on in there?' he asked an orderly lance corporal who was one of Combrink's clerks.

'Damned if I know,' replied the orderly. 'But obviously something serious has gone down.'

'Where's the boss?' asked Andy. He glanced around, expecting Combrink to be hovering about in the near vicinity.

'I don't know. I just work here, remember?' said the corporal. 'Hell, Sarge, I don't even get to go to the bog without signing a request.'

Andy, astonished, moved towards the Major's office, but before he reached it an officer emerged and called him aside.

'Sergeant Mason, a word please,' he said tersely. 'I'm Major Hudson from Special branch.'

'Yes sir,' said Andy, saluting. 'We spoke on the phone. May I ask what's going on?'

'We seem to have a problem in regard to some delicate information,' said Hudson. 'Information that's been withheld and then passed on to persons who have no authority to receive it. Do you have copies of the report you gave Major Combrink on the Mapai issue?'

'There should be a file copy in the vault, sir. That would be the only one other than the copy in the Major's possession. I gave it to Document Security this morning.'

'So you didn't file it yourself?' asked the Major.

'No sir,' replied Andy. 'All filing is done by the document division. The vault is out of bounds to us menials.'

'Who else has access to the vault?'

'All staff with the rank of major and above, as far as I know.'

He wasn't sure where this was going, or what relevance the questions had, but it was obvious that Combrink was in some way under suspicion—implicated in a hidden agenda?

In his mind, Andy began to see a variety of possibilities where someone in Combrink's position could pass on information to the enemy. He thought of the many ops that had gone sour through what can only have been a leak at high level.

Combrink was in charge of groups of intelligence agents who infiltrated the ranks of the guerrilla forces. What would stop him from passing reverse information through the same channels, if he chose to do so? It was an interesting thought, and suddenly it made sense.

Andy had, on occasions, cause to doubt Combrink's trustworthiness, but he'd dismissed this as personal prejudice. He'd chosen not to give the matter much attention. Now it seemed that there could be evidence of a double agent.

If a convoy was to be intercepted near Mapai—a convoy carrying arms and ammunition to bolster the strength of ZANLA forces in the wake of a political settlement—and if it was indeed true that high-ranking personnel from the guerrilla movement could be neutralised near or at Mapai—there were clear grounds for the enemy setting up a decoy to sabotage the intentions of the military.

The impending visit of the VIPs—which Andy had suspected because of what he'd extracted from the snatch, and which he'd reported to Combrink—could easily be cancelled. The information about the suspected visit, held by Combrink, could be withheld from combat unit commanders. The enemy, now forewarned, could then divert the convoy, giving the area a wide berth, while a strong Rhodesian contingent sat in wait, uselessly, for something that wasn't going to arrive. That could be the reason why, as Dawson said, Combrink had chosen not to mention the information gleaned from Mpofu.

It then occurred to Andy that the security inspection that had been reported by Mpofu could be to do with securing storage for the arms shipment, and had nothing to do with an impending visit to the camp by ZANLA heavyweights. If that was the case, Mpofu's disclosure could indeed now be used as a red herring.

These thoughts came to Andy in a flash of inspiration, and it occurred to him why Combrink failed to mention the results of the Mpofu interrogation.

It was obvious:

*Combrink is a mole. He's passed on details of the report to the enemy, and the convoy is no longer going to go anywhere near Mapai.*

But then that didn't make sense either. If the army was to set up an ambush with a view to delivering a tactical blow to nefarious ZANLA operations, would it not make more sense for a mole to put the report before Com-Ops, thus deliberately reinforcing the initial interpretation of Mpofu's information? That way, the planners would have more justification to put troops in place at Mapai, while the supply convoy's other possible routes would get less attention.

He wondered where Combrink was. Had he been arrested, or had he skipped? It was highly unlikely that the activity going on in his office would be happening if the man was innocent, or roaming around free.

He needed to get hold of Greg Dawson and share these thoughts with him. It seemed obvious that the frenzy of activity taking place in Combrink's office was the result of what Andy had disclosed during their conversation earlier that day. Dawson had access to the ears and the confidence of the most senior officers in the army and Andy figured that his thoughts had merit enough for them to be aired.

'I can't disclose anything, Andy,' said Dawson when Andy finally got through to him at Squadron H.Q.

'As far as you are concerned, Andy, there appears to have been a breach of regulations by a high-ranking officer, but you know nothing about it. One thing I can say, though, is that there'll be those who'll want to cover their arses given the fact that an agreement at Lancaster House is looking more likely. The outcome of an agreement will put an end to the war, but we'll be on the losing end and a new government will be those whom we've been fighting for the past seven years. There'll be scores to settle—and as for the likes of you and me, we may be looking for a new address. There'll be those, however, who may wish to change their allegiance and help with the witch hunt. But we're not finished yet. There's still work to be done. Let's just see what happens over the next few days.'

Andy returned home, and went quietly to the bedroom. Alyson hadn't moved from the position in which he'd left her and he gently got her under the covers and crept into bed beside her.

# Chapter 24

THE NEXT FEW DAYS DRAGGED BY. Combrink did not reappear and nobody seemed to have any idea as to why, but it was not uncommon for him suddenly to go missing for a week or more and then resurface and carry on as if he'd not been away. None of the staff mentioned the man's absence, but Andy was convinced that they'd seen the last of Combrink at Com-Ops. He had no idea of the extent of his indiscretions, but he knew enough to realise that they were serious.

Dawson didn't get in touch and it was increasingly apparent to Andy that the discussion about him possibly being wanted for an op into Mozambique had come to naught. He was not entirely unhappy with that; he now spent more time with Alyson and felt that he was gradually breaking through her mindset of distress and self-pity.

They were able to talk without the conversation ending in a bitter argument and he started to feel as though the ice was melting.

Then one morning, for no apparent reason, Alyson made a revelation that shocked Andy to the core, and finally his spirit was crushed. It was something that he'd never have suspected, and his disbelief was absolute.

They'd been out to a restaurant the night before and the atmosphere had been easy and relaxed. It was a pleasant evening. When they got home, they made love for the first time since their wedding night, nearly three months previously, and slept in each other's arms. In the morning they made love again. There wasn't the same intensity of passion that had characterised their relationship before the tragic events of their wedding night, but Andy felt as though they'd turned a corner— he felt that they'd be able to start rebuilding their shattered relationship. It was a dream he held dear, and their lovemaking filled him with optimism.

They lay together in the soft mellow aftermath of their passion. Then, Alyson got up on one elbow. She looked earnestly at Andy and spoke:

'I think you should know, Andy, that I haven't been all together honest with you about something.'

'Oh?' Andy grinned with nonchalance. 'And what horrible lies have I been hearing?'

'Before we got married, while you were away on ops and I was left alone, I was seeing someone else.'

She spoke with casual self-confidence, almost in the same tone as if she spoke about her attendance at a book club, and he thought she was leading up to some kind of playful trap that would make him laugh and feel foolish when he fell into it. He looked at her with mild uncertainty, but was still waiting for the punch line in the hopeful belief that it was a joke.

'Who was the lucky guy?' he asked. His tone too was casual, half-jesting, but now a little less certain.

'Alec,' she replied without hesitation.

Her matter-of-fact response took Andy completely by surprise. He caught his breath, and uncertainty loomed larger in his mind.

'You mean my good mate Major Alec Bradford?' He remembered, for the first time, the epaulette he'd come across in the lounge.

'Yes!'

Andy was shaken, but he remained sceptical—no way would she want to reveal something like that just for the sake of something to say. He clung to the idea that she might be trying to explain something that was entirely innocent.

'Oh?' he said nervously. 'And how long did this go on for?'

Alyson was pensive for a moment. She said nothing, and Andy's concern grew. He realised that he'd just learned something about which he'd rather have remained ignorant.

'You're not being serious, are you?' He hoped that she'd laugh and deny it.

'Of course I'm serious.' Alyson sounded irritated.

Andy was devastated. She wasn't joking at all—she was making a disclosure, the suggestion of which had never so much as entered his head. He still didn't want to believe it. He'd known that there was a mutual attraction, a sort of friendly chemistry, between Alec and Alyson, and that the two of them frequently flirted openly with each other, but he'd dismissed it as friendly banter. He'd never suspected that this flirtation meant anything beyond its face value. His trust had been absolute.

'You're joking, right?' he asked again, with mounting disbelief.

'No, I'm not,' she replied earnestly. 'But it didn't go on for very long. We only met about half a dozen times.'

There was a long silence. Then Andy, reeling from the shock, spoke:

'Alyson—are you telling me that while I was convinced that you were in love with me, you had an affair going with Alec, a married man? Married, on top of it, to one of your close acquaintances? And someone whom I've thought of as one of my best friends?'

'Oh, don't go and make a thing of it now,' said Alyson in an annoyed tone. 'You weren't making much of a confession about your love for me at the time—and, anyway, it's been over for months. Besides it was just a bit of fun and excitement between two people who had the hots for each other. Let it go, Andy.'

He couldn't believe what he heard.

'When, and more importantly where, did all this happen?'

'Why should that matter now?' she asked. 'I've told you it's been over for ages. Don't start tormenting me now with prying questions.'

'Alyson,' said Andy slowly, 'you are my wife. You're pregnant with what I believe to be my child. But you're now telling me that while I had my back turned you were leading a double life and playing the role of another married man's whore?'

'Don't you dare call me that!' said Alyson angrily. She went on immediately: 'Let it go, Andrew, it's in the past. Finito, Over.'

The irritation in her voice dripped like blood from a fresh wound. 'Stop tormenting me.'

'I'm tormenting you?' yelled Andy in disbelief. 'Christ! That's bloody rich! Here you're telling me something utterly incomprehensible—a parallel relationship that's gone on behind my back—and you make it sound as if it was sharing a cup of tea with someone. What exactly do you expect me to do? Ask, in the same tone, if it was enjoyable? I can't believe I'm hearing this. I need to know, Alyson, where this happened and how often.'

'I've told you,' she retorted, 'we saw each other occasionally. He used to come around here to see if I was okay, and one evening it just sort of happened.'

It felt like a physical blow. It felt like his heart breaking. He had never raised his hand to a woman in all his life, but in the face of this torment he knew that if he didn't get away, that distinction might be lost from his grasp.

He got out of bed and headed for the bathroom. His heartache and outrage sat in his guts like a tangled ball of rotting seaweed. It was a sensation not unlike fear. The impact was such that Andy felt like a devout Catholic who'd just learned that the Pope got his kicks out of secretly crapping on the crucifix.

The mental image of Alyson and Alec writhing naked between the sheets of his bed—the sacred symbol of his love for her . . . . It made him nauseous and he thought he was going to throw up. He closed the door and sat down on the toilet lid.

Holding his head in his hands, eyes closed and with his elbows on his knees, Andy tried to control his anger and sorrow. Thinking about the terms of endearment that would surely have passed between the two added to his torment. His mind reeled as it speculated, against his will, on what their secret passions may have been.

'The bitch!' he swore to himself. 'The bloody slut! How could she?' He was shaking uncontrollably. 'I better get out of here,' he thought. 'I could get myself into a lot of trouble by sticking around.'

This was the final humiliation, the ultimate betrayal, the ultimate insult. In *their* home, in *his* bed. The tears welled up in his eyes. His heart pounded. The sense of final and total loss bore down on him in a mindless and ill-defined press of convulsive emotions. He was torn between blind anger, jealousy, hate and love. His mind went back all those years to Doc Morison's lectures during combat discipline training.

'It's a condition of the mind, chaps, and if you don't learn to control it, it will control you.'

The good doctor had of course been talking of fear, but Andy had come to realise a long time ago that the same could be applied equally to all emotions.

'This is how crimes of passion occur,' he thought, 'when the emotions control the individual.'

'Well,' he resolved, 'that's not going to happen here, unless she tries to stop me from leaving. Then my emotions might take control.'

He went out of the bathroom to his closet, pulled out a set of clothes, and dressed quickly. As he went back through the bedroom, where Alyson was sitting up in bed, he looked at her with disgust.

'Where are you going?' she demanded.

'I'm leaving, Alyson,' he said as calmly as he could.

'Oh, don't be so ridiculous, Andrew! You're making a huge issue of something that was over months ago—which hasn't any bearing on you and me.'

'If I'm wrong,' said Andy with dripping sarcasm, 'to be a little more than pissed off by the fact that my wife has used our home as another married man's private playground, where he's been screwing her in my bed—then forgive me for my violating indiscretion. Most married men who need it on the side go to brothels, and that's what you've turned this place into. How does it feel to be the resident whore? No, Alyson,' he continued before she could respond. 'I'm making a huge issue of the fact that you violated the sanctity of the only place that I can call home—and by so doing you have stolen something very dear to me, and you unashamedly shared it with another man. Clearly nothing is sacred to you—and clearly you've got neither morals nor a scrap of dignity or decency. That might mean nothing to you but sure as hell it means a lot to me. Frankly, I really don't give a damn who you screw,' he lied, 'but not under this roof, nor in our bed. That, to me, places you in the class of a dock worker's wife who enjoys the daytime company of the milkman in the back streets of Liverpool.'

'Let me remind you,' said Alyson defensively, 'this is not your house. It was bought and paid for through the tireless efforts of my late parents. Besides, what went on between Alec and I happened before you and I were married and well before I fell pregnant.'

Andy's chin sank onto his chest. He bit hard down on his lip, closing his eyes in his determination to suppress and control the frustration and anger that bubbled within him.

'I think that's a lie,' he said quietly. 'It seems in your rush to get the man's clothes off you tore bits of it away and left the evidence under a chair in the lounge. I wonder how recently that epaulette, that seems to have mysteriously disappeared, was left there.'

He started to turn away. Then he stopped, staring at her with contempt. Anger and grief brimmed into his eyes and his voice.

'You know, Alyson—I have always held the view that a woman who actively pursues a relationship with another woman's husband is cheap and immoral. If the man's wife happens to be an acquaintance of the woman concerned, I would call that cheap, immoral and treacherous. When the man is well known to the woman's husband, I would think of it as being cheap, immoral, treacherous and evil.' He was raising his voice now. 'When all those factors are present in one parcel and the woman then has the audacity to repeatedly bring the man into the home and bed she is also sharing with the man she professes to love, . . . Well! That would rate her among the cheapest, most immoral, treacherous, evil and despicable types of slut on God's earth. Discovering now that I am married to such a person does not rest easily in my guts.'

He paused, breathless, while Alyson stared wide-eyed at him, and then he said softly: 'Well now, my dear, you can do exactly as you please in *your* house,' he spat the words, 'and I wish you luck. It appears that you secretly keep the company of slimeballs whose moral fibre and sense of social responsibility make the ethics of a sewer rat seem appealing. You disgust me.'

He had nothing more to say, and he wanted to hear no more.

With his heart and spirit broken, he strode on down the passage, slamming the door of the apartment on his way out.

He stormed to his car and drove away. He had no idea where he was going, nor what he would do when he got there. He had no idea how his life was about to change.

He drove aimlessly around the suburbs of Salisbury, nursing his pain. He was haunted by the utter devastation of his self-esteem and he wept silently to himself as he drove. The beauty of the glorious summer's day escaped him and he saw nothing of the exuberance of blossoming flame lilies and flamboyants and Bougainvillea that lined the suburban streets of the city. He considered driving out into the country, but checked the urge to do so as he'd not thought to pick up his rifle in his rush to leave the apartment. In any event, he was short on petrol coupons— part and parcel of the strict rationing due to war and economic sanctions. Alyson had always had an unlimited supply of coupons through the supplementary allowance that Ralph had been entitled to as a farmer. This additional grant had allowed them to be a little less cautious than most, but that privilege no longer existed.

He'd given no thought to the fact that he had to return to collect his things, the most important of which was the rifle that for so long had been an extension of his right arm. Since his secondment to Com-Ops it had stayed locked in his gun safe at the apartment.

He drove out as far as Lake McIllwain, a family resort about twenty kilometres south-west of the city on the Bulawayo road. It was a sanctuary still considered relatively safe from the likelihood of guerrilla activity, and a popular family weekend getaway.

The place was deserted. He parked his car and walked up into the hills overlooking the lake, where he found a small rocky outcrop under which he could sit unseen, but still with a view of his surroundings.

It was past midday by the time he gathered his thoughts sufficiently to ponder the reality of the circumstances and to fully taste the bitterness and desolation.

Although he'd labelled Alyson a whore and a slut and a variety of other detestable names that he felt appropriate at the time, he still refused to believe that she was any of those things. The anger he felt was born of love betrayed and it burned a hole in his soul, smouldering with the intensity of a furnace.

Alyson's changed attitude towards him since the death of her parents had been hard to tolerate—but he felt some guilt for not having given her as much support as he might have. She'd made it incredibly difficult for him to get near enough to do so.

Why, he wondered, had she decided to make the revelation of her relationship with Alec? Oh, God! Why did she do it? What motive inspired her to be drawn into something so devious and deceitful? Particularly with Alec, his friend, who was married and could offer her no possibility of anything but the benefits of forbidden fruit in an illicit sexual liaison. What were her thoughts for him while she was having sex with Alec? In the wake of Alyson's confession, Andy couldn't help but believe that his existence and their relationship must, in reality, have been quite meaningless—his role in her life had been nothing more than an expedient toy, until she had fallen pregnant. But—was the baby his? Or Alec's? Had there been others as well?

Alec! The sonofabitch! How could he be such an opportunistic bastard? 'You swine!' said Andy, aloud. 'You treacherous . . . .' He struggled to hit upon an adjective that would adequately describe what he now thought of the man whom he'd trusted implicitly and regarded as his friend. He shuddered with frustration.

Alyson had become friendly with Geraldine . . . . Was that before or after she'd started sleeping with Alec? And how was she able to look Geraldine in the eye one day and let Alec into bed with her the next? What sort of person was she? Oh, God! What had she done, and why? Why, why, why?

His stomach churned in the torment of humiliation. As the sense of despair gripped at his heart, he started to cry. The tears ran down his cheeks shamelessly, like those of a small child who'd been separated from his mother in a supermarket mall, and he made no effort to staunch them. His shoulders convulsed violently under the strength of his despair, and he sniffed unceasingly as he let his tears wash away the pain and anguish that threatened to unhinge his sanity.

After a long time he curled himself up into a ball in the corner of his hideaway and slept.

*   *   *

There was a cool breeze that blew gently across the lake upon which he sailed a small two man yacht. The spinnaker billowed out strong under the touch of the wind, and the water rushed by beneath him, slapping rhythmically against the hull. The sun shone down warm upon his naked torso with sinewy muscles rippling and straining as he leant out and pulled hard on the trapeze, holding the craft steady on its course. In the distance, far beyond the shoreline, the hills shimmered and danced through a mirage of rising thermals and he could see a flight of eagles surfing the currents high above them.

A frustrating sense of urgency consumed him, and he could not understand why. He was tormented by the knowledge that it was imperative that he reach the shore ahead, but it constantly receded and mysteriously remained out of reach as if he were sailing on a watery treadmill.

The power boat that appeared came as if out of nowhere. It cut across his bow at high speed, thirty metres ahead, and then swung back sharply on itself, tilting at forty-five degrees and throwing up a plume of spray as it bit into the turn towards him. He struck the wake of the speeding craft with an exaggerated thump and his little vessel bounced uncontrollably. He lost his footing on the gunwales and he was hoisted high against the rigging of the mainsail. He instinctively released the trapeze line and frantically grabbed for the mast, but as he did so the other craft smashed into his starboard side. The impact sent his boat skidding out of his reach across the surface of the lake, like a toboggan on ice. He found himself falling from what appeared an impossible height, but now he was floating as if suspended beneath the canopy of a descending parachute.

As he looked down, he saw the speed boat swing away—and he stared in disbelief at the departing vessel. It seemed to be Ralph Carstens at the controls but his hair was long and shaggy, and he had grown a beard that hung to his waist and was badly in need of a comb. What astonished him, though, was that Alyson sat beside Ralph, looking back, full of the laughter and gaiety that he so fondly remembered of her.

As the vessel sped away across the surface of the lake, she kissed her fingers and waved happily. Then, in a scene of ghostly mystique that sent a shiver up his spine and brought goose bumps out on his flesh, the boat and its occupants simply faded into invisibility. The surface of the lake was empty and calm. As he tried to make sense of what he had just witnessed, his descent accelerated into a headlong freefall.

# CHAPTER 25

ALYSON HEARD THE DOOR SLAM BEHIND ANDY AS HE LEFT THE APARTMENT. She curled up into the foetal position in bed and pulled the covers over her head in a gesture of withdrawal. The depression that had descended upon her over the death of her parents had started to swing like a pendulum, instead of being a constant deadweight, and she was coming to see—for the first time—how it had affected her.

She reflected on her confession to Andy, and she realised very quickly that it had been a huge mistake.

But there were other, far more delicate, issues that weighed down on her. Her thoughts were tangled with contradictory emotions as she allowed her mind to drift over the events of the previous few months.

\* \* \*

Alyson's liaisons with Alec had been wicked and exciting and had served to satisfy and sustain a flight of the imagination. But she came to realise, too late and at enormous emotional cost, that the best place for those fantasies would have been to keep them in the most private recesses of her own mind.

Alec had called by to drop off a book that Geraldine had offered to lend her—and, over a few glasses of wine, the affair had started: a spontaneous lustful adventure.

It was undeniable that there was chemistry between them from the moment Andy had first introduced them, but it remained an unspoken fact that neither of them was eager to acknowledge or pursue.

Alyson was in love with Andy. She'd been in love with him long before she'd even heard the name Alec Bradford. Her attraction towards Alec didn't change that—but in times of loneliness, imposed by Andy's frequent absences, she had occasionally allowed her thoughts to drift into a fantasy where she imagined she and Alec throwing caution to the wind and exploring the dangerous but thrilling taste of forbidden fruit.

Then, late one afternoon, Alec appeared unexpectedly at the door to deliver the book from Geraldine. Alyson hesitated about inviting him in. But she didn't want to appear rude, and she saw no harm in asking him to stay for a drink.

They sat opposite each other at the small bar in the corner of the lounge and they chatted amiably, cheerfully making their way through the contents of a bottle of wine. It was without question, and quite possibly unavoidable, that the air about them became charged with a sense of desire—a longing that Alyson tried to ignore and reject. The atmosphere in the room led to an odd tension in their conversation and Alec rose to leave. Alyson walked him to the door. There, Alec put an arm around her and placed a friendly peck on her cheek.

His warm breath on her cheek, mingled with the fragrance of his after-shave, enticed from her a mildly intoxicating sensation. She turned her head to return the friendly gesture, but as if by accident their lips touched, and for a moment lingered. There was a hesitation, then lips parted slightly, and tongues touched in a slow exploratory motion. Suddenly their emotions spiralled out of control and their tongues entwined in an oral embrace of searching passion. Her blouse had slipped up above the rim of her skirt and his fingers touch the soft naked flesh of her back, stroking gently as the urgency of their tongues and quickened breath brought them closer together. She felt the hard muscle of his chest against her soft breasts through the fabric of her blouse and she pressed against him, pulling at him as their mutual arousal emerged in a rush of abandoned lust. Electrifying sensations tingled through their bodies.

Overwhelmed by her impulsive need, Alyson wrapped her arms tighter around him, drawing him closer. She closed her eyes, and she savoured the contentment that she found in his arms. She allowed herself to be swept away by the raging wave of desire that now claimed her body with each ravishing kiss.

With each new place his hands touched her, her trembling need grew more demanding. She ripped at his clothing and they stumbled back into the lounge. His hands roamed eagerly over her body, exploring every sensual curve and delicate contour, and Alyson was powerless over her need for him. At that moment she wanted him more than she'd ever imagined, and the intensity of the passion that burst to life inside her was overwhelming.

She broke away and took him by the hand, leading him to the bedroom at a run. They fell naked onto the bed and he resumed his embrace on her, sucking at her nipples and gently stroking the softness of her womanhood. She tossed her head from side to side in her driving passion and, as he rolled on top of her, she raised her hips to meet him halfway, her need now impatient and feverish.

'Make love to me, Alec,' she'd whispered. 'God, I want you so much!'

As he penetrated her, Alyson whimpered aloud. She met every stroke of his with upward thrusts of her hips until the mounting ache that had been created in her finally burst in a magnificent orgasmic explosion, wracking her body with one spasm after another—and she screamed his name as she sensed his simultaneous climax.

The encounter was so draining, so exhilarating, that they lay exhausted in each other's arms for almost an hour afterwards in the soft, mellow aftermath of spent passion, savouring the sensation of having been mutually and so spontaneously rocketed to such heights of ecstasy.

After Alec left, Alyson sat and pondered the experience. A twinge of uneasy guilt emerged and she was in a state of confusion over her feelings. She wondered how she'd face Alec again.

They had impulsively allowed their emotions to carry them down a forbidden path that they had both known existed, but which they'd carefully avoided—like children whose adventurous imaginations had been discouraged by fear of a haunted cave.

But now that they'd taken the plunge and discovered what magic was concealed there, Alyson felt unsure of herself and apprehensive. She knew that what they had shared was something that touched her deeply and felt so right, and yet was so terribly wrong—particularly given the friendship between Alec and Andy. She felt the rub of embarrassment by the fact that she had given herself so completely to the husband of a close acquaintance. She deliberated on how she'd react the next time she saw Geraldine.

After she went to bed that night, the guilt began to ferment. Long beyond the time sleep would normally have claimed her she lay awake, thinking about Andy, wondering where he was and what he was doing.

Was he in danger? Was he under fire by terrorist guns in some distant place? Was he afraid? Where would he be sleeping tonight? . . . How would he react if he found out what she'd shared with Alec? Would he be deeply hurt or would he just let it pass? Would she lose him? Would he even care? The questions rotated in her mind like Catherine wheels, throwing out sparks of misgiving and fuelling her shame.

But then she started to wonder if Andy felt the same way about her as she felt about him. Did it really matter what she did with her personal life while Andy was off on operations, a part of his life that he steadfastly refused to talk about?

He was an amazing lover. Adventurous and uninhibited in his enthusiasm to experiment with new ideas, places and positions, but also gentle and kind, not only in bed but in most things that he did. On the other hand, he'd never even suggested that his feelings for her went any deeper than what they experienced in bed—so why should she feel so guilty about a little bit of fun with someone else in his absence?

Alyson had known Andy for four months when he'd introduced her to Alec and Geraldine, and there was an instant and powerful—if passive—attraction. Now they had consummated this attraction and Alyson was unsure whether to whoop with triumph or to weep with humiliation and remorse.

The next day, Alec phoned her to apologise for what had happened. He told her that they'd made a terrible mistake and that they should avoid seeing each other again.

Alyson wasn't sure whether she should be hurt or relieved, but she told him, philosophically, that it was inevitable.

'We both knew it was there, Alec,' she said. 'A hidden force, bubbling beneath the surface like a volcano, just waiting to erupt. So—now it's erupted, and there's not much we can do to change that. But you're right, seeing each other alone again wouldn't be sensible. For what it's worth, I'd like you to know that it was wonderful.'

'Thanks, Alyson,' he'd replied. 'I thought so too.'

But it didn't end there. A month later, Andy made a brief appearance. He'd been back at barracks for a week, but she saw very little of him because he spent most of the time working with a training team on something that, as usual, wasn't talked about.

When the day came for him to leave, Alyson drove him to New Sarum Air Base from where he and his team were to be flown out to their undisclosed operational zone. She had dropped him in a secure area outside a hangar, and waved him good bye as he ducked through the door and out of sight.

She was walking back to her car when she'd seen Alec emerging from Air Base Security. He hadn't seen her, and her first reaction was to avoid him and get to her car and drive away before he did. That, she thought, would save them both a good deal of embarrassment. But as she hurried to the car, she was stopped by a military policeman, wearing the rank of corporal on his sleeve.

He wanted to know what her business was in the area, and where she'd been. She explained her presence, but this didn't seem to satisfy the man and he requested that she go with him to the Base Security Office. She was annoyed and made no secret of the fact, telling him in clearly defined terms that she had neither the time nor the patience to be marched around like an errant foot soldier.

'Is there a problem here, corporal?' asked an authoritative voice. Alyson knew the voice and turned, looking straight at him, smiling shyly.

'Good morning, Major Bradford,' she said. 'I think this man's trying to arrest me.'

'Are you trying to arrest my friend here, corporal?' Alec grinned broadly at the young conscript.

The corporal saluted smartly as he leaped clumsily to attention.

'Just a routine check, sir,' he stammered. 'She's in a secure area without the correct authority, and I'm just following procedure. I didn't know she was with you, sir.'

'Well done, corporal,' said Alec pleasantly. 'You're doing a fine job and I want you to keep it up. But Miss Carstens is with me and we're leaving now. Carry on.'

'Yes sir! Thank you, sir!' gulped the MP. He saluted again, did an abrupt about-turn and marched away.

'Phew!' said Alec, mockingly. 'That was close. Imagine if I wasn't here to save you from that boy. My God! He could have had you sentenced to a fate worse than death.'

'Well, I suppose you'd know all about that, Major,' said Alyson, laughing. 'And what exactly is a fate worse than death?'

'Not having the time to lunch with me?' Alec raised a quizzical eyebrow. 'Now that could be simply awful.'

Alyson laughed. 'D'you think I'd be any safer with you than I would be if that sexy little corporal had arrested me?'

'You have no idea how safe you'll be with me,' he replied.

And so it began, and three hours later it came to a passionate climax between the sheets of Alyson's bed.

Over the following month, their meetings became more frequent. Alec invented flimsy reasons to come around to the apartment and Alyson put up no resistance. Their escapades took on an attitude of gay abandon, chasing each other around the apartment naked and dissolving into hysterics of playful laughter.

He made love to her over the sofa and on the lounge floor, in the shower and with her sitting astride him on a dining room chair. They performed oral sex on each other and explored each other's bodies with eager fascination. Their encounters were delightfully unrestrained and Alyson thought she'd fallen in love with him.

The nagging guilt that she was cheating on Andy was constantly in the back of her mind, but she chose to keep it there. She justified her relationship with Alec as a fantasy fulfilled, and she reminded herself that Andy, although tender and caring and a wonderful friend and lover, had never offered any expression of devotion. Besides, he was away so much that she sometimes wondered if he ever even thought about her when he wasn't with her. She had chosen to block out the fact that she was sleeping with her friend's husband and Andy's friend.

It came to an end when, lying together naked after an afternoon of breath-taking passion, Alec was pensive and withdrawn. She asked him what was on his mind.

'Guilt, Alyson.' He spoke simply, in a matter-of-fact tone that caught her by surprise. 'Every time we get together like this, I promise myself it'll be the last, and yet I keep getting drawn back. But I go home to Geraldine and I can barely look her in the eye. It's becoming awkward. I know she doesn't suspect anything, but sometimes the guilt gets so bad that it seems like I've got a fluorescent light flashing around me, spelling out the words "I'm cheating on you with your friend"—and it seems impossible to believe that she can't see it.

'I also think about Andy,' he continued. 'I know you're not married to him. I don't even know how you feel about him—and I'm not going to ask. But one thing I'm sure of is this: his feelings for you go much deeper than fondness. He took one hell of a knock a few years ago and he struggled to get over it—but I think it's behind him now and you're in no small way responsible for that. He knows that, although he might not openly allow himself to admit to it. And I know that if he knew what had gone on between us it would break his heart—and probably my jaw. I don't want either of those things to happen.'

'So I guess what you're saying is that you no longer want to see me,' said Alyson. 'Is that it?'

'It's not that I don't *want* to see you, Alyson. If this had happened two years ago they'd have needed a crowbar to get me away from you, but it didn't. As things are, we have to accept that what we've shared has been wonderful. It's been lots of fun but it's been illicit fun and the guilt is making me feel dirty. It must end.'

'Alec,' she replied, 'we went through this after the first time we made love. Do we stay away from each other now until the next time we have a chance meeting, and then pick up again where we've left off?'

'No we don't,' he said sternly. 'We say goodbye, now, and put it behind us. It can't go on, Alyson. It's over.'

Alec got dressed in silence and left the apartment without really saying goodbye. Alyson put on a robe and went through to the lounge while he dressed, and when he left she sat brooding on the sofa with her legs curled up beneath her rump. He'd simply smiled sadly at her as he headed for the door, and said: 'It's been one hell of a ride, Alyson. I'll miss you.' And then he was gone.

Alyson went to bed early and wept silently until she fell asleep. She had started to look forward to his visits with relish and the guilt that had originally plagued her had dwindled to a gentle nudge in moments of reflection.

She felt cheated, but she knew deep within herself that Alec's decision to end their relationship had in point of fact simply proven the inevitable. From the start she'd been conscious of the reality that, sooner or later, their affair would have to end. But she'd stubbornly hidden that awareness in the back of her mind. Now that it had come to pass—after only a month—she felt a worthlessness inside of her that nagged at her self-respect.

Ten days later, Andy returned from the mission he'd been on and her pleasure in seeing him was embodied in such an ardent rush of emotion that any feelings for Alec quickly faded into insignificance.

However, there was a nagging concern and she found this difficult to ignore—her period was five days late.

Andy was given two weeks of R & R leave and they flew to Lake Kariba and rented a chalet at the Carribea Bay resort overlooking the vast dam.

The weather was superb and they spent their days absorbed with the beauty of their surroundings.

They swam in natural rock pools and went water skiing. They went Tiger fishing from a motor raft and took sundowner booze cruises on a luxury barge. They witnessed the most miraculous sunsets over the lake. They sipped ice-cold beer from frosty cans as the orange glow of the sun slipped away beyond the horizon, giving way to a brief twilight before the darkness. They went game viewing from the deck of a houseboat along the shores of the lake from where they watched herds of elephant, buffalo and antelope roaming idly through the savannah grasslands along the water's edge. Zebra and giraffe grazed unobtrusively from the lush vegetation, undaunted by the presence of a pride of lions that lazily preened themselves in the dappled shade of an acacia tree. A pair of lion cubs romped playfully around their mother. A troop of baboons stared at them curiously from the safety of a gigantic baobab tree while scratching their chests and picking at knits. They were enchanted by the graceful flight of a fish eagle that swooped low over the lake surface to snatch a bream from the water and then soared away with the fish wriggling frantically in its talons.

They allowed themselves the luxury of forgetting about the war that embodied their day-to-day lives. They gave themselves as willing captives to the serenity and euphoria of a perfect life where their laughter was spontaneous, contagious and boundless. And they made love wherever and whenever the opportunity arose.

Alyson declared that if they died and went to heaven, paradise itself could not improve on those five days at Kariba.

They flew back to Salisbury on the morning of the sixth day and then drove the sixty kilometres to Golden Acres. There, they spent the remainder of Andy's leave playing tennis and swimming and taking long walks in the fields beyond the confines of the security fencing. They socialised with the community at the club and bonded in a way that made Alyson become conscious how much she was in love.

Alec had been a reckless adventure. While she could not find it in herself to feel regret over the affair, she was now thankful that it was over—and she knew that she'd never want him near her again. Andy was the man she wanted in her life, no matter how long she had to wait for him. Her love for him filled her soul and made her feel as though she'd been blessed by the touch of an angel. But, by now, her period was nearly three weeks late.

They returned to Salisbury the day before Andy was due to report back for duty. It was a Saturday, and they spent the evening with friends at *Le Coque Dor,* one of the many night spots in the city centre. They danced and revelled and laughed jubilantly, and they returned to the apartment after midnight, in a euphoric frame of mind, intoxicated more from their shared elation than from the alcohol they'd consumed.

The passion with which they made love before falling asleep in each other's arms had taken them to heights of ecstasy that magnified the essence of their existence. Neither of them wanted the sensation to subside.

The following morning, Andy left the apartment for Kabrit. Alyson kissed him goodbye at the door with a sense of trepidation. Never before had she felt so insecure. After he'd gone, she spent the day in a state of intense foreboding. She cried uncontrollably, and her tears threatened to overwhelm her. The preceding two weeks had sealed her love for Andy so strongly that, as she closed the door behind him, she felt that her world was about to disintegrate.

But her anguish ran deeper than that. She was now quite certain that she was pregnant, and she was acutely conscious of the fact that she had no way of knowing who the father was. The reality of her circumstances induced a sense of anxiety so intense that it made her nauseous.

The only way out, she thought, was to arrange an abortion, but she had no idea who she should see or how one went about making the necessary enquiries. No legitimate doctor would perform the procedure, so it would have to be done illegally.

She felt desperately alone. Perhaps she should have shared her suspicions with Andy. She didn't have to tell him about Alec—and she felt sure that he wouldn't even consider the possibility of someone else. No, she thought—I couldn't do that. Never!

It was late on Sunday afternoon by the time that Alyson finally picked up the phone and dialled the Mazoe exchange. She had no idea what she'd say when she got through to Golden Acres. She just knew that it was the most sensible thing to do.

Jennifer answered the call, and before the first sentence was complete she could hear the distress in her daughter's voice.

'What is it, Darling?' she asked in alarm. 'Are you alright?'

'Mummy,' said Alyson timidly, 'I'm in a lot of trouble. I'm going to need your help. Can you come into town?'

'I'm not going to ask what sort of trouble it is,' said Jennifer simply, 'but sit tight and I'll be there as soon as I can. It'll only be tomorrow, though. It's too late to leave here now. Take a deep breath, have a hot bath and get an early night.'

Her mother's response was like a tonic. Alyson immediately felt more relaxed. But the gnawing emptiness of Andy's absence did nothing to hold back her tears, and she cried herself to sleep.

Jennifer arrived at Alyson's door at nine on the Monday morning. She left the farm as soon as she'd done her morning routine, and Ralph—who had business to attend to—drove her into town. His business had no great urgency, but he decided to accompany his wife on her sudden impulse to spend a few days in Salisbury.

Jennifer had told him nothing of Alyson's call. She suspected that whatever trouble had to be dealt with, it was best handled between mother and her daughter. If Ralph needed to be drawn into it later, then so be it—but they could address that obstacle when it arose.

Alyson's eyes were puffy and red when she came to the door. Jennifer was shaken at the change that had come over her daughter in the two days since she last seen her. Alyson fell into her mother's arms, amid a fresh outburst of weeping, and Jennifer's heart went out to her. She hadn't seen her like this since the day on the farm, when she was only twelve, that her pet Dalmatian had been killed under the wheels of a tractor. She knew that whatever trouble it was, it was serious.

'It's alright, darling,' said Jennifer tenderly. She guided her through into the lounge. 'Nothing's so bad that it can't be put right. Tell me everything.'

Alyson started at the beginning. She told of the unspoken sexual attraction between her and Alec and how they had suppressed it. She told of how the first encounter had unfolded and how it turned itself into a full-blown and fabulous affair. She gave a colourful account of her feelings towards Andy, and she cried afresh in the telling of her suspected pregnancy and the fact that Andy might not be the father.

Jennifer sat in silence and listened intently. Then she sat back, biting her knuckles as she digested what she'd heard.

'Well, my love,' she said after a few moments of reflection, 'it seems we have to take this one step at a time.' She spoke with a tone of brisk and reassuring common sense. 'The first step is to get you down to Robert Sadler and have you checked out. This may just be a false alarm, in which case you've got yourself into this state over nothing.'

Robert Sadler had been the family doctor since before Alyson was born. He'd been an acquaintance of both Jennifer and Ralph when they were at university and had started his career as a General Practitioner. Now in his mid-fifties, he was a well-respected physician with a successful practice in the wealthy Salisbury suburb of Borrowdale.

'I don't know if this is good news or bad, young lady,' said Robert Sadler after examining Alyson, 'but it's a ninety percent certainty that you are going to be a mum. When did you say your last period was due?'

Alyson gave him the date again and he scribbled a calculation on his desk pad. 'Mmm," he said absently, 'that means you would have conceived around . . . .'

Alyson felt the colour drain from her face as her worst fears became a reality. If the doctor's calculations were correct, the child she was carrying could not possibly be Andy's. The horror that rose up within her made her feel dizzy.

'Are you alright?' asked Robert, observing the sudden pallor about her cheeks. 'Is this bad news?'

Jennifer noticed Alyson go pale at the mention of the conception date, and she knew without asking what had caused her daughter to react that way.

'Robert,' she said without hesitation, 'Alyson and I need a private moment. Is there somewhere we can talk?'

'You can use my office.' Robert indicated the room adjacent to his surgery.

Jennifer rose without replying and took Alyson by the hand. She led her out of the surgery into the doctor's office, and closed the door behind them.

'It's Alec's?' Jennifer's words were matter-of-fact. They were a statement rather than a question. Alyson nodded without replying.

'Well, darling, what do we do? You can live a lie for the rest of your life by telling Andy it's his child and persuading him to marry you. You can tell Alec about it and insist that he takes some responsibility and probably break up his marriage in the process, which will achieve absolutely nothing. You can tell Andy about your affair with Alec and see what happens. Not a good move. Or—and I think this is the most practical—you must consider a termination.'

Alyson sat down on the doctor's chair and gazed out of the window for a long and drawn out minute. Then she turned and looked at her mother:

'Andy once told me that Alec is a clone of his father,' she said. 'If he carries the same strong genes, the lie would not be lived for very long and we both know what that means. Getting

Alec involved isn't an option. Telling Andy the truth would tear us apart as much as if we waited for the child to be born and its features exposed the truth. I don't think I could bear that. Abortion is illegal in this country, mum, and I've heard horror stories about backstreet quacks.'

As she spoke, she became increasingly distraught. By the time she finished she was crying uncontrollably.

Jennifer went to her and took her in her arms, rocking her as she would a troubled child.

'We'll work it out, darling,' she said. 'Let's talk to Robert. I think we've been friends for long enough to be worthy of his help.'

They returned to the surgery where Robert was completing some documentation while he waited for them. They told him as much as he needed to know, and then they asked him what he could do about a termination. He sat pensively for some time, and eventually turned to Jennifer.

'We're old friends, Jen,' he said. 'And Alyson, I've known you since birth. If there was anyone I'd want to help out of this situation, it would be you. But I can't. Not personally anyway. I'm bound by the laws of the land and by the Hippocratic Oath that moulds the very essence of my profession. I would do myself, my calling, and potentially my career more damage than I'd be able to live with. In addition to which, you may hate me for it in years to come.'

'We need help on this, Robert,' said Jennifer emphatically. 'If necessary, we'll fly to England where a termination isn't illegal. Are you able to refer us to a good doctor there who'll make this go away?'

Robert sat with his elbow on the arm of his chair and the knuckles of his right hand under his chin, and he pondered their dilemma. After a few moments of reflection he looked up.

'I'll make some enquiries for you, Jen. I'll call you within a few days.'

'By the way, Robert,' said Jennifer as they rose to leave, 'Ralph will only get to know about this if it becomes absolutely necessary. Until then the only three people on this planet who know anything about it are in this room.'

'I understand, Jen,' he said with reassurance in his voice. 'Don't you worry about that. This is doctor-patient privilege.'

'Thank you, Robert. You're a good friend.' Jennifer placed a friendly kiss on his cheek as they got to the door.

Alyson was quiet while her mother and the doctor set about untangling her life, but now she put her arms around him and placed her head on his shoulder.

'I'm so sorry that we've had to bring this to you, Robert,' she said mournfully, 'but you do understand, don't you?'

The doctor smiled a broad and friendly smile.

'Life doesn't always treat us as kindly as we would like her to, Alyson,' he said. 'And not all the casualties of war fall on the battle field.'

By the time that they got back to the apartment, Alyson had regained her composure. She was visibly more relaxed now that the future seemed a bit clearer. She felt confident that the end of this terrifying nightmare was in sight and that with the help of Jennifer and Robert Sadler she'd be able to get on and put the ordeal behind her. She had a sudden mental image of Andy, and thought she felt her heart skip a beat. She'd have to bury this phase of her life somewhere deep in the back of her mind so that it would never again surface to haunt her.

Ralph took them to lunch at the Salisbury Club, an all-male domain and a legacy of Cecil John Rhodes where, traditionally, ladies were not permitted to enter by the front door. They had to use the side entrance and take the stairs to the first-floor dining room. It was a tradition that Jennifer abhorred with an obsession, but Ralph loved the ambience of place and so, on the occasions when he chose to dine there, she clenched her teeth and enjoyed the cuisine.

As they left the club after lunch they passed a newspaper vendor, shouting the headlines that announced the arrival in Salisbury of a group of international intermediaries. Another attempt at pacifying all parties in the hope of bringing the war to an end.

'Bah!' snorted Ralph. 'As if we haven't done enough to appease the bloody terrorists!' And then, as an afterthought, 'By the way, where's Andy gone off to?'

'That's something only Andy and the people he works with would be able to tell you, dad,' replied Alyson. 'And it would be easier to squeeze blood out of a stone than to make him talk about it.'

At that moment, Andy, Stuart, Rob and Vern were at Deka Drum, preparing for a mission—the outcome of which would end up thwarting the plans that were being made to release Alyson from her anguish.

Robert Sadler phoned Jennifer on the following morning with the results of his enquiries amongst colleagues in England.

'I've chatted to an old university friend, Jen,' he said. 'Do you remember Quintin Burnside?'

'Can't say I do,' replied Jennifer. 'Should I?'

'Maybe not. He graduated with me and went on to specialize in obstetrics. He has a practice on Harley Street in London. He's indicated that he'd be prepared to see Alyson. I don't think he makes a habit of performing abortions unless the health of either the mother or the child is threatened, but he's a man of the world and good at what he does. I've filled him in on your dilemma. Let's just say that I think he's sympathetic to the situation. He's familiar with what happens in circumstances of war, and he's seen the long-term effects that situations like these tend to have on the life of a child.'

Jennifer ignored the inference contained in Robert's justification of Quintin Burnside's involvement.

'So where do we go from here, Robert?' she asked. 'Do I call him and make an appointment, or do we just arrive on his doorstep and tell him who we are?'

'I'd suggest you get there first. Once you're in London, call him to make an appointment. I'll phone him when you're ready to leave and give him the dates you're going to be there. I'll also give you a letter of referral so you can minimize the small talk about the purpose of your visit.'

'You're a darling, Robert! Thank you! I'll let you know once we're set. I'm not sure how I'm going to explain to Ralph why we need to take an overseas trip—maybe we'll have to come clean. He's unlikely to disown his daughter, but I hoped to protect him from this.'

'I don't know why, Jen,' said Robert. 'I'm sure he'll take it his stride. He won't want Alyson to be in the place she is at the moment, any more than you do. He's not a medieval monk who'll have her burnt at the stake, you know!'

'We'll see,' said Jennifer. 'I'll call you when we're ready to go.'

It was only when Jennifer began the process of trying put their travel arrangements in place that she came to appreciate the complications associated with venturing abroad on a Rhodesian passport.

Enquiries served to remind her of the fact that within the restrictions placed upon Rhodesia in its capacity as a political pariah on the global stage, her citizens were not welcome guests in Britain. Jennifer discovered that she was entirely ignorant of the technical hitches involved in making an application for a travel permit. She was aghast at the discovery that it could take two months or more to overcome the mountain of bureaucratic red tape that the authorization needed.

Most frustrating of all was that she couldn't call upon any of Ralph's multitude of well-connected associates to help her, without exposing the reason for her sudden impulse to travel.

'We might have to come up with a plan B, darling,' she told her daughter as they sat in Alyson's apartment sipping sundowners. 'It doesn't look as though this is going to be as simple as we thought.'

Jennifer told Alyson of the information she had gleaned from her enquiries and the unlikelihood of them getting travel documents before it was apparent to all that she was pregnant— and too late for a safe abortion to be performed.

'When do you think Andy will be back?' she asked.

'That could be any time, mum. Sometimes he's gone for weeks; other times for days. It could even be a month or more. Why do you ask?'

'I'm just wondering about how much time we have. Perhaps Robert knows someone in South Africa who can help us. That would be the easiest way out. At least we wouldn't have to worry about what they call "extraordinary travel permits". We could just fly down and be back the next day.'

'Except that pregnancy terminations'—she couldn't bring herself to say abortion, it just sounded so dirty—'are as illegal in South Africa as they are here,' Alyson reminded her mother.

'Yes. But I'm sure there are far more doctors in South Africa than there are here who may be prepared to bend the rules a little . . . . At the right price, of course.' Jennifer said no more.

Alyson's apprehension rose again. The anxiety she'd felt before their appointment with Robert Sadler had returned. The trepidation sat in the pit of her stomach and it threatened to grow into panic.

'This all makes me feel so cheap,' she said, with tears starting to rise to the surface. 'I just so wish it was Andy's baby. I wouldn't want to be rid of it then, even if he didn't want to marry me. But at least I wouldn't have to lie and cheat to protect myself.'

'Are you protecting yourself, or are you protecting Andy, darling?' asked Jennifer sipping at her wine. 'He's the one who would be hurt the most by this if he were to know the truth. And if he finds out, what do you suppose he'll do?'

'I think he'd hate me,' replied Alyson. 'And I don't ever want to see that in his eyes. I love him, mum, more than I can tell you. I couldn't bear the thought of him turning his back on me in disgust—and that's what I think he'd do. I think I'd die. So to answer your question, maybe I'm trying to protect us both but it's me who would be hurt more than anyone if Andy were to walk away and leave me.'

'Well then, whatever we decide to do,' said Jennifer, 'it's going to have to be done before Andy gets back. He only left on Sunday morning, so I'm sure he won't be back before next week at the earliest. Today's Wednesday. Let's hope we can get this over with before the weekend.'

Jennifer left to join Ralph in their apartment next door.

Alyson allowed her mind to dwell on how this nightmare would pan out if she just did nothing.

She could make herself believe that it was Andy's baby she was carrying. She and Alec had resumed their relationship on the same day that Andy had left—but it was a whole week before she saw him again. Robert's calculations of conception being around that date could easily be wrong. They had to be wrong. She could have conceived during the few days that Andy had been back at barracks on his training course. That was close enough to the middle of her cycle as the next time she saw Alec. Of course it was Andy's baby!

She felt a rush of relief so exhilarating that it was like a huge burden lifted off her shoulders and away from her soul. It was Andy's baby! And all this worry was for nothing! A flood of affection swept over her. She felt it with such intense excitement that she started to laugh uncontrollably. She got up and danced around the apartment as if she'd just received news that her lotto ticket had turned up the winning numbers.

She luxuriated in a hot bath, and she climbed into bed. There, she whispered a silent prayer of thanks to whatever power had inspired her to see the situation for what it really was. What she had persuaded herself to now firmly believed what it really was.

# CHAPTER 26

The insistent ringing of the telephone dragged Alyson up through a cloudy stratum of sleep as her mind groped around for consciousness. Suddenly she was fully awake, and she looked at her bedside clock. It was 5.45 am. She rolled over, wondering why anyone would be calling at this time, and she lifted the receiver. She mumbled a sleepy 'Hello.'

'Alyson, its Alec.'

She went cold. Her senses were now on a knife edge.

'What do you want, Alec?' she said petulantly. 'Why are you phoning me? We've got nothing to say to each other and I don't want to hear from you.'

'Alyson, its Andy,' he cut in. 'Andy's been shot.'

The words brought the world around Alyson to an abrupt standstill. A rush of adrenaline seized her stomach and drained her face of colour. Her heart began to race and she felt the palms of her hands break out into a sweat. 'No! No, this isn't happening!'

She sat bolt upright on the side of the bed in silence, clutching the telephone receiver with both hands. Her whole body began to tremble.

'Are you there, Alyson?' asked Alec and it sounded as though he was talking in an echo chamber.

'I'm here,' she said softly after a long pause. 'How bad is he?'

'He was casevacked to Vic Falls yesterday where he had emergency surgery. I believe they're transferring him to Andrew Fleming today, but it depends on whether the doctors think he's stable enough to be airlifted.'

'How bad is he, Alec?' she yelled hysterically. 'Don't try filling my head with bullshit, just answer my fucking question! How-bad-is-he?' She split the question into four unmistakably emphatic syllables.

'He's going to be okay, Alyson,' said Alec defensively. 'He was downed in a contact, but they got him out. He's awake and talking. That's as much as I know. I'm trying to get more information and I'll keep you posted.' He was silent for a moment, and then carried on:

'He's a strong guy, Alyson—and a survivor. He'll be alright. I'm sure of it.'

Alyson's mind teetered on the edge of an abyss. The strain of the past few days had been mercifully assuaged by her personal affirmation that it was Andy's baby she carried and not Alec's. The relief and serenity had been so heart-warming that she allowed all doubt to be erased. She and Andy would share and love this child with the passion from which it had been conceived.

She had gone to bed with these thoughts stored securely and happily in her mind.

The wake-up call she had just received served to shatter her reverie as if it had been a fragile object beneath a hammer blow to an anvil.

She rose from the bed and paced around the apartment restlessly, her imagination starting to play mind games with her.

Alec had said that Andy had to undergo emergency surgery. What did that mean? Had he lost a leg? An arm? An eye? He was awake and talking! Was he in pain, talking from behind bandaged eyes that would never see again? Had he been burned? Would he be an invalid for the rest of his life?

Her anxiety and the frustration of helplessness born of not knowing, coupled with the fact that she was entirely dependent upon Alec for news, infuriated her.

'Oh God, Andy!' she whispered to herself. She so badly wanted to go to him, to see him and be with him.

She boiled the kettle and made herself coffee, but then poured it down the sink after the first sip. She stripped the bed to make it up and couldn't get the sheets straight, so she left it. She picked up and put down ornaments and straightened doilies and coffee tables that weren't out of place. She couldn't keep her hands still. She fidgeted constantly as her sense of helplessness grew.

She tried to resist the impulse to go next door to her parent's apartment and wake her mother, but she finally succumbed— only to find when she got there that the apartment was empty. Ralph and Jennifer had gone off for an early morning stroll through the Avenues.

Returning to her own apartment, frustration and anxiety reaching breakpoint, she pottered around trying to force herself to be positive and find something constructive to do. She checked the time and saw that an hour had gone by since the call from Alec.

She sat by the phone and wrung her hands. She willed it to ring and wondered how she could reach Alec to push him for an update.

When the instrument suddenly jangled to life she flinched in alarm and hurriedly snatched it off the cradle.

'Hello?'

'It's Alec, Alyson. They're moving Andy as we speak. There's a re-supply Dak at The Falls and he's coming back to Salisbury on that.'

'Have they said how badly injured he is?

'He was shot in the stomach. The doctors are happy that he's in no real danger. . . . Listen, you may have a bit of trouble trying to see him immediately so I'd like to offer you my help. Is that okay?'

'What sort of help would that be, Alec?'

'Meet me at the hospital at eleven thirty. I'll pull rank and get you through to the ward. The medics in the war-wounded zone tend to be a bit sensitive about incoming casevacs.'

'I'll be there,' she breathed.

She hung up with a sense of such overwhelming relief that it made her feel light headed.

As she sat beside the phone, gathering her thoughts, she heard her parents returning from their walk. She rushed out into the corridor to intercept them at the door.

'Andy's been shot!' she blurted out.

She saw her mother raise a hand to her mouth, her eyes wide with alarm. Ralph looked at her, calmly taking in what she was saying.

'Is he going to be alright?' he asked in the slow deliberate manner she knew to be his way of taking charge.

She quickly told them of the early morning call and of the news she'd just received, and she noticed the cloud of concern in her mother's eyes. A cloud born not of concern for Andy so much as how this development would affect her plans to have Alyson relieved of the burden she carried.

'I'm meeting someone at the hospital at half past eleven, who'll get me in to see him,' said Alyson happily. She put her arms around her mother and kissed her:

'Everything's going to be okay, mum—so you can stop worrying.'

She wasn't sure if her mother had heard the silent message in her words, but she would explain later. In the meantime, Andy was on his way back and she needed to be there for him.

Alyson was at the hospital entrance shortly after ten. She paced back and forth, impatiently waiting for Alec to arrive.

Just after 10.30 a military helicopter landed on a cordoned-off helipad at the far end of the hospital building, a few metres away from a side entrance to the emergency ward. There was a flurry of activity as a stretcher was offloaded with an obscured form strapped to it. A drip bag with dangling tubes was held high by one of the attendants as they moved the unconscious figure from the chopper onto a hospital stretcher.

From where she stood, Alyson couldn't see who the patient was but she strained to identify any familiar signs. 'Is it Andy?' she wondered, but the gurney was swiftly wheeled away and the party of nurses and white-coated men disappeared with their charge into the building.

The helicopter lifted off scattering a cloud of swirling leaves and dust. Shortly afterwards an army ambulance pulled up in the same area and a repeat performance was carried out, frantically transferring another wounded soldier through the double doors into the ward.

Alyson had never been near the army casualty ward and she was shocked by the frequency of casualty evacuations being brought in.

'Was either of those two Andy? Where's Alec?' She glanced anxiously at her watch, willing the time to have passed, but it was not yet 10.45. Alec had said eleven thirty.

'Why so late?' she asked herself apprehensively. 'Where is he?' Her anxiety was becoming tangible.

An olive green sedan bearing military licence plates eased to a halt close to where she stood at the hospital front entrance. She moved towards it anxiously, but a man wearing a captain's insignia in the uniform of the Chaplain Corps got out and held open the rear door for a man and woman in their late forties. The woman held a tissue to her nose, her eyes red with tears, while the man—himself looking sombre and close to tears—took her arm. They followed the padre into the hospital reception. As they passed her, Alyson heard the woman say quietly through her sobs, 'Roger, please don't let this be true! He was only nineteen!'

She walked up to the cordon that surrounded the helipad, in the hope of reaching a vantage point from where she could see through the doors and into the resuscitation rooms—but the blinds behind the glass were pulled down and she was denied whatever she hoped to see.

Time dragged by. Every minute seemed like an interminable hour, and her annoyance at being kept waiting bubbled within her. She walked around the car park and back to the helipad, then back to the main entrance of the hospital.

'*Come on!*' she begged silently, '*What's taking so long?*'

Alec finally arrived at 11.15, and she berated him for keeping her waiting.

'What took you so long?' she demanded.

Alec was unflustered. He looked at her with mild amusement.

'I said eleven thirty, Alyson. I'm fifteen minutes early. No need to make a fuss.'

'Is Andy here?' She spoke brusquely as if she hadn't heard Alec.

'He should be,' replied Alec calmly. 'He left Sarum by chopper an hour ago.'

Alyson was about to tear strips off him for not getting there sooner if he knew Andy had been airlifted from the base, but she thought better of it.

'That must have been him they brought in while I was standing here!' The thought struck her with a mixture of excitement and irritation.

Alec whisked her through reception and down a long corridor, passing signs in yellow script on a green background inscribed 'military wing.' He spoke briefly to a staff sergeant medical orderly, who consulted a chart and pointed the far side of the ward.

'Right at the end, sir,' he said. 'Turn left to intensive care. But I think you'll find he's not fully conscious right now. He's pretty heavily sedated. Are you a relative?'

'Just a close friend, Staff,' replied Alec, using the abbreviation for the man's rank. He strode away briskly down the aisle between the rows of hospital beds and the wounded men who occupied them. Alyson had to break into an intermittent trot to keep up with him.

They approached the bed to which they had been directed by a matronly nursing sister in the intensive care ward, and Alyson caught her breath.

Andy seemed to have lost weight. His normal healthy colour was replaced with a dirty yellow pallor that made him look shrivelled and ill. His eyes were closed, but they were encircled by dark rings like bruises on a prize fighter, and they seemed to have receded into their sockets behind the lids. Beads of perspiration oozed from his forehead and upper lip and as they rose they trickled down his face leaving streaks of moisture, like snail trails running off him onto his pillow.

There was a drip stand beside the bed, with an inverted bag of clear fluid hanging from it. Droplets of the fluid slowly fell into tubes that ran to a cannular embedded in his arm. Small circular pads were stuck to his naked chest above his heavily bandaged abdomen, with thin wires snaking away to a monitor above the bed that bleeped to the monotonous rhythm of his heartbeat.

Alyson instinctively seize Alec's arm as the shock of Andy's appearance hit her. She turned her head into his shoulder to conceal the tears of alarm that rose in her eyes.

'What have they done to him?' she whispered in alarm. 'He looks so weak—so vulnerable!'

Then she looked up and was gripped by a new resolve. She abruptly released Alec's sleeve as though she was discarding a crutch that was no longer needed, and she strode up boldly to the bed. There, she reached for a towel that lay beside a stainless steel bowl of warm water on the bedside cabinet. She soaked it and then squeezed it out and gently began to wipe away the perspiration on his face.

Suddenly Andy began to thrash and arch in his sleep as if gripped in the embrace of a terrifying nightmare. Alyson doused the towel in the bowl again and wiped his forehead with warm water, softly calling to him. 'Andy—come on, it's okay—come back to me.'

Andy stopped his thrashing and lay quite still for a moment, and then his eyes shot open and he stared blankly—first at her and then at Alec. The confusion in his expression was absolute, as if he recognised neither her nor the man standing beside her, and then Alec spoke in a lightly mocking voice.

'You do realise of course, sergeant, that we cannot have these outbursts,' he said with a goading smile. 'They tend to disrupt the repose and well-being of other patients.'

The recognition flooded into Andy's eyes, and he smiled weakly.

'Piss off, Alec,' he said. 'What are you doing here?'

# CHAPTER 27

Alyson lay silently in the bedroom of the apartment that she and Andy had shared—alone with her thoughts and memories, and beside herself with self-loathing.

Andy had taken the news of her pregnancy in such blind faith, never once questioning her reliability nor suspecting that she had been living a lie with him ever since she had discovered her condition and had so brazenly proclaimed that he was to be a father. It had taken her mother utterly by surprise at Andy's bedside when his disclosure had made it apparent that she had already told him of her pregnancy, and Jennifer had been infuriated by Alyson's indiscretion.

'Have you lost your mind?' Jennifer had yelled at Alyson when the two of them had been alone later that night. 'My God, girl! I've put everything I hold sacred on the line to protect you in this, and you throw it back in my face with contempt! What do you propose doing when the truth comes out? Tell me, you stupid little trollop, what will you do? Do you honestly believe Andy, or any other man for that matter, would stay with you once he discovers that you've been carrying someone else's baby and passing it off as his? I don't have any words to describe the damage you've done.'

In exasperation, with gritted teeth, she had run her hand through her hair and clenched her fists above her head as if desperately appealing for divine assistance to provide the words to adequately express her outrage. The tension and anger displayed in her face had been like a tangible, living thing.

Alyson had responded defensively, with an intensity that matched her mother's:

'Don't be so melodramatic, mother. I know what I'm doing. It was a scare, that's all. This baby is Andy's—I know that for sure. I don't have to hide anything from anyone. I'm sorry I put you through such anxiety, but there's no reason for you, or dad, or Andy or anyone else to worry about it. Mum, it's Andy's baby. And we're going to be happily married and become wonderful parents.'

'Oh, really?. And what makes you so sure, young lady?' Jennifer was unmoved and incredulous. 'Have you magically changed the dates of your indiscreet liaisons with Andy's friend? Or have you just found a way in your mind to make the truth go away? God, Alyson, don't be such a fool! You're throwing away your life and taking on the responsibility of destroying the lives of other people around you. I'm astonished—you're so downright self-centred and stubborn in the face of all the facts.'

Jennifer paced around the room in a state of fuming frustration, while Alyson sat and watched her in silence. Finally Jennifer sat down heavily in an armchair and exhaled with a loud and exasperated sigh.

'I'll go along with you, Alyson,' she ventured after a long silence. 'You're making the biggest mistake of your life and I beg of you to think seriously about what you've done. There may still be ways for us to undo the damage and I'll be there to help. But for now you'll just have to live with yourself and carry on as if everything is normal. It's pretty obvious just from looking at Andy that he's been through hell and it's unlikely that he'll talk to anyone about it, but he's going to need time to recover. Living in ignorance and having you there in the misguided belief that you're the mother of his unborn child will be a help—for now.

'Bring him out to the farm when they discharge him. We'll nurse him back to health there.'

Jennifer then left the apartment without another word. Next morning, before Alyson woke up, she and Ralph had left Salisbury and returned to Golden Acres.

\* \* \*

Now, having taken the plunge and told Andy of her affair, Alyson lay in bed, on the morning when he had left with such haste and anger as the events of recent months pored over her. Remorse, self-pity, vivid recollections, and an overriding fear tipped the delicate balance of her troubled mind.

In her torment and guilt, her self-respect had wilted like a neglected flower in the hot African sun—together with her love for Andy and any hope for their future. Cold reality had returned, and she no longer believed that her unborn child was Andy's. She came to realise with an unquestionable certainty that it was Alec's baby, and she knew that she could never face the consequences of that on her own.

Up until the fateful night of their wedding she had shrewdly and successfully hidden her anxiety from Andy and she knew that he had suspected nothing of the torment that she'd suffered since the confirmation of her pregnancy. She had sat beside Jennifer's death bed willing her to live and be there to help her with the dilemma that she faced—but as her mother's life slipped away, Alyson felt she had nowhere to turn. She withdrew into herself, shutting out the world around her and with it any possibility of resolving her predicament.

Suicide appeared to be the only reasonable escape, and since the moment that Jennifer died, Alyson had pondered this option endlessly. Confessing her affair to Andy was a last-gasp attempt at finding support or justification, one way or another. His reaction, utterly damning but predictable enough, seemed adequate justification for her to end it all.

She'd been constantly preoccupied with the certainty that suicide would solve her problems, but she'd given little thought to the method. Now, imprisoned by her sense of isolation, harrowed by recollections of the idyllic life and love that she'd lost, she felt again the burden of depression that lay on her like an all-consuming black shroud. She lay all day in bed, sleeping fitfully, and each time she awoke her sense of despair deepened.

Suddenly it struck her—she was certain what to do.

She rose, as if on an urgent errand, and out of the drawer in the pedestal on Andy's side of the bed she took the keys for his gun safe.

The rifle stood upright in its bracket. She stared at it for a long time, and then she reached in and pulled it out by the stock. She had never used a semi-automatic rifle before, but she had watched Andy strip and clean the weapon a hundred times. There seemed to be something missing, though, and she reached into the depths of memory to try and work out what it was. *The magazine!* It struck her with a jolt. *There's no magazine.* She frantically pulled open the metal drawer in the safe and, like a chronic alcoholic finding the hidden bottle, breathed a sigh of relief when she saw a pile of loaded clips stacked neatly inside.

Leaving the safe door open, she moved back to the bed. There, she clumsily tried to fit the magazine to the rifle. It took her four attempts before she finally got it right and she felt the solid click as the attachment snapped into place. She placed the muzzle beneath her chin, gingerly flirting with the touch of cold steel against her skin.

*This is for you, Andy,* she told herself. *You'll forget me with time and get on with your life and you'll be free of the torment that our life together will bring. Please forgive me.*

And then she paused and put the weapon aside, staring blankly at the open safe door. With a remote sense of principle, it occurred to her that she should leave a parting message—a note that would make Andy understand. The urge became powerful—she suddenly felt the need to tell him that, despite everything, she still loved him—that her troubled conscience had overwhelmed all emotions other than guilt, fear and anger.

She found writing paper in the bureau in the hall and sat down to write. Three times she crumpled the paper into a ball and threw it onto the floor beside her and started afresh. Then, satisfied, she stood up and returned to the bedroom.

The rifle lay on the bed. She stared at it without expression for a long and indecisive minute, then she sat down and hesitantly picked it up.

Again she placed the muzzle beneath her chin. She looked up at the ceiling, and she reached down with her thumb for the trigger. She gently pressed on it. It did not budge. She pressed harder, but still nothing happened. She thumped the butt on the floor and tried again . . . . Nothing. Then it came to mind that there would be a safety catch. She looked down to where she imagined it would be situated and, finding the change lever, shifted it one position downwards.

Once again she placed the weapon beneath her chin, closed her eyes and pressed the trigger. It moved easily under the pressure of her thumb, but an eerie silence followed and nothing happened.

She was growing frantic. Her heart pounded as if she'd run a hundred metre sprint and her palms were now sweating, her hands shaking. She pressed the trigger again . . . . Nothing! *What's the matter with this damn thing?* She screamed inwardly. *I want to die . . . . Please, just let me die!*

The answer emerged as though a light had been switched on in her mind, and she felt foolish: *There's no round in the chamber!*

And suddenly she was laughing. It was a feverish and high-pitched hysterical laugh. She turned the rifle, took a firm hold on the cocking lever, pulled it back as far as it would go and released it. The sharp metallic reverberation of the slide hitting home echoed through the empty apartment like the clang of a cell gate in a prison corridor.

Touching the cold steel against the soft skin under her chin, she pressed down on the trigger again.

# CHAPTER 28

Andy started awake and stared at his surroundings mystified. The sun hung low over the lake and it took him a moment to realise where he was. He looked at his watch and saw it was just after five. He'd slept for nearly four hours and yet he felt exhausted. He was shaken by the crystal clarity of the dream he'd just awakened from and it left him feeling uneasy to the point of sensing the grip of an anxiety attack.

He became consumed by a premonition that something somewhere was terribly wrong. He experienced a sudden, inexplicable sense of urgency that he must get back to town and he left his place of refuge and hurried back to where he had left his car.

Speed restrictions on the roads outside of the city limits had been cast aside ever since the first civilian ambush casualties of the war and Andy pushed his vehicle to the maximum of its capability.

It took him eight minutes to cover the twenty kilometres back to the outskirts of Salisbury and another ten to get through the traffic to The Avenues and Alyson's apartment.

Under the circumstances of his leaving that morning, and his impulsive vow to himself that it was for good, he had paid scant attention to what subconscious influence had drawn him back there, but as he rounded the corner from North Avenue into Baines, where the apartment was located he felt the icy hand of dread snap around his soul with the force of a bear trap. A flurry of activity outside the building amidst flashing of blue and red lights sent a chill up his spine that caught his breath and raised the hair at the back of his neck.

He pulled his car onto the sidewalk, avoiding a cordon of yellow and black tape that surrounded the entrance to the apartment block and apprehensively approached a sombre looking group of police officers who stood huddled together just outside the double glass doors.

"What's going on?" he asked with an intuitive forewarning that the answer was something he did not want to hear.

"Do you live in this block sir?" asked one of the policemen ignoring his question.

"I did until this morning." said Andy offhandedly, "Am I allowed to know what all the fuss is about?"

"What floor are you on?" asked the officer.

"Why can't you just give me an answer?" asked Andy with irritation. "I come home to find police and ambulance men crawling all over the block I live in, surely someone can tell me what it's all about?"

"These are just routine questions sir" the policeman responded. "We can't let anyone in at the moment unless they reside here. You do reside here I take it?"

"Yes" said Andy becoming exasperated. "My name is Andrew Mason and I live on the third floor"

He caught the collective stunned exchange of glances on the faces of the officers around him and he instinctively knew that he had to get through. He pushed past the policeman blocking his path and headed for the stairs.

"Wait a minute sir . . . !!" shouted the man . . . "you can't go up there"

"Try stopping me" yelled Andy in reply.

He took the stairs three at a time in a panic-stricken dash for the third floor with the shouts of "Stop that man" echoing behind him. As he reached the top of the stairs, he was confronted by a bear of a man wearing sergeant bars on his khaki police uniform. The man put out a hand to stop Andy but with practiced skill that came to him by instinct from long hours in training he was around him and down the corridor before the big man knew what had happened.

He barged into the apartment—and was confronted by a mass of uniformed men and women, all bent on their own activity.

He had started to become frantic. The feeling that he had awakened with after his explicit dream that something terrible had transpired, had increased in intensity as each kilometre had sped beneath the wheels of his car and the spectacle that had greeted him upon his arrival had pushed his foreboding to a point of dread.

At first glance, the apartment looked no different to the way it had been when he'd left that morning, other than the fact that there were far too many people in it now, but as he looked from the lounge down the passage toward the bedroom, his world exploded and the bellow that emerged from the very depths of his soul was like that of a wounded and angry bull elephant.

From where he stood, he could see it—the bedroom wall covered in spattered blood, with small pieces of yellow tissue sticking to it like globules from the aftermath of a mess-hall food fight.

His howl had stopped the bustling crowd of emergency workers and hands were all over him trying to restrain his determined march towards the sickening spectacle that would haunt him for the rest of his life.

He sub consciously but violently threw off the attempts to stop him from entering the room and he approached it as if in a trance. After what seemed like a very long walk he stood at the door and gazed in.

Alyson lay sprawled on the bed with a small black hole just beneath her chin. Her jaw line was still in place and her bottom teeth protruded from it in a grotesque grin. The rest of her head was a shattered unrecognisable mess of bone and blood with thick tufts of twisted hair stuck to the congealing mess of what remained of her skull.

On the floor beside the bed, as if having been carelessly discarded lay Andy's R1 assault rifle.

The voices around him seemed to rise and recede in a meaningless sequence of echoes, his vision blurred and the room began to move as if being viewed through a volume of water. Nausea rose up from deep within him and erupted in a stream of projectile vomiting as he felt his knees lose their grip and transform to the consistency of fresh putty. He staggered, fighting against the all consuming sensation of limbs that had been drained of their strength and as he tried to force himself to remain upright and focussed he was overcome by the awareness that he was losing the battle and for a few moments, a shroud of darkness seemed to engulf him like a black curtain being slowly drawn across his consciousness.

Andy stumbled. He fought to remain upright but his knees folded beneath him. He staggered and fell forward against the bed upon which Alyson's body was sprawled. The bed in which, that same morning, they'd made love.

Through uncomprehending bewilderment, he reached out to touch her, and his stomach churned with nauseating horror. He tasted the sharp bile in his throat. He floundered in utter disbelief—*this isn't happening . . . . It's a hellish nightmare from which I'll wake up . . . . I'll make amends to Alyson and we'll move on into the future with our child . . . .*

He struggled to get his thoughts into logical order, but he heard himself crying out—as if from somewhere far away—*What have you done? Oh God, Alyson! What have you done?*

Strong hands lifted him from the floor, and he didn't have the strength to fight them off. He was being bundled away, but as they propelled him from the room he couldn't help staring back, gazing intently at the spectacle of the unspeakably mutilated remains of the woman he'd so desperately loved and cherished.

He was guided to a chair in the lounge. His escort sat him down and he stared vacantly at the faces surrounding him.

*Strangers. All strangers. What are they doing here? Where've they all come from?*

Someone was gently holding his head, trying to get him to drink water from a glass pressed against his lips. A man, who looked like an adolescent in a policeman's uniform, was talking to him—but the animated voice seemed to come like words piped electronically through an echo-system from another place. They were a mere confusion of incoherent sound. He gazed before him, without blinking, denying that any of this was real. He pushed the glass away and sat forward, his head in his hands, trying to gather his thoughts. Gradually his surroundings cleared and he looked up at the people around him.

'When did this happen?' he asked weakly.

'We received a call from one of the neighbours about an hour ago,' replied the policeman. 'May I ask you what your relationship is to the deceased?'

Andy looked at the man as if it was the most dim-witted question he had ever been asked.

'She's my wife,' he said softly, after staring at the man condescendingly for a long and drawn-out second. He repeated his answer, his tone trailing off to a whisper: 'My wife . . . .'

'May I ask where you were this afternoon, sir?' spoke the man.

Andy continued to stare at him in disbelief. Anger flared, suddenly, and his mind leaped into crystal clarity as sharp and coherent as a highly skilled paratrooper engaged in combat.

'Yes,' he said defiantly, 'you may ask.' He left it hanging there, offering no further response.

'Well?' asked the man impatiently.

'You sought my permission to ask a question,' retorted Andy. 'You have that permission. I didn't say I'd give you an answer. Now may I ask you to do what has to be done here and then leave. I'd like a bit of time on my own—if you don't mind.'

'These are routine questions, sir,' said the officer, "and I'm afraid I must insist on an answer.'

Andy rose from his chair like a striking adder. He had the young man by the lapels of his tunic, slamming him against the wall with an impact that dislodged the paintings that hung nearby.

'I just don't feel up to being questioned by the police on this issue right now,' he hissed, gesturing with a slant of his head towards the bedroom. 'What you see in there is the body of my dead wife, who has clearly taken her own life. What the hell difference does it make where I was when she chose to do that? I don't know what you're getting at, but right now I need to be by myself. So just get on with your job and leave me alone until I've had time to deal with what's happened. Do I make myself clear?'

The policeman stared at him with a look of wide-eyed terror, unable to move from within the grip that Andy had on him.

A second man, wearing the rank of inspector on his epaulettes, placed a hand gently on Andy's shoulder.

'Steady on, sir,' he said calmly. 'We realise it's a terrible shock to you.'

He paused and looked angrily at the dishevelled police officer. 'Constable, would you go and wait downstairs. Where's your sense of delicacy, man?'

Then he turned back to Andy:

'I'm sorry about this,' he said. 'He's young but he'll learn. Are you sure you'll be alright sir? Wouldn't you rather have us take you away from here?'

Andy slowly released the man and turned. A dozen faces were glaring at him as if in suspended animation, displaying frozen stares of mixed sentiment. He looked down apologetically.

'I'll be alright,' he said softly, wondering deep within himself if he'd ever be alright again. His anger was subsiding, but was rapidly being replaced by something else—a deeply bewildering emotion that he couldn't identify. Tears welled up in his eyes and he felt himself losing control again. He walked slowly out through the sliding glass doors onto the balcony, and seated himself on a patio chair.

The sun had fallen beneath the horizon and it was starting to get dark, leaving just a soft blush of orange in the western sky. He gazed out into the gloom of the evening and the magnificence of the jacaranda trees that lined the Avenues in their full December bloom, and his heart broke. The events, the emotions, of the day overwhelmed him. Anger, grief, and disbelief. He let go, and he was convulsed by unrestrained tears.

The police and paramedics left him there, undisturbed, while they completed the gruesome task of moving Alyson from the apartment and down to the waiting mortuary van.

Her revelation that morning, that she and Alec had been lovers while he was away on operational duty, had rocked his self-esteem. He had felt a sensation bordering on what he thought could be loathing. But an event of this magnitude had been so far from his mind that even in the most absurd stretch of his imagination he would never have entertained the possibility. His mind now held no malice—only absolute bewilderment.

*How could she do this?* He ran the scenario in his mind, through tears of frustration. *When did she make up her mind to kill herself? Was her confession this morning intended as a legacy to leave him with? Or, was it his reaction that triggered her decision?*

The questions pounded at his conscience, but there were no answers. For perhaps the first time in his life, he was utterly without the ability to take charge. He suddenly understood the real meaning of being internally crushed.

Time ran by, unmeasured. Then his reverie was interrupted by footsteps on the balcony behind him, and he turned to see one of the police officers standing awkwardly at the door.

'We're finished here for now, sir,' he said uncomfortably. 'But I'm afraid we have to ask you to vacate this apartment for the time being—until we've completed things. Is there anywhere else you can stay for the night?'

Andy looked back over the balustrade and gazed out into the darkness that engulfed his surroundings. Lights were on in the apartment blocks across the avenue and cars moved by at irregular intervals in the street below. *How could everything seem so normal out there?* Nothing unusual had happened in the lives of other people that day, while his entire life had been irreparably transformed.

He turned back to the policeman. He felt the weight of anguish pressing down heavily on his shoulders and in his heart.

'Have they moved her?' he asked quietly, and his voice quivered as he spoke. He cleared his throat and tried again. 'Have they taken her away?'

'Yes. She's been taken down to the mortuary at Andrew Fleming,' replied the officer. His voice resonated with compassion, but his words insisted on reality: 'There'll be a post-mortem, of course . . . . And an inquest.'

'Of course,' croaked Andy. 'Am I entitled to use the phone in there? Or should I go somewhere else?'

'Who would you like to call?' asked the policeman, sympathetically.

'I need to get through to Kabrit barracks,' he said. 'If I need somewhere to live for a while, I guess that's where it'll be.'

'You're with the SAS?' asked the man with a flush of interest.

'I just have friends out there. Do I get to use the phone?'

'I can't think why not,' replied the officer. 'Go ahead.'

He got through to the night orderly and asked if Doc Morrison was still in his office. There was a pause and then the orderly was back:

'I'm sorry—he seems to have left for the day. May I ask who's calling?'

*Damn*, thought Andy. He needed the comforting reassurance that was Morrison's trademark.

'It's Andrew Mason,' he replied offhandedly. 'Is Major Dawson there?'

'Major Dawson's off base at this time.'

'Shit,' said Andy quietly to himself.

'Can you put me through to the duty quartermaster, please?' he said. Nothing was going his way, and there was nothing he could do about it.

When the extension was answered, Andy immediately recognised the voice of Charles Norton. Norton was an ex-combatant. Two years back, he'd lost a leg and half of his left hand when he'd stepped on an anti-personnel mine during a follow-up operation in Mozambique. When he'd recovered and rejoined the Squadron, he'd been put in charge of stores and supplies in the quartermaster's office.

'Hi Charlie,' he said. 'It's Andy Mason.'

'Hey there, Andy! Nice to hear you. What's happening?' There was genuine pleasure in Charlie's voice, and Andy wished he could share it.

'I need a short-term billet, Charlie,' he said sombrely. 'Can you find me a bunk where I won't feel crowded?'

There was a chuckle from Charlie, and he goaded Andy with a long groan of mock sympathy. 'What's happened? The missus sick of you already?'

'It's a bit worse than that, Charlie.' Andy tried not to sound the way he felt. 'But I'm sure you'll get to hear about it. Can you find me a bunk?'

'Come on over, mate,' said Charlie. 'In fact, meet me in the Stagger and the drinks are on you. That way you get to be comfortable tonight. The alternative is a sleeping bag under the stars . . . . Next to the swamp.'

'I might have to settle for the sleeping bag Charlie,' said Andy. 'I don't think I qualify as good company right now. See what you can do—I'll be there in half an hour.'

He hung up and looked around the apartment.

The door to their bedroom at the end of the passage was closed and, he presumed, locked—but he had no desire to go and check. The attractive apartment with all of its amenities looked bare and foreboding. The spacious and brightly-lit lounge with its wide doors to the balcony, the pictures on the walls, the neat and well-stocked little bar in the corner—it all seemed alien, and empty.

He reflected on the contentment he'd enjoyed here with Alyson before their wedding—the love-making and laughter, the games they played and the long-forgotten expectation of happiness that it had presented as their first home. But now there was an almost tangible aura of gloom about the place. It seemed to ooze from the walls, and it mocked him in silent scorn. The heartache caught in his throat and stung his eyes.

The policeman who'd called him in from his vigil on the balcony stood quietly in the hallway, waiting for him. Andy shook himself, deliberately driving out the tormenting demons.

As he walked towards the front door, he caught sight of a yellow envelope on the writing bureau. His name was scrawled on it. He frowned uncertainly and looked at the policeman whose attention, he noted, was taken by a smiling picture of Ralph and Jennifer hanging on the wall.

Andy picked up the envelope and slipped it into his pocket, then walked out of the apartment. He knew that it was for the last time. He never wanted to come back here—ever.

# CHAPTER 29

T he reports of Alyson's suicide were carried on the front pages of the national newspapers.

### Daughter of Ralph Carstens Dies

Alyson Mason, the daughter of Ralph and Jennifer Carstens who were recently killed in a terrorist ambush, has committed suicide at her home in Salisbury.

Carstens and his wife were killed two months ago on the night of Alyson's marriage to a sergeant in the Rhodesian army and it is believed that the motive for her actions stems from depression following the tragic death of her parents.

Alyson's husband was not available for comment and has vacated their residence on The Avenues.

This particular report went on to sketch the Carstens family history. The great grandfather who had ridden with Colonel Pennefather's Pioneer Column in 1890 and witnessed the raising of the Union Jack on a remote and desolate piece of ground which would later become known as Cecil Square in the centre of the bustling city of Salisbury. The emergence and steady growth of a property, farming and financial empire that had been passed down through the generations, and finally Ralph's own humanitarian contribution to his 'beloved Rhodesia'. The storyline concluded:

It is undeniably heartbreaking to witness the tragic demise of this Rhodesian dynasty. The Carstens family have been a part of this beautiful country since its noble birth and it is indeed an irony that, as events unfold at Lancaster House, the name Rhodesia itself may soon suffer the same fate and join Ralph, Jennifer and Alyson in their final resting place.

\*　\*　\*

Sleep did not come to Andy in the bunk that Charlie Norton arranged for him in the NCOs' mess on the night of Alyson's death.

Nothing had prepared him for the events of that day, and he lay awake floundering under the weight of remorseless anguish.

He had known that Alyson needed help, but he'd left it in her hands to ask for it. He had been at the sharp end of her deep depression and short temper since the death of her parents and although he'd found her attitude offensive and infuriating, he had allowed her the freedom to express her grief—even if it meant him having to suffer as the object of her misery.

When he and Alyson had lain together in bed that morning, he'd felt closer to her than at any time since Ralph and Jennifer had been killed, and the sensation had uplifted his spirits.

He'd willingly believed that the rift between them was finally showing signs of healing, and the belief had induced a sense of cautious contentment within him. Then she had dropped the bombshell about her affair with Alec. This had shattered his cautious hope, and cast new ambiguity over everything they'd shared. But not in his wildest flights of imagination did he consider the possibility that Alyson's despair would end up like this. He felt as though he was drowning in a pool of guilt. As a lifebelt, he embraced the expediency of denial. He lay in his bunk and dwelt, continuously, on the illusion that none of it had really happened.

As he lay in the darkness, his mind in turmoil of contradiction, he remembered the envelope that he'd taken off the hall table.

He groped for the light switch, fumbled in the pocket of his trousers, and withdrew it. He turned it over in his hand several times. Then he ripped it open and extracting the single sheet of folded paper. Still he hesitated. He had a pretty good idea what it was, but he was in two minds as to whether he really wanted to read the note. Finally he sat down on the edge of his bunk and unfolded it.

*My Darling Andy,*

*A wise man recently told me that not all casualties of war fall on the battlefield. You have seen the ones whose injuries bleed on the outside and their death is easily explained. My injuries are inside, Andy. They are born of guilt and bleed with a profusion that killed me several months ago. Only I have been able to sense the bleeding and feel the pain and now I feel the time has come for me to put an end to both. Not only for myself, but for my child as well. Yes, I say MY child, not OUR child Andy, because I know that this baby is not yours.*

*I have loved you with a passion that words cannot describe, but I allowed myself the luxury of a bit of illicit excitement with Alec and the consequence is that I am carrying his child. I am not going to try and explain what happened between us, other than to say that you were away so much, I was lonely and Alec was there. What has happened as a result is an unthinkable future for both me and the child. Trying to deal with the death of Mum and Dad, as well as knowing the lie that I have been living with you, has become a burden that I am no longer able to carry.*

*Living without you, knowing that you were somewhere out there hating me for what I have done, would be as destructive to me as it would be for the child. Enough damage has already been done.*

*I know that asking you to find it in your heart to forgive me would be a stupid and presumptuous gesture, so I'll ask you to forget me. You deserve happiness, my*

*darling, and you deserve someone who deserves your
love. I know that I can never again be that someone and
I'd rather be dead all over than just on the inside.
Find happiness, my love. You deserve it.*

*My thoughts and love are with you as I take this final
step . . . .*

*Alyson*

Andy stared at the note with incredulity. Then he read it
again. Rage churned in his guts as the magnitude of Alyson's
posthumous confession descended upon him. He put his hand to
his mouth and he retched violently.

Bounding from the bed he stumbled blindly to the toilet
cubicle and buried his head in the bowl, retching again and
again, choking on his fury and desolation as the pressure of
conflicting emotions swirled around in his mind, blending like a
cocktail of unstable and explosive chemicals.

When the heaving spasms subsided and he was able to
breathe properly again, he remained there on his knees, head
resting on his forearms over the open lavatory, exhausted. He
had reached the end of his emotional tolerance. He felt too feeble
to move.

After what seemed like a very long time, he raised his head.
He wiped his mouth on a wad of toilet paper, staggered out of the
small cubical, and flopped down on the bed. He lay there, wide
awake, with the wreckage of his life lodged in the core of his soul,
until the eastern sky began to pale and a new day dawned.

He looked like a man suffering from an overdose of narcotics.
He was haggard from lack of sleep and profound apprehension.
Stumbling, he somehow made his way early in the morning to
Combined Operations Headquarters. He reported, and put in
for leave of absence. He also put in a request to be relieved of
his responsibilities in Military Intelligence and reassigned to
operational duty when he returned. He needed work that would
give him time to absorb the full truth of things, but the work he

did at Com-Ops was nothing more than a constant reminder of inadequacy. Getting back into combat duty would keep his mind occupied.

His colleagues and superiors showered him with sympathy and offers of support—but it was all very military. Andy could almost read their minds: *People die but life goes on; let's not make too big a thing of this; you'll get over it.*

That would have been the most honest sentiment, and Andy was not unaware of it. His own reaction, when other peoples' relatives were the casualties, had been pretty much the same—so he was under no illusion that everyone else regarded this as just another death in just another family. It happened every day.

'Of course you must have a few days to attend to your affairs,' had been the Adjutant's condescending response to Andy's leave request. 'We'll talk about your return to operations once I've had a chance to discuss it with my counterpart at SAS. Under the circumstances, there may well be reasons why they'd consider such a request inappropriate.'

Andy completed the formalities of leave application. Then he walked down the stairs to the security desk and signed out. As he was leaving the building, he was called back by the orderly:

'Sergeant Mason,' he said, 'there's a phone call for you transferred from upstairs. Do you want to take it here?'

Wondering who it was, Andy took the proffered phone from the corporal.

'Andy, it's Alec. I've just heard the news.' There was as short pause, and then he went on: 'God, Andy, I don't know what to say. Is there anything I can do?'

Andy's blood froze at the sound of Alec's voice. Adrenalin flooded his system as though ice had been intravenously injected from a pressure pump.

'Yes there is, Alec,' he said bitterly. 'You can stay out of my way. If you ever so much as cross my line of sight again, I swear I'll add you to the long list of vermin I've killed over the past few years. I'm not going to explain that. I don't think I need to— but don't put it to the test. You're scum, Alec—and words haven't been invented to describe how I loathe you right now.'

He handed the phone back to the astonished orderly and walked out into the sunlight.

As he strode towards his car it struck him that it was little more than twenty-four hours since he'd angrily stormed from the apartment, leaving Alyson on her own. A surge of intense resentment, mixed with bitter sadness, welled up inside him. It clutched at his throat in a grip of emotional agony.

# CHAPTER 30

THE FUNERAL SERVICE FOR ALYSON A WEEK LATER, WAS ATTENDED
BY ALL OF SALISBURY SOCIETY. There was an atmosphere of
muted horror and disbelief among the mourners and the mood
was appropriately sombre with hushed murmurs and polite
concern.

Dressed in his full ceremonial greens, Andy watched with
morbid fascination, his heart breaking and his emotions in
turmoil as Alyson's coffin, crowned by a vivid garland of red
and white roses, descended slowly into the recently dug grave.
Nothing made sense. The rustic smell of recently turned soil
filled the air and mingled with the fresh fragrance of Jasmine.
Oblivious to the solemn proceedings, birds chirped happily in the
trees and bright summer sunshine smiled down from a clear blue
sky. The setting seemed entirely inappropriate and contrasted
sharply with the dark, heart-rending circumstances of the
occasion.

The casket settled gently at the base of the grave and Andy
stood looking down upon it, still wrangling with his conscience in
his quest to come to terms with the senselessness of it all. After
a while he bent and lifted a handful of damp red soil and tossed
it into the rectangular void. He made no attempt to hold back
his tears as he turned and slowly walked away to the shade of a
nearby flame-lily tree. There he stood numbly, dutifully shaking
hands and receiving the softly spoken condolences of well-wishers
as they filed by on the way back to their cars.

Very few of them were even vaguely familiar, and he couldn't wait for it all to be over. He was overcome with a desire to get away.

A small contingent of S.A.S. men, including Dawson and Doc Morrison, all dressed in camouflage fatigues and distinguishable by the coveted sand berets and blue stable belts were among the recognizable faces, and it meant a lot to Andy that they had come.

Geraldine approached and put her arms around his neck:

'I don't know what to say, Andy.' She released him and took his hand. 'I haven't been in touch with Alyson lately; I knew she was devastated by her folks' death—but who'd have imagined this? She was always so positive and confident. I can't believe it.'

She paused, wiped tears from beneath her dark glasses with the corner of a tissue, sniffed, and continued: 'Alec would have been here but he was called away at the last minute. Some emergency security meeting came up. I'm sure he'll be in touch soon, but he's got to go out of town for a week or two. He asked me to pass on his apologies—and to ask your forgiveness.'

Andy nodded, but he said nothing. Was that some sort of cryptic apology from the man whose duplicity had led to Alyson's despair and suicide?

Obviously Geraldine knew nothing of Alec's affair; or if she did, she wasn't showing any sign. Andy felt sure that she was as ignorant as he'd been, and he chose to leave it like that. All he'd achieve by bringing it up would be to soil Alyson's memory and create more misery in the process.

Andy wondered, not for the first time, if Alec was aware of the fact that he was the father of Alyson's unborn child. Had she discussed it with him? Or had she kept it entirely to herself until she set the truth free after death? He'd probably never know.

He kissed Geraldine lightly on the cheek. 'Thanks for coming.' He said kindly.

Then he turned and walked across to where Greg Dawson and Doc Morrison stood. He saluted them as he approached.

'How're you holding up, Andy?' asked Dawson, returning the salutation.

'Time will tell, sir,' replied Andy. 'I'm still numb.'

Dawson cleared his throat. 'I believe you want to return to full-time ops?'

'I'd appreciate that, sir. I'm stagnating at Milton Buildings—and with this . . .' he gestured towards the open grave, and his voice faltered as he went on: 'It'll drive me insane if I have to continue what I'm doing.'

'Take some leave, Andy,' said Dawson. 'Get away for a while. I'll arrange to have you re-assigned—but I suspect that combat duty may be a short-lived ambition. It looks as though a settlement's been reached at Lancaster House, in which case things are about to change quite dramatically. There are already elements of an advance party of Commonwealth peacekeeping monitors on their way.'

Andy stared impassively at Dawson for a moment, and then he looked away. Will the war abruptly end through suited politicians, whose intransigence gave rise to the conflict in the first place? Adversaries who sit and talk in a conference hall after 27 000 lives have been lost? Manipulators, few of whom have ever seen a day's combat? It seemed so contrived as to be inconceivable.

\* \* \*

ANDY GOT A RIDE BACK TO THE FUNERAL PARLOUR in the undertaker's black Mercedes limousine. He'd left his own car there.

He got in behind the wheel and sat there for a long time, staring blankly at nothing. The power of his despair was so intense, the emotional vacuum that consumed him so devastating, that the world around him seemed to dissolve into shades of grey. This was so reminiscent of his frame of mind after Merryl's funeral—with a profound difference.

The previous occasion had led to his chance reunion with Alec, from where the seed of his decision to come to Rhodesia had been planted. Now the sentiment towards his lifelong friend was so contaminated with malice that he feared the consequences of his actions if he were to encounter him in the same way.

He felt completely lost. He had nowhere to go—and nothing to do when he got there.

He'd been encouraged to join his comrades at a wake for Alyson in the Winged Stagger, but he'd declined. He had no desire to be part of what would inevitably develop into a night of heavy drinking and an atmosphere of jovial indifference.

That was always how wakes ended up, and he'd attended scores of them. For him, this could be nothing like the traditional send-off for another fallen comrade. He wanted to be alone, far from the well-intended but intoxicated expressions of sympathy. He needed a means of escape from the emotional prison in which events had incarcerated him.

The Oasis Inn was a popular meeting spot and watering hole. It was a place where hundreds of off-duty troops from all units of the armed services gathered and revelled over weekends. It was also a place where he and Alyson had shared many happy occasions in the company of mutual friends. Andy knew that the Oasis would be deserted, since it was a weekday, and he decided upon it as his destination. After removing his tunic and other items of military insignia and storing them in the trunk of his car, he drove across town.

The Inn was set in large grounds that boasted a vast, well cared for lawn under a scattering of tall date palms. Beneath the trees stood clusters of tables and chairs, shaded by broad terrace umbrellas. From the car park a shale pathway led to a covered patio, paved in polished slate with an array of tall folding glass doors. Alongside the patio a flowerbed in a blaze of summer colours separated it from a sparkling blue swimming pool set into a rockery of Pelindaba stone. Beyond the pool, fronted by a spacious terrace, stood an open bar under a gazebo of thatch and varnished gum poles. It was here that Andy ensconced himself and ordered the first drink in what would become a long private binge.

\*   \*   \*

THE COMMAND CENTRE AT COMBINED OPERATION HEADQUARTERS in Milton Buildings was a huge area that took up almost an entire floor.

In the centre of the room, positioned at waist height on an enormous platform, was a meticulously constructed papier-mâché model of Rhodesia. Fine detail of the nation's infinitely diverse landscape had been painstakingly recreated, to present an overview of the entire country in a scale of 1:50,000,000.

The mock-up was ornamented with hundreds of colour-coded markers indicating troop positions by number and unit. A remote-controlled mechanical arm, suspended from the ceiling, moved over the structure pinpointing and marking locations of incidents and contact activity as reports were received.

Maps covering the walls in scale of 1:500,000 indicated the positions of known guerrilla bases in Mozambique, Zambia and Botswana where elements of Special Forces were constantly active on clandestine operations.

The relentless sound of ringing telephones, the beep-beep of Morse radio transmissions and the drone of a dozen conversations mingled through the room in a blend of feverish activity.

At the far end of the expansive hall, behind a soundproof glass wall that separated it from the hubbub of the ops centre was the situation room. In here was a long boardroom-style table around which were arranged fifty leather chairs.

The chairs were occupied by the Joint Chiefs of Staff and the commanding officers of all units, who had been summoned to attend a briefing in the wake of the Lancaster House agreement.

At the head of the table sat Lieutenant General Paul Wallace who had arrived back from London that very morning. He was not in an agreeable frame of mind.

'Gentlemen,' he began, 'today is a day I had fervently hoped I'd never live to see. After seven years of conflict, during which time the Rhodesian army has not been the loser in a single battle, we have effectively been forced by circumstances and political expedience to surrender. We are officially, once again, a British colony under the command of the Crown, and we're to be kept in line by Commonwealth military observers.'

He paused and drew a deep breath. Then he continued with the force of his resentment barely concealed:

'We have been ordered to withdraw all troops from the field, and confine them to barracks. Peace-keeping is to be administered by a Commonwealth monitoring force made up in part by—of all things—British policemen.' He glanced around the table with eyebrows raised and shrugged his shoulders, his hands held out in a gesture of appeal. 'What a London bobby knows about containing a hostile situation in the African bush is yet to be established! But that's the way it's expected to be.

'On the flip side of the coin,' he said, 'all communist terrorists have been ordered to report to pre-arranged assembly points under the administration of personnel from this *monitoring force*'—he spoke the words as if trying to drive out a bad taste— 'where they are to register themselves and their weapons and stand down to await relocation.'

He took a fleeting look around the table at the sombre faces of his most senior officers, and then went on:

'At the risk of being accused of scepticism I doubt that this will happen. I don't trust the smiling faces of those talking heads. We all know the methods that they'll use when it comes to campaigning for votes in the run-up to the proposed election, and persuasion by intimidation can't be achieved by idle men in assembly points. So, I'm guessing that some (to show good faith) will be told to go in, while most will have orders to stay out and demonstrate to the rural tribespeople the fate of those who need persuasion on the subject of their allegiance.

'We know that there's no such thing as a nominal role against which names can be ticked off, so it's impossible for us to monitor compliance to the agreement. In a nutshell, gentlemen, we've been sent down the proverbial river without a paddle.

'The so-called monitoring forces are gathering here in Salisbury as I speak, and they'll be deployed within the next few days. Let's see how *that* turns out.'

He took another deep breath and ran his fingers through his hair.

'So, gentlemen,' he continued, resting his hands on the table, 'for now it seems we've got little choice but to stand down and see what happens. It appears our work is done for now. Give the order, please, to withdraw your men. But all units are to be kept on high alert.'

# CHAPTER 31

ALL MASON'S BELONGINGS HAD BEEN DELIVERED TO HIM BY THE POLICE and he'd moved in to the cubicle that Charlie Norton had arranged for him at Kabrit on the night of Alyson's death. This was now his new place of residence and he isolated himself with the completeness of a hermit, until one morning he was jerked awake from a deep alcohol-induced sleep by a sharp rapping at his door.

It was two weeks since the funeral and he'd spent most of his time locked away on his own—brooding and nursing his despair with copious quantities of liquor.

In two weeks he had ventured out only to buy the occasional paltry meal from a take-away kiosk close to the base, or to replenish his supply of booze. He was unshaven, unwashed, and insensitive as to why it mattered. Christmas came and went, and the festive occasion passed him by unnoticed.

Alyson's suicide note lay on the dresser next to his bed and he tortured himself by reading it over and over again. Each time he did so, his bitterness and anger were cranked up to a new level.

The banging on his door startled him and as he came awake he looked around the tiny room. The place was a mess. Clothing that he'd worn on his brief outings was scattered on the floor, a half-drunk bottle of spirits stood on the dresser with an empty glass and an overflowing ashtray beside it. Open take-away food cartons with stale mouldy leftovers dripping over the edges lay untidily on top of his clothes locker.

'Who's there?' he croaked.

'It's Doc Morrison, Andy. Open up.'

He'd been left undisturbed ever since he arrived back from the Oasis in a state of legless inebriation, on the day they'd buried Alyson.

The abnormal wave of incoming troop movement had left him unperturbed and he'd given no thought as to the reason for the unusually high numbers of personnel at the base.

He had lost track of time and he wasn't sure what day it was. He was not in the frame of mind to be pacified or lectured, but he had no right, nor reason, to resist the officer's thinly-veiled order—although it was made to sound like a request.

'Just a moment, sir,' he called.

He leaped out of bed and hurriedly stashed the bottle in his closet, then swept the food cartons up in his arms and deposited them behind the toilet door and closed it.

Kicking the scattered clothing under the bed, he ran a hand through his hair as he went to the door and unlocked it.

Morrison seemed not to notice the odour in the room—nor did he show surprise at the dishevelled appearance presented by Andy. He made no comment on the state of the room. He acted as if everything was perfectly normal.

'It's time, Andy,' he said without preamble as he came through the door. 'It's a new year and time for you to get your ass out of here and face the world. You can't go on hiding forever and you're going to run out of money soon if you keep slipping off down to the liquor shop to feed your newly-acquired habit. Besides, you're contracted to the government to do a job.'

His tone was easy and amicable. There was no hint of disapproval at the state of the wretch that Andy knew he resembled. What Morrison said came across as a friendly and conversational observation from a caring mentor.

Andy sat down on the bed and rested his face in his hands, not sure how to respond.

Morrison watched him for a few moments. Then he spoke:

'Grief is an emotion, Andy. Do you remember what I taught you about allowing your emotions to control you?'

Andy didn't reply. He didn't know how to. He just remained on the bed, holding his face in his hands.

'Alyson is dead, Andy,' continued Morrison. His voice held compassion, but his words were emphatic. 'And no matter how tragic the circumstances, you're alive and you will go on living. Locking yourself away with self-pity and booze isn't going to help anything and it's definitely not going to bring her back.

'But I'm not here to lecture you. Major Dawson wants to see you. I suggest that you take a shower and shave that stubble off your face. You're on in half an hour and I wouldn't be late if I were you.'

He turned to leave, but then as an afterthought he turned back. He laid his hand gently on Andy's shoulder and said, softly but firmly:

'Come on, soldier. Your leave is over. It's time to get back to work.'

The words were spoken calmly, with just enough authority to remind him that he was still in the army, and that soldiers don't question orders.

Andy stripped off his shorts and got under the shower. The stinging jet of hot water washed away the last remnants of sleep but did nothing to salve his depression.

He wondered how come Doc Morrison had been the bearer of his orders. Normally an orderly would have been sent to call him. Whatever the reason, he wished they'd given him more than half an hour. Another day would have been more like it. He was still half drunk and in his state of mind he didn't believe that anything was so urgent that it couldn't wait. He wondered why he was being summoned, other than to tell him that his time for mourning had passed.

\*    \*    \*

ONCE SHOWERED, SHAVED AND DRESSED IN HIS CAMOUFLAGE FATIGUES with his belt and beret neatly in place, Andy felt a slight lifting of his spirits. In some simple way, the uniform brought back a sense of pride and purpose. But the effect of his binge still hung like a fug behind his eyes. He bore the uneasy feeling of not being fully in control and the weight of anxiety bore down in his guts like undigested food.

He entered the admin block exactly twenty-eight minutes after Morrison had left his billet and was greeted by Angela Baxter, a female orderly who dealt with administrative paper work.

'Hello, Sergeant Mason,' she said in a tone that betrayed nothing out of the ordinary. 'Can I help you?"

'I'm here to see Major Dawson.'

'He's been very busy. Is it urgent?'

'I guess it must be,' replied Andy. 'Doc Morrison came and spoiled a perfectly good day by getting me out of bed. He gave me half an hour to get here, and in one minute from now I'll be late.'

'In that case you'd better go through,' said Angela with a half-smile.

Andy knocked at Dawson's door and waited for the word to enter. Moving into the room, he saluted the officer behind the desk.

'Good morning, sir,' he said.

Dawson appraised him with an attitude of dry indifference. Then, after few moments, he spoke:

'You'd better keep your eyes shut, sergeant, or you'll bleed to death.'

Despite himself, Andy grinned.

'They don't look so good from this side either, sir,' he responded.

'I'm not going to ask you how your leave was,' said Dawson tersely. 'I doubt you'd be able to tell me. But I'm curious to know how much booze you think it will take to bring Alyson back to life?' His tone was firm and challenging

'I don't think I'm trying to bring her back, sir,' replied Andy. He was taken by surprise at the severity of Dawson's tone. 'Maybe I'm trying to blot her out.'

'Is it working?' Dawson raised a cynical eyebrow.

'Sir,' said Andy, 'there was a great deal more behind Alyson's suicide than anyone other than me knows about—and those are things that I'm finding very difficult to come to terms with.'

'So the distillers of liquor are now spiking their products with magic potions that help with that condition, are they?' said

Dawson acrimoniously. 'Why don't we invest in a franchise to sell the stuff? We'd make a fortune.'

The disdain was almost tangible—a dry and corrosive acid seemed to ooze from his words.

Andy looked away, not knowing what to say. For the first time in all the years he'd known Dawson, he felt uncomfortable in his presence. Their easy-going rapport was gone. This was the commanding officer, berating an errant subordinate.

'You are to report to Training Troop this morning, sergeant,' continued Dawson after a brief pause. 'And while you're getting back into shape I want you to spend some time with Doc Morrison. Get yourself cleaned up and dried out—and get a decent meal. That shit you've been eating will rot your innards. Oh!—and stay away from the Stagger. Your access there has been suspended. That will be all.'

With that, Dawson diverted his attention to files on his desk and carried on as if Andy wasn't in the room.

Feeling like a spited child, his sense of humiliation complete, Andy saluted and left. He could have done with a drink.

As he was leaving the admin block, Angela Baxter called after him.

'Sergeant Mason,' she said, 'there was a civilian here looking for you a few days ago. I'd almost forgotten. He left his name and telephone number and asked me if I'd get you to call him. He was a very smartly-dressed guy—said he was an attorney.'

She proffered a square of message-pad paper and he took it from her, wondering why an attorney would be looking for him. As far as he knew he didn't need one.

He slipped the paper into his pocket and looked at his watch. It was just approaching 07h30. Breakfast time. He headed for the NCOs' mess hall. Maybe Dawson was right. A decent meal would make him feel better.

\*    \*    \*

DESPITE HAVING TO COMPLY WITH THE TERMS OF THE CEASEFIRE, the SAS remained on high alert. There were concerns for the safety of political figures and refresher courses on VIP protection, crowd control and hostage situations were being conducted by Training Troop. Andy was assigned to join in.

The following ten days were absorbed in repetitive instruction on situation simulation, combined with intense physical workouts. Gradually, Andy's lethargy faded and his sense of purpose returned. He resisted the temptation to devour what was left in the hidden bottle of liquor—even as he refused to give in to the idea that he should pour it down the sink.

While the training provided the distraction of concentrated physical and mental exercise, it did little to relieve the emptiness that was now lodged in his being. Nor did it answer the resentment that frothed within him over the contents of Alyson's confession. The indignity of the betrayal clung to him like an evil spirit that refused to be exorcised. And, all the while, his mind was haunted by the vision, implanted like a photograph, of Alyson's mutilated remains sprawled across their bed.

He listened with patient tolerance to Morrison's analysis of his mindset and the process of healing, but behind his tolerance there lurked a venomous resentment. It seemed to contaminate his thoughts like a toxic virus.

The day after he completed the course he had been assigned to, Mason was again summoned to Dawson's office.

The officer appeared to have forgotten the animosity that had characterised their previous meeting. He greeted him with their old affability and he made no mention of the incident.

'How are you getting along, Andy?'

'Frankly, sir,' he replied, 'I don't know. Physically I'm in pretty good shape—but with all that's happened over the past few weeks life doesn't seem the same. I feel like a stranger living in my own body.'

Dawson appraised him for a moment. Then he said: 'You're going to have to get over it, Andy. I can't begin to imagine how you feel, but you can't spend the rest of your life buried in self-pity. It'll destroy you.'

They sat in silence for a moment, and then Dawson continued:

'We've all suffered losses over the past few years, Andy, but we have to move on with our lives. The dead linger in our hearts and minds, but we have to let them go. Life goes on—and over time the pain will pass.'

Andy wondered if that could possibly be true. Rapid successive events since the day he was shot had changed his life with such devastating consequence that he felt as though he'd been psychically relocated into a chamber of spiritual torment.

Everything, from the circumstances of his ill-fated wedding to the day he returned to the apartment and found the police and paramedics attending to Alyson's suicide, was out of joint with his life to date. And, to cap it all, there was Alyson's posthumous confession—for which he'd been utterly unprepared.

'I guess you're right, sir,' he said evasively. 'Time will tell.'

'Hang in there, sergeant,' said Dawson encouragingly. 'Weaker men than you have conquered worse.'

Then he changed the subject.

'I thought you'd be interested to know that the information you extracted on the Mapai situation was used to successfully destroy that shipment of arms we were worried about.'

'Glad to hear it,' said Andy. He sensed that Dawson was trying to boost his spirits. 'I'd like to have been there.'

Then a thought occurred to him.

'Am I allowed to ask what happened to Major Combrink?'

'He got away,' replied Dawson. 'It's pretty obvious from information we've uncovered since we busted him that he was behind the leaks on most of the ops that turned out to be lemons. He used his network in both directions—giving us what he wanted us to know and giving the enemy what we didn't want them to know. That's probably why he was so pissed off by the fact that you got to do the interrogation on that snatch. It was the last thing he needed. The day you and I had our chat at the rifle range, he just disappeared—but he was recently seen in Maputo by one of Special Branch's operatives. Do you remember Jose Couvallo?'

'Of course I do!' said Andy. 'He left to go and live in Portugal about two years ago.'

'No, he didn't. That was his cover. He left the squadron to join Special Branch and he's been one of our most valuable sources in Mozambique ever since. He was born there and his family came to Rhodesia as refugees when the Portuguese pulled out and left the place to Frelimo in '74. With his fluent Portuguese and his knowledge of the country's culture he was able to get back in and live there without drawing attention to himself. He works as a shipping agent with access to harbours in Maputo and Beira.'

'Was it him who saw Combrink?'

'One of his "eyes" is a driver for ZANLA officials who identified him in the company of none other than Rex Nungu, the ZANLA 2IC.'

'He mixes with high society,' said Andy sarcastically. 'What motivates a guy like that to switch sides?'

'Who knows?' Dawson shrugged. 'Maybe he was never on-sides. But there's the perception where I think we all saw the writing on the wall as regards the end result. Economic sanctions, political leverage being brought to bear by South Africa, increasing shortages of essentials and the endless pressure on our farmers and the economy in general. Not to mention the ongoing bloodshed and the high rate of emigration among the whites. We can win all the military battles they throw at us but it'll never be enough. It had to lead to a negotiated settlement eventually, even if we did out-gun and out-think the terrs. Maybe Combrink thought he'd have a brighter future by being on-side with the likely political winners—he was well-enough connected. It's impossible to assess the number of lost Rhodesian lives the bastard's responsible for, though. And he'll probably be rewarded with a diplomatic posting somewhere.'

'Do you really think it's over, sir?' asked Andy.

'It certainly seems that way Andy. This settlement has the blessing of the entire international community, unlike any of the previous efforts. Whoever breaches this one will no longer just be fighting the Rhodesian war. They'll be up against the political might of the whole planet. Nobody can win that. So, yes. I think it's over . . . . , although having said that, not much attention is being paid to intimidation that's being played out by the gooks. There are constant reports coming in. Most of them finger Zanla as the perpetrators and our so-called monitoring force will do nothing about it.'

'What will you do?' asked Andy. 'I can't imagine that there's a future for any of us in the outcome of an election.'

'The South Africans have put an offer on the table for those who want to take it up,' replied Dawson. 'Sign up in their army for a year in a training capacity, and they'll look favourably upon immigration status.'

'And there we go again,' said Andy with a wry grin. 'Same old, same old. How long do you think it will it be before this conversation is repeated in similar circumstances, down south?'

'That's in the hands of the gods,' replied Dawson. 'But you're right. Now that the Rhodesian problem is out of the way, the heat will be turned up on South Africa. No matter how strong they are in military terms, white supremacy in Africa is doomed. By persisting with the policy of apartheid, they're just prolonging their isolation and it will end up with history repeating itself. It would probably be wise of them to start thinking about that. But then I guess the same could have been said for us, ten years ago. Nobody would have listened then either.'

'My contract with the army expires at the end of the month in any case,' said Andy. 'I'd planned to renew it but that's not going to happen now. Maybe I'll try picking up the pieces and go back to being a civilian. I'm not sure what I'll do, though. It's been a long time.

'You're a good soldier Andy.' said Dawson. 'It may have not have been what you planned to be, but you have the aptitude and temperament that makes you a natural. You should have done an officer's course.'

'My motivation for getting involved had nothing to do with career aspirations sir.' Said Andy. 'Even the cause wasn't a deciding factor at the time. I must confess though, that it pisses me off knowing that the hundred years of honest hard work that it took to make Rhodesia what it is and the lives that have been lost in defence of the achievements will go down in history depicting us as the bad guys. The political victors will get away with making a mockery of all that has been achieved here and only the privileged few will reap any benefit from the ruins.

Those for whom they preached liberation will be worse off than they ever were before and the world will walk away smiling and not give a damn. Hardly what one could call justice'

Dawson's phone rang and he turned to answer it. After listening for a moment he said "Yes, put him through." Then looking at Andy, he covered the mouthpiece with his hand and said.

"I have to take this Andy, we'll chat again. Look after yourself." The dismissal was polite but unmistakable.

# CHAPTER 32

Andy left Dawson's office and headed down the passage towards the exit. Angela Baxter caught him on the way out:

'That attorney guy was here again yesterday. He says you haven't called him.'

Andy had completely forgotten. 'Did he say what it's about?'

'No,' said Angela. 'Just that it's important that you call him. He's a very persistent man. And pompous as well.' She pulled a face.

'I think I washed my shirt with the number in the pocket,' said Andy. 'Have you still got it?'

'I'm afraid not. But he said he represented Boyd, Larson and Partners. Why don't you look it up in the phone book? His name's Cedric Larson.'

'Can I phone from here?' he asked. 'It will save me the trouble of finding change for the pay phone.'

'Sure, go ahead. The phone book's on the table.' Angela gestured across the room.

\* \* \*

'Cedric Larson here,' said a refined but sharp voice when Andy got through.

'Mr Larson? My name's Andrew Mason, and I believe . . . .'

'Mr Mason,' interjected Larson loudly putting emphasis on the "Mr.", 'you're a difficult man to track down.' He paused for a moment and then added in an arch tone, 'must be all that SAS training, what?' He laughed richly, as if his witticism had scored instant favour at the other end of the phone.

*This guy's an asshole,* thought Andy. 'How can I help you, Mr Larson?'

'Well, actually—it's more about how I can help you, Mr Mason. Do you think you could come into our offices as soon as possible?'

'Not unless I know why,' said Andy. 'What's it about?'

'It's to do with your wife's estate, Mr Mason. There are matters that need to be discussed in confidence.'

Andy was taken by surprise. 'My wife's estate?' It had never occurred to him that there would be an estate to wind up—but it now struck him as obvious.

'Yes. There are some rather substantial assets to be transferred. As the beneficiary you need to be appraised of how the estate is to be handled.' He paused again as if waiting for Andy to say something, but when there was silence he went on:

'You understand—there are asset transfers, various taxes, and of course the estate fees. All of which will require your participation.

'Define substantial, Mr Larson.'

'I don't think this is a matter to be discussed over the telephone. When can you come into the office?'

The training programme had been completed the previous day and personnel were stood down to await further instructions, but they were still on standby.

'I'll have to call you back,' said Andy.

'It's a matter of great importance, Mr Mason,' came the plummy voice. 'Sooner rather than later, I strongly suggest.'

'Mr Larson,' said Andy firmly, 'I'll thank you not to instruct me. I said I'll call you back. Is there a part of that that you don't understand?'

Self-importance, such as that displayed by Larson, irritated him. He felt no inclination to roll over before that high-and-mighty summons.

There was a stunned silence on the line. Then Larson said, hesitantly, 'As you wish, Mr Mason. I'll await your call.'

'Thank you.' And Andy hung up without saying good bye.

*'He probably thinks I'm an arrogant prick'* thought Andy *'Good. Let him come down to where he's playable.'*

Two days passed, during which Andy reflected on the conversation with Larson. It struck him only now, in these reflections, that Ralph Carstens was indeed a man of considerable means and not the type to leave loose ends untied. His affairs would have been meticulously in order when he was killed. Alyson and Jennifer were obviously his heirs, and Andy was disturbed over what that meant. If Alyson had made him the beneficiary of her will, which he had never so much as considered, it would mean by extension that he was the beneficiary of Ralph's estate—a very substantial estate.

Andy entered the well-heeled offices of Boyd, Larson & Partners.

Larson was a tall but stout man in his early forties. His hair was combed straight back with a middle parting and held in place by a light coating of hair cream—something that Andy thought had gone out of fashion when he was still at school. The man was jacketless and wore light beige suit trousers, a pale blue shirt and a broad yellow tie speckled with tiny black spots. He had on a pair of braces to match the tie.

'Mr Mason,' he said effusively as he swept into the reception area. He extended his hand, along with a charming professional smile. 'So good of you to come.'

Andy took the proffered hand and squeezed it with more force than was necessary. He felt the bones crunch under his grip and Larson flinched visibly, his smile turning instantly to a wince.

'Please, come through to the boardroom,' he said in a more moderate tone, surreptitiously flexing the injured hand.

Andy was ushered ahead of him down a long and richly-carpeted passage to a room that was furnished with all the trappings of a successful law practice. The table was of solid Rhodesian teak and the surrounding chairs of genuine polished cowhide. The walls were adorned with original artworks of African scenes and a teak wall unit boasted a glass front with shelves that displayed silver trophies for archery and polo. In the centre of the unit was a fully stocked bar and Andy recognised the labels of expensive whiskeys and liqueurs that had not been available in Rhodesia since before UDI. The thick carpet had a woven design of elephants at a waterhole.

'Please have a seat, Mr Mason,' said Larson. He was no longer quite as breezy and self-assured as he'd been when he first pranced into the reception area.

They sat opposite each other at the table and Larson opened a bulky file.

'I'll try to be as brief as possible, Mr Mason,' he said. 'But there is a great deal to get through, so I hope you're not in a hurry.'

'I've got all afternoon.'

'Good! Now, I don't know if you are aware that Mr Carstens had all his assets tied up in a variety of trusts. To all intents, he as an individual was practically penniless. Mrs Carstens and their daughter—your wife Alyson—were the beneficiaries of those trusts and we at Boyd, Larson are the trustees. Your wife was in here only a few days before her untimely death, and she drafted her will in your favour.'

Larson rambled on about the structure of the trusts and how the assets were divided between them. Share portfolios were in one trust, the farms and properties in another. Valuable artworks formed the assets of a third, and offshore assets a fourth. A safety-deposit box with undisclosed contents remained Ralph's only personal asset and that was held in the bank vault. Larson had one key and the other was held by the bank.

As Larson went through the details, Andy became more and more uncomfortable. The values attached to the trusts ran into millions and Alyson, as Ralph's only heir due to the death of Jennifer within thirty days after him, had bequeathed all her worldly goods to her husband, Andrew James Mason.

Nearly two hours had elapsed by the time Larson looked up from his file. He grinned, and he said: 'You seem to have been blessed by good fortune, Mr Mason.'

The unfortunate remark stung Andy like a cattle prod. He stared at the attorney with open contempt until the other man looked away.

'If one day you walk into your bedroom, Mr Larson,' said Andy coldly, 'and see your wife lying across your bed with half her head missing and her brains spread across the walls, call me. I'd like to get your perspective on good fortune under those circumstances.'

Larson recoiled. 'Dear God, Mr Mason! I'm sorry! I had no idea.' He fumbled for words, and then he gave up. Weakly, he said, 'I was referring to the fortune that has now become yours.'

'Perhaps you should take a course on how to phrase your comments, Larson,' said Andy, deliberately dropping the 'Mr'. 'Will you please have copies made of all these documents? I'd like to go through them in my own time. When I've done that, I'll call you with instructions.'

'May I recommend that you consult Mr Carstens' accountant to assist you,' said Larson. 'As a soldier, I'm sure you don't have the required experience.'

'Throw away the shovel, Larson,' retorted Andy. 'You're just digging yourself deeper and deeper into a hole. Will you have the copies made, please? I'd like to get back to barracks.'

\* \* \*

THAT NIGHT, ALONE IN HIS ROOM, ANDY SCRUTINIZED ALYSON'S WILL. The will itself was simple and to the point. Other than her wish that he was to be the sole beneficiary and that all her worldly goods were to become his in the event of her death, there was nothing to it.

It was the copious documents detailing what those worldly goods consisted of that astonished Andy.

The impact of her will only served to deepen his depression. It had been an unspoken but irrefutable fact that the Carstens family were enormously wealthy; it was there for anyone to see, but Andy had never once thought of that wealth as something from which he would benefit. It had simply never crossed his mind.

Now, looking at the extent of what Alyson had left him, he dwelt on what they could have done together. The life and love they could have shared, and the joy it would have brought them.

If he couldn't share it with her, he really didn't want any of it. Now it was his, and Alyson was gone.

Images of her drifted through his mind: her smile, their love-making, the laughter that gave them so much pleasure. The time they'd spent together at Kariba and at Golden Acres. Dwelling on these memories, he could almost feel her presence. The recent phase of her hot temper, the resentment that she'd displayed after the death of her parents, faded from his mind. What lingered there, and in his heart, were the high spirits, the passion, and the warm sense of well-being which she'd given him.

The pent-up emotions burdened his chest like a lead weight and, as he pondered the terrible finality of loss, he began to cry. His body was wracked with sobs, and the tears were unremitting.

Then, through his anguish, he thought of Alec. He'd heard nothing from him since the phone call that he'd taken at Milton Buildings the morning after Alyson's death. No attempt had been made reach him again, not even through Geraldine—and Andy assumed that Alec knew he'd found out the truth and was eaten up with guilt. But *did* Alec know the full truth himself? Had Alec ever considered the possibility that he was the father of Alyson's baby? He knew that she was pregnant.

Andy was haunted by a mental picture of Alec making love to Alyson on their bed. Impregnating her and leaving her to face on her own the consequences of his lust. Leaving her to take her own life rather than live with the shame that he'd brought upon her. Next, a vivid and very real image ran in his mind—Alyson sprawled across their bed; his rifle on the floor; the contents of her head splattered across the walls of their bedroom—and bitter anger flared up in him.

At that moment he could have killed Alec. Doing so would have left him as indifferent as he felt towards the many guerrillas who had fallen victim to his combat skills. The disturbing depth of loathing that replaced his state of gloom came upon him with such force that it shocked him. But the satisfaction that he drew from the idea of taking Alec down slowly fermented, until it developed into an irresistible fixation.

*   *   *

THE FIRST DECISION ANDY MADE IN RESPECT OF ALYSON'S WILL was to sell the apartments on the Avenues. He would rather have given them away than ever go back there.

The scramble by white Rhodesians to emigrate in the face of an uncertain future in a country which would soon become known as Zimbabwe under a government of doubtful civility, had reduced property values to an all-time low. It was not uncommon for homes to be summarily abandoned, leaving them to be repossessed by the mortgage underwriters.

When Andy phoned Larson the following day and asked him to arrange the sale, he wasn't surprised at the objections that the attorney raised.

'Mr Mason,' he began, 'you do realise that it's hardly the time to be selling property? If anything, I'd be buying.'

'Well, in that case Mr Larson,' replied Andy, 'buy the ones I'm selling. Name your price.'

'Those are valuable properties, sir,' said Larson. 'And once the dust settles the market will stabilise and you'll fetch a far better price for them.'

'There is no such thing as valuable property in Rhodesia at the moment, Mr Larson,' said Andy. 'Why do I get the impression that you are trying to control me over this? You're my attorney, are you not?'

There was a short silence while Larson struggled with his words. Then:

'I don't have that mandate. I'm the executor of Miss Carstens'—er, er—Mrs Mason's estate. But I'm sure we could represent you.'

'Well, then. Represent me and stop opposing me. I want those properties sold. Take whatever you can get for them. Just get rid of them. Am I clear on that?'

'Quite clear, Mr Mason.' Larson spoke flatly. 'Anything else?'

Andy heard the tone in Larson's voice. It was obvious that he was unaccustomed to being ordered in this way, and he didn't know how to deal with it.

'I'd like to have a look at the contents of Ralph's safety deposit box. When can I pick up the key from you?'

'I'll leave it in an envelope with my receptionist,' said Larsen. 'You'll need a letter of introduction from us. I'll include that in the envelope.'

'Thank you,' said Andy. 'I'd also like you to have Golden Acres valued for possible sale.'

'Mr Mason! Really!' blurted Larson, his astonishment profound. 'That farm's been in the Carstens family for seventy years!'

'And what exactly do you suppose the Carstens family are going to do with it now? Unless I'm mistaken, the Carstens family have ceased to exist.'

'What about all the staff and their dependants? Mr Carstens was deeply protective of their well-being. If the farm were to be sold, what would happen to them?'

'What's going to happen to them when the incoming government nationalises the land and takes away the farm, Mr Larson?' retorted Andy. 'Have you any thoughts about that?'

Larson was quick to respond:

'We've been given assurance that this won't happen. I've read the terms of the Lancaster House agreement and the land ownership clause is quite clear. Private property is protected.'

'The next time an agreement of that sort is honoured in Africa will be the very first time, Mr Larson. I'm sure you know that.'

There was an audible sigh from Larson. 'This will be different,' he said.

Andy was not convinced.

'Will you please see to the valuation, Mr Larson? Or would you prefer that I engage another firm of attorneys to attend to it?'

Later that day Andy received orders that he had been assigned to a team, giving close-in protection to the former Prime Minister and his wife. It meant that he'd have to move into quarters at the official residence and his spare time was going to become scarce.

Before reporting for duty, he went to Larson's office to pick up the envelope and he arranged with the bank for access to the safety-deposit vault.

He was shown into a secure cubicle, and when he was left alone with the box he opened it. He recoiled from what he saw, as if confronted by a nest of snakes.

The inside of the box was split into two compartments. On one side there were two holstered Smith & Wesson 9mm pistols with what seemed at first glance to be a dozen or more boxes of ammunition. But what astounded him was the other compartment. It was filled to capacity with neatly-stacked piles of banded one-hundred-dollar bills in American currency.

He stared incredulously at what he saw and hesitantly lifted one of the piles out. Within the band were ten separate batches of ten bills each. *Ten thousand dollars.* He quickly counted the number of piles. There were fifty of them. *My God! There's half a million US dollars here!*

His mind reeling, he put the money back and took out one of the pistols. It was clean and lightly oiled. He popped the magazine and pulled back the slide. It moved smoothly under his hand. He checked the breach, released the hammer, slid the magazine back, and re-holstered the weapon.

Andy was stunned. It was no secret that most people who could afford it had spirited money out of the country. Nest eggs that escaped the scrutiny of the reserve bank's stringent exchange control regulations. Documents associated with Alyson's will included a statement showing nearly two million British pounds in one of Ralph's offshore accounts. So why the stash of dollars? And why the hidden weapons?

He had no way of getting answers to the questions, and he was running late. He put the pistol back into the box and locked it. He called the security marshal and took the box back into the vault where they double-locked it in the safe from which it had been drawn.

# CHAPTER 33

ANDY'S OBLIGATION TO THE ARMY UNDER THE CONTRACT HE HAD SIGNED WAS COMING TO AN END. The timing couldn't have been better.

The assignment of giving close-in protection to the former first family of Rhodesia was uneventful. Much of the time was spent standing outside closed doors waiting for meetings to end. It was only out on the streets and in the car, between venues, that a high level of vigilance was needed. He had lots of time to think about his next move.

He resolved to get the contents of the safety-deposit box out of the country as soon as the opportunity presented itself.

He was undecided on the sale of Golden Acres. It was still functional and highly profitable under the management of Louis van der Berg, an Afrikaans immigrant who had worked for Ralph for twenty years. Louis seemed confident that he could keep the farm going. Andy had decided to give him half shares as an incentive to stay on, although he had no faith in the long-term future of such a plan. It was a beautiful place, but for Andy it held far too many fond memories and going there was something he chose to avoid.

The sale of the other properties would have to be registered with the relevant authorities and this meant that any proceeds from the sales would have to remain in Zimbabwe. He had no idea what would become of those proceeds.

Among the military personnel, there were rumours of a witch hunt once a new government was installed. No direct threats were known of but warnings had been issued to men of the SAS and other Special Forces units that their safety could not be guaranteed if they stayed in the country. That was something else to consider. Everything was utterly uncertain and unpredictable.

But there was one thing that he could not leave to fate, and he allowed his mind to dwell on it without respite.

\*　　\*　　\*

OFFICERS' CLUBS AT MILITARY BASES AROUND THE COUNTRY HAD ALWAYS BEEN CONSIDERED POTENTIAL TARGETS and, in consequence, the security around them was tight. The RLI officers' mess at Cranbourne barracks was no exception.

Andy stood in the darkness of a nearby tree line and surveyed the high-security fence with the hedgerow that grew around it, and he devised his plan.

He had waited for three consecutive nights, hoping to see Alec's car arriving and passing through the gates, and finally it happened.

The armed personnel patrolling the area did not look all that alert. Andy surmised that this mundane duty wasn't taken too seriously. He was looking for a pattern in the patrols.

He wanted to be in the car park when Alec came out—but entering through the gate was not an option. He couldn't afford to be recognised, and what he'd come for he didn't wish to be questioned about.

He had borrowed a pair of wire cutters from the stores at Kabrit, and he went back to the bank to retrieve one of the weapons from the safety-deposit box. It was comfortably tucked into a shoulder holster under his arm.

He was dressed in dark clothing and his face was covered by a balaclava. He couldn't afford to be seen. The balaclava itself would have raised some embarrassing questions, but at night a white face would stand out like a beacon.

The two sentries moved from the boomed gate, along the perimeter fence and around a corner. There, the boundary ran up to the back of the mess where it ended. From that point they did an about-turn and retraced their steps to the gate.

Andy timed how long it took them from turning the corner until they re-emerged. He was repeating the same routine that he'd made on his previous visits to this spot. Four times he watched their patrol, and each time their re-appearance was within seconds of two and a half minutes. As they disappeared around the corner on the fifth occasion, he sprinted noiselessly from his refuge, across the open space, to the hedgerow. He tucked himself in underneath it, and then he waited.

The sentries returned and walked, unsuspecting, past his position. One of them was smoking a cigarette. Neither of the two seemed very observant.

He waited for them to go past again, and then he quickly cut through six squares of the diamond mesh fencing. He hid, and waited. He repeated the exercise after their next pass, and again after the third. He pushed the fence inward and slipped through the hole that he'd cut, letting the wire spring back into place. He was in.

Hugging the line of the fence, he made his way around the boundary to the point where the mess building met the fence. He took off the balaclava. From here, he could make out as if he belonged.

He went along the side of the building, into the open, and set out with a confident stride towards the car park. Finding Alec's car, he moved away into the shadows and waited.

He remained hidden in the shadows, watching the coming and going of officers he knew, until an hour later he heard the crunch of footsteps on the gravel near the car and saw Alec approaching.

He was on his own. He walked with confidence, whistling a tune.

From out of the darkness, Andy stepped towards him.

'Hello Alec,' he said quietly. 'Long time no see.'

Alec stopped in his tracks and looked up sharply.

'Andy!' The surprise in his voice was heavily laced with fright. 'What brings you here?'

'There's something I want you to read, Alec.'

'Under the circumstances, don't you think you should address me as "sir", sergeant?' Alec tried to make it sound light-hearted but it was obvious that he was sparring for high ground.

'Fuck you, *sir!*' said Andy. He took Alyson's note from his pocket and thrust it across to him with a map light. 'Read this. Take it all in and then look at me, you scum.'

Alec took the proffered items and ran the beam over the text. Andy noticed the instability in his hands and the note quivered like a leaf in the wind.

'Oh, my God!' Alec looked up. He'd only read halfway down. 'I had no idea.'

'Finish reading, Alec,' said Andy menacingly.

Alec looked down and read the rest of Alyson's confession.

When he raised his face again, Andy had taken the pistol from its holster—and with a steady hand he aimed it at Alec's forehead.

'Andy!' he exclaimed. 'Please don't be foolish! Don't do this!'

'You didn't even bother to come to the funeral. You knew she was pregnant. You knew that we got married when we did because of it. And you knew that it was entirely possible that the child was yours—but you did nothing! You stood at my side as my best man at the wedding, knowing all along that you could be the father of the child she was carrying.'

'What could I have done, Andy?' pleaded Alec. 'I was in as much of a situation as Alyson.'

'You had no problem going into my home to fuck her when it suited you. *Friend.*' He raised his voice slightly and spat the word. 'But when the consequences had to be faced you ran like a frightened dog.' The gun in Andy's hand was rock steady and he stared at his former chum without emotion. 'She's dead because of you, Alec. Doesn't that mean anything?'

'Andy, I swear I didn't know! I had no idea of her anguish. You have to believe me.' He was pleading, and his voice trembled with fear. 'Put the gun down, Andy. This isn't going to solve anything.'

Andy kept his unflinching glare on Alec. He made no move to lower the weapon and the seconds ticked away like a tangible thing between the two old friends. When he spoke, Andy's words were as cold as an Arctic winter.

'I think I'll let you live with what you've done, Alec. We were friends from childhood, but that wasn't enough to stop you from destroying everything precious to me. Killing you right now would give me more pleasure than you can imagine, but I reckon I'll deprive myself of that. I hope that you live for a very long time—and that you remember this moment every time you look in the mirror.'

He released the hammer on the pistol and holstered it, and then took a pace forward so that his face was within inches of Alec's.

'I spit on you, you bastard! Even if you didn't know it was your child, you knew you were screwing the woman I loved.'

If Alec saw it coming, he made no effort to evade the blow. It swung up from the region of Andy's midriff at lightning speed, and it carried with it all the anger and loathing that was lodged in his gut.

The swinging right hand connected Alec under his jaw, slightly to the left of his chin. Andy felt the bone give way under the force of it and teeth slam together. In a blur of speed, seemingly in the same movement, he pirouetted and his foot shot out backwards in a perfectly-aimed mule kick to the groin.

With a groan, Alec dropped to the ground like a bag of cement. Andy was on him, driving the air from his lungs with a knee into his midriff. Blood ran from Alec's mouth and nose and Andy saw that an incisor had broken off. He grabbed Alec with both hands, by the front of his shirt.

'Don't ever come anywhere near me again, Alec,' he hissed, 'or so help me God I'll finish this. You're scum, my friend! Now fuck off back to Geraldine—and tell her who did this, and why.'

He got up, retrieved Alyson's note and his torch from where they'd fallen and strode back to where he'd entered the club grounds. Within a minute of leaving Alec, he was gone into the night.

\*　　\*　　\*

ANDY LEFT THE NEWLY-NAMED COUNTRY OF ZIMBABWE AND RETURNED TO SOUTH AFRICA. With him were half a million US dollars in cash, hidden behind a panel between the trunk and the rear seat of his car. He also carried with him a heart filled with sorrow.

It seemed to him as if fate had conspired that he should depart from this land in much the same frame of mind as when he'd first arrived: bitter, angry, resentful and alone.

He was leaving a place that had given him the best and worst years of his life, and his parting held all the emotional turmoil of a five-year-old given up by its parents for adoption. Behind him, he left an attachment that had seeped into his soul, which had moulded him in ways that defied definition.

As part of cleaning up after his discharge from the army, he had driven out to Lake McIllwain and hired a boat. He had then rowed out to the deepest part of the lake and dropped the two pistols overboard. He couldn't think of any reason why he'd want to keep them.

Larson had turned out to be an efficient and scrupulous executor. His bombastic manner had mellowed, and Andy came to respect the way that he got things done.

The apartments on the Avenues were sold for half of what they might have fetched, and he signed over half of Golden Acres to Louis van den Berg. The farm was in good hands for as long as it would be allowed to stay that way.

The remainder of Alyson's legacy was left untouched. Andy was still undecided how to handle the fortune contained in offshore accounts and share portfolios.

His newly acquired wealth did nothing to improve Andy's sense of well being. It was as though it didn't belong to him and had been achieved by default through ignoble circumstances undeserving of ownership.

He resolved to use only as much as he needed to re-establish himself.

He would need to find a job.

# CHAPTER 34

## 1980
## Johannesburg, South Africa

ANDY'S FIRST ATTEMPT AT FINDING EMPLOYMENT DID NOT GO WELL. He had sent his CV to an institution called Impact Finance, in response to an ad in the careers section of the newspaper. He wondered later why they'd bothered to invite him for an interview.

'This is all rather impressive,' said Mr Smithers, the bespectacled little man who had been assigned to interview him, as he browsed through Andy's CV. 'But your version seems quite inconsistent with what our personnel department has uncovered in their enquiries."

'Oh?' asked Andy. 'And what is it that has been uncovered?'

'Well, it seems that you were fired from Highgate and Savage in 1974 for breach of confidence and that you left the country to avoid prosecution.'

Andy was taken completely off guard. Sinclair had given him a firm undertaking that none of the issues leading to his departure from H&S would be disclosed, even though he had nothing to feel guilty about. But the bit about a pending prosecution was just a blatant lie. So—Sinclair had not only reneged on his promise, but had twisted the knife as well!

'May I ask where your personnel department dug up that bit of rubbish?'

'We follow a procedure in which we investigate candidates who make application for employment with us, Mr Mason, and our sources are very reliable.'

'Well, Mr Smithers, I'm sorry to disappoint you, but your sources seem to have bungled this one. I left Highgate & Savage after uncovering corruption within the executive suites of the bank—and I left the country for reasons totally unrelated to that. There was certainly never any suggestion of prosecution.'

'Let's get back to your CV,' said Smithers. 'The last five years seem a bit vague. "Selected to serve with Rhodesian Special Forces" doesn't provide much in the way of detail. Would you like to elaborate?'

'No,' said Andy.

'Just "no"? Could I not glean a little bit of what those five years may have taught you that could be of some benefit to us?'

'What would you like to know, Mr Smithers?' asked Andy. He felt his anger rising. 'I honestly don't think that anything I've learnt over the past five years would be of benefit to you at all—unless I've mistakenly strayed into a military institution.'

With some difficulty, Andy collected his words and continued:

'I think my background in asset-based finance is what we should be talking about, right now. But can we stick to the first matter? I'd like to know where the information came from. Where you got it from. It's libellous and I have no intention of allowing it to remain on record. If you'd care to find out the truth, get hold of Sam Cohen, Singer and Associates. Speak to Sam Cohen. He knows what that scandalous setup was all about.'

Smithers appraised Andy for all of a full minute. Andy stared straight back at him, unflinching. Then the little man spoke again;

'I cannot imagine that any of what we have here would have been placed on record if it were untrue, Mr Mason. Especially in the light of the fact that Highgate & Savage were the complainants. They're a highly respected institution, with a highly respected board of directors.'

'They're highly respected for all the wrong reasons, Mr Smithers,' retorted Andy. 'If high respect were to be accorded to crooks, they would be first-class candidates. You're misinformed if you think respect is due to them as honest bankers.'

'You're making serious allegations here, Mr Mason.'

'They're not allegations. What I'm telling you is the truth. However, I don't see why it should concern you. What you have disclosed to me is an issue between Highgate & Savage and myself. I think that this meeting's over. Please don't be offended, but I'm leaving now.'

He picked up the file that provided all the information he'd thought would have been necessary for the interview.

'I intend to find out where you source your information from, Mr Smithers, because you're clearly way off the mark.' Andy's cold voice barely concealed his anger and contempt. He turned and walked out—with a new resolve to clear up a few things with the executive at Highgate & Savage.

*Maybe I don't need a job,* he thought, as he left the building and headed for the nearest bar.

\*     \*     \*

ALONE IN HIS APARTMENT, ANDY DOZED, trying to shake off the affects of the previous day's binge and the consequent night of folly. His reminiscences flowed clearly in his mind, as the mental tour of events that had mapped and dominated his life washed over him.

His thoughts moved to identify and separate the turning points and how they all seemed to have been part of an incomprehensible plan of fate, put together as a sequence in which to play themselves out.... Scholar cum-Laude and successful young financial executive to a skilled and ruthless killer in a war he would never have thought to be a part of. Now, by default and tragedy, the wealthy young widower with a drinking problem and allegations of pending prosecution over issues he had long since put out of his mind.

He idly wondered, not for the first time, what course his life would have taken if he had been in Mozambique as he had planned to be on the night he'd received Merryl's call.

He pondered at the significance of uncanny coincidence; him being in the same place at the same time as Alec and his men on the day of Merryl's funeral, and how different things may have been if he had chosen another venue to drown his misery, or if it had not been Alec's team on fire force duty at the time of the ambush on the tourist convoy.

The incidents were so completely unrelated in nature and yet inseparable in the way they had come together to play their part in changing the course of his destiny....

Had there been some rogue celestial puppeteer with a warped sense of humour pulling the strings of providence? Manipulating and twisting the shape of events to form a pattern in an inventive, self-satisfying but cruel game of mortal Tetris? That would be an acceptable explanation for someone who believed in the supernatural. Andrew Mason never had but was now considering the possibilities.

But why would he have been singled out as a guinea pig in this weird test of human tolerance? What was the purpose of it all?? What had been achieved other than to leave him hardened to death and carnage, emotionally damaged and haunted by the experiences? The questions kept coming and he had given up trying to match them to answers.

He was still smouldering over his humiliating encounter with the woman at the night club that had resulted in the theft of his wallet and watch. He now knew, as he should have done from the outset, that the seemingly eager 'come on' by the woman, whose name he couldn't remember, was just a contrivance by an attractive con-artist who'd suckered him. The reality of it made him feel soiled and resentful.

The morning light intensified and stirred Andy from the drifting miasma of his reverie. Opening his eyes, he turned them to the window. The curtains were open and the casement framed the spectacle of a glorious African sunrise

As it had done, time and time before, the sight enthralled him. The splendour of the fiery orange streaks that ran across the vast morning sky seemed to speak to him,. It called him up out of his self-pity. It unlocked a part of him that seemed bound fast by anguish, disappointment and remorse. It spoke, with all its power of newness and hope and possibility.

He got up off the bed to stand again at the tall French window. He gazed out at the inspiring view and the magnificent dawn; the clouds that drifted beneath it flecked with gold

'Yes, he resolved. Yes. A new awakening..... Time to move on.'

**END**

Lightning Source UK Ltd.
Milton Keynes UK
UKOW04f0411130214

226360UK00002B/67/P